MW01440956

# 111 Souls

by
Justin Bohardt

Book 1 of the Infinite Universe
(Finite Ways to Make a Living)
Series

**111 Souls**
Justin Bohardt
CreateSpace Edition
Copyright 2014, 2015 Justin Bohardt

# Dedication

*When the writer pours hours of his life into the simple endeavor of telling a story, it is the writer's fondest and perhaps most desperate hope that someone will take a few minutes to read and perhaps even enjoy the story he crafted. Sadly, I have found that this hope (expecting someone to read your story, that is) is often too great an expectation. My wife's parents, however, have been kind enough to read my stories, even the ones that were truly horrible, and I will always be grateful to them for that.*

*In addition, whether it is reminding me that I should not curse as much as I do in front of my child, debating with me over alternate ways the Civil War could have ended, providing me with homemade cards for holidays I was not familiar with, or discussing the latest <u>Buffy the Vampire Slayer</u> fan fiction, my in-laws are always there to keep me on my toes.*

*Mostly, I am just thankful that they are always there.*

*As such, this book is dedicated to Bill and René. Thank you.*

# Table of Contents

Chapter 1 ................................................................................ 1

Chapter 2 ................................................................................ 9

Chapter 3 ................................................................................ 22

Chapter 4 ................................................................................ 28

Chapter 5 ................................................................................ 42

Chapter 6 ................................................................................ 50

Chapter 7 ................................................................................ 588

Chapter 8 ................................................................................ 666

Chapter 9 ................................................................................ 766

Chapter 10 .............................................................................. 811

Chapter 11 .............................................................................. 88

Chapter 12 .............................................................................. 95

Chapter 13 .............................................................................. 1033

Chapter 14 .............................................................................. 1088

Chapter 15 .............................................................................. 1177

Chapter 16 .............................................................................. 126

Chapter 17 .............................................................................. 138

Chapter 18 .............................................................................. 147

Chapter 19 .............................................................................. 155

Chapter 20 .............................................................................. 163

Chapter 21 ............................................................................... 173

Chapter 22 ............................................................................... 183

Chapter 23 ............................................................................... 209

Chapter 24 ............................................................................... 222

Chapter 25 ............................................................................... 227

Chapter 26 ............................................................................... 242

Chapter 27 ............................................................................... 249

Chapter 28 ............................................................................... 256

Chapter 29 ............................................................................... 263

Chapter 30 ............................................................................... 271

Chapter 31 ............................................................................... 279

Chapter 32 ............................................................................... 285

Chapter 33 ............................................................................... 294

Chapter 34 ............................................................................... 303

Chapter 35 ............................................................................... 317

Chapter 36 ............................................................................... 331

Chapter 37 ............................................................................... 341

Chapter 38 ............................................................................... 357

Chapter 39 ............................................................................... 364

Chapter 40 ............................................................................... 373

# 111 Souls

by
Justin Bohardt

# Chapter 1

A light flickered on overhead, and Captain Matthew Jennings heard the unmistakable electronic whirring of plasma weapons being charged. At least eight of them occupied the room, a small, circular, windowless steel trap. *Correction*, Jennings thought to himself quickly as he heard the delicate drawl of a woman clearing her throat. There were nine of them.

Jennings turned his head slightly to size up the lady stepping from behind one of the leather-clad muscular behemoths who appeared to be in her employ. The woman was short and squat with matronly gray hair pulled back into a bun. She wore a bright red suit which screamed colonial housewife trying to pull off administrative assistant in the capital city of some back berth abortion of a Terran settlement. One glance into those cool, steely gray eyes though, and Jennings immediately changed his mind. Her eyes whispered that she was just as comfortable wading hip deep through blood as hosting tea at the governor's mansion (*Or viceroy's*, Jennings's brain corrected, sidetracking his thoughts for a moment. *Governor implied democracy*.) Those cold irises even introduced the woman before she had spoken a word.

Jennings flashed a winning grin. "Anastasia Petrova, I presume."

Her stride forward faltered for a moment, and Jennings allowed himself a brief moment of self-satisfied congratulations. Anastasia Petrova had been a bounty hunter for over a decade and unofficially started before then by capturing T-Fed Army deserters during the Gael War. That success allowed her to take on partners and understudies until she employed an entire army of hunters. From what Jennings knew, she mostly sat back these days, growing rich off ten percent of her army's bounties. It was rare for her to actually pound the pavement anymore, or so the rumors said. Naturally, Jennings felt honored to have gathered her personal attention.

"You seem quite pleased *vith* yourself," Petrova spoke at last, her voice baring a hint of an old Earth Russian accent. "Especially considering the precariousness of your position. Nine guns against only one."

"Well, it so happens I carry four guns- two on my spine, one at my hip and another at my ankle. I also have a couple of knives you may not have taken into consideration, so I am still willing to consider your surrender," Jennings said, getting a few chuckles from Petrova's lackeys. Adopting a contemplative countenance, he pretended to give it more thought and then shrugged his shoulders. "Besides, if I'm going to die, I might as well go contentedly." He paused once more before allowing his eyes to travel to where his right hand grasped the shoulder of the man next to him. "There's also the possibility I might take something you want with me."

Tension pulsed through the neck of Jennings's prisoner, and he wondered for a moment what was going through Ciarin O'Sullivan's mind. Here he was, a black bag over his head, arms bound behind him, and now two different sets of people were about ready to kill each other for the right to bring O'Sullivan to the authorities. Certainly, it could not have been young Ciarin's best day ever.

"You *vill* kill the bounty? I think not," Petrova said. "Besides, a corpse can still be carried in."

"Wrong again, my dear," Jennings said. "You really need to read the postings more carefully. This one's wanted alive only. Dead, he isn't worth two cents a kilo."

Again, Petrova's pacing halted, and she eyed Jennings. He could see her mind working, wondering if he would really kill his own mark just to spite her. Jennings had no intention of killing O'Sullivan- that was not the way he operated. Besides, it was plain rude to shoot someone on the way to their own funeral. However, he was hoping Petrova did not know that.

A smile formed in the corner of the Russian bounty hunter's mouth, and Jennings immediately knew his bluff was about to be called. "I have read your combat files, Lieutenant Jennings," she said.

"Captain Jennings," he interrupted.

She ignored him. "You can learn much about a soldier in his record: his actions, his motives, his- dare, I say- heroism. *Vould* a decorated officer of the Gael War murder a mark in cold blood rather than hand him over to a fellow seeker of justice?"

Jennings rolled his eyes and muttered something about, "Seeker of profit."

"No," she said. "Lieutenant Jennings is a good man."

"Captain Jennings," he growled. "And Captain Jennings is a bad man."

In one swift motion, he threw O'Sullivan down to the ground with his right hand, while reaching behind his back with his left. His left hand whipped back around and produced a plasma pistol with a rotating six charge cylinder. With astonishingly fast reflexes, Petrova dove behind one of her men- the one who captured the first blast of red energy from the pistol and flew back into the steel wall.

As the other shocked hunters tried to bring their rifles to bear, Jennings drew a second identical pistol off the right side of his spine and opened up with both weapons. Red energy ripped through the air bringing down two more of Petrova's goons before a well-aimed blast of green energy from the Russian's own weapon struck Jennings in the chest and sent him sprawling, both weapons spilling from his hands as he fell.

Desperately gasping for breath, Jennings barely heard Petrova order her men to pick up O'Sullivan and follow her to one of the room's two egresses. One man remained behind and walked over toward Jennings's body. He wore a cocky half-grin on his face made all the more ridiculous by the stupid supernova tattoo which adorned his left eye. His rifle leveled at Jennings's face, and Petrova's lackey did not even notice the little red dot appear on his forehead. After a brief flash, Petrova's man collapsed to the ground.

"*Mon Capitaine?*" came an anxious, whisper.

"Marquis?" Jennings tried to respond, but it came out as "Mmmaaa."

"Not exactly, *cher*," came the Cajun drawl.

Familiar hands grabbed hold of Jennings as a sensation of rapidly approaching unconsciousness set in. He felt himself being dragged across the steel floor as the world faded into darkness.

~

General Dominic Ounimbango watched with mild interest from behind a two-way mirror as Anastasia Petrova handed custody of Ciarin O'Sullivan over to four men dressed in the black uniforms of the Terran Gael Force. The Terran Gael Force was the only standing military which Earth and her allies fielded any longer, and it was a complete farce.

While Ounimbango emerged as the leader of the newly constructed puppet army after the crushing defeat the Terran Federation had suffered during the Gael War, everyone knew the Gael actually pulled the strings. Ounimbango himself had been an obscure major in the African 432nd regiment, but he had been left in charge of the Lunar Defense Base when the Gael made their last push toward Earth. With an order to defend his home planet no matter the cost, he surrendered the Lunar Base without a shot fired and gave the Gael the command codes to disable the defense net surrounding Earth. He saved the countless human lives which would have been sacrificed in a last-ditch defense of Earth (except for those in the center of the North American continent. Even with the Terran defense grid down, the Gael felt obligated to make a point about how powerful they were.).

Ounimbango rationalized this by telling himself that by refusing to send his men out to be slaughtered and giving the Gael what they demanded, Earth was preserved for the most part, and millions who would have died at the hands of a superior enemy were spared. Of course, it did not hurt that the Gael Occupation Force had offered him the position of general-in-chief of the Terran Gael Force, making him the commander of the only human military power allowed to remain after the unconditional surrender of the Terran Federation.

The General threw a curious eye toward the other man in the room. "Tell me again why this O'Sullivan is so important to you?"

Man, of course, was an incorrect term although the Gael were mostly humanoid. The Gael stood almost seven feet tall, and he wore long flowing robes. In general, the Gael were completely hairless and had larger craniums than humans. Their faces were similar, although their eyes were more narrowed and completely black.

The one with Ounimbango was named Pahhal, and he served as the Overseer for the Terran sector. In essence, all decisions in regard to the Gael military, Terran Gael Force, and Terran Autonomous Region Ruling Council went through him. Very few people though had actually heard his name mentioned or were even aware of his existence. That was the way the Gael preferred- always working behind the scenes, letting the general public believe humans still ran their tiny little corner of the galaxy.

After a long pause, as if in contemplative thought, Overseer Pahhal at last answered the general, "I don't recall telling you a first time why we are interested in Mr. O'Sullivan, General. In point of fact, I don't recall ever giving you a reason for any of my orders. I simply give them and you obey them, isn't that correct?"

"Of course, my friend," Ounimbango said quickly in his Oxford-educated East African accent, his hefty frame shifting nervously from foot to foot and his hands suddenly finding tiny imperfections in his olive-green uniform which needed to be corrected.

"One hundred and ten," Pahhal whispered more to himself. "Only one remains." He then spoke to Ounimbango. "There will be a transport ship arriving here at midnight for O'Sullivan. Make sure the prisoner transfer paperwork is in order."

"Of course, Overseer," the general said. "In regard to the last one, are you sure you wish to use this Matthew Jennings? Petrova just proved how capable she is by bringing us O'Sullivan."

Pahhal let loose a derisive cough, the closest the Gael ever seemed to laughing. "Petrova is the epitome of the laziness that defines your species. She is a vulture, taking from those who do legitimate work and making it her own. Jennings captured O'Sullivan, and I believe he is our best chance to capture this last piece of the puzzle."

"Understood, Overseer. I shall begin making the arrangements," he said.

"No, general, I will set this deal myself," Pahhal said with an icy edge to his tone. "There must be no mistakes."

Pahhal vanished into the shadows of the small room, and Ounimbango felt the weight of his presence vanish. He let out a sigh of relief, and his copious gut relaxed, spilling out over his belt. He turned his attention back to Petrova as the bounty hunter finished handing control of O'Sullivan over.

*Better start that paperwork for the transfer*, he thought to himself. He had no idea where any of the previous one hundred and nine captives taken by the Gael had been transferred to and he truly did not care (save for a bit of morbid curiosity). The Gael could- and did- do whatever they wanted as far as he was concerned. His focus now, as he left the small room and headed for an office that had been set aside for his use, was to make sure number one hundred and eleven was captured without any further problems.

As he wended his way through the maze of offices, returning nods from black uniformed security officers, a rare moment of motivation seized him. Ounimbango certainly did not trust Matthew Jennings to get the job done- he had never even heard of him until today. He would much rather have regular Terran Interplanetary Security or Terran Gael Force personnel bring in the mark, but the Gael did not want any kind of official presence from the government involved in these abductions.

*That was fine with him, but why did Pahhal trust Jennings when Petrova had a long history of successful work?* Ounimbango usually did not do anything to upset his Gael superiors, but his ambition every so often outweighed his caution. *What if he were to take steps which ensured number one hundred and eleven was successfully brought in?* His esteem in the eyes of the Overseer would certainly rise. That potential made it well worth the risk.

Striding into his makeshift office in the government facility on the planet Mariador, ignoring the beautiful view of the skyline edifices adorning its capital Centuria and the flurry of personal transport craft swirling around, he sat at his desk and pulled up the Nucleus. Accessing the secure server of the government site, he input a series of at least a dozen passwords to activate the Classified-Your-Eyes-Only archive. Another few moments, and he at last had the details for Operation Aurora pulled up as well as all the information on the last free target from the list of one hundred and eleven names.

~

"Where am I?" Matthew Jennings whispered, his voice scratchy and his throat parched.

"The hell you think you are?" came the growled reply.

"Fix?" Jennings asked as his eyes fluttered open.

"It sure is nae your mother," Fix said, his Scottish accent coming out in his annoyance.

Jennings's eyes finally focused, and he realized he was lying down on a surgical bed in the small closet which served as his ship's sickbay. Fix, the ship's medic, stared over top of him, his trademark scowl creasing his dark skin. Fix was tall, thin, and the fact that he was pushing fifty was evident by the gray hair at his temples and the crow's feet and worry-lines on his forehead. The fact that he was a convicted felon was evidenced by the long string of tattoos running down his arms and peeking out above his shirt at the collar line. He was born Angus Ferguson, but he would be damned if he answered to it.

"What happened?" Jennings managed.

Fix shrugged. "Lafayette said something about your brilliant arse stopping a plasma pulse with your chest."

"Lucky for me, I wear body armor," Jennings said, swinging his legs off the operating table.

"Lucky for you Lafayette was watching your back. Otherwise there'd be a smoldering hole where your face used to be," the medic said.

Jennings flashed a white-toothed grin. "That would be a real shame considering how pretty I am."

"Mother of God," Fix groaned. "I'm guessing we did nae get paid today." When Jennings shook his head, he asked, "Russian bitch?"

"I think she was born on Monument actually," Jennings said, but got a cold stare from Fix in reply. "Russian bitch," he acknowledged at last.

"Shite," Fix cursed. "We have no money."

"No money. No fuel. No spare parts. And I think we have a small can of sausages left for dinner," the captain agreed.

Fix swore again.

"Give me a minute here and gather everyone together in the Caf," Jennings said.

"Aye, captain," Fix said before disappearing through the hatch.

Jennings hopped off the table and walked over to the small sink and mirror in the corner of the room. He was dressed only in his olive-green cargo pants; Fix must have removed his shirt to make sure the plasma shot he had taken had not burned any of his skin. A massive bruise started at his sternum and spread across his muscular stomach. He would not be doing any sit-ups any time soon, he thought to himself. Turning on the sink, he bent over and splashed some water in his face. Catching his reflection in the mirror for a moment, he saw a flash of worry in his hazel eyes. Angry at himself for the instant of fear, he set his lips in a thin line of determination and pushed some more water back through his brown hair. Another moment's study in the mirror revealed he could use a shave and some more sleep, but otherwise the twenty-eight-year-old looked as he always did- flat broke.

"It was easy money," he said to the mirror. "How did it all go so wrong?"

# Chapter 2

*Several hours earlier…*

Captain Matthew Jennings had seen the potential in the opportunity immediately when the message flashed into his Nucleus inbox. He and his ship, the *Melody Tryst*, were already in the Proxima Centauri system, and the fugitive request was being posted by Terran Interplanetary Security's field office on Mariador, the largest planet in the Proxima Centauri system. The fugitive was one Ciarin O'Sullivan, an accused Resistance supporter, wanted for suspicion of terrorism and murder. The reward was twenty-five thousand dollars, easily enough to keep the *Melody Tryst* in repair and her crew paid and happy for a few months.

Generally, Jennings did not like working for the Gael's puppet human government, but the money was right, and more importantly, he did not care for the Resistance. He certainly may have agreed with their politics. They demanded that the Gael remove themselves from Terran space; that the Terran Federation Government be allowed to reform; that the Terran Gael Force and Terran Autonomous Region Ruling Council be disbanded; and they called for free elections once again. All of those were things Jennings wanted to see happen himself.

As a veteran of the Gael War, he wanted to see the Gael's collective butts kicked all the way back to their home system as well. However, the Resistance carried out their little war by bombing civilian targets, hoping to hit Gael officers or human collaborators. They did not care about the humans who got caught in the crossfire or the collateral damage which ensued. According to the warrant, O'Sullivan helped plan a bombing attack on Firefall a few months previously, killing three hundred civilians. Jennings would be only happy to bring him in.

"Are you sure about *dis, mon ami*?" Lafayette asked, his Cajun patois coming through with more severity whenever he was nervous.

"Sure about twenty-five thousand dollars, hells yeah."

An imperious harrumph escaped the Cajun's throat, and Jennings turned an eye to his first officer. Remy Emmanuel Lafayette was a middle-aged man who had let himself go slightly since his military days (taking plasma shots to both legs toward the tail end of the war did not help), but still packed a decent bit of muscle under the gut he had formed. He had blue eyes and a receding hairline which was more gray than its original black.

Lafayette had been at Jennings's side for twelve years, ever since Jennings was churned through T-Fed Army officer training at the tender age of sixteen. By that point in the war, the T-Fed Army was fleeing before the Gael advance and taking volunteers as young as fifteen to defend Earth. Already ten years and two wars his senior, Sergeant Lafayette stated he had expected to despise the little twerp who was technically his superior officer. It did not take Jennings long to earn respect from Lafayette and his men however.

Natural tactical brilliance came rather easily to young Lieutenant Jennings, and he combined that with a genuine compassion for the men under his command. With a drink or three in him, Lafayette would confess that Jennings impressed him in a way no commissioned officer ever had. They fought together so well and so long during the Gael War that when Jennings said he was getting a ship after the decommissioning of the T-Fed Army, Lafayette came along without needing to be asked, even if it still clearly annoyed him that Jennings insisted on calling him Marquis.

"I don't like working for TIS," the Cajun clarified.

"And you think I do?" Jennings countered. "Terran Interplanetary Security is yet another Gael puppet factory, but at least it's slightly better than the TGF. Besides, we need to find something; otherwise, Mariador is going to be the final destination of the *Tryst*."

Lafayette nodded. "*Je comprends, mon capitaine.* I don't have another idea, but we should be on our guard when dealing with *dem*."

"Hey, don't worry," Jennings said with a grin. "Besides, Frank still owes us a favor."

"*Mon Dieux*, not Frank," Lafayette protested, but Jennings merely grinned and swung the *Melody Tryst* down into the atmosphere of Mariador.

~

Francis Xavier Barlow watched the *Olympus*-class shuttle screaming in toward him with a sense of wry amusement. He stood outside a rusted square of metal sheeting pieces nailed together over plywood which he called a home. A small sign hanging from the roof of the hover-port swung in the breeze. *Barlow's Best* was stenciled on it in crude red letters. Behind the building sat a huge mass of small starship hulls, junk parts, piles of metal scraps and some complete ships which had seen better days.

One could argue the same about Barlow himself, although he would scarcely admit to it. The fifty-something with the prominent beer gut, gray beard tucked into his belt, and the pink Hawaiian shirt wrapped over a stained undershirt was dead certain he was the sexiest thing alive. And he was damned determined to prove it to the cute Frenchman that Captain Jennings always dragged around with him. The shuttle set down, and Barlow raised a friendly arm as the cargo ramp opened and Jennings and Lafayette strolled out.

"Howdy boys!" He waved exuberantly in their direction. "Matthew, my friend, what brings you here? You need some more parts for that scrapper of yours?" A boisterous laugh accompanied his extending his hand to Jennings. "Where is it by the way?"

The captain took it and shook his hand warmly. "The *Tryst* is flying fine, thank you very much. We set her down in Centuria."

"Well, how 'bout you, Monsieur Lafayette?" Barlow intoned with his most seductive voice. "You lookin' for anything in particular?"

Jennings allowed a long moment of uncomfortable silence to unfold before he said, "Jesus, Barlow, you're scaring the straights."

The scrap merchant guffawed mightily. "Well, let's get out of this cursed heat and have ourselves a beverage. Maybe, we can relax a bit and talk some business, eh?"

He laughed again and led them across the dirt field toward the house. It was hard to call it a dirt field actually, because all of that part of Mariador was covered in the same red dirt. It never rained in Barlow's part of the world, so there were no crops, no vegetation and no people. That was a good thing for someone whose business transactions were less than legitimate; it was bad because it was pushing one hundred and twenty-five degrees.

Lafayette muttered something in Acadian French as they stepped inside into the slightly cooler garage which passed for Barlow's living space. To the right were a bar and a couple of stools and to the left sat a small bed and a dozen shelves with random assorted junk on it. Directly in front of the door was a small round table with ejector seats serving as chairs where Jennings and Lafayette dropped themselves. Barlow first headed behind the bar and opened the cooler before coming back with two beers and a soda pop for Jennings.

"Still yet to embrace the dark side, eh?" Barlow joked as he sat down and then pulled in a long slug of beer.

"Just like to have all of my wits about me," Jennings said.

A loud belch was Barlow's witty retort, and Lafayette rolled his eyes.

"Well, gents, as much as I enjoy the company, I do figure you didn't drop by just to socialize," Barlow said at last. "If you're not here for parts, what's your business?"

"Did you see the Nucleus bulletin for O'Sullivan?" Jennings asked.

"Come on, you're not working that job, are you?" Barlow protested.

"*Dere* aren't a whole lot of other offers, *cher*," Lafayette pointed out.

Barlow shrugged an agreement. "Still don't see what that has to do with me though. Not that I mind visitors," he added hastily, his smile flashing toward Lafayette again.

"You work on both sides," Jennings said carefully. "Thought you might be able to point us in the right direction is all."

"You want me to cross the Resistance? Hell no," he answered immediately. "Not only are they better customers than you, Matthew, but they're eleven times more vicious."

"Come on, Frank, you know how the Resistance operates," Jennings argued. "Once their men are made, they sever ties in order to minimize collateral damage. You'd actually be doing them a favor to help us pick up O'Sullivan."

Barlow scrunched up his face in thought and heaved an enormous sigh. "All right, all right. I don't know exactly where he is, but there's an old school pub in the Émigré section of Centuria. Name of Sullah's. It's been known to harbor a few characters of ill repute. Good place to start."

Jennings nodded, stood and gave a half-bow to Barlow. "Catch you on the other side." The two men shook hands.

Lafayette offered his hand as well, which Barlow immediately grabbed and pulled up to his lips before the Cajun could react. "Such lovely hands," Barlow whispered. "Do come back soon."

~

Centuria was a colossal city, one of the oldest in human colonial terms, the very first founded on Mariador when humans arrived in Proxima Centauri. Somewhere deep in the bowels of the city sat an old closed museum which had been built around the first transport ship to land on Mariador. Now, it lay buried under an enormous superstructure thousands of stories high.

On Earth, as humanity ran out of space to expand their cities outward, they started expanding upward. Centuria now rivaled New York City or Dubai in terms of which city stretched the tallest toward the sky. Unlike on Earth however, Mariador was not the most hospitable of locations even with the terraforming that had been done. Colossal storms would build over the distant mountains, far stronger than even a Level 5 hurricane in old Earth terms, and would savage the long open plains upon which Centuria sat. The city had magnetic and electronic storm shields of course, but they consumed too much power over a long stretched-out city. It was far easier to keep the shield smaller horizontally and let people build the city up toward the sky.

The base of the city was now at least twenty-five stories above sea level, and Centuria was a beautiful sight. Everything sparkled with modernity, beautiful steel, synthetic concrete and glass shimmering in the afternoon sun. Green grass in clean parks, children playing, the latest model shuttles and hovercars whipping about the city- it was a testament to all humanity achieved (or had achieved before the Gael showed up, Jennings thought to himself).

Jennings set the shuttle down in an alley between a couple of smaller thousand story edifices, and he and Lafayette got out. Only barely bothering to keep an eye out for anyone watching them, Jennings pried open a utility hatch in the street, and he and Lafayette climbed their way down.

The underbelly of the city, the lower levels, had been officially closed off to public use for some time. Not only was it a matter of structural safety (when a new level was built as the base level, engineers reinforced the structure holding the city together in the now unused sub-levels), but the closure might be considered an open invitation for criminals, the homeless and the psychotic to take up residence and get up to no good. Despite the city's best efforts, this is exactly what they did.

Once the underworld had been established, Terran Interplanetary Security and the local cops all turned a blind eye to the place. Jennings supposed they figured it was better to at least have it all out of sight. The small utility tunnel they were in opened into a larger expanse of tarmac, which had once been a normal four lane street. On either side were dark and shadowy shops, illuminated by the occasional light. The entire area had a feel of night despite the early afternoon hour. The streets were not crowded, but business was definitely being done. On Jennings's right were a series of open windows and the faint glow of red light. A few overly made-up eyes tracked Lafayette and Jennings as they passed. On the left, goods changed hands at a sort of black-market bazaar. It might have been drugs, maybe guns or even sex, but Jennings was not concerned with it in the slightest as his eyes locked on a glowing neon sign with a few letters missing in the distance. Even without all the lights, he could make out *Sullah's Level 24*.

"There it is," Jennings nodded.

"Right, how do we want to do *dis*?" Lafayette asked.

"Carefully," he said without slowing down.

"I'm starting to really not like *dis* day," Lafayette muttered. "First, Barlow. Now you have to go all cryptic."

"Barlow's not so bad," Jennings said.

"He's not always trying to *touch* you, *mon ami*," he countered angrily.

A roll of the eyes was all Lafayette received.

"I'm not kidding," he said. "He does it every time."

"Probably because it bothers you so much, genius," Jennings pointed out.

Lafayette seemed to consider that. "Next time, you take Fix," he said at last as they crossed the last few feet of street and headed into the pub.

The double doors swung inward, and a dozen pairs of eyes turned toward Jennings and Lafayette. The place was old- old enough to still have walls of cold gray concrete instead of synthetics. Also, the tables were all wooden just like the bar set against the back wall. The tables were about half full, and everyone stared at the new arrivals. Most of the men in the bar appeared a bit on the shady side. Of course, if they were legitimate, they would all be top side.

"Something we can do for you?" a loud, disgruntled voice demanded from across the room. It belonged to the burly, grizzled bartender wearing a T-Fed Marine Corps camo-jacket.

Jennings strode into the bar past onlookers who seemed as if they were waiting for something violent to go down. "Looking for someone."

"Look elsewhere," the bartender, whose jacket's name tag read Rafiq, growled.

"No can do," Jennings said good-naturedly as he allowed a fake smile to cross his face. "I have it on good information that he's here."

"Bounty hunter scum!" one of the older customers shouted as he drew a short knife and made toward Jennings.

The captain drew his plasma pistol before the man made it out of his chair, and he did so without ever taking his eyes off Rafiq. "I'd appreciate it if your patrons restrained themselves," he said toward the bartender. "And if you would take your hand off the slug-thrower you're palming under the counter there."

A dark shadow of anger crossed Rafiq's face, but he slowly raised both his hands and put them on the bar.

"Thank you," Jennings said. "Now, we're looking for a man named Ciarin O'Sullivan."

"We're not appreciative of Gael lackeys here," he spat out, staring daggers at Jennings.

"I don't work for the Gael," Jennings said sternly, his eyes narrowing in anger. "I work for myself."

"By bringing in Terran freedom fighters? You're a traitor to your race," another patron shouted from behind him.

Lafayette's hand went to his gun, but Jennings waved him off. "Freedom fighters? Funny, I call them murderers. How many innocent people have died…?"

"They're not innocents! They're collaborators!" Rafiq thundered.

"Not your targets maybe, but what about everyone else who is killed in the Resistance's bombings?" Lafayette asked. "Are you content with all the collateral damage? As long as you kill your target, your actions are justified?"

Rafiq glowered with rage. "The Resistance doesn't bomb civilian targets."

"Then who does?" Jennings demanded.

Rafiq did not appear as if he had an answer, but Jennings would not have heard it anyway as a flurry of activity came from the kitchen in the back of the pub followed by the sound of broken glass. Quickly running past the bar, Jennings kicked open the kitchen door and surveyed the scene. A window leading to the outside alley had been shattered and half of a bloody handprint lay on the sill.

Turning back to Lafayette, he shouted, "Outside. He's on the run. Move."

Lafayette was already out the door with Jennings hot on his trail. No one made a move in the Resistance-friendly pub until the door swung shut and then everyone went back to their drinks.

Rafiq followed Jennings to the door and watched them run for a moment. "Foolish boy," the bartender whispered to himself. "Now, you're as good as caught."

~

General Ounimbango was out of uniform, wearing a long trench coat, milling about on the street outside of Sullah's pub when a young, red-headed man raced around a corner and start heading down the street. A moment later, he saw another two men come running out into the avenue, chasing O'Sullivan top side. The woman at his side made a comment in a language he did not understand.

"I didn't catch that, Ms. Petrova," he said.

"It's of little consequence," she said. "So, that is our mark, *da*?"

"Yes, he is a highest priority case, almost worth his weight in gold," the general said.

"If you knew he was here, why bring me in?" she asked.

"I have my reasons," he said. "One, the Gael prefers this to be done unofficially. Two, there's no reward for criminals captured by Terran Gael Force or Terran Interplanetary Security."

"Ah, you want a commission?"

Ounimbango laughed, a deep robust sound, very foreign in the underworld. "A commission? I want half."

Petrova's eyes narrowed. "That's outrageous."

"Is it?" the general asked. "The other bounty hunters have already flushed the quarry. I provided you with this location in the first place. You really only have to put a couple of hours of work into this one, so I think half is quite generous on my part."

"Very *vell*," Petrova conceded after a moment's pause. "I appreciate the fact that you brought me into this, and in anticipation of a positive future *vorking* relationship, I shall accept your terms."

"Excellent," the general nodded.

"Now, if you'll excuse me," Petrova nodded to the general. "I've got some *vork* to do."

She vanished into the shadows of the dark underworld street, and Ounimbango suddenly felt very isolated and alone in the lower power neon lights and tough characters walking the streets of the underworld. With as much dignity as he could muster, he scampered his way down the street heading in the direction of the surface.

~

"Marquis! Make for the shuttle! Get airborne!" Captain Jennings shouted as they raced back into the daylight in pursuit of O'Sullivan.

"*Oui, mon capitaine!*" he called as he took off in a different direction, headed back to where they had left the shuttle.

O'Sullivan had a decent lead, but Jennings was gaining, and all he needed to do was keep him in sight until Lafayette arrived with the shuttle. Then, it would be a matter of just pinning him down. They sprinted down the central thoroughfares of Centuria, but the road was mostly clear.

Traffic in the city sprouted in an upward direction, so hundreds of hovercars sped about the hundreds of levels above their heads, but very few transports flew near the ground. A couple of people walked casually around the city, but only a few. The bottom levels of Centuria were mostly industrial and warehouse areas. Most of the public resided much higher up in the structures, and the general public areas were built atop some of the wider buildings. There was nowhere for O'Sullivan to hide.

The fugitive must have realized this as well, because he suddenly stopped in the middle of the street and turned toward Jennings. Instinctively, Jennings threw himself to the ground and managed to barely avoid the red plasma bolts raking the ground behind him. Coming out of the roll, Jennings drew his own weapon and squeezed off several shots, one of which glanced off O'Sullivan's arm. He cried out in pain, and his weapon went flying from his hand. Spinning around wildly, he appeared torn between trying to retrieve the weapon and whether he should start running.

With a sudden whoosh of repulsor lifts engaging, a small shuttle swung over the street, pinning O'Sullivan between the ship and Jennings. Very reluctantly, O'Sullivan raised his hands above his head, and Jennings walked over to him, clapped some binders on his arms and led him up the shuttle's ramp. The ramp closed behind them and the hovering shuttle took off into the sky.

~

Anastasia Petrova watched from the shadows and smiled to herself. She had guessed correctly when choosing to follow the older of the two men, and placing the homing device on the shuttle had been easy. Calling the local police to advise them of the firefight and giving them the exact names and physical descriptions of the two bounty hunters was a rather inspired move as well, she thought to herself. The bounty hunters would have to try to bring in O'Sullivan to the Terran Gael Force while avoiding the local police, which would give Petrova the perfect opportunity to snatch the mark right out from under their noses.

~

The three of them sat cramped into the small cockpit of the *Melody Tryst's* only shuttle, aptly named Shuttle Four. (The first three had been, in order: blown up; crashed into an asteroid; lost in a card game by Lafayette.) The Cajun was at the stick, gaining altitude as he traversed one of the vertical skyways marked by the lighted buoys on repulsor-lifts, which formed the city's skylanes.

"Captain," a harsh voice came through the squaw, and Fix's face appeared on the screen.

Lafayette glanced worriedly at Jennings. The *Melody Tryst* did not break radio silence with them unless there was a problem.

"What is it, Fix?" Jennings asked quickly.

"Your faces just flashed over the Nucleus," he said. "You're wanted in connection with a shooting on one of the many fashionable streets of Centuria."

"Last I checked, we received most of the fire, *non*?" Lafayette muttered.

Fix ignored him. "According to Minerva, an unknown female called in a report. Accent sported a trace of old Earth Slav to it."

"Dammit!" Jennings swore heavily. "Petrova."

"You can bet your arse," Fix agreed.

"I'd rather not," he said. "Can Minerva find us an underground to Security Central?"

"It better not involve a sewage system," Lafayette grumbled.

"Maybe you should let me go and give up, considering I'm not a member of the bloody Resistance," Ciarin offered.

Lafayette smacked him on the back of the head as Fix ran some numbers. "Quickly, *mon capitaine*. We're running out of sky."

"There's a back door you can use," Fix said. "Power sub-station. Fully automated. Powers the central hospital and admin building in the event one of the storms knocks out main power."

"Navigating..." Lafayette studied the intel being fed from Minerva, the *Melody Tryst's* Near-Artificial Intelligence system.

Jennings's stomach lurched as Lafayette threw the shuttle hard over and headed for what looked like an orange, five-story metallic tumor growing on the side of the Government Administration Tower. He landed on the roof, and the three of them exited, Jennings pulling Ciarin behind him.

"The door," Jennings said as he pointed at the black aperture set in a bump-out on the roof.

Its security was fairly intensive, two-foot-thick steel and an LBT Tumbler Encrypt with retinal and fingerprint scanners. Jennings guessed the roof had sensors as well. They probably had about sixty seconds before alarms went off. Lafayette took out a small sliver of plastic, similar to a credit chit, and slid it into the ID slot. The computer interface gave the appearance of shuddering as the screen flickered maniacally and then blanked out.

"Minerva is in," Lafayette said.

"Come on. Come on," Jennings intoned as the computer on his ship linked with the card and hacked its way into the system.

With an explosive decompression, the door locks gave, and the door slid open a little bit. Jennings opened it wide and shoved Ciarin through the door. Lafayette went to follow him, but Jennings held him up.

"Stay with the ship." He took off into the doorway and called from inside, "But keep your comm open. Just in case I need rescuing."

~

Gael Overseer Pahhal finished studying the report he had collected detailing Captain Jennings's pursuit of Ciarin O'Sullivan, fugitive number one hundred and ten. His resources were far greater than someone like General Ounimbango could understand, and he had garnered enough information to piece together exactly how the O'Sullivan situation played out. The more he read about it, the more confident he was of his decision.

Captain Jennings had contacts, investigative prowess, strength, improvisation, and a certain finesse most bounty hunters did not. They tended to prefer brute carnage, which ended up with the target being dead more often than not. Even Jennings's failure at the hands of Petrova told Pahhal a great deal about what type of man Jennings was. He had been outnumbered and outgunned, and he still walked away to tell the tale.

His service record said the same. In the Gael War, he turned a number of hopeless situations into small victories over the Gael forces, or more often Terran defeats which were horrifically costly to the Gael military. Still, he supposed, all situations were hopeless for humans in the war. The fact that anyone might grab even a small victory was miraculous in and of itself. On top of that, when things got really bad for his side and defeat was imminent, he took prisoners of war rather than murdering any pockets of surrendering Gael. He was one of the few who did. Jennings was a man of honor, and that defined him above all else. That was why he did not mind hunting the Resistance; he deemed people who killed civilians to be worse than the Gael.

And that is what Pahhal would use against him- his honor. If he painted the proper picture for a man like Jennings, the captain would feel obligated to bring Pahhal fugitive number one hundred and eleven. A light flicked on in the cockpit of his transport shuttle, advising him that the autopilot had activated the landing gear. His ship started to set down in the Western Docks on the outskirts of town. He stared through the ship's viewscreen and found the *Melody Tryst* resting before him. A small smile crossed his face as he realized one other thing he loved about Captain Jennings and his crew: they were starving.

# Chapter 3

The Caf was the unofficial name of the galley on the *Melody Tryst*, and it was where most of the crew could be found in their off-hours. The *Symphonic*-class cargo-conversion was a tri-level ship: two levels to the aft compromising the majority of the spacecraft and a lone level flight deck to the fore connected to each level by a sloping gangplank. The Caf sat at the center of the top level, separated from a lounge by a thin plastic partition. Eight doors and two small hatches led to crew and guest quarters or gave access to the ship's two wings. The guest quarters were convertible to prison cells when the situation demanded it, which seemed to be more and more frequent as real work was snatched up by legitimate contractors and post-war profiteers. The ceiling of the Caf housed a ladder that would drop down to give access to the shuttle locked into place atop the *Melody Tryst*. Beneath their feet on the lower level sat the cargo hold, small arms locker, armory (or large arms locker as Lafayette liked to say-where the ammunition for the *Melody Tryst*'s weapons was kept), a few smuggler's holds and the engineering section.

When Jennings walked into the galley, he saw Fix and Lafayette already there. Fix sat at the long table where most of their meals were held, and Lafayette bustled about the kitchen, preparing something. Jennings had no idea what Lafayette might be cooking as there was an extreme dearth of edibles onboard, but the Marquis had done more with less before. Despite being multiple generations removed from the French mainland, Lafayette knew more about cooking than the rest of them put together. Jennings did not know what half the contraptions in their kitchen (most purchased or brought in by Lafayette) were for, and Scottish blood ran deep in the veins underneath Fix's black skin. From what Jennings understood, his only requirement in food was that it be dead and preferably deep fried. Even the former was flexible given the circumstances. Lafayette caught Fix making haggis once, and the two almost came to blows.

For a moment, Jennings took a long look around, then checked under the table, in the corners of the ceiling and pulled out each chair.

"He's nae here yet," Fix said without looking up from the tablet he was scrolling through.

"Squawk!" Jennings roared, his voice echoing in the small space.

One of the access panels to the wings sprang open and out flew a whirling ball of energy. "Inertial dampener is shot. Needed overhaul six months ago. Wait and see. Wait and see, captain says. We waited and we saw, and we need a new part. Yes, yes, yes. Wait, could bypass it through a power coupling, could work, could work. Yes. For a while anyway. Yes. Yes. Maybe. Try it and see. Good idea."

"Squawk?" Jennings interrupted his diatribe.

The tiny engineer glanced up as if noticing everyone else for the first time. With a sudden expression of recognition, he straightened up swiftly, saluted Captain Jennings and leapt up into a chair. Stifling a yawn, Jennings sat down beside him. Squawk's energy was enough to make anyone tired. The ship's engineer was a Pasquatil, one of the three races humans met when they began exploring the galaxy. Combined with the Merquand and the Uula, they joined with humans to form the Terran Federation, although the Uula only did so in a desperate attempt to beat back Gael incursions into their space.

The Pasquatil were a diminutive race of "hyperactive chipmunks" as Lafayette once said. Squawk stood about three feet tall on legs which could only be described as kangaroo-like. Although able to walk, he preferred to jump and spring almost everywhere. Claws on his toes allowed him to cling to almost any surface, and a short, fat, furry tail extended from a hole in his engineer's coveralls. He had long thin arms that allowed him to reach into nooks and crevices in the ship's inner workings and a four fingered hand with an opposable thumb. His body was covered in a kind of downy gray fur from his head on down, but he had a vaguely humanoid, although dark gray, face- a prominent wet nose and whiskers being the main distinction.

Pasquatil were born engineers. Something about their brains just intuitively understood how things worked. They probably could not tell you the physics or mathematics of it all, but they understood it inherently all the same. The downside of that was they tended to talk constantly, mostly to themselves, and very few Terrans had the patience for their obsession with the work they did. His name took about thirty seconds to say when not being pronounced by a fellow Pasquatil so Jennings simply called him Squawk.

A delicious aroma now emanated from the kitchen, and Lafayette emerged carrying a frying pan and a sauce pot. As he set the sizzling frying pan in front of everyone, he said, "*Bon appétit.* Enjoy the meal for it may be our last."

"How bad is it?" Jennings asked.

"This magnificent feast represents the last of our dried fruit, canned meat, powdered potatoes and pasta," Lafayette replied.

Squawk pulled out a large bag of chocolate covered peanuts from his greasy coveralls. "Fine. Fine. Fine. Everything I need for a while." He threw two into his mouth, and after a moment of frenzied chewing, he let out a contented sigh.

Eyeing the small amount of spaghetti in the pot carefully, Jennings took a third and spooned it onto his plate. There was no sauce, so he piled the small portion of fried sausage and dried apples in some kind of wine sauce over top of it. Fix divided the rest of the meal up between himself and Lafayette, and everyone dug in with a kind of grim resolve.

After a moment, the food was gone, and Jennings said, "Remember Riverfront?"

"*Merde*, don't remind me," Lafayette said, pushing his plate away. "I ate my own belt."

"I ate the soles of my shoes," Jennings said.

"Think we're headed that way again?" he asked.

Fix grunted. "We do nae have any coin, any credit. The larders are empty, and the tank is dry. We've no work on the horizon and no way to get to it. Oh, and you two are wanted by the local cops."

"No fuel, we have no fuel," Squawk said, his voice jittering. "Need parts. Need fuel. No fuel, no flying. No parts, we're crashing. Fuel or parts? Which or both? Need both, want both. Can we have? Must have."

"We're in deep shit," Jennings muttered at last.

"Not as deep as Wolf VI," Lafayette reminded. "We're not chest deep in Gaels trying to kill us."

"You sure about that?" Fix nodded toward the gangplank leading up from the cockpit.

"Son of a bitch," Jennings swore, immediately standing and going for a weapon.

"I assure you that is not necessary." The Gael raised two placating hands. "I mean you no harm. In fact, I have a job for you."

Not lowering his weapon in the slightest, Jennings gestured the Gael into one of the empty chairs around the table. With a swishing of flowing robes, the Gael sat and affixed its black eyes on the captain and his sidearm. Fix continued eating, barely paying attention to what was going on, while Lafayette eyed the captain closely, waiting to see what move he would make. The Pasquatil had vanished into one of the air shafts when the Gael first arrived. After a long moment of stony silence, Jennings holstered the pistol and sat back down.

"I don't work for the Gael," Jennings said flatly. "Could've saved you a trip down here."

"Are you in a position to turn down work, Captain Jennings?" the Gael asked.

"Why ask questions you already know the answers to?" the captain countered quickly.

The Gael attempted to feign surprise. "Whatever do you mean?"

"You know my name. You know my ship. No one comes offering someone a job if they don't know who he is. If you know who I am, then you know that my crew and I have seen some bad luck recently. A Gael such as yourself would know exactly how many cents we have in our accounts and how much fuel we have in our tanks," Jennings said. "A Gael never makes a move without seeing all the pieces. So, quit dancing with me. You're not my type."

The Gael bowed his head slightly, and the faintest trace of a smile crossed his lips. "Very well, captain. We will cease dancing, as you say. I admire your candor, and I hope you will appreciate mine. My name is Pahhal, and I am a person of some import among my people. Important enough to have been given a special charge: the humans of

Terran Gael Force call it Operation Aurora: the elimination of the Resistance."

The muscles in Jennings's arms tightened as his hands squeezed together. "What makes you think I would have any interest in taking on the Resistance?"

The Gael eyed Jennings with bemused curiosity. "I am well informed. Perhaps I shall just say I admired the way you handled the Ciarin O'Sullivan situation."

"That didn't work out so well for us," Lafayette pointed out.

"Due to some circumstances with the humans I have working for me I am afraid," Pahhal said. "Corruption is a vice which extends deep into the power-hungry members of your race... as is avarice."

"You son of a..." Lafayette stood up from his chair angrily.

"Sit down, Marquis!" Jennings snapped out an arm to restrain his overeager first mate. "Don't be rude to our guest." He turned back to Pahhal, who seemed entirely nonplussed by Lafayette's outburst. "You're saying someone in TGF is skimming off the bounties on Resistance captures?" He turned to Lafayette. "Bet you ten bucks it's Ounimbango."

Pahhal did not make any indication that he was correct, but Jennings read something in his expression all the same and smiled.

"Regardless of my direct report's prerogatives in matters of fugitive retrieval and commission structures," Pahhal said. "I was suitably impressed by the way you and your crew handled yourselves in the last endeavor. It is that type of touch I need to see in the apprehension of our next target."

A frown crossed Jennings's face, and he said, "What good is the job offer if Ounimbango farms it out to Petrova again just so he can take a slice? We've gone up against her once and come out on the wrong end. You want us to go into debt with the sharks so we can fuel the *Tryst* and go off on a mission where even if we grab the mark, there's a decent chance Petrova or Ounimbango screws us out of our shares? No, thank you."

"I don't want this matter handled by the likes of them," Pahhal said, leaning forward and locking eyes with Jennings. "They are thugs, criminals, blunt force trauma as opposed to surgical precision. You are a cunning warrior and a worthy adversary of conflicts past. As much as one of my kind can trust one of yours, I trust you to get the job done. You and no one else." He paused and sat back. With a purposefully careless wave of his hand, he added, "Certainly, you might have to take on Petrova or some other puppets who get wind of the mark, which is why I am willing to be exceeding generous."

"How generous?" Fix piped up for the first time, still not taking his eyes off his plate.

"Ten thousand dollars up front," he said. "Certainly enough to get your ship up and running, outfitted, and supplied. Perhaps I can even throw in some items if you make me a list. Two hundred and fifty thousand when the job is done, minus the ten paid up front of course."

"And if Petrova gets there first?" Jennings asked with a raised eyebrow.

"Then we'll consider the ten an apology for what happened with O'Sullivan," Pahhal answered. "We'll walk away owing each other nothing."

"Sweet deal," said Fix as his eyes met Jennings's. "Take it."

Pure anguish filled Jennings's mind and probably crossed his face. Lafayette stared at him with a concerned expression as the debate raged in Jennings's mind: protect his honor or protect his crew. For a man like Jennings, there was only one choice.

"We'll take it," Jennings said quietly. Pausing long enough to lean forward, he then asked, "Who's the mark?"

# Chapter 4

*Two Weeks Earlier…*

Michelle Williams stared out at the skyline of her parent's four-story condominium on the 234th floor of the old Monument building. She could see White Tower, the mammoth edifice which used to house the senate and presidential offices of the Terran Federation. Formerly a bastion to freedom, now it was the home of the Terran Autonomous Region Ruling Council.

A hundred other skyscrapers dotted the sky of the Washingtonian district of Seaboard, most topping off at the one hundred and seventy-five story mark. Somewhere deep below where she stood, the leafless cherry trees on the tree-lined streets were festooned in Christmas lights. A moment of sadness spoiled the view as she thought about what used to stand on the grounds of White Tower and what the giant white obelisk had now come to represent. She considered her parents' own role in its conversion and how they afforded this massive home in the richest neighborhood on the planet, and she felt shame.

The megalopolis of Seaboard stretched down nearly the entire east coast of the area that was once the United States of America, now part of a greater governing zone simply known as the Americas. The Washingtonian district stood on the capital of that former nation and had become the capital of first a unified Earth and then the Terran Federation as an acknowledgement to the role the Americans played in unifying the planet. The Gael had simply swooped in and corrupted the entire district from a bastion of democracy to the hand puppet of a totalitarian state. Michelle hated the Gael for what they had done to her nation and her planet with a fury generally reserved for the few human soldiers who survived the war- those who failed to protect their planet. To be fair, most of that fury was the fault of her parents.

James K. and Madison Williams were both career politicians from wealthy families who had served in government for as long as anyone cared to remember. James's family came from a long line of

Congressmen and governors in the old United States, one even having been a vice-presidential nominee. The family of Madison had dominated Toronto politics and ruled Canada the way the Kennedys once ruled the world. They had both been representatives to the Terran Federation Senate during the war, and both called for Earth's surrender long before it came. When the Gael arrested and disappeared many of Earth's prominent leaders, her parents sidestepped the problem by welcoming the invaders to Earth with open arms and accepting senior leadership positions in the twelve-man Terran Autonomous Region Ruling Council.

While they managed to have a platitude or a rationalization for every action they committed, Michelle considered them to be traitors nonetheless and hated them with every ounce of her being. When she was in high school, she decorated her room with old-fashioned posters of Abraham Lincoln, George Washington, and Che Guevara along with copies of the Declaration of Independence, Magna Carta and *cahiers de dolerance* brought to the Estates General in France in the eighteenth century. As frequently as she dared, she wore shirts which featured the Resistance logo: the clenched fist on fire against a starry backdrop.

Now a senior at the prestigious and historic College of William and Mary, Michelle had blossomed into an intelligent, thoughtful, idealistic young woman, but her opinions had not changed. Flowing red hair, ivory white skin, and deep green eyes combined with a voluptuously full figure and "legs that went on forever" (as a drunk English professor once shared with her) made her an object of a good deal of attention from the young men at the university. Only one had really turned her head though, and it was for his beliefs not his looks. His name was Tanner Rice, and he was the founder of an on-campus organization which called itself Common Sense. He was on his way to her parents' apartment that very night, and they were out of town for Christmas break.

Although she did not plan to sleep with him, Michelle had not ruled it out entirely either. Tanner had such a way with words. For hours, she had listened to him rail on issues that hit her deeply: bringing back control of the Terran government to the people, kicking the Gael influence out of human affairs, finding small ways to legally support the Resistance like staging sit-ins, nonviolent protests, and rallies. Several times he had invited her to come to demonstrations he planned. They were not always successful, and sometimes only a handful of fellow students showed up, but she believed in her heart that they were making a statement just by doing something.

The day they truly lost to the Gael was the day they stopped trying to resist them. Those were the words he had whispered in her ear the first time she let him reach up under her shirt, his tongue flicking her earlobe in between each bit of political rhetoric. Tanner was the same as she- one of the fighters. Michelle believed that to the bottom of her heart, and she could not wait to see him again.

The doorbell chimed, an annoying reenactment of the new Terran Autonomous Region anthem, and Michelle checked her appearance in the ornate antique mirror in the foyer of the condominium. Her make-up was on perfectly, her hair straight, a political T-shirt wrapped tightly over her chest highlighted her curves nicely, and a black skirt with black stockings said that she was accessible, but not easy. It was perfect, she thought to herself as she swung the door open.

"Hey," Tanner said, his eyes trapped on her shirt for a moment before raising them to meet her smile.

"Come on in," she said with a star-struck grin plastered on her face.

Sweeping past her through the foyer and into the living room, he appraised the high-end furniture, the antiques, and the artwork with a clear disdain. Michelle understood completely.

"Sorry it's so bourgeois," she said. "It's kind of embarrassing."

"Yeah, definitely." He dropped his leather jacket onto the floor and pushed his sunglasses back up into his long black hair.

Tanner wore a sleeveless black faux-velvet shirt and blood red denim jeans tucked into black military boots. Seven or so bracelets adorned each wrist, and he had a tattoo of some Asian characters on his right shoulder.

"This isn't really my vibe," he said. "Too rich. Why don't you show me your room? You said you had some cool posters, right?"

"Absolutely," she said excitedly. "Up this way."

Taking his hand, she led him up the circular, open-air stairs past the second floor, which she said was her parents', and to the third where her room was. Everything so far was going exactly as Michelle hoped.

~

*Finally,* Tanner thought to himself as they made their way upstairs. He had already put in more work closing escrow on Michelle Williams than on any conquest he had ever pursued. *With that kind of body, she would be worth it, but still…* Pretending to be the exact man she thought him to be was utterly exhausting, and if he did not close the deal soon, he would certainly slip up.

Fortunately, Michelle did not seem to notice the involuntary eye roll Tanner performed as she took his hand and led him upstairs. Or that he lingered a step or two behind her so she would not see him already straining against his pants. Just seeing her in that tight T-shirt… *Easy, Tanner,* he told himself. *You don't want to do anything prematurely.*

They crossed the third floor's landing, and Michelle swung open a door emblazoned with a Resistance fist. Shaking his head slightly at such lunacy, he followed her into the room and spent a perfunctory amount of time admiring the political posters she had gotten from God knew where. They made a little small talk about what each one meant to her, and he feigned enough interest to make her happy.

Michelle sounded like she was about to launch into some political tirade, and Tanner decided he was going to make his move and live with it. He just could not take it anymore. "Kinda dangerous wearing that shirt." He indicated the white stenciled letters which read RESIST with a nod of the head.

"In my parents' apartment?" she said. "I think it's safe."

"Just to be certain, you'd better take it off." With a wry grin, he then held up his hands as if in apology. "I'm only thinking of your welfare and what might happen if a Gael saw you."

Understanding crossed her face, followed by a coy smile, and Michelle slowly pulled her shirt off showing a white bra barely containing her beautiful breasts. An incredible hunger took over

Tanner, and he pulled her close, panting as he ran his tongue over her. Immediately his hands went under her skirt and pulled her stockings down to her knees.

"Tanner, I don't--"

"Shh..." He held a finger to her lips and then kissed her passionately on them.

Fear surrendering to passion, she returned the embrace, and Tanner fumbled quickly with his zipper and his denim pants fell to his ankles, but he was too late. "Oh God!" he groaned as he grabbed her breasts once more. It was all over.

Though flushed, short of breath and entirely obsessed with his own coming back to reality, Tanner still noticed the expression equal parts confusion and revulsion on Michelle's face. This was replaced by a questioning countenance which seemed to ask, "Was that what sex was supposed to be like?" Quickly, it was subsumed by an expression of realization. She had just been with her first lover, and Tanner could see love blossoming in her eyes as she moved closer to embrace him.

"No cuddling, sweetie," he said, quickly stepping back. "You need to clean up first- probably a shower and a change of clothes."

"Oh," the sound escaped her lips, followed by a long pause. "Right, I'll just do that then," she said before heading into the adjoining bathroom.

"I'm going to climb into bed," he called after her. "Need to get ready for round two." The last was spoken more to himself as he pulled back the flower petal designed covers on her bed and slid in, hoping he would be able to hold his wad until the actual intercourse next time.

~

For a building which housed some of the wealthiest people on the planet, security was surprisingly lax, Pascal Jacobin thought to himself as he stood in the elevator riding up to the 234th floor. The front desk did not even bother to call up to the Williams's condominium to advertise he was coming. All he needed to say was that he was a friend of Michelle's from college coming to visit, and he had been waved through security.

Places like this relied way too much on their technology to deter people such as him, and Jacobin did not entirely fault them. The technology was fairly impressive. All floors used motion, thermal and chemical sensors. Holographic cameras covered in detail every square inch of the building; there were no blind spots. Entry into the individual units involved knowing a rotating twenty-digit alphanumeric code, and no cracking software could break through in anything less than a decade. Without a keycard, entry was impossible. Although human security officers existed, the whole thing was run by a computer that existed off the mainline and could not be hacked. Knowing all of that, Jacobin still smiled to himself: this would be a piece of cake.

Jacobin came across as younger than he was and presented himself as utterly non-descript in every way. He wore a charcoal gray suit with a white dress shirt, tieless as the fashion of the day dictated. His hair was short, but not in a militaristic way, nothing which would give the hint of aggression. He was Caucasian and clean-shaven in a way that was wholly unremarkable. In a city of one hundred million people, at least three million looked exactly like he did, blending into society perfectly. He could be a young lawyer, banker or the aide to a politician. Just as easily he might be a salesman or a man on the way to a funeral. His expression was perfectly even and deliberately aloof as he stepped out of the elevator and came to a stop.

Taking out a pair of eyeglasses from his shirt pocket, he put them on and the built-in heads-up display kicked on, immediately feeding lines of information on lighting, power consumption, oxygen levels, distances between objects in his line of sight, and where the holographic cameras and sensors were located in the walls. He casually stared directly into the nearest camera and clicked a small button on the side of his glasses frame.

Imperceptible to normal eyesight, an ultraviolet beam of light shot out from the bridge of the glasses and hit the nearest set of sensors and cameras. It was state of the art technology and a brilliant way to upload code into a computer which controlled sensory apparatus. The code went into the system as data saved within the image itself and then wormed its way to its real target, causing the system to enter a five-minute loop which began ten minutes before the code had been triggered. The computer deceived itself into looking at video data from the recent past rather than the present, leaving Jacobin to carry out his mission without any interference. Had a person glanced at the video monitor, they would have seen exactly what Jacobin was doing, but no one bothered as the computer was supposed to handle alerting them to any threats.

Heading down the corridor, Jacobin smiled and gave a small nod to an elderly couple headed toward the elevator. He rounded a curve and came to the door of the Williams's home. Taking a look at the overly complex electronic lock, he had to restrain a laugh at the simplicity of his method for bypassing this obstacle compared with the techno-espionage required on the cameras. He took a keycard out of his jacket pocket and slid it into the slot. No door in the world was secure when the right amount of money could buy you a copy of the key, he thought to himself.

The door swung open, and he cautiously stepped inside, swinging his head back and forth to see if his glasses picked up any heat signatures. Seeing none, Jacobin turned his glasses toward the condo's illumination controls and sent another fragment of code into the system. This one would allow him to turn off the lights in the house at a simple command. Moving silently, he began making his way up the stairs to sweep the upper floors and find his quarry.

~

Stepping out of the shower, Michelle wrapped a towel around her torso and grabbed a head towel to take care of her hair. She had taken a brutally hot shower and had stayed in too long, mulling over the decisions she made as she tinged her skin pink. The encounter with Tanner had been what she wanted, or so she thought, but it did not make her feel any different. He seemed colder somehow than when they had spoken for hours on ending the occupation or returning freedom to the Terran Federation.

She wiped some of the moisture off the mirror, but it started to fog up quickly again. Staring at her own hazy reflection, she asked a dozen silent questions of herself, but got no satisfactory response. An overwhelming sadness welled up within her, and silent tears began to stream down her face. This was not what she wanted at all- not how she imagined it. Michelle had the horrible feeling that some part of her was gone- something she would never get back. Staring into the mirror, she tried to put herself back together as she knew she would need to go back out and face Tanner. But then, the lights went out.

~

Intel had been right for once, Jacobin thought to himself. The parents were indeed gone, and the house was deserted except for his target. Jacobin found it odd that they wanted the daughter dead and not the parents. The parents were known collaborators and high up on the Resistance's list of most hated humans, but the order came down to him for the girl, so he was here for the girl.

The glasses fed a heat signature through to Jacobin, showing the girl in bed lying down, probably asleep. A lot of residual heat flared in the bathroom- she had probably just taken a bath or a shower to relax and then curled up in bed for a nice evening nap before heading out to party or go clubbing. Young people, he thought to himself as he sent the command that killed the lights in the apartment just to be safe.

Counting to two, he swung open the bedroom door silently as he withdrew his small plasma pistol with an oblong sound suppressor attached to it. The target did not even wake up before he fired six shots into the bed and heard the customary sound of plasma striking flesh and flashing through. With the heat vision on his glasses, he saw that two of his shots struck the woman's forehead and four more hit her chest.

His target was definitely dead, but he was thorough and needed to check. As he reached to pull back the comforter, he switched out of heat vision and over to night-vision. Pain then exploded through his eyes, sending him reeling backwards and out through the door. Alarms sounded, loud klaxons screaming into his ears, and he ripped off the glasses. The lights had come back on, and white strobes had been added. Someone was trying to break into the apartment.

"You must be joking," Jacobin said to himself.

"Kill that alarm," came an authoritative voice from downstairs.

The reply was inaudible from where Jacobin stood, but it did not matter. Quickly, he put his weapon back into his shoulder holster and raced up the stairs to the fourth-floor loft. Another exit to the 237th floor hallway there, but the security systems would not be neutralized. Not knowing who he was dealing with, he was not certain if he had the time to try and upload the code into the hallway monitors. If it was the police who had busted down the Williams's door, they would be locking down the building shortly.

Taking only a moment to decide, he quickly took off his jacket and shirt, leaving only a black undershirt. He wadded the clothes into a ball, hiding his plasma pistol within, and he hit another button on the glasses tinting them black. Opening the door and stepping into the hall, he tossed the clothing into one of the handy garbage incinerator chutes and strode toward the elevator, looking like a man about to step out into the evening and head to a nightclub or discotheque.

~

The door to the bathroom had been slightly ajar when the lights went out, and Michelle peeked out to see if Tanner was messing with switches, trying to create some mood lighting. The room was jet black save for the little bit of neon from the streets outside sneaking through the drawn shade. She did not know why, but a nervous tremor starting at the base of her spine made her swallow back the interrogative she was going to call out to Tanner.

Without warning, her bedroom door swung inward, and she saw someone's silhouette. A whirring sound of something powering up hummed softly, and the room filled with silent flashes as bright beams of energy blew apart her bed. And the man in it, she realized in horror a split second later. Fear paralyzed her; she could not take her eyes away from the ghostly visage in front of her.

Michelle wanted to scream as the unknown intruder made his way forward to inspect the wreckage of her bed. At last, she pulled herself slowly away from the door, backing around the sink and crouching between a shelf and the commode. As she hid, her hip brushed against something on the back of the toilet, and she sensed something falling in the pure darkness. Terror gripped her as she knew she had just revealed her location.

Alarms exploded all around her as the lights came back on. She never heard her makeup box hit the floor in the cacophony, and neither did the intruder apparently. When she looked again, the shooter was gone. Moving slowly, she crept her way out of the bathroom, still wrapped in a towel and made her way toward the bed. The thought of defense crossed her mind slowly, and she reached out to a shelf to grab a trophy for an equestrian event she won when she was twelve. Michelle brandished it like a club and turned back to her door, waiting for the intruder to return again, but he did not.

Moving slowly, not wanting to look but knowing she needed to, Michelle reached out and pulled back the blood-soaked, burned-out bedspread. Her hands instinctively went to her mouth to stifle a gasp of horror. Tanner's face was gone- melted by the heat of the plasma shot. A violent spell of nausea hit her, and she doubled over, vomiting onto her carpet. She heaved over and over again as tears began to stream down her face.

"Do you hear that?" a voice called from the hallway.

"In here." A second voice.

The sense of sickness vanished, and she gripped the trophy harder. The door swung open and a short, squat man with a thick jaw and three days stubble walked through it. Michelle let loose a primal scream and hurled the trophy through the air. The golden horse atop it struck the man right in the face, and he cried out in shock and pain.

"Are you all right?" a man asked from the hallway.

"No, I'm not all right!" the short man thundered. "She hit me right in my teeth. Son of a bitch!"

The second man stepped into the room and sized up the completely unarmed, mostly naked woman. He was tall compared to his companion and better dressed, clean shaven and younger. Deliberately, he pulled a weapon from his suit jacket. It was not a pistol, Michelle realized, but rather it was a shock stick.

"We're not here to hurt you," the tall one said calmly. "Now, I must ask you to co-operate with us, so I don't have to use this."

"Maybe you should have thought of that before you shot Tanner!" she screamed.

"Shot? Who's been shot?" the short one grunted through his hand as he tried to rub the teeth hit by the trophy.

The tall one sniffed the air. "Plasma residue," he said darkly as his eyes fell to the bed and he stepped around Michelle and the puddle of sick. "Good God." Covering his mouth with his hand, he stumbled backwards after pulling back the comforter. "What the hell is going on?" His attention snapped over to Michelle.

She finally collapsed to the ground, the tears beginning anew. "He killed Tanner." She repeated it over and over.

The tall one's next few statements sounded as if they were being spoken from across a chasm. "Paul, you better call this in. We need the police now."

"Whatever you say, Gil," he grumbled.

Gilbert turned back to her. "Ma'am, my partner and I are licensed private investigators and fugitive retrieval specialists here in the Seaboard district." He flashed out an official looking ID card. "We were here to place you under arrest under a warrant issued at 4:30 this afternoon by Terran Interplanetary Security and the Ministry of Justice. We were going to bring you into the police ourselves, but considering…" His voice trailed off.

Michelle curled herself up into a ball as the tall one found a blanket on top of her antique hope chest and wrapped it around her shoulders. Her stare was a thousand yards away, and Gilbert frowned down at her as if he felt a little sorry for her. He said as much to Paul when he returned, but Gil's partner pointed out that she certainly wasn't the first person to murder a lover and regret it afterward.

~

The place was already a zoo, Detective Lieutenant Pierce James thought to himself as he arrived on the third floor of the condominium. He was impeccably dressed in a light brown suit and an old-fashioned gray fedora no modern white cop would have been able to pull off. James took off a khaki overcoat and passed it to a uniformed security officer, who took it wordlessly.

A feisty energetic man with pale skin and shockingly red hair spied James and hustled over to him. "This is shit," Palmer announced as he began to lead James through the scene.

Terry Palmer was a young detective, fifteen years James's junior and still passionate about the job. That probably explained the shirt and tie with food stains on it that all looked like they had been slept in the night before. Palmer had probably crashed in his office chair. James sighed, remembering when he had that type of energy for solving homicides.

"Who called it in?" James asked as he stuck his hands in a black box set on a portable table the Crime Scene Unit had set up. His hands were covered in a latex sheen, and he turned back to Palmer.

The younger cop nodded toward two men talking to uniformed officers. "These two bloodsuckers. They broke into the place to perform a snatch and grab on the daughter of two Councilmen."

"Local?"

"Nope, Councilors James and Madison Williams," he said.

"Fuck me," James muttered. "We've got to keep the press out of this as long as possible. If they find out we've got a TARC member's daughter here, we're going to get filleted."

"Tell me about it."

"Are you holding these two?" James asked, pointing back to Gilbert and Paul.

"Nah, they're licensed," he said, checking his notepad.

James came to a sudden stop. "Wait, you're telling me there's a legitimate warrant and bounty on the daughter of two TARC members? On what charge?"

Palmer locked eyes with him. "Conspiracy to commit terrorism."

An open-mouthed expression of incredulousness passed James's face. "This is shit," he said at last.

"Gets better," Palmer said. "Follow me."

James entered the bedroom behind Palmer and found a room that any late teenager might have, especially if they fought a lot with their parents and their parents were TARC members. A bunch of political propaganda posters adorned the wall along with shelves full of old textbooks, political treatises and pictures of younger, happier times with her parents. Then there was the dead body lying fragged in the bed.

"Who the hell is this then?"

"Tanner Rice, age twenty-one," Palmer read off his tablet. "Student at William and Mary with Michelle Williams." He nodded toward the girl getting medical treatment from a crisis counselor. "Apparently, they are in some student organizations together. He came over here to *discuss his politics* if you know what I mean. And then this." He waved his hand in the direction of the body.

"You're saying the girl did it?" he asked incredulously.

"Killed him without anyone hearing the shots, setting off the weapon alarms, or arousing any suspicion, and then took a shower…" Palmer nodded, although he did not appear convinced. "While still managing to vanish the gun before the two bloodsuckers showed up."

"How do you know that?"

"Didn't use it on them," he said. "Chucked that at them instead." He pointed to the trophy lying on floor with a duct tape circle running around it.

"What's her motive?" James asked.

"She didn't finish?" Palmer suggested wryly, shrugging his shoulders.

James scowled at him. "You realize there are about ten thousand holes in your theory."

"Yeah, but it sure as hell beats her story," he said as he checked his notes again. "An unknown assailant breaks into the apartment, kills the lights and then opens fire on Mr. Rice here. This mystery assassin becomes scared when the lights come back on and the two bounty hunters enter and vanishes into thin air."

"Security cameras?"

"Nobody comes in after Mr. Rice and before the bounty twins," Palmer said. "There wasn't anyone else in the condo."

"Shit, this stinks," James mumbled as he stared at the pretty young girl who was their best murder suspect.

"Yeah, like I said," Palmer said. "Look, she's wanted on the terrorism count already. With shit that complicated, there might be an explanation for what happened here that you and I are never going to explain."

"What are you suggesting?"

He shrugged. "We run her in on that beef and keep investigating. A murder rap is not going to be that big a deal when we drop the word terrorist into the mix."

"Yeah, you're right," James sighed. "Get her dressed, slap some binders on her and let's take her down to the station."

"You got it, boss." He gave a curt nod and quickly grabbed a uniformed officer to start relaying instructions.

James took another glance at Michelle Williams as the crisis counselor held up a blanket for her to get dressed behind. She looked so scared. Her makeup was running down her face and was smeared from her attempts to wipe away her own tears. She sure as hell did not give the impression of terrorist or murderer, but what the hell did he know? If you believed the Gael, the terrorists were everyone and could be anyone. Williams fit the profile as well as anyone: idealism mixed with education and youthful desire to rebel. He sighed again. The Resistance just did not realize how futile it all was.

# Chapter 5

Sitting in his small shuttle on the street level, Pascal Jacobin cursed his luck. The police had arrived, but they were not the first on the scene. The building's security station had been a bit chaotic, but he had been waved through without any commotion. His ID said he belonged there, and he was dressed far too nicely to be breaking into someone's house. (He wore thousand dollar loafers, for God's sake.) After exiting the building without any fuss, he had waited a good six minutes before the first security shuttle arrived. The cops docked at a loading valet on the 200th floor. Another three minutes later, additional units arrived, docking at the 100th and 300th floors, with a few more arriving on ground level.

Jacobin was tempted to take flight and see if anything was happening at the loading docks, but then he saw a black shuttle labeled CORONER landing right behind him, and he saw no further need. He would need to follow the medical vessel to the hospital to verify his kill, but breaking into a hospital was easy, especially if he waited for later into the night.

Time drew out slowly, and hours passed, but Jacobin was patient and his eyes tracked everything. The press arrived but was being kept out of the building. A few more officers threw up cordons to keep them at bay. Pointless trying to limit the press, Jacobin thought to himself. Soon enough they would have their story: rich student daughter of powerful *blah blah blah* horribly murdered by *blah blah blah*. It would make the news for a few days, then the Gael would cover it up. The Resistance would claim a quiet victory, and the world would keep on turning.

Finally, he saw the coroners coming out of the lobby pushing a hover sled through the overly ornate gold plate doors. The flash of digital imagers and holographic cameras snapped around the body like fireworks. As quickly as the coroners could, they slid the hovering gurney into the back of their shuttle. Jacobin prepped his shuttle to take off as well, but immediately killed the engines when he saw the police emerge with a young redhead in binders.

"Son of a bitch." Quickly, Jacobin punched in a long sequence of numbers into the screen of his shuttle's computer panel. "Cipher griffin four-four-two-one," he barked at the static filled screen. The screen shifted to black, but Jacobin knew someone was listening. "The mark eluded. Repeat the mark has eluded."

"Stand-by," a voice said. "Patching to CL."

The Cell Leader appeared in silhouette against a dark blue background on the screen. "What the hell happened?"

"The party got crashed before the job was complete," he reported. "Collateral damage down."

"Dammit, man. It's one girl."

"I didn't know the local bounty hunters would come swooping by her place looking for an easy payday," he spat back. "The Gael didn't post any of the others this quickly."

"She's number one hundred and eleven on the Aurora List. Out of one hundred and eleven, Mr. Jacobin," he said. "With O'Sullivan in the wind, guess they couldn't hold their wad."

"I can still get to her," he said.

The Cell Leader's silhouette shifted in surprise. "She's not in police custody?"

"No, she is, but I can hit them en route to the station," he said.

"Jesus," the Cell Leader swore, before sighing. "What do you need from me?"

"Their likely course and a roadblock where it's most advantageous and least conspicuous," Jacobin said. "And fast. They're leaving now."

"Working," the Cell Leader said. "Okay, we've got Gillespie in the area. She can rig a fire show at 42nd and Constitution. Industrial sector- no witnesses. It should give you a clean shot. Don't fucking miss!"

"Roger," he said as he punched the ship's throttle.

The police shuttle was already getting out of his eyeshot, but he programmed his boat to follow it from a safe distance. Meanwhile he turned around in his seat and reached into the storage area behind his ship's two seats, pulling out a long cylindrical bag and placing it into the seat next to him. According to the GPS system, he had five minutes until they reached Constitution. It was more than enough time he thought to himself as he began assembling the weapon.

~

"Sorry about the press," Detective Pierce James muttered as he shut the shuttle's hatch and nodded at Detective Terry Palmer to take off.

Michelle did not reply. She sat in the back seat of the police skiff, her mind reeling from everything she had seen. Detectives James and Palmer had both been unfailingly polite when they questioned her in her bedroom, but her answers had been cold and distant. Nothing about what happened made sense to her, and Michelle felt she must be missing just as many pieces to the puzzle as the detectives were.

The officers told her she had a warrant out for her arrest on suspicion of terrorism- that is what the two men who showed up first had been doing in her home. They were two of the luckiest bounty hunters in the world- showing up at her house on the highly unlikely chance that a wanted fugitive would be found at the address listed in the Nucleus's directory. She supposed she should thank them, interrupting her would-be assassin before he confirmed she was not the one lying dead in her bed. Palmer had grumbled something about bureaucratic inefficiency- if the police had known about the warrant before the bounty hunters, the government wouldn't be out of a quarter of a million dollars.

Perhaps that was the most outrageous bit of it all, she thought, suppressing the mournful laugh rising in her throat. Not only was she a terrorist according to the Ministry of Justice, but her capture was worth more than bounty hunters would receive for taking out an entire cell of Resistance members. On top of that, the warrant specified Alive Only. The Gael generally did not care what condition Resistance members were in when they were taken, even if it was just a smoking corpse. *Why would they want her alive?*

That being the case, why was there a man in her apartment trying to kill her? He couldn't have been a bounty hunter as he wouldn't miss out on the chance to pick up his cash. The police told her there was no evidence of another person in the apartment, so the man was obviously very good at what he did. That led to a whole slew of other questions beyond why anyone would want her dead- who wanted her dead so badly that they would hire a highly skilled, professional hitman to kill her? Perhaps it had something to do with her parents, she thought. They could be trying to send her parents a message by killing their only daughter.

Anything seemed possible at this point, she thought to herself, fighting back an overwhelming feeling of despair. She had not even taken a moment to mourn for Tanner, she realized as the skiff rounded a turn and accelerated through the end of a residential district and into the Mall Memorial Commercial Park. Residential towers vanished, and a surprising amount of darkness enveloped them as the only illumination in the park came from the street lamps hundreds of feet below them. The cab of the skiff fell into shadow, and Michelle at last began to cry.

~

Detective Terry Palmer felt awkward as hell knowing a cute girl was crying in the back of his shuttle, but that she was also a murder and terrorism suspect. Was she feeling regret or was the sense of loss starting to hit her? One never knew with these types of cases. He wanted to pity her, place his hand on her shoulder and tell her it would be all right, but if she was what she was accused of...

In the end, he tried to stay down the middle. "We tried to call your parents, but they were unavailable. Your father's assistant's secretary has a call into their lawyer's office, and an attorney will be meeting you at the station. If you need to talk-"

"Thanks, I know my rights," Michelle spat back harshly before she took a breath and visibly calmed. "Sorry, it's been a rough day."

"You know we want to believe you," Palmer began, which caused James to throw a glance his way. "But things don't add up."

"We went over this at my house," she said, clearly exasperated. "I don't know what else I can tell you that's going to make you believe me."

Putting the skiff in automatic, Palmer turned around to face her. "I'll tell you what. We're going to follow the evidence. That means we're not handing you over to the Gael until we are utterly convinced you deserve to be locked up."

A sad sigh escaped from the back. "You don't think they can manufacture whatever evidence they want?"

James glanced back at her as well. "That sounds sort of conspiratorial."

In response, Michelle growled, "A man broke into my home in a secure high-rise, bypassed all of our high-tech security, and managed to murder my friend without showing up on any security cameras, and you think I sound like a conspiracy theorist?" She drew a sharp breath. "You don't have to believe me, but I know Tanner was murdered by someone else in that room and I know I've never committed an act of terrorism in my life, unless attending anti-Gael Occupation Force rallies is an act of terrorism. I know- Look out!"

The skiff entered the Suitland Industrial District and was met with the harsh halogen glare of industrial lighting on the skyway. The skyway swung left and ran between two enormous four hundred story factory buildings, hulking masses of steel and stone which spread the equivalent of twenty city blocks lengthwise. In the middle of the street about one hundred yards in front of them, an inferno raged. A stalled hovercar lingered in the skyway, spewing fire high into the air as well as toward the ground below: a pure, unbreaking column of greenish-yellow plasma fire.

There was no way to get through the column heading down to the surface, and they did not have enough time to climb up and above the firestorm. Palmer quickly switched the control back over to manual and fired his retro-rockets full burn. With a sickening lurch, the shuttle screamed to a stop, and all three occupants slammed forward.

~

"What the hell?" Palmer groaned as he pulled his face out of the control column. A trickle of blood ran down his forehead.

The skiff hovered only about twenty feet from the blazing vehicle- Michelle could almost feel the heat coming off it. She had hit her head on the seat in front of her, but fortunately not too hard. The pain was much worse in her wrists though. The binders wrapped around her and chained to the floor had caught her hands as she was flung forward. She was pretty sure she was bleeding.

"You okay?" James asked, looking back to her. In the soft light, he looked like a zombie with his broken nose and cut lips.

"I don't know," Michelle said as the pain in her hands intensified. "My wrists are ripped to shreds."

James slid back the partition between them and leaned through it. "Let me see."

Examining her hands gingerly, he produced a laser-cut key, inserted it into the lock on her binders, and turned it. He did a cursory examination of the cuts- they weren't deep, but they would still need medical attention. Dropping the binders in the front seat, he said, "I don't think you'll need those for a little while," before turning to his partner. "We better call this in."

"Yeah, right." Palmer punched in a code into the secure comm in the dashboard. He swung his head to the left, to the right and back to the left, cracking his neck each time. "Oh shit!" he swore vehemently as he suddenly punched the throttle up and pushed the shuttle into a dive.

"Palmer, what the hell are you doing?" James cried.

The explosion rocked the shuttle, flinging Michelle against the window. Everything moved in slow-motion for her: the fast-blinking alarm lights warning of their impending doom; the ground rushing up to meet them; and the streak of smoke as another torpedo sped its their way toward them took an eternity to process. Just before the second impact, she swore she saw a shuttle behind them with an open cockpit and a man with a rocket launcher pointed at them. For just a moment, she knew that was the man who killed Tanner. Then, there was a sickening crunch and everything went black.

~

The first shot took out the shuttle's rear thrusters, but it had not been a kill shot thanks to some excellent piloting on the driver's part. The ship was careening so badly that Pascal Jacobin's second shot impacted on the exposed belly of the shuttle, one of the more reinforced areas on it. Most of the repulsors cut out, and the ship fell another fifty feet to the ground, the twisted and mangled aft end still burning. A third shot would have taken them completely out, but he passed up on it for two reasons. One, he needed to make sure the girl was dead with absolute certainty, and that meant watching the life drain out of her eyes. Second, that was the part of the job he enjoyed the most.

As swiftly as possible, Jacobin set down his shuttle next to the flaming wreckage and opened the cockpit. He swung his legs up and over the side of the ship and allowed himself to drop to the ground as he drew his plasma pistol from its holster. There was no movement inside the wreckage, but he took no chances. Carefully, Jacobin stalked up to the police shuttle at an oblique angle, making sure they would not have the opportunity to fire off a few potshots at him if there were survivors.

The shuttle had landed on its belly, but it seemed as if one of the landing gears had at least partially descended as the ship was resting at a strange angle, tilted toward the ground on the side he approached. The pilot's head lay against the window in the front hatch. The hatch refused to open as the bottom portion of it was pinned by the ground, so Jacobin put his pistol to the glass and fired straight through, splattering blood and gray matter across the cockpit's cracked windshield. Sirens began to blare in the distance so he hurried around to the front of the ship and grabbed the handle at the bottom of the hatch.

Opening it, Jacobin saw the older, black detective's body lying sprawled across the control console. Casually, he fired two rounds into the cop's chest. The body spasmed, but did not move. Jacobin's eyes tracked through the back seat, but it was empty. He flipped on his glasses and switched them to night vision mode so he could stare into the blackened recess behind the seats which served as the shuttle's storage area. The girl was huddled in the back, pressed in between a storage bin and the rear hatch. A small smile crept across his face as he climbed into the back seat and took aim at Michelle's face. Her eyes were brilliantly beautiful in the emerald green night vision, Jacobin thought to himself as his finger began to squeeze the trigger.

"Hey," a voice gargled from behind him.

Whirling around, Jacobin found himself face to muzzle with the well-dressed black detective's service pistol pointed through the partition. "Fuck you," the voice rasped as James pulled the trigger, blasting a round of superheated plasma through the assassin's high-tech glasses and into his eye.

~

The assassin's corpse fell to the floor of the shuttle in between the rows of seats, and James's gun hand fell down to his side. He then fell over, letting his head land on the lap of his partner. Immediately, Michelle rushed forward, stepping on the assassin's body accidentally, and leaned over through the partition.

"Are you okay?" she asked James.

"Peachy," he said, his face ashen. "That was the guy, wasn't it?" His voice was barely a whisper now.

"Yes," she whispered back, leaving out the, "I think so," that sprang to mind. The sirens were getting louder.

He nodded. "Get the hell out of here. Don't stop running."

A few more tears welled in Michelle's eyes, but she forced them back and crawled out of the shuttle. The sirens sounded as if they were coming from behind her, but she could not go forward as the blazing inferno (which she was now certain had been set by the assassin who lay dead in the police shuttle) blocked her escape forward. Sprinting as fast as she could, she raced away from the industrial area, making a few turns to hopefully clear the path of any incoming police shuttles, and made her way to the park, vanishing into the night.

# Chapter 6

Matthew Jennings dropped the tablet onto the table, having just finished reading Pahhal's report for the second time. A bitter sensation crept over him, starting with his gut and worming its way up his throat like bile. They were going after an idealistic college student, one supposed to be a terrorist. Personally, he did not buy anything Pahhal had said, but he ran over the conversation once more in his head.

"As you can see, she went into hiding after the detectives bringing her in were murdered," the Gael said. "We don't know if the unidentified man found dead on the scene with the two officers was there to rescue her or not. It seems the likeliest scenario."

"My arse," Fix grunted, which drew an amused head tilt from Pahhal.

"You don't launch torpedoes into a shuttle carrying someone you're trying to rescue," Jennings clarified.

"Perhaps," the Gael said. "But you know it wasn't us, if that's your concern. We very much want her alive."

"And why is dat?" Lafayette asked.

"We will make an example of these terrorists," Pahhal said. "Humans appreciate spectacle, and so we will create one in an effort to discourage those who would perpetuate acts of terror against their fellow citizens."

Something did not add up about what Pahhal said, but Jennings could not put his finger on it, and he did not let that stop him from accepting the job. What was more important to him was that they had some cash, some supplies, and some work which promised more of the same. They would find the girl and let the Gael worry about her trial.

With Pahhal now long gone, Jennings continued to sit at the table in the Caf, lost in his own thoughts when Lafayette came up the gangplank pushing an anti-grav cart stocked high with supplies.

"*Mon capitaine*, a hand *s'il vous plait*," he called.

Ignoring him, Jennings kept staring down at the tablet. "If the Gael want her alive, who the hell is trying to kill her?"

Sighing as he began to singlehandedly stock the galley, Lafayette said, "I suppose it's too much to hope *dat* it was random. Some sort of psychopath."

"We both know it's not that," he countered. "You don't attack the police with rockets if you're a psycho looking for a thrill." Still preoccupied, he took a deep breath and then stood up to begin helping Lafayette. "It's not a bounty hunter either. One, it's too high-tech and well organized to be anyone but the largest players. This guy was too fast, too good to be a mere cellar dweller like us."

Lafayette feigned offense.

Jennings continued, "He had connections; he knew he was going to kill the girl before the warrant crossed the Nucleus." He eyed a package contemptuously. "Canned beats? Really?"

"Don't like it; don't eat it," he shot back.

"Anyway, second, this assassin they found dead with the two cops," Jennings said. "No ID, fingerprints had been stripped off, he had new retinas, and DNA was entirely inconclusive. The guy's a ghost."

Lafayette stopped and locked eyes with him. "I know what you're getting at. If this girl is getting hunted by the Resistance…"

"They would kill us all and a million more around us to get to her," Jennings finished. "I know, but we took the job. What other choices do we have?"

"Take the money and run," he countered quickly. "We could find more work…"

Jennings shook his head. "Do you think we're going to be able to find anything after we get a rep for welching on a deal? We won't be able to get a sniff, honest or not, and then we're dead in space."

"*Merde*," Lafayette muttered under his breath. "Can't get out from under the lion's paw, can we?"

"We always fight our way clear," Jennings said calmly. "Sooner or later."

Lafayette nodded and went back to placing some more items into the galley storage cupboards, grunting with effort with the heavier items. "What's next then? Where do we start looking for her?"

"Upper class girl on the run with no underworld contacts to sneak her off-world? She could be hiding with a friend, but the Gael would have found her if that was the case. So, she managed to get smuggled off-world somehow," Jennings mused. "The number of people she knows who could pull that off for her must be slim." Jennings glanced up to the ceiling as he always did when he talked to the near-artificial intelligent computer system onboard the *Melody Tryst*. "Minerva, my dear?"

"Captain Jennings," the pleasing female voice intoned. "What can I do for you?"

"I need a full profile on a Michelle Rachel Williams of Seaboard, North American continent, daughter of the TARC councilors," he said. "Focus on friends or relationships which might produce a tie to off-world shipping or smuggling."

"Processing," Minerva said. "It will be approximately 2.3 hours before search is complete."

~ .

Things were proceeding quite nicely, Jennings thought, and that was always a grave cause for concern. Lafayette had finished stocking the kitchen, and he was already making plans for actual cooked meals involving real food, non-canned vegetables and meat that came from real animals. Squawk was running around like a hyperactive hamster, tweaking items, fixing things that had not worked in months (like Lafayette's bathroom) as well as prepping the ship for takeoff, stocking the parts shed in the cargo bay, and refueling the ship's tanks and massive reserves. Meanwhile, Fix was busy changing out the *Melody Tryst's* spent plasma chargers- the space cannons had been mostly decorative for the last few months- as well as fixing the anti-personnel weapons systems and loading the space-to-space and air-to-surface missiles they had purchased. The database search was almost complete, and Pahhal had sent a message that their warrants would be quashed as soon as they took off.

Captain Jennings sat in the pilot's chair on the bridge, going over the pre-flight checklist. The bridge was small, just the six stations- pilot, navigator, tactical, communications, science and engineering- situated in a semi-circle in front of the viewscreen. Computer screens flashed with activity all around him as Minerva continued her search; security cameras jumped from signal to signal; the Magellan computer calculated navigational co-ordinates; and the flight HUD indicated one by one each aspect of pre-flight being completed.

Punching the intercom, Jennings sounded throughout the ship, "All hands report."

"This is Fix. External defenses online. Internal defenses not yet ready," came the terse reply.

Jenning nodded to himself. "Squawk, your status?"

"Go, go, all systems are go. Go!" came the excited reply.

"Once we're spaceborne give Fix a hand with the internals," he ordered.

"Roger!" the Pasquatil shrieked in manic glee.

Jennings could not help but smile. "Lafayette?"

"I don't think we can leave yet, *mon capitaine*," he said.

"Why not? What's wrong?"

"I can't find my favorite bouillabaisse pot," Lafayette said after a moment.

Jennings rolled his eyes. "Activating thrusters. Perhaps you could set aside your aspirations to haute cuisine for a moment and haul ass to the bridge." He paused. "Unless you want me to take a turn at using Magellan."

"*Non!*" Lafayette shouted. "En route!"

A wry smile crossed Jennings's face as he remembered the first time he attempted to use the navigation computer. The *Melody Tryst's* course skirted a little too close to a black hole for everyone's comfort, although Jennings still maintained they would have been fine. Ever since, Lafayette did not allow him near Magellan.

"Interstellar travel is far too complex and variable to allow for your kind of cowboy push the button and go mentality," Lafayette said as he stepped on the bridge and sat on Jennings's right at the navigator's seat, where he began gingerly touching Magellan's touch-screen interface. "Don't worry, *ma cherie*. I will not let him touch you again."

Jennings smiled as he activated an external comm line. "Mariador Control, this is *Starlight Minstrel* requesting permission to exit gravity."

"*Starlight Minstrel*. This is Mariador Control. Stand-by," came an automatic space traffic control reply.

"Let's hope the fake ID holds," Lafayette muttered.

"It'll work," Jennings said, expressing a confidence he did not exactly feel.

A female voice came on the line, "*Starlight Minstrel*, you are clear to enter the pattern. Engage thrusters only until above hard deck, then proceed on gravity exit vector eleven."

"Thanks, control," Jennings said as he kicked on the thrusters, and the *Melody Tryst* lifted off the ground.

"Safe sailing," the controller said.

Jennings punched a few commands into the computer, grabbed the control stick and the throttle, and began easing the ship up into the sky. A satisfied smile crossed his face, and a sense of ease flowed through his entire body. No matter how many times he performed the simple act of taking his ship into the sky, he never got over the thrill of it. The city of Centuria became smaller and smaller as Jennings continued to follow the elevator- the vertical airspace above each individual dock going from ground to the hard deck at ten thousand feet- skyward. The docks were a no-fly area without clearance, a prescribed elevator shaft, and docking port as dictated by the tower.

"Eight thousand. Nine thousand. Here we go," Jennings said to no one in particular.

The thrusters disengaged as the atmospheric engine cut in and the ship leapt forward up its exit corridor- another no-fly zone to all but those trying to escape planetary gravity. The inertial dampeners kicked in as they reached breakaway speed, and the feel of the acceleration vanished. However, those few seconds of breakneck velocity were all that mattered to Jennings, and he could not help but grin. The *Melody Tryst* broke through the atmosphere within two minutes, and the roar of the engines vanished. The hull rumbled with a slight vibration under his feet as the *Melody Tryst* continued to accelerate rapidly now that it had escaped the confines of gravity, but the silence of space was an eerie and mesmerizing thing.

"It gets quiet fast," he commented to Lafayette.

"Until the screaming starts anew," he said without looking up from Magellan. "All right, where to?"

Jennings thought about it for a long moment. "Earth."

~

Long after Magellan finished its telemetry calculations and the FTL engines sent them rocketing out of Proxima Centauri and into the darkness between solar systems, Jennings was enjoying a nice cup of tea in the tiny lounge with his boots up on the coffee table in front of him. Fix was in the rec room, lifting weights, and Squawk was catching some sleep. Lafayette had bridge duty, and Minerva at last advised him she had completed her evaluation. Jennings hoped his presumption of Earth was the correct one. He wanted to get Mariador far behind him, but it would not help to send them on an incorrect course.

"Good evening, captain," the pleasing female voice of Minerva said. "You look comfortable."

"I'll be more so if you have some good news for me," he said, before taking another sip from his cup.

"Perhaps," the computer said coyly. "Begin report. There have been no sightings of Michelle Rachel Williams since her escape from police custody in the incident contained within your briefing. The high-profile nature of Ms. Williams's parents, the level of news coverage of the incident, the high reward for the safe return to police custody of the fugitive, and psychographic profiling compiled from Ms. Williams's psych screenings and current affiliations suggest a 71% chance she is no longer on Earth."

"Any suggestions where she might be?"

"No known inputs to satisfy said logic," Minerva said. "No found friends, family or acquaintances on outlying colonies. All possibilities present nearly equal probability."

Jennings figured as much. "What's the other 29%?"

"9% chance she has already been killed. 7% chance she is still in hiding," she explained. "13% miscellaneous and highly unlikely possibilities."

"Right," Jennings nodded, pulling his feet off the table and sitting forward in his seat. "Makes sense. Whoever is trying to kill her would make damn sure everybody knew it was done."

"Unless it was a non-Resistance related murder," Minerva corrected. "Given the likelihood she has needed to deal with the underworld as a part of her flight, the majority of the chance of her being deceased relates to that element, not the assassins chasing her."

"If a friend were hiding her, the police or the bounty hunters would have found her already," he said.

"Correct," Minerva agreed. "However, her attractiveness matrix scores very high with most males of the human species. There is the small possibility she is being hidden by someone outside of her normal circle for sex or for the promise thereof."

"Thanks for your high opinion of our species," Jennings muttered.

"Don't take it personally. It's only mathematics."

Rubbing at his eyes, Jennings scrunched his face in thought. "Working under the parameters that she got off-planet before they found her, what's her most likely escape route?"

"93% likelihood she was smuggled off planet by illegal shipping activity," she replied. "6% chance she stowed away on legitimate transport. Less than 1% chance normal shipping or passenger methods due to interstellar travel advanced security precautions."

He nodded. "Any associates or friends who might make an introduction to anyone with smuggling associations?"

"Probabilities suggest this man," Minerva said as a holographic emitter on the table showed an outline of a young man, probably twenty, tall, muscular with dark brown skin and light brown eyes.

"Jacq Clemmons?" he asked Minerva as the personal details of the man displayed in a holographic image next to the picture.

"Though not friends, our fugitive shares three university affiliations with Mr. Clemmons," Minerva reported as Fix came in and sat on the couch opposite, still sweating from his workout. "They would at least be aware of each other, maybe even acquaintances."

"He is nae a smuggler," Fix said.

"Mr. Clemmons comes from a privileged background, but his father did not make his wealth with one hundred percent legitimacy," she said. "Although much is classified, he was a duty-free smuggler who became a useful tool for the military during the war when they needed to resupply besieged planets. Not only did it make him rich, but the government turned a blind eye on all his past discretions. His father legitimized the business after the war and became a regular trader."

"I guess you don't care so much about doing end-runs on import taxes once you get wealthy enough," Jennings said.

"His father would likely still have connections to the underground," Minerva said. "He is by far your most likely source. Combined, all other options only have a probability of 7%."

Nodding, Jennings said to Minerva, "Connect me with Lafayette please."

"Go ahead, *mon capitaine*," Lafayette said through the intercom.

"How long to Earth?"

There was a moment's pause. "1.4 hours present speed."

"You ready to play?" Jennings asked Fix.

The Scotsman gave a curt nod. "I'll put my game face on, and I'll make sure my tool kit is fully stocked."

As he headed into his cabin, Jennings said to Minerva, "Download all data to flashport."

"Of course."

Jennings stood and walked over to the wall where one of Minerva's terminals was built in. Inserting a flash drive, he watched the download bar shoot from left to right across the screen and then removed it. Shoving the drive into the receiver on his tablet, he sat back down on the couch and began deciding what his move would be on young Jacq Clemmons.

# Chapter 7

Colonial Triangle was a massive anachronism located smack in the middle of about forty TGF military bases, planet-side shipyards, and skyscrapers which housed the giants of the military-industrial complex. Stuck in between the former tobacco lands and the ocean, Colonial Triangle was home to the re-creations of some of the first European colonies on the North American continent. Stuck in the middle of that was the historic and prestigious College of William and Mary.

The core of its campus was a series of buildings arranged around a sunken garden that had existed since the nineteenth century, but the university radically expanded after its popularity skyrocketed in the latter half of the twenty-first century. There was no space-to-shore landing area for a ship the size of the *Melody Tryst*, so Fix and Jennings hopped into the shuttle and followed Antarctica Traffic Control's directions to their entry vector. A couple of hours of speeding through different skyways brought them halfway around the planet and to the Colonial Triangle section of the city of Seaboard.

The shuttle circled around Lake Matoaka, around which a huge section of the dormitories for the university lay, for the better part of half an hour, looking for a landing space, but they were all full or more annoyingly tagged for residential use only. At last, Jennings piloted the shuttle to a parking facility which stood about twenty stories high and two miles across just outside of campus.

"Parking in this town sucks," Fix said as he jumped out of the open cockpit and landed next to Jennings on the tarmac.

The cockpit sealed shut behind him, and the two took off to find an elevator which would take them to the ground floor. From there, it would be a beautiful but long trek through the forested waterlands within which many of the university's halls were located. The large brick institutes of higher education held no interest for them though. They were headed to the residences around the lake, where fraternity row had been relocated after the first one burned to the ground.

According to Jacq Clemmons's file, so expertly organized by Minerva, he was a member of the Phi Theta Gamma fraternity and lived in their house. It was Friday planet-side, and evening was approaching quickly. Everyone was back on campus with winter break coming to an end, and there would naturally be a lot of parties before classes started up again. Disappearing someone from a loud, raucous group of mostly inebriated morons was not the most difficult thing in the galaxy. Finding a place to work on him would be a little different, but Minerva had already sorted that out for them. The music department had soundproof rooms, and no students would be using them at the hour they planned to arrive.

The forest that had surrounded them since they began their walk from the parking structure vanished suddenly as they came onto the lake. Consulting the microlink to Minerva on his left wrist, Jennings pulled up the holo-map as discreetly as possible, consulted it, and pointed for Fix to take the right hand fork of the path which completely encircled Lake Matoaka. As they continued down the path, they began to pass four and five-story brick buildings with Greek letters branded into the brick.

A couple of female joggers passed them by, and Jennings smiled and nodded, receiving a few grins in return. Fix carried all of his equipment in a black book bag, and Jennings looked young enough to pass as a student. Minerva had even forged a couple of functional student IDs for them. They kept their pace at an even clip as they passed the Phi Theta Gamma house, which Jennings only gave a brief glimpse to. Locking eyes with Fix for the briefest of moments, he still managed to convey his plan.

They continued walking until they entered a wooded area again and were certain no one else was within their line of sight. Winter had not truly hit this far south yet, and the trees still clung to their last vestiges of red, orange and yellow leaves, providing all the cover they needed as they darted into the woods. They circled back through the forest, Jennings with the learned stealth of fighting the Gael on a dozen different worlds with hundreds of different forest types, Fix with the learned skill of whatever the hell he had done before they met. The forest was cleared only around the very edge of the lake and where the dormitories had been built, so they were able to creep within sight of the building easily.

"This is good," Fix whispered.

"All right, let's get comfortable until nightfall." Jennings dropped with his back against an impressive oak, out of sight from anyone who might peer out one of the building's windows.

Fix did the same. "Let's hope Minerva's on point."

Jennings gave a thought to the computer system which helped run his ship. He had never seen an NAI like her, or like it, he corrected himself. Most ships used NAI central computers, but none seemed to have the intelligence or the emotional range Minerva expressed. He asked Minerva about it once, and she accused him of flattery, but did not comment anymore on the subject.

"Minerva's always on point," he said at last. Despite her only being a computer, Jennings still felt an attachment to her, as if she were a manifestation of the ship he loved so much, and he felt an obligation to defend her.

"Whatever you say, cap'n," Fix said quietly.

Fix never did talk much, so waiting until darkness fell and then another three hours until the thump of an overly loud bassline started hitting them was a long stretch of boredom. Jennings spent the time going over the plan in his mind. Snatch the kid. One point one miles to the music building. Fifteen minutes. Seventh floor. Password for admin would be hacked by Minerva once they got there. Anywhere from a few minutes to a few hours for him to wake-up. Then they had about seven hours at best until someone would be looking for him. It was tight- hopefully the kid would be a pushover, and Fix would not need to get nasty. Other than the war, Jennings's nastiest memories involved watching Fix get desperately needed information out of someone who did not want to give it.

"Party's started," Fix said.

"Give it a few more minutes," Jennings said. "We don't want to be the first guests."

Fix grunted in reply.

"You have the injector ready?" Jennings asked.

A stare from Fix essentially communicated a dozen curse words and an affirmation.

"Just checking," he clarified, holding up his hands in placation. Jennings took in another breath. "Okay, let's move in."

The two of them stalked their way through the forest back to where they had jumped off the trail, waited until the coast was clear, and then walked back onto it about one hundred feet behind a group of seven girls, dressed to party. The music got louder as they approached, booming through an open double door. A dozen or so people mingled outside, smoking dried fruit cigarettes, sipping beer from synthetic cups, or chatting up the few ladies out there. A beefy guy with a flattop and a badly fitting black suit stood outside the door with a tablet, checking names for the guys who wanted in. The seven girls in front of them he just waved right through.

He stepped out in front of Jennings. "ID cards." Once produced, he scanned them through his tablet and shook his head menacingly. "Sorry, but you're not on the list."

"Come on, man, we're here to party," Jennings said in his most jocular, beer-addled tone.

"You're not on the list. You don't party," the security guard said, stepping forward and staring up at Jennings. "Plus you brought your father with you." He nodded toward Fix.

Looking over at Fix himself, Jennings nodded and then accepted from him a small plastic bag no bigger than one inch by one inch. He leaned down to the security guard's ear and said as he pressed the package into the man's beefy hand, "We're here to *help* the party if you know what I mean."

The guard eyed the small package in his hand and turned his gaze back to Jennings.

"Reasonable rates. Satisfaction guaranteed," Jennings continued with his sales pitch.

"All right, come on." The guard waved them through as another group of girls arrived behind them.

Stepping into the darkness which lay beyond, Jennings immediately felt a migraine beginning to grow. The music throbbed through his skull painfully, colored lights and strobes danced like a horrible hallucinogen stinging his retinas, and a sea of drunken future leaders of the world thrashed about as if they were being hit by some sort of stun gun. Fix nodded toward a bar situated toward the back of the room, and Jennings dragged his feet forward until he was at a bar stool and seated.

An interrogative glance from a goateed bartender prompted a response from Jennings of, "Anything. Fast."

"Hurting?" Fix asked in his ear, slipping him another one of the small plastic bags with a little green pill in it.

"I'm not taking that," he nearly shouted back.

"It's prosenipal," Fix said. "It reduces input from the senses, leaves you a little numb to all this chaos."

"That's what you gave the kid up front?" he asked.

Fix snorted. "You could give one of these kids a breath mint, and they would swear they were trippin'."

"Fine." Jennings downed the pill with the shot of vodka the bartender threw down in front of him. The cheap vodka burned badly, reminding Jennings of why he almost never drank.

Fix glanced around the room. "No eyes on target. How the hell are we going to find him in here?"

"Minerva?" Jennings said.

"One moment, filtering out background noise," Minerva's voice said through the small earpiece Jennings wore. "Ah, hello, Captain. Enjoying the party?"

"Cute," he whispered back. Minerva had filtered out all the surrounding noise, so she could hear him quite easily although Fix probably was hard pressed to. "What do you have?"

"Satellite data show Mr. Clemmons left his dormitory apartment seven minutes ago. I convinced the satellite to lock onto his heat signature, and I am currently tracking him at approximately thirty feet from your position," she said.

Jennings scanned the room, feeling the pill Fix had given him alleviating the harsh burn of the lights and strobes, and reducing the cacophony to a more controlled din. He spied Clemmons almost immediately- he was one of the only black members of this fraternity apparently. The young man was dancing with two women simultaneously. Jennings tapped Fix on the shoulder and jerked his head toward Clemmons. He nodded in reply and pulled out a small hypodermic injector, just big enough to fit in the palm of his hand.

Taking a breath, Jennings almost fell off his bar stool and began to stumble his way forward through the crowd of dancers drunkenly. As he passed by Clemmons on the left, moving around the brunette of the two women he was dancing with, he purposefully lost his balance and fell directly into Clemmons, sending him sprawling.

"Oh shit, I'm sorry, man," Jennings said as he pulled himself to his feet gingerly.

Jennings had pushed Clemmons directly into Fix, who if everything went to plan, hit him with the injector while they were trying to untangle themselves from each other. Clemmons pulled himself to his feet, rubbing his wrist subconsciously. Fix flashed a slight grin as he too got up and vanished back into the dancing throngs.

"Why don't you watch where you're going, you son of a bitch," Clemmons snapped as he cocked his fist back and let his punch fly.

The punch vaguely connected with Jennings's chin, the pain reduced by an iron jaw (and Fix's medicine). Nonetheless, he threw himself backward and cried out in imagined pain.

"Damn man, I'm sorry," he managed as he pulled himself back up.

Feeling Clemmons staring daggers at him, he made his way back to the bar and signaled the bartender for another shot of vodka. Fix had vanished into the periphery, but Jennings knew exactly where he was headed- the nearest bathroom on this floor. He threw back his vodka, barely tasting the burning alcohol in his mouth as the drug continued to shut down his senses. Spinning on the bar stool, he stared out into the grind, keeping an eye on Clemmons in his periphery. If Fix was right, it should be any moment now.

The young man had one girl grinding in front of him and another on his rear when it struck. Without any hint of anything being wrong, Clemmons vomited violently into the hair of the girl dancing in front of him. His body spasmed, and he wrenched his head back, head-butting the girl dancing behind him. Blood blossomed out from her nose as another gut-wrenching heave overtook Clemmons, and he spewed onto the floor. Furiously clutching at her broken nose with her left hand, Clemmons's companion took her right fist and brought it up between his legs. Clemmons let loose a cry of pain as more vomit forced its way out, and he collapsed to the floor. The two girls ran away from him, one screaming, and Clemmons took advantage of a twenty second break between heaves to half-sprint and half-limp toward the bathrooms. Laughing quietly to himself, Jennings took a circuitous route through the party, which started back up as if nothing happened.

The communal bathroom was at the end of a long, poorly lit hallway with a couple of dozen dorm room doors leading off of it. A putrid smell emanated from the door marked BOYS. Perhaps more fitting was the crudely carved phrase Abandon All Hope Ye Who Enter Here dug out of the wood just below the sign. Fix waited outside the door, leaning inconspicuously against the cinderblock wall of the hallway.

"You ready?"

Jennings nodded in reply, and Fix swung the door inward. "Should be empty save one," Fix said against the sound of more retching.

"You all right in there?" Jennings asked as they both stepped into the bathroom.

"Do I fucking sound all right?" Clemmons managed to bark out in between gasps.

"Not really," Jennings said. "My partner here has something that might help."

"What are you? Fuckin' drug dealers?" came the response.

"Ethnopharmacology majors," Fix said.

"We've got synthetic virulax, one of the best anti-nausea medicines you can buy. It comes in handy at these parties," Jennings said as he stepped out of sight around the stalls.

The stall door flew open, and a very sweaty and deathly pale Jacq Clemmons emerged, staring vaguely at Fix. "I'll try anything." Without preamble, he took the pill and threw it into his mouth.

"Feel better?" Jennings asked as he came around the corner after a moment to let the pill do its magic.

"Yeah, that's fast… Wait. You're…" his voice trailed off as his eyes rolled back into his head and he collapsed to the ground.

# Chapter 8

Selena Beauregard was washing the vomit out of the back of her hair and trying to clean it out of her dress, cursing silently as she did so. Her long, blond hair was matted with her target's regurgitation and attempting to wash it out in the sink proved pointless. Her ten thousand dollar black and red party dress was ruined as well. Her plasma pistol was still tucked into the garter on her left leg, and she still had the straight razor concealed in her strapless bra, but they would both be useless now.

Until the vomit incident, she was simply one of the dozens of tipsy college students grinding on some random guy. Not anymore- people tended to remember the girl who got puked on. Glaring daggers at her reflection in the mirror, she silently chastised herself for not being professional. She did not anticipate a move from another hunter, as she assumed only she had the contacts to figure out that Clemmons was most likely the man who helped Michelle Williams off-planet.

The two men who arranged the bump'n'drug were not her caliber either, which made it all the more infuriating. It had been decently well executed, she supposed, but it was way too public- especially when a woman with Selena's skills could have Clemmons tied down to a bed with truth serum injected into his arm before he realized he was not getting laid. This was supposed to have been so easy too.

~

*One Day Earlier...*
God, Selena hated coming to Midway. She found it dreary and depressing as she looked out at the junkyard of ruined buildings that were just shells crumbling away before her eyes. The war-torn landscape had barely changed since the area had been the only part of the Terran homeworld obliterated by the Gael invasion fleet when they began their planetary bombardment. They deemed it a punishment for daring to resist in the first place; then later on, covered it up. To this day, all news agencies referred to the *accident* which

happened in the heartland of the North American continent. Volunteers who knew the truth still scoured the devastated buildings and homes, looking for bodies and bones to bury.

The Resistance loved the area because everyone except for the grave diggers avoided it. On top of that, the residual signature of the Gael energy weapons played havoc with anyone trying to get a sensor reading on the place, and in Old Chicago, there were miles upon miles of tunnels which went back hundreds of years. Only the Resistance knew the ways in and out, and they had more emergency egresses and contingency plans than the Gael could imagine. Factoring in sub-levels and old underground rails that connected several cities, the Resistance was hiding in a place roughly the size of France. It would take legions of Gael troops a year to search the place, and they still might not find a single cell. Suffice to say, the Resistance valued their privacy.

It had not been particularly difficult for Selena to sign up with one of the charity groups who wandered out to the wastelands, and was even easier for her to lose her companions. People generally understood why someone would want to be alone in the face of so much death. The buriers would be wandering from dawn to dusk, so she had plenty of time to make her way to an old subway station entrance and head down the cracked and crumbling stairs into the darkness without anyone missing her.

Within fifty feet, the darkness completely overcame her, but Selena kept walking forward. The stairs flattened out into a platform, and her footsteps became more tentative now, then stopped. She could tell she was no longer alone.

"That's far enough," a nearly imperceptible voice whispered from behind her.

The gentle caress of a standard issue T-Fed plasma rifle kissed the back of her neck, and sent a deliciously pleasurable shudder down her spine. "No need for that. I was requested."

"Turn around," the voice commanded.

Selena did so and immediately a burning sensation bore in her eyes as a red light flashed from somewhere in front of her.

"Apologies, Ms. Beauregard," the voice said. "Your identity is confirmed. We were expecting you. Kindly follow me."

"How do I...?" she started before a pair of glasses were pressed into her hands.

Putting them on, nothing changed, so she searched along the frame and found a small button. Once pushed, the world became visible in a brilliant emerald hue. She found herself standing on an old underground transit platform only a few feet from a drop onto the tracks. A destroyed locomotive, a mesh of twisted and contorted metal, was rammed halfway up onto the platform only ten feet from where she stood.

Her escort waited for her to acknowledge that she could see him, or at least his silhouette. The Resistance soldier was dressed completely in black, armored from head to foot and wearing a black battle helmet with a mask pulled down in front of his face. He beckoned for her to follow him as he leapt from the platform to the track below and took off at a stiff-paced march past the crashed train and into the tunnel.

For the better part of two hours, she followed him as he led her in silence through subway lines, utility tunnels, part of the sewer system, and through God knew what else as they trudged through the bowels of the wasteland. Every fifteen minutes or so, they encountered a new checkpoint where they were confronted with more men with plasma rifles before her escort provided a password and identification. She wondered if he were leading her in a winding pattern on purpose so she would not be able to remember how to find her way, or if the Resistance really was this spread out in their underground metropolis. She thought the former more likely and more annoying. She had no desire to come back to this place.

At last, they arrived at a large tunnel with a pressure door on one end which looked like something from an old-fashioned bank vault. Two soldiers stood guard outside of the door and another dozen or so milled about, smoking cigarettes in the dim light afforded by a few electric lanterns.

"New recruit?" one of them asked as they approached.

"A visitor," her escort said as he pulled off his helmet, allowing the others to confirm it was really him.

Beauregard was surprised by his appearance as he could not have been more than sixteen years old. He must have noticed because an arrogant smirk crossed his face, and he tossed his helmet toward one of the tables set up in the hallway.

"Major's on the other side of the door," her escort said, before gesturing to the two guards. "Let her on through." He collapsed into an office chair and leaned his weapon against the wall.

One of the two guards wheeled a handle around in a circle until the door unlocked, and he swung it open. "Up the stairs and to the left," he said as she stepped through and heard him begin to close the door behind her.

She was in a strange room with row upon row of locked compartments, each with their own number. It was like a morgue, but the compartments were too small. Some kind of private storage, she thought to herself. The whole thing was lit eerily by orange lantern light, and she moved quickly through the room, heading up a flight of marble stairs and turning to the left like she was directed.

This room was impressively larger and quite ornate, or rather had been at one time. Chandeliers on the ceiling had been wired with cheap electronic torches. A beautiful marble parquet spread under her feet, and the pieces of furniture pushed up against the wall were antiques of some type. The furniture had been replaced with row upon row of bunked beds stacked three high. Many were occupied. She turned her head around to the sound of some muted noise coming from behind her. A couple of soldiers in tank tops were playing billiards, and a few sat on couches watching vid-screens.

Turning her back on the recreation room, she continued her way forward, passing the beds. A few people stirred as she passed, but no one said anything to her. At the end of the long line of bunks was a crude curtain partition strung up to give the sleepers some privacy from what lay on the other side. Selena stepped through and into the command center for the cell, immediately spying her contact: Major Geoff Paulsen.

Paulsen was no major in reality, having been a corporal in the real T-Fed army during the war. However, he joined the Resistance early after the Terran surrender and shot himself up through the ranks because of his willingness to do anything to inflict damage on the enemy. He was short and wiry with buzzed down brown hair with the beginnings of a bald spot setting in. He rarely smiled, which most considered a positive, as he without a doubt suffered from a horrific case of English teeth. Twice she had worked with him before, both times when members of the Resistance failed to complete a job. Selena succeeded each time. She supposed Paulsen trusted her as much as a man of principle could trust a hired gun.

A semicircle of control stations with portable computers were arranged around a series of large vid-screens mounted onto the wall. The screens displayed everything from patrol routes, sensor readings, a news ticker, and a giant map of their sector of the underground labyrinth. Paulsen stood behind one of technicians whispering something to her, when he sensed Selena approaching.

"Madame Beauregard," he said in his rough North London accent.

"Major." She nodded her head slightly. "You sure know how to pick a meeting spot."

"Humph," he snorted. "Follow me." He beckoned with his hand.

"What was this place?" Selena asked as she fell into step behind him.

"Bank for rich pensioners," he said. "Treasury vaults below for valuables, reception area up here so they could check on their wealth without being disturbed by the middle and lower classes."

She did not reply as he led her into a small office and waved her into a chair in front of his desk. A small halogen light flickered above them, casting a sterile glow. It was better than the darkness of the world outside the door with its dim orange halos barely permeating the blackness.

"D'you want a drink?" he asked as he poured himself a whiskey.

"It's still morning."

"Not down here," he said before swallowing back a mouthful of the dark brown liquid.

"No, thanks."

"Always business." He gave her a satisfied smile, showing his teeth. Selena tried not to think about them as he said, "You're probably wondering why I sent for you."

"Not really- you have a job for me," she said. "Now, why I had to come to this God forsaken place... that is a good question."

"That came on from down high," he said. "The only reason the brass are letting me touch this is because they wanted you and we've had cordial business dealings in the past."

"I'm always happy to provide a service." She tried to hide her sarcasm as much as possible. "What's so important that it necessitated me coming down here?"

"They wouldn't trust putting this on normal communications even as good as our encryptions are." Paulsen sighed. "Especially considering how delicate and severely fucked the situation is, brass wants this run by the numbers. No more mistakes."

Shaking her head, Selena said, "Start at the beginning and tell me what the fuck you want from me." She paused, smiled and then added, "And how much you'll pay me to do it."

"Ten times our last transaction," he replied quickly.

Selena's eyes popped open, and she began spending money in her head very quickly.

"That's the easy part," he said as he tossed her a tablet. "Here's the target."

Quickly, she scanned it. "If it's a simple kill order, why the theatrics of bringing me here?"

He eyed her appraisingly for a moment. "It's because of Aurora," Paulsen said at last.

"What's Aurora?"

"It's a list," he answered curtly. "A list with one hundred and eleven names on it. The Gael have now arrested one hundred and ten. With Ciarin O'Sullivan being found on Mariador, Williams is the last."

Selena blinked in surprise. "Are they your people?"

He shook his head and poured himself another drink. "O'Sullivan was friendly to the cause, and a few friends in the service got him out through unofficial channels before the kill order came down from the brass. Some off-world cell, also friends, took him in while neglecting to pass the word that they had him." He downed his glass of whiskey. "Bloody colonials."

"Wait. If none of them are yours, then why are the Gael arresting them?" she asked.

"The Gael, of course, claim they are all Resistance members and make up crimes for which they are arrested," Paulsen said. "In truth, we have no idea why the Gael want them. They're not ours. They're not spies. They come from all walks of life, political affiliations, geographies; some military service, some not. That last one there is the daughter of two of the largest collaborators on the planet."

"If they're not compromised agents or Gael spies, why do you want them dead?" she asked.

"Because the Gael want them alive," he said as if it were obvious.

That seemed pretty brutal to Selena but she did not say anything. Brutality was part of the game in her line of work.

"We sent in one of our own to take care of this," Paulsen said. "He got sloppy and killed the wrong person. A second chance came his way, and he got himself blown apart by a bloody copper. There's heat on all sides of this thing now. The Gael have posted a huge reward, so every lowlife douchebag in nine systems is going to be looking for her. I need you to find her and make her go away. Permanently."

"All right," she said after a long moment. "You know where to put the money once you receive confirmation."

He nodded and stood up, gesturing toward the door. "Oh," he added as he opened it for her, "She's most likely not on-planet any longer. Included in the data is her most likely contact for getting off world. Intel has been working all week on that."

"Thanks," she said.

"Head back to the portal," he said. "I'll signal ahead that you're coming and that you'll need an escort back to the surface."

She nodded, thanked him and headed back toward where she had come from. One last question sprang to mind, and she turned to face Paulsen. "So, you have no idea what this Operation Aurora is all about then?"

"None," he said. "But it's the Gael. Whatever it is, it isn't good. You'll probably be doing her a favor when you consider what they might do to her if they can capture her."

~

After reviewing the file Paulsen had given her, Selena had come to the same conclusion. Jacq Clemmons was Michelle Williams's only ticket off Earth. What intrigued her far more were the circumstances around Ms. Williams's disappearance. She had left a trail of bodies behind her. Fairly strange for a pretty young college student, she thought to herself.

More disconcerting for her was the notion of this Operation Aurora. According to her files, the hackers who loved to play havoc in the Terran Gael Force servers had stumbled upon this by pure chance. They did not finish the decryption until number one hundred and nine had been found, had failed in killing Williams, and had been unable to prevent O'Sullivan's capture. All without even understanding what Operation Aurora was. If Selena were calling the shots in the Resistance, she would want Williams alive- give them a better chance to find out what the hell the Gael were up to. It was odd for the Resistance to be so adamant she be killed, and Paulsen was extraordinarily nervous, far more so than she had ever seen him. Sure, he played everything cool, but deep down she knew he had been sweating.

A realization dawned on her, and Selena found it an all the more frightening prospect. What if the Resistance did know why the Gael were taking these one hundred and eleven people? Could that be what had them so scared that they would order the assassination of a college-aged civilian? What the hell could Aurora be that had them that frightened?

Selena examined her contract and found another interesting bit of bonus information: collateral damage had been authorized. The Resistance did not care how many people she hurt to accomplish her mission. Normally, she did not allow such thoughts to concern her. Compassion was not a luxury afforded a business woman, but at the same time she did not relish her work the way others did. No matter what the psych screening tests which kept her out of the military said, she was not a sociopath.

At last satisfied that her appearance was as good as she was going to make it without a shower and a change of clothes, Selena stopped washing and put her hands under the thermal unit to dry them off. She then reached into her stylishly tiny handbag and pulled out a small receiver. It located the tiny tracking device she had dropped in Clemmons's first beer and provided her with his current location and a map overlay.

"Good boy," she said. "Didn't throw that up at least."

Concealing the small device in her hand, she stepped out the woman's lavatory and headed for the exit. The night had grown much cooler, and she regretted not having brought a coat with her- warm and useful for concealing weapons, but not revealing enough to get any man she wanted like a nice low-cut dress. As she got clear of the party and into the dark once more, she checked the position of her targets again. They were moving slowly down one of the wooded paths headed toward the older campus and the sunken gardens at its center. Selena guessed the two men were carrying Clemmons, making it seem as if they were helping a friend who had partied a little too hard back to his dormitory, just in case they ran into anyone. Maybe they were a little better than she had given them credit for.

Over the course of ten minutes, she got within sight of the two men in time to see them break into one of the academic halls, still carrying the unconscious Jacq Clemmons. This was a move she had not expected. She figured they would take him to a vehicle or a safe house they had set up and interrogate him once they were certain they were safe.

Selena pulled up in the shadows outside the old brick building and took out the handheld device once more. Punching in a few commands, she found a detailed map of the building called Ewell Hall, home of the music department, and she realized where they were going. They were in one of the soundproof rooms.

"Damn," she swore under her breath.

She had definitely underestimated these guys. None of the devices she had which could eavesdrop on a conversation through a brick wall were going to be any good. That only gave her three options as far as she could see, none of them particularly appealing. An attempt to rush the two men would result in too much death, possibly even the death of Clemmons. It was too messy- way too many things might go wrong. She could wait until the two men were done, reacquire Clemmons and acquire the information she needed, but that also had its disadvantages. What if these two men killed Clemmons when they were done? Not to mention, she would be losing a lot of time and falling behind her fellow hunters. The only other option that she saw was to allow her competition to get the information she needed and then either get it from them or follow them.

Following them seemed to be the better option. She had already made a bad habit of underestimating these two and a confrontation might go horribly wrong, especially with so little time to plan. The better choice was to wait until she had the advantage again. Yes, that was best, she confirmed to herself. She checked the map again. There was only one good egress from the building- the same way they had gone in. Walking slowly, she picked a spot in the shadows of another academic building and curled up against a tree, waiting for the two men to leave.

# Chapter 9

"Morning, starshine," Jennings said with false gusto as Clemmons's eyes fluttered open.

Fix stepped back from Clemmons withdrawing the hypodermic which had rapidly sped up the reawakening of their captive. "I give it three seconds," he said as he went back to a table set against the wall.

Clemmons eyes darted around the room furtively, desperately taking everything in. He was strapped to a chair (a cello chair- just to make it slightly more uncomfortable for him). The lighting was dim as there were no windows in the room, and the wall was covered with a type of egg crate material for soundproofing. The room was only about twelve feet by twenty, with one door almost invisible as it was also covered with the soundproofing material. The door was fitted with a heavy lock to keep unwitting souls from interrupting recording sessions. A cluster of microphones hung down from the ceiling, and a powered down switchboard dominated the left-hand wall. Clemmons's eyes were more drawn to the table on the opposite wall where Fix had unrolled his black nylon tool carrier and was inspecting different sharp and dangerous looking objects.

Clemmons at last came to his senses when he saw Fix turn back around toward him with a scalpel in his hand and a pair of pliers. He screamed, "HELP!!!" as loudly as he could.

"Fifteen seconds," Jennings said, glancing to Fix. "Braver than you thought or stupider?"

Clemmons screamed again.

"Stupider," Fix said.

Taking out his own knife, Jennings gently placed the flat of it against Clemmons's cheek. "No good screaming," he said matter-of-factly. "This is a soundproof room." Disbelief crossed Clemmons's face, and Jennings chuckled. "Not a music major evidently. Let's put it this way. No one can hear you. You can choose to believe me, or you can choose to keep screaming. Keep in mind, if you choose to keep screaming, I will need to cut out your tongue."

A profound terror widened Clemmons's eyes, and he wet himself. It was not turning into a banner day for his clothes.

"Bear in mind that the choice to cut out your tongue would be for our own benefit alone," Jennings clarified. "Screaming will do you absolutely no good. We just find it annoying. It's in your best interest not to annoy us, understand?"

Clemmons nodded, his upper lip shaking as tears began pouring out of his eyes.

"Excellent," Jennings said as he grabbed a chair, spun it around and sat on it with its back to his chest. He stared directly into Clemmons's eyes. "We're going to play a little game with you, Jacq. This game is called the truth. As long as you keep telling the truth, you keep winning. If you win, you get to keep your life. If you answer questions incorrectly though…" He glanced over at Fix, who smiled darkly. "You will need to forfeit pieces of your body." He let that revelation sink into Clemmons's mind. "My friend here will start with your teeth and then your fingernails. If we're still playing, and you're still not answering questions correctly, we move on to round two, which will involve losing your fingers and toes." Jennings cast his eyes downward to about Clemmons's belt buckle. "You really don't want to know what happens at round three. What do you say? Are you ready to play?"

"Yes, sir," Clemmons said weakly.

"So polite," Jennings said as he smiled at Fix. "We'll start with the easy questions. Do you know Michelle Rachel Williams?"

He nodded.

"Well?"

A shrug.

Fix stepped forward, opening the pliers.

"No, no," Clemmons protested, trying to throw himself out of the chair he was in. "Look, yeah, I know her. We're on a couple of committees together, different school organizations, that's all. I didn't know her all that well."

"Until?" Jennings led.

"I saw what happened on the news, man," he said. "I never expected her to show up at my parents' place. I don't know how she even found it."

"The school directory, genius," Fix muttered.

Jennings held up a hand to Fix. "Continue, please."

"Michelle was confused as hell. All she knew was that some guy tried to kill her twice and that she was being falsely accused of some kind of espionage or treason charges," he said.

"You were willing to help out a wanted felon? Very compassionate," Jennings said.

"Hey, man. The Gael put that on her. Do you actually believe anything they say?" Clemmons asked.

Jennings's thoughts darted to their current mission, but he quickly pushed them back down to the surface. "So, you did help her get off-planet?"

Clemmons nodded. "As much as I could, I mean. It's not like I have a shitload of underworld connections or anything."

"Who'd you set her up with?" Jennings asked, leaning closer.

"An old friend of my father's," he said. "Vesper Santelli. He said he could get her out to the Wolf System."

Fix and Jennings shared a glance. "Vesper Santelli?" Jennings snarled. "Don't you know who he is?"

Clemmons seemed taken aback. "He's a transport merchant. I know he does some smuggling, getting items in around tariffs, but that's all."

"Tariff running?" Jennings snapped. "That's his most legitimate enterprise. Not only is he one of the largest pentamethaline dealers in the galaxy, but he also runs a lucrative side business supplying the outer worlds with kidnapped young girls to be wives and haremites of the outer world colonial barons. You probably signed her death warrant by sending her to a man like Santelli."

"And her rape warrant," Fix added darkly.

"I didn't know," Clemmons protested.

Jennings decked him across the face so hard his body rocked against the restraints keeping him in the chair. "Consider yourself fortunate that's the worst you're getting," Jennings growled as he got up and kicked his chair out of the way.

"You're not going to kill me?" Clemmons asked hopefully, despite the blood running down his face.

"Never was," Jennings said.

"I considered it," Fix added as an afterthought, as he turned back to his bag and withdrew another hypodermic.

"We're going to give you one last dose," Jennings said. "When you wake up, it'll be all over."

"Unless we're lying," Fix said as he depressed the button on the syringe, "And this is drain cleaner."

~

They left Jacq Clemmons unconscious but relatively unharmed from the ordeal and headed back toward where they had parked the shuttle. Jennings was working under the assumption that Clemmons would be too frightened to mention to any authority figures about what happened to him tonight. However, even if he did talk to anyone and he convinced them that what he was saying was true, Clemmons's blood work would show the young student was delving into the pharmaceutical experimentation common in most universities among the teenagers. Crazy kids, Jennings thought with a smile as they arrived at the garage.

"You got a ticket," Fix said as they arrived at their ship.

"Son of a bitch," Jennings muttered as he pulled the electronic tag off the hatch. "Three hundred bucks! That's robbery."

"Parking here sucks," Fix observed once more as they climbed in.

"We'll bill it to the Gael under expenses," Jennings said wryly as he punched several controls, closing the hatch, engaging the thrusters, and warming the engine.

~

Selena Beauregard watched as the small shuttle left the parking structure and sped off toward one of the skyways, heading eventually to a ship in orbit, she would guess. The small electronic device in her hand had already tracked the engine signature of the shuttle and locked in on it thanks to the network of satellites the Resistance had access to. In a short while, she would know what ship they were heading to, but to track them she would need a ship of her own.

Pulling out her communicator, she punched in a series of numbers, which resulted in an electronic squelch that was quickly shut out. "En-Enter Cl-clearance," an electronic voice said.

"Foxtrot Tango Golf two-two-five-nine-seven."

"Paulsen," the voice of the major came on immediately.

"I need a ship," she said.

"Have you not your own?"

"Mine's not appropriate for this type of mission," she said. "I need something a bit bigger, but discreet. I'm going into some dangerous areas; don't want anything too flashy or that will be noticed by anyone."

"I have a ship you can borrow that would do you," Paulsen said. "Sending co-ordinates to you. The shipyards. Paulsen out."

A coded sub-file popped up on her display showing a mapped location outside of the military base not far from where she stood now. "Great. Now I just need a taxi," she said to herself.

# Chapter 10

"How'd it go?" Lafayette greeted them as they slid down the ladder which led from the shuttle hatch to the living quarters.

Jennings stepped past him. "As expected."

"Did you find out where she is?" his first mate asked, falling into step behind him, headed through the kitchen.

"We've got a good idea," Jennings said. "But we're lacking details."

"She's been sold most like," Fix said, bringing up the rear.

"Slavers? She's got wonderful friends," Lafayette said as they all crashed down on the couches in the lounge.

"Not bad people, just stupid," Jennings said. "This Clemmons guy thought he was helping her escape off planet, but he had no real idea who his father's old buddies were."

"So who is it?" Lafayette asked.

Jennings sat forward on the couch, sniffed the air and let out a long sigh. "Did you make dinner?"

"You know I did, but answer the question," Lafayette said.

"You will nae like it," Fix said as he stood up and went to the reefer and pulled out a container. "What is it?"

"Does it matter?" he retorted.

"Nae."

Fix scooped whatever was there onto two plates and then threw them in the convector. Half a minute later he grabbed two sets of silverware and brought a plate over to Jennings before setting himself down in a chair opposite the captain. Jennings began shoveling what turned out to be a very tasty parmesan rigatoni with arugula and spicy Italian sausage into his mouth, completely aware he was ignoring the hard stare from Lafayette.

At last, Jennings relented. "Santelli."

"Santelli?" Lafayette repeated incredulously. "Vesper Santelli?"

"It sure is nae his nicer cousin," Fix said.

"*Merde, Capitaine*, we can't go up against Vesper Santelli," he protested. "*Dat* guy is insane. Remember Aric Tyson- guy in our unit who leased out his ship to Santelli for some illicit bullshit or another. He had to drop his shipment in order to avoid being caught with it by the tariff inspectors. Do you know what happened to him?"

"I know," Jennings said.

"Santelli chopped him into tiny pieces, but kept him alive long enough to throw him out into space and watch his eyeballs freeze and his heart explode," Lafayette continued anyway. "*Dat* was of course after he murdered his parents and his sister and her whole family. There's no way we can tangle with this guy."

Fix grunted. "He's right."

"Both of you want to give up now?" Jennings asked incredulously. "You'd have the Gael hunt us down?"

"I'm not saying *dat* it's a good idea, *mon capitaine*, but what else is there?" Lafayette protested.

"Santelli's protected," Fix said. "Guy like him has protection everywhere he goes. Probably lives in a very lavish and expensive fortress. Security. Cameras. Lethal response systems. Guns. More guns. Shields. If he's flying, he's got escort ships. We would nae be able to take him."

"And we don't have the connections to even think about approaching him as legitimate fellow criminals," Lafayette pointed out. "We wouldn't get a meeting. No way to parlay *dat* into an information exchange."

"No one's untouchable," Jennings said.

"And if we had months to observe, plan and execute, that would be true," Lafayette argued. "We don't."

Somberly, Jennings let his eyes fall to the floor, conceding the point. "Maybe we're looking at this the wrong way," he said suddenly, looking back up. "Maybe we don't need to go to Santelli at all."

Lafayette sat forward, intrigued. "What do you mean?"

"Well, we know Santelli wouldn't really have anything to do with the girl anyway," he began. "He was just someone Clemmons knew. He's certainly not taking the girl in- it would be too much risk for him. Probably never came within a thousand miles of her."

"The guy certainly would nae captain his own ships anymore," Fix agreed.

"So what you're saying is that it doesn't matter if we can't get to him, because all we need to do is find which of his ships took Williams off-world and squeeze one of the crewmen or the captain or something," Lafayette said.

"Exactly," Jennings said. "Hell, my guess is that Santelli told one of his captains to take her off Earth. We don't know if he ordered her sold into slavery, or if they decided to do it on their own and make a little money on the side."

"Technically, we do nae know she was sold into slavery," Fix pointed out.

"She had no money and no connections, and I doubt Santelli's people operate a charity for wayward damsels," Jennings said. "I don't see them getting her off world out of the goodness of their hears. But either way, the person who is going to know where she is would be the captain of the ship who took her out. We find that captain, we'll find Ms. Williams."

"How do we find that out?" Lafayette asked.

"Minerva, my dear," Jennings said. "Have you been eavesdropping?"

"It's not my fault you're having a conversation where I can distinctly hear every word you're saying," the female voice replied condescendingly.

"*Dat's* a lot of data to pour through, most of it unofficial," Lafayette said sotto voce. "How do we know she can do it?"

"Please don't speak about me like I'm not here, Sergeant Lafayette," Minerva chided. "It is a simple matter of coordinating data available from traffic co-ordination satellites, public flight plan data, known real estate holdings of one Vesper Santelli, and suspected illicit subsidiary holdings of his."

"How do you find those?" Lafayette asked.

"My source is the *New York Times*," she said. "Data is compiling. Estimate forty-seven minutes until relevant probabilities are available."

"Fine by me." Jennings shoveled the rest of his dinner into his mouth, earning a reprehensive stare from his chef. Noticing the look, Jennings said to Lafayette, "Outsmarted by the computer again?"

Grumbling something in French under his breath, Lafayette vanished toward his cabin and disappeared inside, probably to grab some rack. It was running almost four a.m. ship standard time, so that sounded like a terrific idea, but Jennings would need to wait until Minerva finished her calculations and then get them on course before he could think about sleep.

"You need me for anything else, Cap'n?" Fix asked as he stood up to carry his plate into the mess.

"No, catch some rack."

"Are you going to pilot us out of here after Minerva gives us a destination?" he asked, probably thinking about the last time Jennings had used Magellan.

*Why didn't anyone let that go?* he wondered to himself. "Naw, Squawk should be up soon. I'll let him take the bridge."

Fix nodded and headed off to his cabin as well. As fatigue grabbed hold of him mercilessly, Jennings recalled once again what a blessing it was to have a Pasquatil on his crew. The hyperactive maniacs slept only four hours per day, but they were immobile and mostly comatose during those four hours. Generally, it would take a nuclear blast of an alarm clock to wake them up. However, that sleep cycle and relentless energy made it useful to have a Pasquatil to take the night shift. Normally, Squawk manned the bridge from midnight to six a.m., but Jennings had told him to rest during that time as he did not expect them back from their mission until late, and he wanted to be able to crash as soon as they got back.

*So much for that plan,* he thought to himself wryly, cursing Jacq Clemmons for opening up so easily. If they had gotten back after six, he could have climbed into bed and let Squawk handle everything. A long sigh turned into a massive jaw-unhinging yawn as Jennings stood, stretched, and went into the kitchen to make himself a cup of tea.

*Why are they just sitting there?* Beauregard wondered to herself from the cockpit of the small *Trenton*-class ship the Resistance had fashioned for her.

What it lacked in size (It was hardly larger than a standard fighter- just the cockpit, a small living space with barely enough room for a Mason cot, a mini-reefer, and a thermal unit for cooking, and a small access hatch which led to the crawlspace in the rear of the ship and the engine.), it made up in being the stealthiest ship the Terran military had ever produced. The outer hull was covered with a material T-Fed R&D discovered about halfway through the war. They called it Light Shroud technology. Essentially, it was a material with a negative refraction index.

Beauregard did not know what that meant, but she was told the material essentially bent light around it. All tracking systems were built on lasers and light beams, so the *Trentons* were very difficult to detect. Unfortunately, the material was hard to produce and highly unstable during the manufacturing process. T-Fed had only been able to build a few of these ships, but they were the only ones which showed any combat effectiveness against the Gael onslaught during the war. Some said if humanity had prolonged the war further and had the opportunity to perfect the technology, T-Fed might have beaten back the Gael in the end.

As it was, there were very few of these ships in existence, and she doubted the Resistance could afford more than a handful. It had taken seven security codes to gain access to the massive stellar cargo container that housed the ship. The fact they trusted her with one only re-emphasized how important this kill was.

Selena once again cursed her luck at being beaten to Clemmons as she stared at the *Melody Tryst*, drifting in a parking orbit around Earth. She was completely dependent on the bounty hunters on that ship to figure out where Williams had gotten off to. Based on the fact that they had not immediately taken off in pursuit meant Clemmons did not know where she was, had only been able to give them a little information, or they simply did not break him. She had considered breaking into the soundproof room after they left and doing some interrogation work of her own, but the two men were a step ahead of her once more, calling the police anonymously and leading them to Clemmons.

Waiting was not Selena's strong suit, and she began drumming her fingers on the control panel in front of her. It would be so easy to take a shot with the cannons on her little ship, slag the *Melody Tryst's* engines, board it and kill the crew. She could not take that chance though. There was too much traffic in the shipping lanes around Earth, stealth ship or not. Sensors were bound to see the plasma blasts, and even if they did not, the ship might still get off a distress signal, and she had no guarantee they would not be equipped and ready to repel borders.

"Patience, Selena. Patience," she said through gritted teeth.

To calm herself, she read the files on the suspected crew members of the *Melody Tryst*- three men and one Pasquatil. Pasquatils were worthless in a fight, but the others were a concern. The ship's doctor was a convicted felon- had probably shivved a few in his day- but Angus Ferguson was not the primary concern. Matthew Jennings and Remy Lafayette were both veterans of the war with about a dozen medals of commendation apiece. Lafayette had been a simple sergeant, but one with an impressive record. On the other hand, Lieutenant Jennings was the prototypical hero- member of the elite Immortals (an inter-branch military special force equally adept and used on ground, air and space missions), Councilor Medal of Valor, Silver and Bronze Stars, even an old school Victoria Cross and four purple hearts. Not only was he a hero, but he was apparently impossible to kill. Jennings's fighter was one of seven ships to limp away from the Battle of Monument. He had eighty-seven enemy kills in that one battle. At the battle of Urakt Creek, he led a platoon of forty and a crew of fifty-five Uula against a Gael force of near one thousand. They held the village for three days before the Gael retreated. Were it not for the Gael, Matthew Jennings would be running for Council in a few years and probably President of it within twenty. Killing him would be a true challenge, but she honestly hoped it did not come to that. A very small part of her, buried under layers of professionalism, admired Matthew Jennings.

A flurry of movement from outside drew her eye, and she saw the *Melody Tryst* moving out of orbit and making for one of the designated FTL zones, areas where ships were allowed to jump to light speed without having to worry about crashing into local traffic. It must have been a slow day, because they were only fifth in line queued up behind the stellar buoys that marked the FTL zone. She brought her ship in behind them, marking them as closely as she dared. If someone else got in line too close to the *Melody Tryst*, they might crash into her accidentally.

Her Magellan computer was plotting the course Jennings's ship would be taking. A program of hers had wormed its way into the *Melody Tryst's* Magellan, hiding as background data when Space Traffic Control gave the *Melody Tryst* permission to depart orbit. The program had then hacked its way from the main computer system to the Magellan interface. The navigational computer in her ship was now copying exactly what the *Melody Tryst's* was doing.

Following them would be a piece of cake, she thought to herself as the *Melody Tryst* jumped to lightspeed, followed a moment later by her.

# Chapter 11

"This is nae gonna be easy." Fix's observation came as they gathered in the dining area for one of the meetings becoming all too common in his voiced opinion.

"It's not supposed to be, *cher*," Lafayette said. "If it was easy, everyone would be hitting smugglers, *n'est-ce pas*?"

"There isn't another way around it," Jennings said authoritatively.

Fix and Lafayette continued to glare at each other, but that was fine as far as the captain was concerned. That animosity would come in handy in a matter of hours. Minerva had determined which ship of Santelli's had a ninety-seven percent chance of being the one Williams escaped on: the *Brigandine*. Unfortunately, the ship had already stopped at three systems and twelve settlements. Williams could have been sold (or gotten off if she was lucky) at any of them, or she might still be on the ship. With no way to be certain, they did not have the time to search all the available areas. Even more unfortunately, the ship was a fairly new DC-MAC 1400 Corvette. The *Brigandine* outclassed the *Melody Tryst* in every tactical way possible: speed, shields, and weapon number and power. As far as Jennings saw it, their only option was to hit the *Brigandine* in between systems where security patrol response would likely be low, and hope an ambush gave them enough tactical advantage to cripple the ship and then board her. Once aboard, there was only the problem of the *Brigandine's* crew compliment being eighteen to their boarding party of three.

"Squawk, do you have the gravity generator online?" Jennings asked the Pasquatil engineer.

"Captain, aye, aye, captain." Squawk saluted three times as he chittered away. "Weapons and more weapons are online. Stealth mode is acting stealthy, and shields are ready to shield."

The Pasquatil did not have synonyms in their language. They found having more than one word for an item redundant, but they also refused to allow the same word to have multiple definitions. It made their attempts to learn English amusing for others, and it drew a small smile from Jennings.

"Well, gents," he said with grim resolve. "We're as prepared for this as we're going to be. Be on the bridge in one hour. The *Brigandine* is coming through this sector in two, and hell's riding in with her."

~

Captain Jennings always liked to give his men an hour to themselves before going into battle. It had been that way when he was a lieutenant in charge of Lafayette's platoon, and he carried it over to their operation on the *Melody Tryst*. More than any other commander Lafayette had ever reported to, Captain Jennings understood the psychology of soldiering. Instinctively, he knew exactly how far he could push each man, how to motivate them for the battle ahead, and how to extract the most from each soul who served under him. He did not waste his men needlessly, and he was not afraid to send them to their deaths either if the mission required it. Lafayette hoped the latter would not be the case with this mission, because he had a bad feeling about it.

Of course, Lafayette had a bad feeling before every mission-Jennings called it his pessimistic French blood. The truth was he had never been cut out to be a soldier, but was never any good at anything else. Well, that was not quite true, he thought to himself as he opened the refrigeration unit's door and pulled out a banana pudding he made earlier. He took a moment to inhale the sweet scent of the dessert before heading to his cabin to enjoy it. It was a true shame they would only be able to spend one hour together, but it was bad luck to die hungry, and he sure as hell was not going off to die while leaving this little slice of heaven in the reefer.

~

The room was spartan, but that was the way Fix liked it. After living in a maximum-security prison for more years than he cared to remember, regardless of his own personal opinion about his guilt, he got used to not having anything. In those days, he considered himself lucky if he had a phosphorescent light above his bed, the rack itself, a sink and a commode. Little had changed.

The bathroom was a small, separate room off his bunk now, the lighting less harsh, and the bed more comfortable, but he still had the dog-eared copy of the King James Bible. He had it out now as he knelt before his bed. Fix was not one to think about the past, to dwell on what he perceived as injustice in his imprisonment. Yet, in these moments, before he would go into battle, he always thought on it. Those thoughts would coalesce into memories from prison itself: fighting off the various gangs looking to beat him down, getting caught up in one riot or another, avoiding being knifed. And the worst memories of all: when he would fail and wind up in the prison hospital, sometimes for months. Fix had survived worse than the battle upcoming. He had endured more than the men they would face. He repeated that mantra over and over to himself as the impeding battle drew nearer.

~

It was difficult to describe what might have been going through the Pasquatil's mind before any fight. Squawk's race was a naturally docile group, whose evolution did not focus on combat, war, or the need to prove one's superiority the way humans and other species had. Efficiency was the hallmark of the Pasquatil's course from primordial ooze to spacefaring race, and so the little Squawk made himself happy and relaxed by running about the ship a mile per minute making sure that shields, weapons, the gravity generator, and the boarding hatch were all in working order.

~

Jennings sat on the bridge and stared at space through the viewscreen. This kind of star gazing was not any kind of appreciation for the aesthetics of space, but a visualization process he started learning when he was a teenager playing war simulations on the home computer or even commanding his 9-year-old troops when playing capture the flag on his birthday. Preparedness was not enough when he was going to put his and his men's lives on the line in battle. Sure, most things turned into a clusterfuck pretty quickly when in the shit, but that was where preparation came in handy. It was easy to improvise when he had already planned on a hundred courses of action based on every conceivable variable. Some would call it a waste of time, but as far as Jennings was concerned, they were the ones who got fragged by the Gael back in the war. His skin was still intact, when eighty percent of the military could not say the same at the end of the war. No, he would stick with his preparation no matter what anyone said. And so, he watched the battle unfold a thousand times as he stared off into the stars.

~

"Are we ready?" Jennings asked, the countdown on the computer having reached ten.

"Oh, yes, yes, yes. Gravity generator ready to generate," Squawk buzzed before making a sound like electricity hissing.

Ten seconds. Jennings eased his hands around the fire controls. The problem with setting up an ambush like this was that at the speed the *Brigandine* was traveling, it would only be in sensor range for about .2 seconds before already past them. That meant leaving the springing of their little gravity trap to Minerva, who was giving them the countdown. Five seconds. Jennings instinctively re-checked the charges on all his shields, cannons, interceptors and torpedo launchers. All were ready. One second.

"Here!!!" screamed Squawk as the *Brigandine* lurched into view.

The false gravity generator the *Melody Tryst* employed would cause the *Brigandine's* onboard navigation computer to force stop the ship, yanking it out of light speed, as the computer registered the *Melody Tryst* as a planetary body. Planets were such horrible speed bumps to faster than light travel, Jennings thought with a smile as he depressed his finger on the twin triggers. A shudder ran through the hull as a salvo of torpedoes launched toward the *Brigandine*. He followed it with pin point plasma cannon fire designed to hit the *Brigandine's* shields before the torpedoes impacted, softening them and allowing the concussion explosives to plow through to the hull.

The plan worked to perfection, which was a pleasant change, Jennings thought to himself, as he watched the explosive impacts on the three-dimensional holo-display. He had successfully hit the power plant, the primary cannons, and the communications array with the first salvo. Now, as the weapons system automatically reloaded, he could easily open a breach to space in the living areas, killing or incapacitating all except those on the bridge. It would help even the odds when it came time to board them. He pulled the torpedo trigger again and nothing happened. Jennings swore and tried it again, but again the system would not fire. This time the computer system flashed a warning in red letters: RELOAD FAILURE- TORPEDOES OFFLINE.

"Squawk!" Jennings yelled.

The Pasquatil squeaked and raced from the bridge down toward engineering, chattering excitedly to himself the whole time.

"We've got problems," Jennings said through the intercom as the *Brigandine* slowly turned its auxiliary weapons to bear. "Hang on! Going evasive!"

The *Brigandine* was essentially unmovable without primary power, and her torpedo launcher was destroyed, but the plasma cannons could function on reserves, and they packed a lot more punch than the *Melody Tryst* did. Fix and Lafayette both arrived at the bridge from where they had been standing by at the boarding hatch just as the first salvo of flak ravaged the *Melody Tryst's* shields. Lafayette was thrown sideways as the ship lurched violently to the starboard while Fix easily got settled and fastened in.

"Shields are down to sixty-seven percent," Fix said, his tone grim as usual. "Moderate leakage through to the hull. No breeches."

"Marquis, dammit, sit down and find me an approach vector!" Jennings ordered.

Lafayette pulled himself into the co-pilot's seat. "Keep circling."

Another salvo sailed passed them, barely missing. "Squawk, where are my torpedoes?" Jennings shouted into the intercom, barely avoiding another barrage as the *Melody Tryst* did a flip-roll.

"Working! Working! Working!" came the excited shout over the sound of what could only be a sledgehammer smacking against a bulkhead.

"They're trying to keep their engine away from us," Lafayette said. "If we can move around them to the stern, we'd have a straight shot in."

Jennings shook his head. "They have an aft reserve launcher on that ship."

"Use the interceptors and punch through," Lafayette fired back. "It's the only path that doesn't allow their guns to get a bearing on us."

"Fine, give Minerva the telemetry," Jennings said as another blast rocked the ship.

A cacophony of alarms and red lights sounded all around them as Jennings tried desperately to keep the ship under control.

"Hull breech, guest quarters," Fix said calmly. "Drop doors are in place, but shields are buckling. Hull showing severe portside damage."

"Minerva, are you ready?" Jennings shouted over the caterwaul.

"At your leisure, captain," the cool female voice said.

"Punch it!"

The sublight afterburners on the *Melody Tryst* kicked on, taking the ship on an elliptical path toward the rotating *Brigandine* so as to always keep the rear of the ship at the *Melody Tryst's* nose. They were essentially hiding in a narrow blind spot for the *Brigandine's* weapons as they made their approach.

"Torpedo launching!" Lafayette announced.

Quickly Jennings activated the interceptors, and a column of blue fire raced from the *Melody Tryst* and intercepted the white streak which would have turned his ship to slag.

"Firing again!" the first mate said. "And a third!"

"Interceptors running hot," Fix said.

The interceptors were only able to lock onto one target at a time with how fast torpedoes moved. They blew up the first of the two, and Jennings had to throw the ship into a complicated swoop roll to buy the interceptors enough time to take out the last torpedo. As he came out of the maneuver, Jennings locked his plasma cannons onto the aft launcher and sent a green cannonade which reduced the launcher to slag.

"Ten seconds, and then we're past the *Brigandine*!" Lafayette said.

"And in her gun sights once more," Jennings said through gritted teeth. "Squawk!"

"Now!" the engineer shrieked.

Without hesitation, Jennings depressed the torpedo trigger and sent a new salvo of explosives streaking toward the *Brigandine*. The massive fireball which ensued took out the *Brigandine's* guns and opened holes in the hull in the cargo bays, crew quarters and engineering. The *Melody Tryst* streaked past the now crippled ship without drawing more fire, and Jennings gently turned her back around.

Flicking on the ship-to-ship transmitter, he said, "*Brigandine*, prepare to be boarded."

Fix eyed Jennings curiously. "Why are you warning them?"

"It's what they always say in the movies."

# Chapter 12

The *Brigandine* drifted slowly in space, rotating slightly as Jennings came back around and matched its rotation so they could dock with it. He had already sent Lafayette and Fix back to the breach hatch, and turned on the ship's automatic internal defenses, just in case the crew of the *Brigandine* thought their only hope was to charge the *Melody Tryst* as soon as they docked.

Jennings checked the readings- they were within a meter of the other ship's hull. With the press of a few buttons, he heard the whirring of the umbilical being extended echoing through the ship, and then felt a shudder as it connected and formed a seal against the *Brigandine*. Quickly, he leapt up from the pilot's chair and hot-footed it out of the bridge and down to the hatch.

"You've got the conn," he called over his shoulder back to Squawk, who pulled himself to attention and saluted.

As he approached the other two men, Lafayette said, "They've got air on the other side. They might be waiting for us. Grenade?"

Jennings nodded. "Grenade."

"Hurry up and get ready," Fix growled.

The other two were already in their space suits and battle helmets. With the *Brigandine* open to space in several areas and the possibility of her emergency airlocks being compromised, they might run into vacuum while they were onboard. As fast as possible, he jumped into his space suit and locked the gloves and boots to the rest of the suit. The helmet came next; it was sleek compared to most EVA gear, but it would still be cumbersome to fight in. The helmet snapped into place, and he picked up his gun belt, reattaching the firepower around his waist. Fix tossed him a compact automatic plasma weapon with a flashlight on top. It looked rather tiny in his hands.

"Is this really enough?" he asked as he slung the weapon's strap over his shoulder.

"That's your back-up piece," Fix pointed out as he handed over a four-foot-long ammo-box fed rail gun with a collapsible tripod.

"That's what I'm talking about," Jennings said as he hefted the massive weapon. "Long time no see, darling." He patted the weapon gently while noting the sniper rifle and the rotating eight-barrel automatic Lafayette carried, and the incendiary round pump-action shotgun Fix held. "Now, we've got enough firepower. But what's with the crossbow?" He nodded to the weapon on the back of Fix.

"You never know," he said cryptically. "Now, let's get this fuckin' show on the road."

Jennings punched another command into the console at the floor hatch, and a sudden burst of light flashed across his retinas as the laser saw created an aperture in the *Brigandine*'s hull. As soon as it opened, Lafayette yanked up on the floor hatch, hurled a grenade through the umbilical and the hole in the *Brigandine*'s hull. He slammed shut the hatch just as quickly and waited until another flash of light pulsed through the window plate.

"*Après vous.*" The Cajun shot a smile to Jennings as they pulled the hatch open once more.

Jennings dove head first into the umbilical, allowing his momentum to carry him through the gravity-less atmosphere until he popped through the opening in the *Brigandine*, arriving in a hallway. The ship's artificial gravity grabbed hold of him hard and slammed his feet back to the ground, giving him a weird feeling of nausea. The grenade had seared the hallway they stood in, and had taken out one of the *Brigandine*'s crew. The body lay against the corridor's wall, a long scorch mark running the length of his uniform.

With amazing speed for a dead body, the crew member whipped out a plasma pistol, but Jennings casually raised his rail gun and sent a stream of energy through his entire torso. He was definitely dead the second time.

"Problem?" Lafayette asked as he arrived in the corridor, followed a moment later by Fix.

"Nope," Jennings said. "Let's see if we can find a working computer outlet. And be careful."

The *Brigandine*'s internal alarms had been thankfully silenced before they arrived. However, the flashing red lights on the ceiling and the pulsing emergency lights on the floor combined eerily with the smoke from the explosions and damaged ship components to create the sensation of wading through a bloody mist. It was a hellish sensation, Jennings thought to himself.

They had not come across anyone else since Jennings took out the one stray crew member, and that made the captain nervous. All of them knew they were outnumbered, and there was no way they could have been lucky enough to take out nearly the entire crew with their attack. With each corridor they navigated, Jennings expected an ambush to come out of every open door. That necessitated a certain amount of deliberation in how quickly they moved, and it was a very slow process to move toward the ship's bridge. That surely worked for the crew of the *Brigandine*- the longer they kept the boarders at bay, the more likely help might arrive from another of Santelli's ships. The *Melody Tryst* would not stand a chance in another battle, especially not with Squawk in command.

"Here," Fix suddenly snapped, pointing to an open room that was still well-lit.

Stepping through carefully, Jennings swept his rifle from left to right, making sure the room was empty. It was. Two surgical beds lay in the room, along with a shelf full of medical supplies and cabinets with missing doors that had apparently spilled their contents of bandages, needles and sundry during the battle. Much more importantly though, a clearly functioning computer sat mounted on the counter next to a pile of surgical equipment.

"Minerva?" Jennings whispered.

"On-line, captain." The computer's voice came through clearly in his earpiece.

"I'm plugging you into their network." He connected the portable CPU to the desktop system.

"Unbelievably, captain, their password is *Brigandine*," Minerva said as she hacked her way through the ship's defenses.

"Are internal sensors online?"

"Sort of. Only a partial scan available."

Jennings chewed on his lower lip for a moment. "Show me."

The heads-up display in his helmet showed a neon-green outline of the *Brigandine* and a dozen glowing orange dots. Two were trapped near the engineering section, emergency bulkheads, showing as bright red on the display, keeping them in place. Much of the rest of the ship was unavailable as the internal sensors in those areas had failed. That left the section they were in and the majority of the middle of the ship with no intel as to how many crewman might be out there waiting for them. At the bow of the *Brigandine*, where sensors began working again, a solitary orange dot sat on the bridge, whom Jennings assumed to be the captain. Nine more dots clustered together along the sole path from the central body of the ship to the bridge at the fore.

"Well, that's a rude way to welcome guests," Jennings grumbled as switched off the HUD.

"What's up?" Lafayette asked.

"An ambush. Right near the bridge," he said. "Nine of them clustered together."

Fix rolled his eyes. "Morons. One grenade and they're done."

"We've got to be close to lob one," Lafayette pointed out. "That's a long bit of corridor with no cover- basically a shooting gallery. We get near enough to do anything and *au revoir*."

"Oh, but there's a better way," Jennings said. "We can always take a walk around them."

Lafayette groaned as realization flashed across his face. "*Mon Dieux*, I hate space walking."

"Don't bitch, you could still get shot on the way there." Jennings smiled before readying his weapon and leading them down the corridor.

~

After moving through three corridors, two bulkheads and into the ship's secondary cargo bay, Jennings was beginning to think about how easy everything was when a burst of green-yellow energy slammed into the wall above him and sent him diving behind a stack of steel power-lift-only crates. Fix and Lafayette had not come through the doorway yet, so they still had cover enough, but neither was apparently able to track where the fire had come from.

The silence in the room was punctured by a burst of static from a comm unit. Fix immediately targeted where the sound had come from and sent a barrage of incendiary rounds across the bay toward a stack of spare parts, shelves of tools, and more steel crates. The area lit up in a massive orange fireball, and a man in overalls came running out from behind it, screaming wildly, his torso and head on fire. A single shot from Lafayette's sniper rifle ended his suffering.

As Jennings emerged from cover, Lafayette asked him, "You think he sounded the alarm?"

Before he could answer, the loud sound of footfalls clamping on steel echoed from the hallway on the opposite end of the cargo bay. "That answer your question?" Jennings asked as he open up full with the rail gun, sending a salvo of fire into the opposite corridor.

The bodies of two men skidded out across the steel floor as an answering barrage came from the defending crew members. Returning to cover once more, Jennings and his crew were able to keep the *Brigandine's* crew from advancing, but from the angle of their cover, they could not hit anyone in the corridor. There were only three exits from the bay: the way they had come, the corridor the *Brigandine* crew held, and the airlock.

"This is a stalemate," Jennings said. "We're going to need to go outside early."

"*Merde*," Lafayette said.

"I'll hold them down as long as I can," Jennings said as he let loose a shorter burst of fire that was immediately answered. "Once you clear the bridge, you'll probably need to come back and give me a hand."

"We can't just leave you here, *mon capitaine*," Lafayette said.

"Long walk, Cap'n," Fix pointed out. "Plus we got ten guys to take out ourselves. That's going to be a little more difficult without you."

"Damn," Jennings swore as Fix fired again. "Alright, I'll come with you. Just give me ten seconds."

Falling to the floor on his belly, Jennings slithered to the edge of the crates they were using as cover and pulled open the tripod on the rail gun. Punching a few commands into the small interface near the trigger, he then switched the scope from human sight to target acquisition.

"Cover me!" he hissed as he jumped out from behind the crate, set the weapon down, and then scrambled back as fire raked where he had stood.

The rail gun started opening fire on its own, tracking the movements in the corridor opposite them. While in sentry mode, the rail gun could track any movement and open fire on it. They would need to be careful that they did not pass in front of its line of sight while making their way to the airlock, because it did not know the difference between friend and foe.

Hustling as the rail gun fired almost continuously, they made their way to the airlock, and Jennings punched in the necessary commands to open it. They passed into the intermediate zone where all atmosphere was drained and the artificial gravity kicked off. The doorway to space opened in front of them, and all three stepped out, activating the magnetic boots they wore as they did so. The magnets were not strong enough to inhibit walking, but were excellent at keeping people from flying off into space, which was something that all three of them wanted to avoid. Slowly, they began the march down the hull of the ship, headed toward the bridge, not seeing the fourth man dressed in an EVA suit coming up behind them with a knife drawn.

The man slashed for Lafayette first, but the attack deflected partially off the breather unit on the back of his EVA suit. Over their comms, Jennings heard Lafayette cry out in surprise and saw him fall forward, bouncing off the hull of the ship and slowly bounding up and away from the hull. Jennings went to grab him to keep him from floating off into space, but the assailant slashed out at his reaching arm and forced him to back away.

"Fix!" Jennings brought up the small back-up rifle Fix had given him and depressed the trigger instinctively, forgetting that smaller plasma weapons needed oxygen around them in order to fire.

The weapon seized up in Jennings's hands, but he reacted quickly as the *Brigandine* crewman struck again, bringing the malfunctioning weapon up to block the knife attack. Out of the corner of his eye, Jennings saw Fix make for the Cajun in a rescue attempt, but he was already too late. Lafayette had already drifted too high off the hull for

Fix to reach him without jumping. If the Scotsman did jump after him, he too would be drifting away through space.

Jennings needed to act fast, and he tried to swing his rifle into his attacker's face, missing badly. The *Brigandine* crewman brought the knife down, but his whole body suddenly jerked as an arrow flew straight through his faceplate. With the rupture, the atmosphere within escaped his suit, and he immediately began to decompress. Jennings supposed it was a small mercy the man was probably already dead.

"Captain!" Fix shouted as he leapt off the hull and grabbed Lafayette's outstretched hand.

As fast as possible, Jennings bounded over to where they were and was just able to grab Fix's ankle without his magnetic boots coming off the hull. Easily in the weightless environment, he pulled the two men back down until their boots were back on the hull.

"That was overly exciting," Jennings said as he tried to catch his breath.

"Now you know why I brought the crossbow," Fix said.

"Bring whatever the hell you want from now on," Jennings said as they started off once more to the bow of the ship.

The rest of the operation went far more smoothly. They had successfully pinned half of the crew in the aft of the ship, and the half who waited in the atrium leading up to the bridge did not apparently expect a half-crazed Cajun to throw open the emergency hatch and toss a couple of grenades on top of their heads. Those few who survived were more than willing to surrender as they hacked acrid smoke out of their lungs. Fix bound the four survivors together against a pylon with some cable he found.

"The captain?" Jennings asked the most conscious looking of the four.

"On the bridge," the captive said, his voice barely more than a growl.

"Any surprises?"

"Open the door and find out," the man spat.

"Do you want to be the first one through?" Jennings asked.

Defeat passed across the man's sweaty, smoke-stained face. "We were the last line of defense. Bridge defenses are down. I think Captain has a pistol." The last came as an afterthought.

"That wasn't so bad," Jennings said. "You might just survive this yet."

Lafayette was already at the door leading to the bridge. "Locked, *mon capitaine.*"

Once again removing the small CPU, Jennings plugged it into a flashport next to the bridge hatch. "Minerva, if you would be so kind."

"You know I am a highly sophisticated artificial intelligence system," Minerva protested.

"Near-artificial intelligence," Lafayette corrected.

"I'm just pointing out that breaking and entering could be done by a far less important system," she said.

A half-smile crossed Jennings's face. "But not as quickly or as well."

"Flatterer," Minerva said, her voice shining as with a smile while the door slid open.

They were greeted by a salvo of plasma fire which caused Jennings and Lafayette to scramble out of the way. Very calmly, Fix stood still and fired his crossbow into the bridge. With a yelp of surprise and pain came the unmistakable sound of a plasma pistol clattering to the deck floor.

"*Mon Dieux*, do you sleep with that thing?" Lafayette asked.

"Every night." With that, Fix stepped onto the bridge, the other two falling into step behind him.

The captain of the *Brigandine* was an older man named Javier Rodriguez, who looked like he handled more the money side of the smuggling business than the ruffian side. He was small, thin, with a well-manicured beard and a ring of silver hair running around his head. Teeth grit, in pain, he slumped on the deck next to the captain's chair, an arrow sticking out of his leg below the knee.

Rodriguez stared at the three men and managed to stutter out, "What the hell do you want?"

The captain answered for the three of them. "We're looking for a girl."

# Chapter 13

"Has there been any movement on the other matter we spoke of?" General Ounimbango asked vaguely.

"The line is perfectly scrambled," Anastasia Petrova replied with a hint of disdain. "You can speak as you *vill*."

Ounimbango slumped in a chair in his office onboard the *TGFS Intrepid* en route from Mariador to Earth, and he did not like discussing his end-around on his Gael superiors on any channel, scrambled or otherwise. The Gael had shown an amazing ability to decipher and decrypt even the most advanced communication codes T-Fed had used during the war. His split of the two hundred and fifty thousand dollar bounty was enough to override his sense of caution, however. He wanted to know what the hell was going on.

"Fine," he said at last, exhaling mightily as he stared at the small vid-screen. "What is the status of the Williams retrieval mission?"

"Proceeding much better," Petrova said. "Your intelligence reports on *vhat* Captain Jennings is up to have made it quite a bit easier, of course. At first, *ve veren't* able to determine how Ms. Williams made it off-planet, but the government's investigation into the attack on the *Brigandine* revealed it must be Jennings behind it. Once I had that, I was able to backtrack his logic and determine the *Brigandine* was the ship which took Ms. Williams away. *Ve* still don't know *vhere* they took her, but I am now pursuing some… diplomatic options, general."

"You're sure Jennings is on the right track?"

Petrova's eyes narrowed at Ounimbango's questioning of her. "*Da.*"

He ignored her annoyance, and he pressed, "How do you know it wasn't a simple act of piracy on Jennings's part? Men like him…"

"Men like him are something you'll never understand," Petrova said. "Jennings considers himself above all else a man of honor. Men of honor don't commit piracy. Not to mention that it *vould* be unbelievably stupid for a small *Symphonic*-class vessel to take on a fully armed DC-MAC 1400, or for a three-man crew to attack an eighteen-crew ship, *pravda*?"

"He might be working another job," Ounimbango protested vehemently.

"According to your report from the Gael, Jennings was broke and his ship was grounded before getting this job," she countered. "Do you really think he *vould* be *vorking* on something else?"

Ounimbango was forced to concede. "Very well. What are these diplomatic angles you intend to pursue?"

"That's my business," Petrova said darkly. "Your only concern need be your cut once the operation is complete."

"But..." Ounimbango tried to protest, but the vid-screen went blank.

He sat back in his leather chair and swiveled around to peer through the portholes out into space. The stars were stretched out to star lines with the speed they traveled, a beautiful sight. He let his eyes become unfocused as his thoughts became lost. Perhaps he should not have brought Petrova into the operation, he thought to himself. The Russian was turning out to be a loose cannon, cutting him out of her strategy, refusing to update him. Impotent anger welled up inside of him, and he slammed his meaty fist inside an open palm.

~

"Everything all right?" asked Vosler.

Petrova spat out a few curses in Russian as she locked eyes on her lieutenant. He was overly tall, but muscular so it did not appear disproportionate. His blond hair was growing in gray, and the scar which ran down his face clipped through one of his blue eyes. She still remembered when he got that scar, back when their little operation was just the two of them.

"It's fine," she said at last in English. "That man is an idiot."

"But he does feed us rather lucrative work," Vosler pointed out.

Bitterness colored her tone. "And takes a hefty fee for his lack of trouble."

Vossler shrugged. "You could always not pay him. It's not like he can take you to court."

She shook her head slightly. "Ounimbango is a puppet, but he still has power, as much as any human. Crossing him would be dangerous."

"You're the one bringing the Gael what they want." Vosler sat down in one of the chairs opposite her desk. "That should turn their favor toward you, I would think."

"*Ve'll* see," she said with a sly smile.

"Then there's the other possibility."

She raised her eyebrows interrogatively.

"We kill him and then keep the money," Vosler said.

"I do love your deviousness," she said, her eyes flirting with him.

He did not respond, but he never did. That had never stopped her from having him before. Focusing herself to the business at hand though, she brought the communication system back up and punched in a communication code only a few dozen people in the universe knew.

A well-tanned face displaying dark Mediterranean features under a full beard appeared on the screen in a moment. "Santelli," he said shortly.

"Ah, Vesper, it has been too long," Petrova said.

"Now's not a good time, Ana."

"Yes, I know," Petrova said. "The *Brigandine*. I heard about it."

"Then you know I've no time for pleasantries no matter how amenable are previous meetings have been," Santelli said. "Farewell."

Petrova held up a hand. "I also know who is responsible for it."

Santelli had been halfway out of his chair and about to turn off the comm system before stopping short. He sat back down. "An interesting claim to make. Many have offered their theories as well. All wrong."

"I offer no theory," Petrova said.

"Of course not," he said sarcastically. "Very well, Ana. We've had enough dealings in the past for me to know this isn't free. Nothing with you is." A strange smile as of a pleasant memory passed his face and vanished just as quickly.

"I *vant* a favor in return."

"Of course, the gratitude and generosity of Vesper Santelli is known throughout the nine systems," he said. "Did you already have a favor in mind or would you like it to be added to the books, redeemable upon request?"

"I know *vhat* I *vant*," she said. "The men who did this to your ship were looking for a girl. So am I. Your ship sold… I should say, dropped her off somewhere and the price of my knowledge is that location."

"A fair price," Santelli said without hesitation. "According to the captain of my ship, the men who boarded them asked about a girl they sold to the Raw Mind on Strikeplain. It's a club in Storm Haven."

"I'm familiar *vith* it."

"And the name of the ship and its captain?" Santelli asked.

"Captain Matthew Jennings of the *Melody Tryst*," she said. "If you hurry, you should be able to reach Strikeplain before he can leave."

The information did not appear to faze him. "Thank you, but several of my ships are on their way there now. It wouldn't have been too difficult to track down which of the ships on the planet had mounted this attack against me and mine, but your little piece of information will save me a few minutes."

"Of course, I'm glad *ve vere* able to help each other," Petrova said. "I'll try to stay clear of your men *vhen ve* pick up the girl."

"Oh, I'll be picking up the girl well before you arrive," Santelli said.

Fury flashed in Petrova's eyes. "*Ve* had a deal."

"We had a deal for information," Santelli said coldly. "I have provided that. Don't dare accuse me of reneging. This girl must be truly valuable based on the lengths everyone is willing to go to for her. I would say that is a profit that should belong to me. Don't take it personally, Anastasia. It's just good business."

As he signed off, Petrova shrieked in frustration. Immediately, she stood, walked over to Vosler, and pulled him to his feet. She poured all her strength into her fist and belted him in the gut. Vosler doubled over and let out the barest hint of a grunt, before pulling himself back up to his feet and smiling at her.

"Feel better?" he asked.

"*Da*, get everyone onboard the *Grey Vistula* as fast as possible. I *vant* to be ready to leave in an hour," she said.

"Of course," he nodded and immediately left.

Petrova took a moment to glance around her office on Firefall, lush and lavish, many old Earth antiques, some replicas, but all very expensive. The office was a tribute to her success, her indomitable nature, and now she felt it mocking her. She had given away a priceless piece of information to one of her biggest rivals. This was the first time she could ever remember being tricked in such a way, and it caused a burning sickening sensation in her stomach.

"Focus," she said sternly as she slapped herself in the face.

There was still time. Santelli had a huge head start, but Firefall was closer to Strikeplain than Earth. She was willing to bet she could make it there in time or close enough to make it interesting. Plus, Santelli's men still needed to make it back to Earth with the cargo intact. There was plenty of time, she reiterated to herself, allowing a grim smile to cross her face as she set about to the work she needed to do.

# Chapter 14

"Ugh, Strikeplain," Lafayette said as the *Melody Tryst* rocketed into the atmosphere, headed for the dark gray maw that was the near permanent cover of the planet.

"It's going to be fun," Jennings said as the ship immediately lurched wildly when they entered the cloud cover. "The shields are up, aren't they?" He turned to Squawk, who stared through the viewscreen at the numerous flashes of purple energy. "Squawk?"

"Shiny! Pretty! Shields!" squeaked the engineer.

"How much further?" Jennings asked as another lightning strike hit the ship so hard it managed to shake Fix awake for a moment.

"Thirty seconds," Lafayette reported over Fix telling them all to shut up.

With a few more held breaths released and a collective sigh, the *Melody Tryst* blasted through the cloud base and headed toward the surface of the desolate planet. Strikeplain was in the outer reaches of what used to be Terran controlled space, and the terraforming was not exactly completed. That of course did not stop the mining companies from moving in, so a dozen or so cities dotted the mostly rocky planet. All were settlements for miners, their families, and the assorted other necessaries that went with a town. No water could be found on the planet, save for the sooty water vapor blasted out of the long line of volcanoes running along the planet's equator. Rather than spewing magma, the volcanoes erupted with superheated water, which went into the atmosphere and became the super storms that forever encased Strikeplain.

Temperature and oxygen levels were all Earth standard, however. So, when Jennings set them down in the sparsely populated docks, and they stepped outside, it felt rather pleasant despite the ominous roiling of the skies above. Squawk as usual stayed with the ship, supposedly keeping it on stand-by in case they needed to make a sudden exit. More likely though, he was staring up at the skies from a porthole. The Pasquatil were fascinated by those powers of nature that were the most destructive. Supposedly, an entire Pasquatil settlement once had been destroyed by a tornado, and they all died standing there, watching it come closer.

Jennings, Fix, and Lafayette made their way toward the exit of the fenced-off space dock. Inside a glass dome, a dowdy security guard who looked two shades of ennui from being bored to death processed their disembarkation.

"Anything to declare?" he grumbled.

"No."

"Any weapons?"

Jennings rested his hands on one of the holsters on his belt. "No."

"Purpose of your visit to the wonderful world of Strikeplain?"

"Just looking to shoot in and out," Jennings said. "The crew needed some shore leave, and I being a benevolent captain allowed it."

"Yeah, right," the guard snorted, before turning to Fix and Lafayette. "You guys should seek new employment."

They both shot him grins in return.

"Actually, we were hoping to check out the Raw Mind," Jennings said.

"Ah…" The guard started to say something, thought better of it, and seemed to come to attention a little bit more. "Yes, sir. You'll be wanting to head straight to town center, take a right down the alley next to the inn. Can't miss the sign."

"Thanks for your help." Jennings hid the sense of puzzlement he felt as the guard stamped their falsified paperwork. *Why had the guard's demeanor changed when they said they were heading to the Raw Mind?*

They left the docks and made their way down the central avenue of Storm Haven. There was very little foot traffic as it was after eleven planet time, but the streets were lined with ground speeders and a few shuttles. Three-story buildings lined the street, most of them shops or cafes of the more eccentric kind with apartments over top. The grocers, restaurants and clothiers would be found in the city center.

The center of Storm Haven was where two perpendicular thoroughfares met, and that part of the city was still awake. Late night revelers spilled out of the middle-class taverns and pubs, while a few outdoor restaurants still had clientele sipping cups of ridiculously expensive imported coffee. The city center was better lit, and the dreariness of Storm Haven seemed to wash away in the glow of the light.

"*Dis* is more like it," Lafayette said as a group of drunken revelers ambled past singing something unintelligible.

"We're not here to party," Jennings said, trying to get his bearings.

A twenty-foot-tall statue stood in the center of a plaza with a roundabout encircling it. "Wonder who *dat* is," Lafayette pondered.

"Some arsehole or another," Fix said.

To their left and straight ahead, the neighborhoods got dimmer, and the housing became more matchbox tenement high-rises- housing for the low-income miners almost certainly. The affluence of the town seemed to be to the right, which was where they had been directed, but Jennings did not see anything called the Raw Mind amid the many lighted signs in that direction.

Fix pointed down an alley. "There."

He led them across the plaza past the statue of the arsehole and a building on the right which said Strikeplain's Finest Inn. Based on its shabby appearance, Jennings hoped that was not the case. Fix led them past the hotel entrance and halfway down the block until they came to a small alley between the inn and the first tenement high-rise. None of the street light reached into the narrow maw, and the three men stopped for a moment.

"We're not really going in there, *mon capitaine*, are we?" Lafayette asked.

"It's what the man said," Fix stated.

"I don't see anything down there," Jennings said.

"It's what the man said," Fix reiterated slowly.

Slowly, Jennings led them into the alley, his eyes gradually adjusting to the near dark, until he saw a small neon purple glow on the left. It was above a small non-descript door and read RAW MIND. Two men in expensive suits stood on opposite sides of the door. The place appeared to be for a reserved clientele, Jennings noted as he picked up on the trademark jacket bulge of concealed plasma pistols.

"Good evening, gentlemen," Jennings said as he walked to the door.

In perfect tandem, both men stepped in front of him.

"Members only," one of them said sternly.

"Excellent, where do I sign up?" Jennings asked.

"It's forty thousand," the other said. "I can summon the manager if you like."

"That seems rather extravagant for what is surely going to be a one-time visit to this charming little world," Jennings protested. "Don't you have an option for well-to-do spacefarers who want to take in the best of Strikeplain for the short time they're planetside?"

"Well-to-do?" one of them echoed, eyeing Jennings's denim and leather clothing with clear disdain.

Jennings's eyes narrowed, feigning insult. "I dress how I see fit. And I don't like when I am insulted, which is why I pay these two very well to get angry on my behalf."

Lafayette and Fix glared at the two guards.

Behind them, the door opened and a nasally voice announced, "I do appreciate the work you're doing Mr. Stone, Mr. Cahill, but perhaps I should speak to our guest."

The guards stepped aside to reveal a man wearing a red tuxedo with a pencil thin moustache sitting on the top of his upper lip. His hair was slicked back and greasy- Jennings disliked his obsequious smile on sight.

"Gentlemen, please do come in to the Raw Mind." He swept them in through the door with an open arm.

"Thank you, Mister…"

"My name is Sinclair." He did not indicate if it was his first or last. "I believe you were interested in a one-time visit to our fine establishment, something that is not customary here for us." Sinclair led them into what reminded Jennings of an Old Earth hotel lobby with red velvet carpet, and old-world furniture. "However, we are perfectly willing to work out an… a la carte deal for the well-financed individual."

Jennings forced a smile as a scantily clad woman grinned at them as she took their coats, and brought back three dinner jackets for them to put on.

"House rules, I'm afraid," Sinclair said.

"Of course," Jennings said as he put his on. "A perfect fit, thank you."

"Yes, Ms. Madeleine sizes men up well," Sinclair agreed. "Now, let us discuss your interests, and we will work something up that would hopefully be amenable to you."

"What do you offer?" Jennings asked.

"Whatever the gentleman requires, sir," he said. "One thousand will provide you with the company of a lady for as long as you desire her. But that only covers certain items and certain ladies."

"Where can I make a selection?" Jennings asked.

Sinclair swung his arm toward a double door made of solid oak. "This way, please."

The manager swung the door open, and they stepped into an expansive room with a stage across from them, booths around most of the walls except where the bar was located on their left, and a dozen or so tables and lounge chairs placed around the room. A soft ambient music was being piped in from somewhere, more erotic than the techno-driven thump of most clubs of this type that Jennings had seen. A fog machine created a mist over the stage where two topless women moved and intertwined with each other slowly and sensually. Maybe twenty or thirty men sat at the tables, some enjoying the company of beautiful women, some chatting with their friends or watching the show, and others downing drinks at the bar. Women moved slowly from man to man chatting, laughing, flirting, and every so often one would lead a man over to a spiral staircase, past another security guard.

"Look around, talk to the girls, have a good time, then come back to me and we'll discuss anything extra you might wish to purchase." Sinclair took a small bow and bustled off.

For Sinclair's benefit, Jennings said, "Gentlemen, I don't think I will need you for a while. I feel quite safe here." He smiled at the manager and gestured toward the bar. "Please help yourself to a drink."

He handed over his weapons to the two of them, knowing he would never be allowed to keep them if he were to get Michelle Williams alone. Fix and Lafayette made their way to the bar and ordered drinks, keeping their eyes open for their girl. Jennings made his way through the tables, saying hello and shaking hands with those less reserved in their tipsiness. There were worse places to search for a bounty, he thought to himself as he passed the fourth unbelievably beautiful woman he had seen. Looking over at the bar, he met Fix's eyes, who glanced over to his left where a few men were smoking cigars and laughing uproariously. In the middle of them stood a college age girl wearing knee-high boots, a short skirt and a low-cut top. She held a box of cigars, handing them out to her customers upon request and lighting them.

Nodding only slightly to Fix, Jennings turned and raised his hand, beckoning Sinclair. The manager hustled over immediately. "Has sir made a decision?"

"Yes," Jennings said. "That one with the cigars is exactly who I am looking for."

Sinclair became noticeably uncomfortable and turned his gaze to the floor. "Sir, I am afraid she is unavailable. But we have many fine other selections…"

Jennings cut him off. "She is the one I want. Why is she unavailable?"

"We have been saving her," Sinclair explained, choosing his words carefully. "As of yet, she's untarnished, and we have some members who enjoy that sort of thing."

"Sinclair, you strike me as a pure capitalist, and I mean that as the greatest compliment," Jennings said, to which Sinclair smiled and nodded. "And as such, I am sure a deal could be struck. You said one thousand, but I will give you two."

"I'm afraid I cannot…"

"Five then," Jennings said quickly. "Four for the club and one for you, as a gratuity if you take my meaning."

Jennings could see Sinclair adding the money in his mind. "I believe, sir, we have a deal." He offered a hand which Jennings took.

"Excellent." Letting his voice drop to a whisper, Jennings said, "I've been disappointed with women who were supposed to be... What was the word you used? Untarnished? Alas, they have not been so."

"Sir, you have my personal guarantee," the manager protested.

"All the same, if I am going to pay five times the going rate for a night's company, I would want certain assurances," Jennings said.

"If sir wishes to place a deposit and would like to deliver the rest upon the morning, I am sure that would be fine," he said.

"Capital." With a flourish, Jennings produced his credit chit and authorizing it for one thousand dollars.

Sinclair took out a small card reader out of his pocket and scanned the chit through. Jennings was glad he allowed that little bluff to go through, because the way his luck ran, God only knew how much of the Gael's advance would be needed to actually bring the girl to justice.

"Shall I introduce you?" Sinclair asked.

"Lead on." He wrapped an arm around Sinclair's shoulders and steered him through the tables toward Michelle Williams.

"Miss Melody, you have a guest," Sinclair said, beckoning Michelle over with an outstretched finger.

Terror crossed the pretty face of the young girl, but she visibly recovered quickly. At a snap of Sinclair's fingers, another raven-haired beauty took the cigar box from Michelle, and the girl stepped forward.

"You're very beautiful," Jennings said honestly.

"Thank you," she said, her eyes refusing to meet his gaze.

"Come now, don't be like that, this gentleman has paid a good deal of money for the pleasure of your company, the least you could do is smile for him," Sinclair chastised.

"Sorry, sir." She glanced up and did her best to force a smile.

"Shall we head upstairs?" Jennings placed an arm around her bare waist and steered her toward the spiral staircase.

"Have a nice night," Sinclair said as he then scuttled off to some other duty.

As soon as he was out of earshot, Jennings said, "Don't be afraid. I'm not going to hurt you."

Before he could explain anything further, they arrived at the security guard standing in front of the spiral staircase. The guard patted Jennings down for weapons and then gave him the stereotypical "if you try anything foolish or hurt the girl" speeches.

"I understand. You've nothing to worry about from me," Jennings said.

"Seriously, no funny business," the guard said in a Polish accent. "The rooms are miked to ensure the girls' safety."

This did concern Jennings, but he kept the smile plastered on his face. It would be hard to explain to Michelle that they were here to rescue her with someone listening in.

Jennings and his crew had already decided before landing at Strikeplain that her cooperation would be necessary to facilitate getting her out of the Raw Mind. Outgunned as they were, they could not afford to be dealing with a prisoner as well. Michelle would need to want to go with them in order for their plan to work. The Raw Mind did not strike Jennings as an institution which allowed their customers to openly discuss escape plans with the club's "property."

The guard gave them a room key and some directions, and they headed upstairs. Michelle opened the door, her hand shaking so hard that it took a moment to stick the key into the slot. The room was smallish, but lavishly done with a four-poster king-size bed, a fur rug next to a fake fireplace and some reproductions of classic art adorning the walls. There was a small buffet with a selection of alcohol and a music player.

Michelle had already headed nervously toward the bed, but Jennings called her back by asking, "Do you dance?"

She nodded.

"Excellent, let's see what we have." Humming to himself, he looked through the computer files on the music player until he found something he liked. "This is one of my favorites." The opening serenade of Shostakovich's Waltz from his Jazz Suite no. 2 began playing.

Slowly, Michelle came over towards him and allowed her body to be pulled into his. Hoping the music was loud enough to make his whisper inaudible to the listening devices, Jennings put his lips to her ear. "Whatever you do, do not speak louder than a whisper, do you understand?"

A bolt of fear appeared in her eyes, but he did his best not to project any malice, so she just nodded.

"I'm not here to spend the night with you," he said softly. "Not that you're not lovely, of course." Having her this close to him messed with his mind a bit. She was stunningly beautiful; she had an intoxicating aroma of wildflowers; and the way she moved against him deviated his thought process considerably. *Focus, Jennings*, he thought to himself. "We're here to break you out of here."

"A rescue?" she mouthed back.

He nodded.

"Who do you work for?" she whispered. "My parents?"

He shook his head to say, "Not now," and glanced up to the ceiling to indicate the listening devices. Gently, he put his mouth back to her ear. "We need to find a way out of here. We have a ship, and I have two men in the club, but we'll need-"

He was interrupted by the unmistakable sound of plasma fire ripping through the air. "Now what?"

# Chapter 15

Remy Lafayette ordered a beer and nursed it slowly, waiting for whatever was bound to go wrong to occur. Some people called it pessimism, and he would not disagree. However, when you had already thought about all the horrible things that could happen, it made it a lot easier to deal with when they did.

"Do you think the girl will be able to get us out of here?" he whispered to Fix.

The Scotsman eyed him sourly. "The hell would I know?" With that, he took a belt of sake.

Lafayette stared at the choice of beverage with an inquisitive look. "You like rice wine?"

"You don't?"

"Never mind," Lafayette muttered.

"I find it relaxes the tension nicely without interfering too horribly with the reflexes before a firefight," Fix explained further, one of the longer sentences he had been known to utter.

"Yeah, but…" Lafayette protested.

"You're the one expecting the worst aren't you?" Fix said. "Yet I'm the only one drinking like it."

The Cajun conceded with a slight bow of the head. "Touché, *mon ami*. Besides they've only got three or four security guards. They're not going to stop us from getting out of here."

The oaken double door they had entered through to reach the salon suddenly flew open. Eight men armed with plasma rifles stepped through the door, the leader firing into the ceiling to capture everyone's attention. The one security guard at the steps drew a weapon as did another who had been masquerading as a guest. Both fell under a column of green fire before even getting a shot off.

"Your attention, please, ladies and gentleman," said the leader, a beefy man with an American accent, wearing a suit too expensive even for the nicest brothel on Strikeplain.

Sinclair moved forward slowly from where he had been glad-handing several of his clients, his hands raised in the air. "I am the manager of this establishment, gentlemen. What can we do for you?"

The leader turned his weapon on Sinclair and fired, sending the small man's body flying back into a table. He crashed into it hard, already dead, sending the drinks of the four men seated there flying about. No one else in the establishment moved. It seemed as if the cigar smoke that lingered in the air had even stopped drifting.

The leader glared down at the corpse. "I hate being interrupted." He turned to his men. "Fan out. Martinez and Roma, upstairs."

The men spread out through the room, forcing those seated to stand up and make their way over to the bar. The leader continued, "We are looking for four people: three men and a girl. If they are given over to us, we will leave this charming establishment with no more injury. They are one Captain Matthew Jennings, one Remy Lafayette, one Angus Ferguson, and the girl Michelle Williams. If you would care to step forward, we won't have to execute anyone."

Well toward the back of the people corralled over to the bar, Lafayette bent over to Fix to whisper, "Santelli?"

The Scotsman grunted and turned to the bartender. "Sake."

Lafayette stared at him. "Really?"

"Why the hell nae?" Fix asked. "We need to wait for Cap'n to make his move."

"What?" Lafayette hissed.

"They only sent two men upstairs," Fix said, eyeing him coolly. "You don't think Cap'n can handle it?"

~

Michelle was shaking, and her tone was frantic. "What's happening?"

Jennings turned away from the door he had opened a crack. "Apparently there are some other interested parties. Two of them coming this way, clearing out all the apartments." He closed the door fully and locked it. "Quickly, take off your clothes."

Her mouth fell open in shock. "You want to do it now?"

"No! It's a… just do it," he said, as he took up position behind the door.

Michelle did as she was told and had just finished when the door was kicked open. There was the briefest moment of hesitation that tended to accompany most men, even the most dedicated soldiers, in the presence of a beautiful, naked woman. The barrel of the man's rifle dropped to the floor, and Jennings took advantage of the distraction to ram the door back against the intruder. A cry of pain came from the other side as the rifle clattered to the ground and Martinez stumbled back into the doorway. Jennings slammed the door a second time and felt the brief satisfaction of the wood slamming into Martinez's nose. In one fluid motion, he scooped up the dropped rifle and started to bring it to bear on the second man. Roma was faster though. He brought his rifle down on Jennings's head, sending him sprawling, and he then kicked Martinez's rifle out of his hands. He brought the rifle down two more times to make sure Jennings was truly down, before turning to study the girl.

"Get dressed, Ms. Williams," he said softly.

~

The fight upstairs was over quickly, and Lafayette swore under his breath as Roma escorted Michelle onto the landing.

"Mr. Sciavella, I've got the girl and Captain Jennings up here," Roma said. "Jennings is out."

Sciavella nodded to two of his men, and they headed up the stairs to help Roma. "Excellent," he said, turning back to the Raw Mind's guests. "Two down. Two to go. I'm afraid my time is almost up. So, I'm going to start shooting the ladies here as I already have the one I want if Mr. Lafayette and Mr. Ferguson don't show themselves. I'll give you ten seconds."

Lafayette turned to Fix. "Now what?"

"Interesting tactic from the Cap'n," he muttered in reply. "We could take'em."

"Without getting all these people killed?" he hissed.

"Nope."

Lafayette sighed. "I guess we have no choice. We're right here." Hopping off his bar stool, he pushed his way through the crowd. Fix followed, still carrying his cup of sake.

Sciavella's eyes narrowed. "I had friends on the *Brigandine.*"

"Your friends were wankers," Fix retorted.

This earned him a slug in the gut from Sciavella's meaty fist.

"A small down payment on the torture Mr. Santelli is going to bring to you," Sciavella said.

"Is that before or after he's done shagging his sister," Fix said.

This time he was sent sprawling by a fist across the face.

"You made me spill my sake, tubby," he grumbled as he tried to pull himself to his feet.

Sciavella grabbed him by the shoulder, intending to yank him up so he could pound on him some more, but Fix was far faster. He grabbed hold of Sciavella's wrist and pulled himself upward, drawing his pistol at the same time and sticking it in the gangster's throat. Fix had him rotated around as a human shield before the others could even react.

"Drop the weapons or I drop him," Fix said.

There was no reaction from Santelli's men, so Lafayette slowly made the move to draw his own weapon. As he brought it to bear, a horrific burning sensation surged in his fingers and the pistol was ripped from his grasp. From the stairs, Roma had a pistol trained on him. The man was a good shot to take his weapon right out of his hand and leave him mostly intact.

"Let him go," Roma said. "Or I kill your Captain." A nod indicated the blood-soaked man propped between two more of Santelli's goons.

"Do nothing he says," Jennings rasped.

Fix allowed a second to pass, and Roma dropped his pistol down to Jennings's knee and fired. The captain's left leg buckled, and he fell forward, rolling all the way to the bottom of the stairs.

"What else do you think I can do to him before you lay down your weapons?" Roma asked. "Or to this pretty young thing?" His eyes went to Michelle who was being held by the broken-nosed Martinez. "The warrant specified alive. It did not specify her condition."

"Shite," Fix swore as he took the barrel out of Sciavella's throat and pushed him forward. He dropped the pistol on the ground.

"Lucky for you Santelli wants the pleasure of killing you himself," Sciavella said before turning to his men. "Take their weapons, bind their hands, and let's go. Sorry for the inconvenience, ladies and gentleman. The constables will be here in a few hours to clear up this mess. It would best if everyone developed a case of amnesia."

With that, he turned around and followed his men and the four prisoners out the door and into the lobby. The door to the alley was blown open, and the two men guarding it lay dead, their bodies splayed haphazardly about the lush confines of the lobby.

"Told you we should've killed the captain," Fix said as they emerged out into the alley underneath the sky that continued to roil with incredible power.

"So noted," Jennings said, the stress evident in his voice as he was partially dragged and partially limped through the alley.

"No talking," one of their captors said harshly.

"Sorry the rescue isn't going to plan," Jennings said to Michelle.

Before she could reply, the captor who ordered their silence punched Jennings in the kidney. "Stop it!" she shrieked. "Leave him alone."

"Thanks," Jennings whispered as Lafayette did the best he could to help the captain stagger back to his feet.

They emerged from the alley, and Sciavella held a communications device up to his mouth. "We've got them. Rendezvous at extraction point alpha."

Their captors steered them all to the right, heading into the poorer sections of the city. It wasn't a bad idea, Lafayette thought. Police response times were slower and people were more likely to simply hide instead of calling the police if they saw a bunch of men armed to the teeth marching down the street with several prisoners. They walked several blocks without encountering anyone until they came to a small park that was probably a haven for gang activity. Most of the wall going around it was falling down, and the little bit still standing was tagged with dozens of graffiti markers.

Sciavella signaled everyone to stop once inside the park. "This is where we wait for our ride."

"They're not going to be too long are they? I've got places to be," Jennings said.

Sciavella laughed. "You don't stop, do you, Mr. Jennings?"

"Captain Jennings."

"Tell me, is it a true lack of fear that you experience, or do you use this banter to mask the terror inside you?" he asked.

"What do you think?" Jennings asked, a half-smile crossing his face.

The unmistakable sounds of an approaching shuttle cut through the night above the rumble of the storm clouds above. "I think we'll find out when Mr. Santelli begins to work on you," he said.

"Unfortunately for you, that will never happen," Jennings said.

"Oh, and why is that?" Sciavella asked.

"I have powers beyond that which you can understand," the captain said, his tone mysterious.

Fix and Lafayette exchanged a glance. *What the hell was he talking about?* Lafayette wondered. The captain bantering with a captor was not surprising, but claiming some kind of telepathy? This was new. Perhaps Jennings had his bell rung harder than Lafayette thought. A flash of movement drew Lafayette's attention down Fix's hands- he had managed to free himself from his bindings somehow.

Meanwhile, Sciavella was laughing even harder. "Why don't you give us an example of this power then?"

"As you wish," Jennings said.

The captain scrunched up his face as if trying to focus all aspects of his life force on a single act as the shuttle appeared from over top of one of the tenement buildings and started to descend toward them. Sciavella looked away from Jennings for a moment to watch the shuttle's approach. He appeared about to spit another mocking retort at Jennings when the ship incinerated before them. The wreckage slammed into the far side of the park and sent a six-story high fireball skyward. The force and the heat of the explosion hit them as far away as they were and pushed Lafayette several steps back.

"That's but a small sample of my power," Jennings said mysteriously.

Sciavella placed his plasma pistol to Jennings's temple. "How the fuck did you do that?"

Turning to face him slowly, Jennings said, "I didn't. I just happened to notice the guy with the rocket launcher who did."

"What guy? What the hell are you talking about?" Sciavella said.

Jennings nodded back to the park entrance. "I imagine he's with her."

Lafayette turned back around to see a woman wearing a green business suit armed with a plasma rifle that somehow coordinated nicely with her outfit. She had a dozen men behind her at least, one of whom toted a rocket launcher. Sciavella and his men immediately drew a bead on this new group.

Anastasia Petrova spoke clearly, "I *vill* be taking the prisoners, *da*? Or you *vill* be killed."

"These people belong to Mr. Santelli. If you're wise, you'll know that name and you'll piss off," Sciavella threatened.

"I know Mr. Santelli *vell*," Petrova said. "And he has betrayed me for the last time. He must be taught the price of his betrayal."

"The prisoners are ours," Sciavella reiterated.

"Perhaps we should get out of the way while you resolve this dispute," Jennings suggested.

Sciavella slapped Jennings across the back of the head. "Shut up." To Petrova, he said, "How about a deal?"

Petrova smiled her shark-like grin. "*Vhat* type of deal?"

"You take the girl, and we keep Jennings," he suggested.

"That *vas* the deal I originally proposed to Santelli, and he rejected it in favor of betrayal," Petrova said. "*Vhy* should I make the same deal *vith* you?"

"You've killed two of Mr. Santelli's employees and destroyed his property," he said, gesturing to the shuttle for a moment. "I would think your revenge has been satisfied."

"Russian revenge is eternal," she spat. "Lucky for you, I am from Firefall, *da*?"

"I wouldn't trust him, Anastasia," Jennings said. "They've already betrayed you once. Don't you think they'll just follow your ship, shoot it out of the stars, and then take back the girl?"

"Enough!" Sciavella thundered, smacking Jennings in the face and sending him to the ground.

That was apparently the opening Fix had been waiting for. While everyone was distracted with Sciavella and Jennings, he grabbed the rifle out of the hands of the nearest man and elbowed him in the face. Rather than turning the weapon on his captors though, he whirled and fired a barrage of plasma at Petrova's men. The bounty hunter's team quickly scrambled for cover behind the park wall, taking pot shots as cover fire. The rest of Sciavella's men quickly opened up as well in the confusion, probably thinking that one of their men had seen Petrova's men making a move. Sciavella was the only one other than Lafayette who seemed to realize what was happening, but his orders and protestations were inaudible over the cacophony of shots fired and his men diving for cover behind park benches and the few statues in the park.

At Fix's urging, Lafayette dove behind a small statue of the Strikeplain colonial founder while Fix pulled out a small blade they had evidently not found on him. He sliced through Lafayette's bonds and handed him the rifle. Where they currently crouched in the park, the flaming wreckage of the shuttle was behind them, but all of Sciavella's men hid in front of them, firing at Petrova's men. The girl had been dragged behind an overturned park bench by the rearmost of their captors, and Jennings lay on the ground next to Sciavella himself.

"Cover me," Fix whispered to Lafayette as he made his way forward and darted out toward Michelle Williams.

Sneaking easily in the chaos of darkness and battle, Fix crawled right up to Michelle's captor, Martinez, and slit his throat. Quickly, as a grenade exploded near Petrova's men, Fix sliced through Michelle's bonds and pointed to where Lafayette hid. Grabbing the fallen Martinez's weapon, he fired vaguely in the direction of Petrova and then slithered forward to where Jennings lay and started working on his bonds.

Perhaps sensing something amiss, Sciavella cast his eyes down to where Jennings lay. "Son of a bitch," he started to yell before Lafayette filled his body with bright green plasma pulses.

Without exposing himself to Petrova's snipers, Fix dragged Jennings back to safety under the cover of Lafayette's rifle. The battle still raged out of control, and their movements had not been noticed. If they were going to use the battle as a distraction to escape, now was the best time, the Cajun thought.

"Can you walk, *mon capitaine*?" Lafayette asked.

"Barely, Marquis, barely," he said weakly.

"I'll help," Michelle said as she pulled Jennings to his feet and put his arm across her shoulders.

"I'll lay down cover fire," Lafayette said. "On three, make a break for the eastern wall. One. Two. Three."

The Cajun spun out of cover and open up full with the plasma rifle, raking the distant wall with fire, forcing Petrova's men to seek cover. At full auto, the rifle's charge was gone quickly, but it was enough. He dropped the gun and took off at a run after everyone else. Overtaking Jennings quickly, he immediately grabbed his captain under the other shoulder and helped Michelle half-drag, half-carry the captain to the wall. With Fix's help, they got him over and hustled through the side streets of the city, trying to put as much distance between themselves and the firefight as possible. They stopped to catch their breath several blocks away.

"Were we followed?" Fix asked.

Lafayette shook his head as he was too winded to speak.

"The docks are this way," Fix said, pointing south.

"Then we better get there fast," Jennings said. "I can't wait to put this planet behind me."

# Chapter 16

As quickly as they could move with the injured Captain Jennings, the four of them made their way through Storm Haven. Despite the ruckus the fight had almost certainly caused, there were no police hover cars or shuttles responding. That meant the police must have been bought off by Santelli or Petrova or both. That was fine with Jennings as he was just as glad they would not need to fight their way past anyone else. He was not in much of a condition to do any fighting anyway, but he did have a small pistol he had taken off Sciavella's corpse just in case. There was not even any extra security at the docks when they arrived, just the same surly guard at the customs booth.

"I need to process you out," he called as they walked past him purposefully.

Jennings turned and stared at him. The guard flinched as he noticed Jennings's blood-covered face and the heavily armed nature of his companions and waved him through without another word. As they walked up to the *Melody Tryst*, Jennings realized that either Sciavella or Petrova had been there as the ramp lay open and Squawk stood at the end of it, a small stream of blood matting his fur. Two men stood on either side of him.

A growl escaped Jennings throat. "Son of a bitch."

One of them spied the quartet coming at the ship and pointed his weapon down at Squawk. "That's far enough, Jennings."

Without hesitation, Jennings raised his pistol and fired twice, one shot into the face of each man. They fell backwards onto the ramp. Squawk immediately ran forward, got their guns and headed up into the ship.

"Get her ready for take-off!" Jennings yelled after the Pasquatil. "Lafayette, kick that shit off my ramp." He gave a dismissive wave to the two bodies. "Fix, go find Squawk, make sure he's all right, and see to the lady."

"I want to stay with you," Michelle said.

"You're in worse shape than Squawk, Cap'n," Fix pointed out.

"Ms. Williams, this is for your own safety, and I'll be fine once we get the hell out of here," Jennings said to each in turn. "Marquis, meet me in the conn once you've disposed of these. We need to get Magellan up and spinning."

"*Pas de probleme.*"

Jennings limped his way up the ramp and then traversed the gangplank to the cockpit. Fix and the girl followed for a moment, before Fix offered to showed her up to the second level and one of their guest quarters. Jennings began running preflight, and a few moments later, Fix reappeared, carrying a medical kit.

"Told the girl to stay in the cabin for now," Fix said. "No matter what."

"Roger, go check on Squawk," Jennings said through grit teeth, fighting the pain and the fatigue threatening to slow him down.

~

The Scotsman did as he was told and left the conn, although he was not thrilled by the captain's triage. Jennings was quite protective of his crew, but the Pasquatil with the small cut was in less need of Fix's attention than the man who got shot in the leg and brained with the stock end of a plasma rifle. Still, he made the trek to engineering as orders were orders. Amidst the mechanical innards of the Melody Tryst, the engineer jumped about quickly, prepping the engines for launch. However, he slowed down long enough for Fix to diagnose the injury as superficial and slap a bandage on it.

"Thankfully thankful," Squawk squeaked as he immediately bustled back to work.

Fix felt the ship lift off as he headed back toward the conn. For a moment, he lost his balance before the inertial dampeners kicked in. He would need to tell Squawk to fix it, he noted to himself before continuing on to the cockpit. Lafayette had beaten him there and was coaxing jump data out of the Magellan computer as Jennings steered them higher up through the storm.

The captain threw a glance over his shoulder and saw Fix coming in. "Get a communication out to that Gael bastard, Fix. Might as well let him know we have his package."

"Aye." Fix took a seat at one of the computers and pulled up the communication system. After receiving a dozen different errors, he shook his head. "It's nae good. The storm's causing too much interference. We'll need to be clear of the planet before we can send a signal."

Jennings grunted in reply.

"I also need to take a look at your injuries," he pointed out.

"Once we jump," the captain said.

Fix stared at the back of his head. "Cap'n…"

"After the jump, dammit," Jennings said without turning around.

Quietly, Lafayette said, "We should be coming out of the storm now."

Jennings turned back to Fix, who nodded and started trying to acquire a signal once more. "Message away," he said after a moment as black atmosphere turned into space and starlight shone through the cockpit window.

"Do we have a jump solution?" Jennings asked of Lafayette.

The Cajun shook his head. "Magellan's still computing. Twenty seconds."

"We got a reply from the Gael," Fix said. "Ordering us to rendezvous with him at Barnard's VI."

Jennings nodded. "Update Magellan."

Lafayette's gaze lingered on Jennings for a moment, and Fix understood why. The first mate was worried, and he had every right to be. The captain's face was turning pale and beads of sweat pooled on his face. It did not seem as if all his wounds had clotted either.

"Cap'n, you need my help. Now," Fix added for emphasis. "You can come down to sick bay, or I can brain you and drag you down there."

Jennings laughed slightly, which triggered a horrible cough. "All right, Fix. Doctor's orders, right? Lafayette, take over and get us to Barnard's VI as fast as humanly possible."

The captain had just stood up when an explosion rocked the *Melody Tryst* and sent her careening wildly off course. The captain crashed into the side of the cockpit, and Fix fell over on top of him.

"Marquis, bring the shields up and grab the stick," Jennings ordered as he and Fix tried to disentangle themselves from each other.

Lafayette jumped a seat over and grabbed the controls as another salvo hit the *Melody Tryst*. "I've got something off the starboard stern," he said. "But I can't get a solid lock on it. Weapons won't target, but shields are up and holding."

"Now, what the fuck?" Jennings demanded as he scrambled to his feet. "Switch aft cannons to manual and create a cone of fire in the direction of that sensor ghost. Scan for impacts and follow up with aft torpedoes." As he barked orders at Fix, he hurriedly sat back down and punched data into Magellan.

Lafayette threw the ship hard over to avoid another burst of fire. "All this movement is going to play hell with the navigation system."

"Tell me about it," Jennings said as Magellan reset its jump calculations once again.

"Weapons ready," Fix said.

"Fire!" the captain said immediately.

With the press of a button, Fix opened up with the aft cannons in a blaze of energy, carefully targeted across a wide swath of space. The ship's sensors, unable to detect anything about the ship attacking them, were able to register the impact of the weapons energy on the shields of the enemy ship. Fix fired torpedoes into the presumed ship's course, but his entire barrage missed.

"Missed her," he said. "She's too agile for manual targeting."

"Dammit," Jennings swore.

Lafayette pulled them through another complicated series of maneuvers. "We only need ten seconds of constant course in order for Magellan to finish. But this bitch isn't going to let me have it."

"How about a full stop?" Jennings asked, his tone implying he already knew the answer.

"That would work," Lafayette agreed. "Might even cut it down to seven seconds." There was a pause. "Wait a minute. You don't mean… A Dime Gambit?"

"They won't be expecting it, Marquis," Jennings said.

"That's because they're not crazy."

Jennings grinned ruefully. "Good thing we are."

"It's the oldest trick in the book," Lafayette protested.

"Maybe they do nae read," Fix pointed out.

"*Merde,*" the Cajun swore.

~

Selena Beauregard had been in orbit above Strikeplain forever. She was not one to be bothered by tight spaces generally, but she had been in the tiny ship for far too long and was starting to get a little stir crazy. That might have accounted for her opening fire on the *Melody Tryst* before being in proper range for a kill shot. The nervous energy and excitement that came with the hunt was even more hyper-acute with the prolonged wait for her quarry.

When she intercepted and decoded the message sent from the *Melody Tryst* that they had the girl, she immediately fired. Based on the recent higher level of traffic she had observed entering the otherwise backwater berth in the past few hours, she assumed other parties were attempting to capture Ms. Williams as well, and she had worried the crew of the *Melody Tryst* would not be able to acquire her. Her ship was not matched to take on the ship she had decoded as the *Grey Vistula*, belonging to one Anastasia Petrova, or the *Marathon* owned by Vesper Santelli.

All those doubts were behind her now though as she dodged an interestingly designed attack from the fleeing ship. Again, she was impressed with the guile of Captain Jennings. Had she not altered her approach vector at the last moment, she would have been in a lot of trouble. It was a nice try, but Captain Jennings and his associates were running out of lives, she thought to herself as she depressed the firing trigger again.

The shot should have taken out the *Melody Tryst's* engines, the aft shields being as weakened as they were, but the shot missed entirely, going past the nose of the fleeing ship. *That wasn't possible*, she again thought to herself. *They can't be slowing down.* A split second too late she realized what they had done. Desperately, she jerked up and away on the control stick, but she had already shot past the *Melody Tryst*.

"No," she managed to whisper as the *Melody Tryst's* weapons opened up full.

~

The Dime Gambit tended to wreak havoc on ship and crew, but it was well worth it if pulled off successfully. It involved disengaging the majority of the ship's inertia dampeners, combined with a cold cut off of the sublight engines, and a full firing from the ship's retro-rockets, which were only designed for atmospheric use. It resulted in a gut-wrenching change in momentum as all were flung against the safety harnesses they had quickly scrambled into.

The cockpit was showered in sparks as electrical conduits blew. A pipe overhead burst in a billow of steam, and red lights everywhere flashed warnings of damage to various ship systems. Only two concerned Jennings though: the FTL engines and the Magellan computer system. Both were still in the green.

Once they stopped, the computer immediately began its calculations, while Fix fired a salvo at their passing attacker. He scored multiple hits even as the ship tried to veer out of the way. Jennings could tell it was not a fatal attack, but that was all right with him as long as they got the seven seconds they needed.

Lafayette looked over Jennings's shoulder at the computer. "Ready," Jennings said. "Punch it!"

Lafayette hit the FTL Engage button, and the *Melody Tryst* rocketed out of the system.

~

Selena Beauregard restrained a scream of pure frustration as her instrument displays went dark. The ship's sensors had been knocked offline from the final barrage from the *Melody Tryst*. Because of that, she would not be able to calculate in which direction they left. Perhaps more importantly for her was the fact that the stealth ship's Light Shroud had been damaged in the battle. She was visible on sensors once again. Even if she could have followed the *Melody Tryst*, they would see her coming from a parsec away. Without the cloaking technology, the *Trenton*-class ship was outgunned and outclassed by most ships.

She had failed. It was an entirely new sensation to her, and she was anathema to it, but her sense of professionalism quickly took over.

"Computer activate scramble code Omega and send subspace relay via Wyvern channel," she said.

The Resistance had their own communication systems hidden throughout the known galaxy that operated independently of the major channels. Paulsen had given her the code to report on the success of the mission. She never thought she would need it to report the opposite.

"Ms. Beauregard." A shadowed version of Major Geoff Paulsen's face appeared on her screen.

She scowled in return.

"The line is secure," he immediately said, apparently realizing why she was annoyed.

"Then why the shadow?"

"No line is that secure," he said.

Selena could not see it, but she was sure he was smirking.

"I trust you are calling to inform of the mission's success?" he asked.

Wincing noticeably, she said, "No, mission is a failure."

The aspect of the shadowy face flinched, and Paulsen's tone turned dark. "I suggest you remedy that situation, Ms. Beauregard, or things could become very unpleasant for you."

"No remedy is available," she said. "They have escaped, and my ship is damaged. The ship was unable to decode the response from whoever is buying the girl from Captain Jennings, so I don't know where their rendezvous is. My sensors were down when they jumped, so I don't even know what their telemetry was. Nothing more I can do. It is over."

"We'll see about that," was all Paulsen said before he signed off, leaving her alone, drifting in space.

"Well, that was comforting," she muttered as a new alarm started going off. "Even better."

Another ship had closed on her and began grappling onto her ship. They were going to pull her into their cargo bay. With an annoyed sigh, she pulled out a plasma pistol, checked its charge, and clicked off the safety. This mission was becoming a colossal pain in the ass.

~

As he stepped out onto the bridge of the *TGFS Intrepid* and stalked towards General Ounimbango, Gael Overseer Pahhal announced, "General, you will immediately set the ship's course for Barnard's VI."

The *Intrepid* was one of the larger ships in what remained of the Terran space force, and the bridge accurately reflected that. The bridge sat at the very top of the ship, enclosed in a rectangular glass dome which sank on pistons and was covered with solid tritanium during battle. While cruising normally, it gave an unparalleled view of the stars, and Pahhal wondered often how they could work while something so beautiful lay all around them.

Apparently seething, General Ounimbango sat in the middle of an up-raised dais, surrounded by six officer stations and two small sets of stairs which led to a general systems control area wrapping around the dais. In that section, enlisted men and a few lower grade officers handled the actual operation of the vessel, and their eyes darted between their commander and the Gael. Human senses of hierarchy made little sense to Pahhal, which was one of the reasons why he did not understand the reasons behind Ounimbango's barefaced ire. He had seemingly embarrassed the general in some way.

Pahhal glided onto the dais as Ounimbango stood and pulled in closely to Pahhal. "You have embarrassed me in front of my men. I am in command of this vessel. And I say where it goes."

"You go where I tell you," Pahhal whispered back darkly, before adding at a more audible level, "Apologies that my excitement got the better of me, but the package we have been waiting for has been found and is being taken to Barnard's VI."

"Oh, Jennings captured the girl? Fantastic," the general said without any enthusiasm as he tried to force his face to appear neutral.

Pahhal had his own suspicions as to why that was, but it did not matter any longer.

Seemingly uncomfortable and desperate to fill the growing silence, the general turned to the navigation officer, but stopped before issuing any orders. With a glance turned back to the overseer, he asked, "Why Barnard's VI? It's a little out of the way."

"We will be picking up additional cargo there while we wait for Captain Jennings," Pahhal said cryptically.

The general waited a moment for the Overseer to clarify, but he did not. "As you wish," Ounimbango replied at last before relaying the new course.

*It was almost time*, Pahhal thought to himself. The Gael had fought wars, subjugated races, and hunted across space and time, and now Operation Aurora was finally coming to fruition. *At last, at long last,* the words echoed in his mind.

~

Vesper Santelli had been having a decent evening. There had been a very enjoyable cocktail party that one of his friends was throwing on his old-fashioned water-based luxury liner. Three thousand people cruising from Italy to Greece for the night, and there was enough alcohol, partying, and joviality for everyone. It was especially enjoyable for Santelli because he stumbled upon Tricia, the wife of one of his old business rivals. She was a trophy certainly, young, blonde, and stupid, and her ferocious love-making was more than adequate (on his rival's own bed no less).

He had promised her that his ability to father children had long since been surgically eliminated, and that simple lie allowed him to forego the use of protection. It was not true, of course, but the idea of his enemy being forced to raise a child of his was too awesome a possibility to pass up. It aroused him so greatly that their first congress was over in a matter of moments. Santelli assuaged her anger quickly and was on to round two before Tricia even realized she had agreed to more sex. Much more satisfied by his second effort, she moaned his name, and Santelli captured the whole liaison with a small camera.

Useful footage in case Tricia's husband should make a nuisance of himself further down the road.

After leaving the satisfied Tricia in her husband's cabin suite, he returned to his, but not before tempting a waitress who was a little on the heavy side into joining him for a little frottage. He sat at a desk in his suite, staring at his reflection in one of the wall mirrors, admiring what he saw. At sixty years old, he passed for forty with just the slightest bit of silver in his gray hair and beard. He was lean, muscled and tan, and had dark, intelligent eyes which appraised others easily and gave little away. He shuddered in pleasure and cast a glance down at the waitress who knelt in front of him, and ran a hand through her hair.

A knock on the door interrupted the moment, and the waitress stopped.

"Come in!" he called.

Salv Rocca, one of his most trusted aides, strode in wearing a frown of some seriousness and an expensive, poorly fitting suit. "Apologies, Mr. Santelli. But I have some news I thought you would want to know immediately."

"Go ahead," he said to Rocca before looking down at the waitress and saying, "No one told you to stop."

As the waitress returned to pleasuring Santelli, Rocca remained undeterred. "It's about the Strikeplain expedition." He paused, apparently not sure how to phrase what he needed to say around an outsider. "There was a setback. Unfortunately, the endeavor failed and a new mission team will be required."

"Out," Santelli immediately growled at the waitress, his eyes narrowed. He fumed as he waited for her to leave, not even bothering to zip up his pants. "They're all dead?"

"Yes, sir."

"Cocksucker!" He smashed his hands down on the desk. The night had been going so well too. "Get everyone together. It looks like we're going to war."

~

The plasma pistol ended up being completely useless for Selena Beauregard. Whoever captured her had simply gassed the entire cargo bay, taking her without a shot fired. Her failure was becoming more and more unbearable as she sat in a small cell, a force field protecting the small aperture in the four gray walls. There was a tiny bed, a sink and toilet in the cell, all crammed together. Beauregard sat on the bed with her long legs pulled up to her chest, chin resting on her knees.

Her first and only visitor was a short woman wearing a green business suit. Her captor's hair was pulled back, but Selena instinctively recognized the woman as a predator. Something about the way she sized up a human being in a cage was too damned eerie.

"A Resistance member, *da*?" Anastasia Petrova asked.

"No."

"Of course not," she said. "You're clearly not with Santelli's group. Even he doesn't have the resources for a *Trenton* stealth ship, not to mention he *vanted* to capture Captain Jennings and the girl alive. Based on the fight the two of you had, you *vere* trying to kill them."

"Maybe Captain Jennings broke my heart," she said.

Petrova laughed heartily. "He has that reputation as *vell*, but this is not the truth, *da*?" She paused. "Maybe I'll ask him *vhen ve* catch him."

"*Nee puha nee paira*," Selena said.

Petrova smiled. "Luck has nothing to do *vith* it. *Ve* know his telemetry, and *ve'll* follow him."

"What makes you think he won't change his course?" she asked. "He got out of here in a hurry, and I am willing to bet you couldn't decode the transmission he received back from his buyer."

"I didn't have to," she said. "A little-known fact about the Dime Gambit is that it tends to ruin engines. The *Melody Tryst* will die shortly. There's only so far he can go."

Curious, Selena hopped off the bed and stepped closer to the barrier. "Why are you telling me all this?"

"*Vhy vouldn't* I?" she asked. "*Vhat* could you possibly do *vith* it?"

Selena was silent.

Petrova's eyes narrowed, and her voice became harsher, her accent more pronounced, "I *vill* capture Captain Jennings, and I *vill* take his bounty from him. No one *vill* ever dare question who the best bounty hunter in this galaxy is. You *vill* bear *vitness* to this."

"Minor inferiority complex?" she responded with an upraised eyebrow, trying to convey a sense of being unimpressed.

"Humph." Petrova started to stalk away from the cell. As she was about to be out of Selena's narrow sightline, she stopped and turned on a heel. "The buyer is a Gael. I *vonder vhat* he *vould* pay for a member of the Resistance?" A ruthless smile turned the corners of her lips. "Enjoy your stay, *da*?"

# Chapter 17

Black spots swarmed in front of Matthew Jennings's eyes as the *Melody Tryst* rocketed through the darkness between systems. The adrenaline of the past few hours finally seemed to be wearing off, and his body was realizing just how hurt he really was. Pushing the feeling of queasiness down into the pit of his stomach, he turned to Lafayette. "I need you to compile a damage report. Stay here though. I want someone in the conn at all times until we have some more distance away from Strikeplain. Work with Squawk and find out how bad everything is."

"Yes, *mon capitaine*."

"Fix, I think I'm about ready for your services," he managed to say to the doctor before passing out.

~

When he awoke, Jennings had the feeling that several hours had passed. He lay on a surgical table, strapped down. While he could have reached the buckles and let himself free, he was too tired and sore to move. Lifting his head up slightly, he found that Fix had been forced to cut through his pants to get to the plasma burn that had gone straight through his leg. The various cuts, scrapes, and bruises had all been tended to. His naked chest seemed to have more red and purple skin then normal light tan, but he supposed he would live… at least until the next time. The door to their small infirmary slid open, and Fix walked in.

Jennings smiled at him. "I'm getting awful tired of waking up in here."

"Aye, Cap'n," Fix agreed. "But if you do nae spring a leak every so often, you might start to doubt if you need me on this tub."

"Good point."

Fix turned serious for a moment. "I had to dose you with perimescaline to do the surgery- you'll be a little groggy for a while."

"How long was I out?" Jennings asked.

"Eight hours," he said. "You were lucky. The shot ripped through the flesh just above and to the right of your knee. No ligaments damaged- just the meat. It did nick the femoral artery, which is why I had to do surgery. Something that big will nae respond well to bio-engineered adhesives. You'll be sore for a while, but you will nae need any more surgery, and you will nae need rehab."

"Any other good news?" Jennings asked.

"I gave you a pint of synthetic O positive," he said. "That's a lot of wounds in one week. I thought it better to be cautious."

"Thanks, Fix." Gingerly, Jennings unbuckled himself from the surgical bed and stood up.

In his shorts, he walked slowly to his cabin, putting as little weight as possible on the injured leg until he got used to what it could handle. Moving rather slowly, he put on a new pair of cargo pants and a fresh T-shirt- ones without bloodstains were running in short supply, he noted. Sitting on his small bed, he put on his boots and then pushed the intercom button on the wall next to his bed.

"Marquis?" he called.

*"Oui, mon capitaine?"*

"Any contacts?" he asked.

"Negative," Lafayette said.

"Pull everyone together in the Caf for a status update," he said and then signed off.

His leg seemed to feel better and more relaxed with each step he took, and he was almost back up to full speed as he made his way to the common room. Fix was already there, seated at the table. As Jennings approached, he tossed him a small pill bottle.

"Some of what I gave you earlier," Fix said. "Use as needed."

"Thanks," Jennings said as he sat down, placing the bottle into a pocket as he did so.

Lafayette was the next to arrive, followed by a rather wearied Squawk. It was the first time Jennings could remember seeing him like that beatdown.

"We've got problems," Lafayette announced as he sat down.

"When don't we?" Jennings said.

"Won't work, won't work, won't work," Squawk grumbled, slamming a small fist down on the table.

Jennings eyed the Pasquatil. "What won't work?"

"All won't work," the engineer explained.

"The power plant is in trouble," Lafayette translated. "Apparently, the ship didn't like the Dime Gambit very much."

"Engines overloaded!" Squawk exclaimed. "Caused a cascade failure in power systems!"

A shiver ran down Jennings's spine. "What the hell are we running on then?"

"It hasn't gone critical yet," Lafayette said. "We've got about forty minutes."

"Almost nine hours since we left Strikeplain," Jennings mused aloud. "Barnard's VI is about…"

"Seventeen hours beyond that," Lafayette finished. "At sub-light, we'd be looking at…"

Silence dragged out for several moments before Fix broke the silence. "A bloody long time."

The captain chewed his lower lip for a moment. "Can we make repairs in space?"

"Componentless," Squawk said sadly.

"Maybe we can change the rendezvous with the Gael," Jennings suggested. "They can meet us out here. Maybe we can negotiate a tow for good measure."

"Sorry, Matthew," Lafayette said. "The communication system was fried in the firefight. With main power the way it is, weapons are also offline. Once the power plant dies, we have ten hours of auxiliary power from the batteries where we can run the entire ship, then two hours emergency power where we'll only have life support and thrusters, no engines."

Jennings rubbed the fatigue from his eyes. "And you couldn't have just let me sleep? What's the nearest habitable planet?"

Lafayette shook his head. "I've already changed course, but it might not make a difference, captain."

"Why not?"

"We're headed for an asteroid belt in the Beta Durani system," he said. "We'll hit the outskirts of Beta Durani right when main power goes according to Magellan. Minerva confirmed."

"How far to the settlement?" Jennings asked.

"Ten hours."

"What's the problem then?" he demanded. "It sounds doable."

No one spoke for a moment and a voice above them chimed on. "The settlement is a former mining facility on one of the larger asteroids of the Durani belt," Minerva said. "The Comet Corporation removed its presence from the asteroid as it felt all tritanium that could be profitably removed had been successfully mined."

"How long has it been abandoned?" Jennings asked, his voice laced with fatigue.

"2.4 Terran years," Minerva reported.

"What's the probability that it still has any staffing or life support in place?" he asked of Minerva.

"Staff reported as zero. Probability of life support less than three percent with known variables."

Jennings nodded, his mind running through the limited possibilities. "We've got no other choice then. Squawk, I want you to do anything and everything you can to squeeze every last minute out of that power plant. Shut down anything non-essential. I don't care if that means pulling every light bulb out of the wall."

Squawk saluted and sprinted off to engineering with a new sense of purpose.

"Cajun, you've got the best relationship with Magellan," Jennings said. "Do anything and everything to shave a few parsecs off our travel distance."

"*Bien sur, mon capitaine.*" The Marquis stood and headed back to the conn.

"Fix, I want you to get all of our EVA suits prepped," Jennings said. "Any tool, device or equipment we have which uses oxygen fuel tanks, I want pulled and jury-rigged to be a back-up O two supply, understood? A few minutes of breathable air might make the difference here."

"Aye, Cap'n," he agreed before starting to head down to the cargo bay. Before reaching the gangplank, he turned around. "You know there's something else. The Gael might think we are attempting to welch on our deal if we do nae show up at Barnard's VI on time."

"I'm well aware of that," Jennings said quietly. "If we can't get things turned around on the ship fast enough, they will start hunting us."

Fix nodded. "That ship which attacked us did not belong to Santelli or Petrova."

"I'd considered that as well, and I think I have an idea as to who to ask about that," Jennings said as he stood and walked over to the guest cabins.

~

Michelle Williams had not left her cabin since first being brought onboard the *Melody Tryst*, but that had nothing to do with what the black man with the strange accent had told her. He said she was safe, and that staying in the small dingy cabin would keep her so. She did not think this was true as the ship was rocked by explosions, and she did not believe it now.

The man who told her he was there to rescue her, the one the others called Jennings, had been lying to her. She was certain of that now. Left with hours to ponder her plight, Michelle had decided that her situation had actually gotten worse. The fear of being assaulted on a nightly basis by anyone who could afford it had terrified her, as had being on the ship with the slavers. The *Brigandine* was possessed of an entire crew which had only one thought on their minds once they saw her. If her value had not been so significantly increased by her virginity still being intact, the crew would have taken it forcibly from her. They tried twice anyway, and only the bosun arriving in time to whip those responsible had spared her. The bosun spit on her and called her a whore. The other men called her a cocktease. And somehow, things were still worse. The men of this ship were not her rescuers. They were liars, and they were taking her to her doom.

But they did not realize she had figured them out. So, when the man who the others called the captain limped into the cabin and stopped to glance down at her prone form lying on the bed, he was not expecting her attack. He stood over her appraisingly for a moment, perhaps trying to figure out whether or not she was awake, when she lashed out with her legs, catching him in the shin. A cry of pain escaped his lips as she reached for the lamp on the table beside the bed. Aiming for his head, she swung it as fiercely as she could, but her arm was stopped as a powerful grip seized her about the wrist. There was a sudden twisting sensation, a sharp pain, and the lamp fell out of her hand.

"Would you not fucking do that please?" the captain asked. "It's been a rough day already."

There was a pause while her eyes frantically darted around the room looking for another weapon.

"Are you okay?" Jennings asked out of nowhere.

"What?" she demanded, clearly taken aback.

"Are you hurt?" he asked again softly.

"No," she growled.

Nodding, he gently pushed her back to a seated position on the bed.

*So, now is where we get to it,* she thought darkly, but Jennings merely walked to the opposite wall of the small cabin and collapsed in a small chair against the wall.

"Sorry about the wrist," he said. "But my mom happens to like my face the way it is, and I can't have you rearranging it."

Michelle did not reply.

"I assume by the nature of your welcoming that you have deduced that we are not in fact a rescue party as I mentioned," Jennings led.

"What are you then?" she asked softly.

"Just working men offered a plum job who felt obliged to take it," he said.

"Bounty hunters."

"When the need calls for it," he agreed. "Believe me, if we could find honest freight jobs to keep our bellies and the fuel tanks full, you and I wouldn't be having this conversation."

Anger flashed in her eyes. "So why are you telling me this?"

"I just wanted you to know that there wasn't anything personal in this," he said. "We mean you no ill will, and as long as you are in my care, you will be treated kindly. You need not fear anything of the like you may have experienced with Mr. Santelli's men or at the club on Strikeplain."

She remained silent as a single tear rolled down her cheek.

"As long as you do not attack me or my people, we will continue to see to whatever needs you have, but you will have to remain here," he said. "Any nonsense and we will lock you in here. The door will not be opened until the Gael are here to take custody."

As he started to stand up, a confused expression crossed her voice and her voice dropped to a whisper. "The Gael? It was the Gael who hired you? What the hell do they want with me?"

"I'd imagine it has something to do with the charges of terrorism pending," Jennings pointed out, sitting back in the chair.

"I've never committed a terrorist act in my life," she said.

Jennings raised an eyebrow. "You've no affiliation with the Resistance?"

Shrugging her shoulders, she said, "Politically, I support them, I suppose. They're the only ones who are fighting the Gael."

"Fighting the Gael," Jennings sneered. "They bomb public areas, killing civilians to get one Gael agent or one collaborator. Women. Children. Thousands of dead chalked up as collateral damage by the bloody Resistance- and you support them?"

"I'd expect to hear that from a Gael lackey," Michelle fired back.

Jennings rocketed to his feet and crossed the distance to Michelle incredibly fast. She recoiled as she expected to be hit, her back thudding against the cabin wall.

"Listen to me, you self-righteous deluded school girl," Jennings said coolly, his calm voice barely containing a torrent of rage. "I fought the Gael for three years. I was just a boy and I led men into battle. I watched the Gael tear them to shreds, leaving nothing but hollow shells and piles of rotting meat. Have you ever seen a friend's body ripped in half by a Gael plasma cannon? I somehow doubt it. I watched my friends fragged in their own cockpits because we were totally outclassed in every battle. Everything I knew and loved was taken from me because of the Gael, and still I fought them, and occasionally I beat the fuckers. If the puppet regime fell and we declared war, a real war- not some bullshit terrorist political statement- I would sign back up in a heartbeat. I would fight for my people and gladly lay my life down were it required. The upper-class daughters of collaborators and puppet government representatives are not allowed to question my loyalty to Earth or my willingness to fight for my world."

Michelle stared intently into the floor and did not respond.

That appeared to be fine with Jennings as he headed for the door. He stopped short though and turned around, adding, "Before you extol their virtues too much, you might want to ask yourself why the Resistance wants you dead."

"What?"

Jennings smiled slightly. "It might have been confusing with all the different people trying to kill us in Storm Haven- Santelli and Petrova both have issues with me and getting you would have been a nice bonus or vice-versa- but the attack that came at us once we hit space…" He paused and locked eyed with Michelle. "That was a *Trenton*-class stealth ship. Not too many were made before the war ended, and it is well beyond the reach of bounty hunters or criminal overlords to have one. Only the Resistance can both afford it and has access to contacts in the military that can get that kind of technology."

"But why would they?" she asked aloud.

"That's the question, isn't it?" he said. "Bear this in mind too. If you accept that it was the Resistance who tried to kill us a short while ago, it seems safe to assume they killed your friend and tried to kill you in your apartment before you were arrested."

Again surprise gripped her. Her mouth fell open, but she said nothing.

"The level of technology needed to break into a high-security building like that added with the fact they broke in to kill you before the warrant and bounty for your arrest were issued," he led on. "It points to a level of sophistication far greater than any bounty hunter or common criminal would have. The Resistance wants you dead, Ms.

Williams. But I'm sure it's for the greater good." With that, he opened the cabin door, left, and then electronically locked it behind him.

# Chapter 18

As Matthew Jennings left the crew and guest cabins on his way to the bridge, a great feeling of unease grabbed hold of him. He felt it before when he first read her file, but he had buried it deep under the logical need to provide for his ship and crew. Nothing about the situation with Michelle Williams made sense. She could have been a young recruit for the Resistance, he had supposed, but she would not be so bright-eyed and naïve about their methods. She also would not have been so surprised the Resistance was trying to kill her. It would not have been the first time the Resistance offed one of their own in order to protect the cause. *And if she was a terrorist, why did she not go to the Resistance once freed initially?*

None of it made any sense to him, but Jennings was becoming more and more certain that the girl he was holding was no terrorist. If that was the case, why the hell would the Gael want her so badly, and why did the Resistance want her dead? There were so many unknown components, and Jennings hated operating in the dark. Silently, he cursed himself. The Gael set him up perfectly. They played on his dislike for the Resistance's methods while simultaneously offering his ship and crew a kind of monetary salvation. The most annoying thing was Michelle had been right to call him a Gael lackey. That was exactly what he had become by taking this mission. Maybe that was why he almost lost his temper with the girl. Her being right had touched a nerve.

"Damn," he muttered under his breath as he headed down the corridor.

"What did she say?" Fix asked as he met Jennings on the way to the bridge.

"Nothing I shouldn't have expected her to," he said as he stepped into the cockpit where Lafayette was arguing with Magellan in Acadian French.

"*Qu'est-ce que pensez-vous vous faire? Idiot!*" he yelled at the computer.

Jennings sat in the pilot's chair and swung to face Fix as Lafayette continued to fight with Magellan. "She said she doesn't know why the Resistance is trying to kill her or why the Gael want her in the first place."

Fix grunted. "Believe her?"

Jennings sighed. "I do."

"Did you tell her we're turning her in?" Lafayette asked after a final curse at the computer.

A bemused smile crossed Jennings's face. "She figured that out for herself."

"Did you tell her we're all gonna die?" Fix mumbled.

Shaking his head, Jennings chuckled ruefully. "I didn't want to ruin her day." The three shared a sad laugh, and Jennings turned back around to stare at the starlines through the viewscreen. "Time to Beta Durani?"

"4.6 minutes, captain," Minerva reported.

"Squawk, time to power plant fail?" Jennings called into the intercom.

"Five minutes now!"

"Twenty-four seconds. Twenty-four seconds is all we were able to shave," Jennings said.

"Twenty-four seconds is a lot of time at light speed," Lafayette pointed out.

He had a point, Jennings supposed, but he did not acknowledge it. He simply stared out into space, ignoring Lafayette reporting their entering the Beta Durani system outskirts. It seemed like only a breath later that the starlines shrank back to stars and the ship came to a shuddering near-stop. Klaxons blazed in his ears as red lights flashed all around him. The cabin lights dimmed, and all non-essential instrument panels went out simultaneously. A quick series of commands killed the alarm and the red warning lights.

"Time to target," Jennings barely whispered. The universe suddenly seemed very quiet.

"Calculated at nine hours and thirty-five minutes," Lafayette said.

"Minerva, confirm," Jennings said.

There was no response.

"No main power, no main Minerva," a frazzled voice called behind them as Squawk came in and jumped into the engineer's seat. "All possible modifications have been modified."

"Very well," Jennings said. "If anyone would care to say a prayer, now would be a good time."

"You took the words right out of my mouth," Michelle Williams said.

Jennings whirled around in surprise to see Michelle holding a small plasma rifle on all of them. With an exasperated sigh, he glanced at Squawk. "Let me guess. You disabled all the door locks as part of your power saving modifications."

"Non-essential," Squawk said.

"We're going to need to have a talk about what constitutes an essential program," Jennings muttered before appraising the plasma rifle in Michelle's hands. "Well, Ms. Williams, you certainly have gotten the drop on us, so to speak. What is your next move?"

"Take me somewhere else and let me go," she said.

"Nae possible," Fix said.

She pointed the rifle at the Scotsman. "I could kill all of you."

"So you could," Jennings said. "But that doesn't change the impossibility of taking you somewhere else right now."

Michelle's tone became incredulous. "You would die rather than let me go?"

"How to put this delicately," Jennings mused. "Well, our ship was badly damaged in the fight against the Resistance ship we previously discussed- damaged to the point we lost primary power. Hence, the ease of your escape and your ability to access a normally locked weapons locker. Without main power, we have no light speed. We also have no communications and no weapons. The only things we do have are ten hours of auxiliary solar stored power and two hours of emergency battery power. We are hoping that is enough to get us to an abandoned mining facility in the asteroid belt in the Beta Durani system. If we're lucky, we'll make it. If we're really lucky, there will still be life support. If not..." He let his voice trail off.

Realization dawned on her face. "Are you telling me we're all about to die anyway?"

"About sums it up," Fix said.

"So, as I said, you can continue to hold the gun on all four of us, but it will be a trifle difficult to save all of our lives if you do," Jennings pointed out.

"Maybe that's better," she spat. "I don't know what the Gael want with me, but it's not going to be good. That's one thing I am certain of."

"Probably true." Jennings looked around at his crew. "Very well. If you hand over the gun now and allow me to try to save all of our lives, then I will take you as far away from the Gael as I can."

"*Mon Capitaine?*" Lafayette stuttered out, completely surprised.

"Marquis, you know as well as I do that handing her over to the Gael is a death sentence for her," he said. "She dies here with us or with them as it stands now. Were I in her situation, I would choose to die before those bastards got their hands on me. So, either we all die, or we all live and go our separate ways. I'll choose the latter, thank you."

"But she's a terrorist," he hissed.

Jennings shook his head. "No, I don't believe she is."

"*Capitaine,*" Lafayette continued to protest.

"Marquis, this is my ship and you're part of my crew," Jennings said coldly. "You will obey my orders. Is that understood?"

"Yes, sir," Lafayette said, although he was clearly unconvinced.

Jennings eyed the medic next. "Fix?" He received a non-committal shrug in reply. Taking that as a sign the doctor was onboard, he turned to Squawk. "Do you have an issue with my orders?"

"Sir, no, sir," Squawk said and then saluted.

"Well, it's up to you now," Jennings said to Michelle. "Do you hand over the gun and trust me, or do we all die?"

"I don't trust you," Michelle fired back, but her conviction was not as strong as before.

"You don't have to," he said. "There are only two possibilities. Choose to think I am lying in which case we all will die together. Or choose to believe me, and then it's a fifty-fifty shot as to whether or not I keep my word."

She appeared to consider that for a moment while Lafayette said, "*Mademoiselle*, if Captain Jennings gives you his word, you may rest assured he intends to keep it."

After another long moment of indecision, she at last lowered the weapon and handed it over to Fix. He pulled the power charge out of it and then lay it down before turning back to his station. Michelle crossed her arms awkwardly and refused to make eye contact with any of them. She still wore the mini-skirt, low-cut top, and knee-high boots from the brothel in Storm Haven, and her make-up had streaked across her face though from her earlier tears.

"Marquis, please keep me apprised as we approach the asteroid in question," Jennings said as he stood up. "I'm going to help Ms. Williams get more comfortable and maybe find her a bite to eat. In point of fact, why don't you make us one of your fine culinary creations? Since we may be about to die anyway, we certainly could use a decent final meal."

Lafayette nodded. "Once the auto-pilot is secure-synched, I'll get started."

Jennings gave a slight bow in deference to the chef and gestured Michelle out of the cockpit.

"You're not taking me back to that closet you call a cabin, are you?" she asked as they headed back to the living area.

"No, not that it would do any good considering the locks don't work," Jennings pointed out. "I thought you might like to change out of those clothes. It's been a few hours, and I am guessing they weren't really your choice to begin with."

"What? You don't think I normally dress like a middle-class prostitute?" she asked.

"Well, sometimes it's hard to differentiate between the ways a college student and a hooker dress, but you strike me as a T-shirt type," he replied as good-naturedly as possible.

"What makes you say that?" she asked as they arrived at the captain's cabin and he opened the door.

"I'm guessing with your family's money and connections you went to some sort of extremely prestigious boarding school back in Old Europe," he explained as he stepped inside and started rummaging through some drawers. "The kind where you had to have a specific school uniform which you wore every day, plaid skirts, white dress shirts, et cetera."

"So what if I did?"

"If I had been forced to wear the same damn overly formal and stuffy clothes for twelve years, I would wear a T-shirt when I got to college," he said.

She laughed. It was a pretty, bright sound. "You're not nearly as stupid as you look."

"No, I probably am," he pointed out. "I just wore a uniform every day too. Now, I can't stand the fucking thing. A-ha!"

With his cry of victory, he tossed her a green T-shirt which had GROPOS stamped in blocky, black letters, a pair of black sweat pants, and a white pair of space socks. "It's been a while since we had any women on the crew. Well, never in point of fact, so we don't have any…um," Jennings mimed wrapping his hands around his thighs and buttocks.

"Panties?"

"Exactly," he said, pointing a finger at her for emphasis.

"I'll make do," she said as she stripped off the top. She was not wearing a bra.

"Whoa," Jennings said as he spun back around. By a strange instinct, he raised his hands in the air as if about to be arrested.

"Something you've never seen before?" she asked as she continued changing.

"No," he said. "It's just…"

"Gay?"

He almost turned around to argue, but caught himself in time. "No, ma'am, I'm just exceedingly polite. It doesn't seem right to be ogling a young woman you're not in a relationship with. A much younger woman."

"I turned twenty-two yesterday," she pointed out.

"I turned twenty-two too many yesterdays ago," Jennings said.

"You look fine to me," she said. "What are you? Thirty?"

"Twenty-eight," he replied defensively.

She laughed. "I'm done; you can turn around."

Michelle Williams had turned into a beautiful college student once again, too frazzled to care what she was wearing and still managing to be unbelievably cute. The hormonal side of Jennings was kicking the chivalrous side for not getting a better peek at her a few moments before.

"If you want to wash up, the bathroom is right there." He nodded in the direction of the small alcove that barely qualified as a bathroom, and she headed in that direction. "Shower won't be working with the mains down, but you should be able to wash your face."

"Wow, I look hideous," she muttered from the bathroom as she turned on the faucet. There was a long pause until the water was shut off at last. "Why the sudden change?"

"What's that?" Jennings asked.

She stepped back out, the long streaks of mascara and eyeliner gone. "You could have waited for me to make a mistake or pretended to cooperate with me. I didn't even know how to use that gun for God's sake. Either you're an exceptional liar and have me convinced you're actually going to let me go, or you've done a remarkable about face."

Jennings sighed. "I was never a big fan of working for the Gael in the first place, and I suppose I rationalized it a little bit because we needed the money badly." He crashed into an easy chair, a fine layer of dust billowing up from it as he did. "It was even easier when your file said you were a member of anti-Gael, pro-Resistance groups at school; your parents were collaborators; you were a confirmed terrorist. I told myself it was all right to do this for the Gael, because I hate the way the Resistance goes about its business. I loathe self-righteousness being used to excuse terrorism. Until we talked for the first time, it never occurred to me how badly the Gael were using me. It wouldn't surprise me if they doctored your file and tailored it specifically to play upon my own emotional reactions, the manipulative bastards. You called me a Gael lackey, and you were right."

"I'm sorry I said that," she said. "I was just trying to lash out."

"But you're right," he said. "Well, you were right, but no more. Assuming we survive the next few hours, I'll tell the Gael something, anything. We'll send them a new message letting them know you escaped in our shuttle, and we're back in pursuit. Eventually, we'll lose your trail."

"Do you think that will work?" she asked.

He shrugged as he pulled himself back up to his feet. "Better than the alternative. Because I am not giving you to those Gael bastards."

Faster than he would have expected, she rushed forward and wrapped her arms around his back. Within another few moments came the unmistakable sound of sobbing, and Jennings felt her body tremoring against his. Gently, he placed his own arms around her and squeezed her softly. As her tears began to soak his T-shirt, he placed a hand on her head and stroked her hair gently.

"You're all right now," he whispered.

"It was horrible," she stammered. "It was so horrible."

"Do you want to tell me about it?" he whispered.

For the next hour, she stayed in his arms and told her the epic of her ordeal. Once in a while, Jennings would offer some small word of comfort, but for the most part he let Michelle talk of what she would, how she would, and gave her what little comfort he could.

# Chapter 19

Onboard the *TGFS Intrepid*, General Ounimbango watched a Gael become unnerved for the first time. Ever since Pahhal ordered the *Intrepid* to Barnard's VI, there had been a growing level of excitement with the Overseer. It persisted as mysterious shuttles came up from the planet below and the Overseer ordered the hangars cleared of humans as the cargo was offloaded by a few Gael and transported to a secure storage area onboard the *Intrepid*. Now that they had been sitting in orbit of Barnard's VI for five hours however and the Gael cargo shuttles were long gone, that sense of excitement had vanished to be replaced with what seemed to be worry.

Surely enough, the Gael appeared to be quite serene. He was not pacing or fretting or repeatedly asking questions about what time it was like a nervous human might, but something was just off about him. His lips were pursed a little tighter than normal, and his eyes tracked the room like a hunter looking for his quarry. On top of that, he never left the bridge. In Ounimbango's experience, the Gael never liked to be seen, did not like humans to form the impression the Gael actually ran the Terran government, and yet he was seated next to Ounimbango on the bridge for all to see.

"They are late," Pahhal said quietly. "By four hours."

A dozen reasons why Jennings could be late jumped into Ounimbango's mind, but were quickly quelled again. There was no reason, or more specifically no profit, in making excuses for Captain Jennings. Furthermore, if Jennings had run into trouble, it might give Petrova a chance to get the girl back.

"It must be something innocuous, Overseer," Ounimbango intoned. "Surely, Captain Jennings would never betray your confidence."

"His psychographic profile suggests he places his honor above all else," Pahhal mused.

"Psychographic profiles can be wrong, and humans can be irrational," Ounimbango pointed out. "Not to mention, it's been a long time since the war. Like most of his particular type of scum, he exists to make money. Perhaps he received a better offer for your girl."

Pahhal's slit eyes narrowed further, and he scowled. "Let me know when he arrives. I've a call to make."

~

The Overseer left the bridge and headed for his quarters, a suite large enough for a fleet admiral. He walked into the massive four room domicile and wondered to himself why the humans would waste this amount of space when space was at such a premium on a starship. A few button presses on the panel next to the door, and the room was locked to all human personnel. Even if there were a hull breach in his quarters, the humans would be able to do nothing about it, but that was how he preferred it. He could take no chance that a stray human would come wandering about his private office. The cattle might begin to suspect they were not the evolved creatures they presumed they were. Like many things, they were a means to an end.

Stepping through the living room briskly, he deactivated a force field designed to exclude anyone from entering his office. The office was nothing like standard Terran fare. There was no desk or chairs or any kind of presumed work space, but a few strange metallic disks protruded from the walls. When he stood in the center of the room, they began to pulse with a purplish-black energy. That energy suddenly shot out of the disks into the center of the room, penetrating the entire area except for a small halo which perfectly encased Pahhal. The energy eventually coalesced into a solid purple sphere around him, and he felt his feet leave the ground as the confines of artificial gravity vanished within the Construct. He folded his feet underneath him and sat serenely as program filaments stretched out like white lightning and entered his eyes, nose, mouth and ears. With a sharp crack and an explosion of consciousness, Pahhal became linked to the Construct.

The Construct was an artificial collective consciousness- a repository for all Gael knowledge and memories- and an amazingly efficient communications system which allowed the Gael to co-ordinate anything with utmost celerity. When plugged in, Gael brains could communicate, interact and learn at the speed of thought, a thousand times faster than regular communication. Scientists could perfect new discoveries by working collaboratively- their minds linked; historians had full access to the memories of millions of Gael who had passed this world and onto the next; and military commanders could plan, adjust and defeat their enemies with the greatest of ease.

Pahhal focused his thoughts on the communication grid of the Construct and began accessing the military section of the grid. His mind reached out, seeking to connect deeper and deeper into the Construct. Bearing in mind the sensitive and classified nature of what he was trying to access, his mind was challenged for algorithmic passwords and impossible equations to verify he was who his mind claimed he was. After what felt like an hour's worth of communication (which passed as about fifteen seconds in the real world), his mind joined with the one Pahhal sought.

"Greetings, Fleet Master Varenhas," his mind spoke.

"Overseer Pahhal, my old friend," the reply came in fast as a tachyon from several hundred light years away. "I trust Operation Aurora proceeds on schedule."

"That is the purpose for my joining with you," he said. "We have a complication."

"Oh?" The concern in Varenhas's mind was palatable. He was as desperate for Operation Aurora to be drawn to a swift conclusion as Pahhal was, as all Gael were. "What is the problem?"

"The last soul has been captured by a human, whom I hired for this purpose," Pahhal explained. "I have reason to believe he has betrayed me. And when we are so close to success." He paused for a moment. "I fear for what might happen. We must take decisive action or I fear the soul may be lost."

"You want us to expose our involvement?" Varenhas interjected. "You know the humans must never know the reason behind the war. If they were to discover what we were looking for, they might kill the souls we need."

"There is only one left," Pahhal hissed. "After this one, the humans no longer matter. They can think whatever they want about their backwater berth of the galaxy. We need that soul, and we need to go home."

Varenhas's voice became indecipherable as a loud torrent of simultaneous thoughts escaped his mind. After a few moments, it quieted and his mind settled on, "What do you need of me?"

"A super-cruiser, armed to the teeth."

"Accessing," Varenhas said. "Thirteen hours to Terran Autonomous Space. It will begin a systematic hunt of all the systems at your direction."

"I will keep you informed of whatever information I find," Pahhal said. "The Terran who runs this ship keeps a retinue of louts outside of the normal chain of command who pay him a cut when they fetch one of our targets for us. I suspect one of them will turn up something before the cruiser arrives."

"Understood. The dream of home go before you, Overseer Pahhal."

"And you, my old friend," Pahhal replied before his mind disconnected from the communication system.

Knowing he needed to go back to the bridge, Pahhal lingered for a moment in the Construct. His mind called up a historical record, the most widely experienced archive in the Construct. It focused on a single prophecy and the long road home.

~

Onboard the bridge of the *Grey Vistula,* Anastasia Petrova sat in silence, her teeth grit in annoyance. The bridge on the transport was small, barely room for her chair in the center with all the stations crowded around. Six others sat on the bridge crew, including Vosler, who looked over the shoulder of the young, overly muscled man at the science and tracking station. This was the part that Petrova hated, the searching. It had never been her forte- it required a patience she never possessed. That was why a man like Vosler was so handy- one of the many reasons, she thought to herself. He was patient, methodical and thorough; everything she was not.

"I think we've got it," Vosler announced at last.

"Finally," Petrova said under her breath. "It only took seven hours. *Vhere* are they headed?"

"Based on our calculations, Beta Durani," he said.

"*Vhy vould* they be heading there?" she muttered. "There's nothing there but some old defunct mining colonies."

Vossler's forehead wrinkled in thought. "Good place for a rendezvous."

"If that's *vhere* they are meeting the Gael buyer, *ve'll* be too late," she said as she slammed her fist into her hand. "Damn!"

"I think we still have a card to play," Vosler said. "If you think Ounimbango will be stupid enough to fall for it."

"Always," she said. "*Vhat* card do *ve* have?"

"It would be presumptuous to assume the rendezvous Jennings set up just happens to be in the nearest system," he said. "It would seem more likely that he is limping to the nearest place he could put down and make repairs after the Dime Gambit blew out his systems. There are plenty of old mining facilities that have since been abandoned, but might provide a safe haven temporarily for Captain Jennings."

"So, *ve* talk to Ounimbango and see if he knows Jennings is in Beta Durani," Petrova mused, catching on to Vosler's notion.

"If he doesn't, we can still beat them there or even sell that information to the Gael," he finished.

A self-satisfied expression settled onto Petrova's face. "Get Ounimbango via subspace," she ordered her communications officer as she sat back in the command chair.

~

"Understood, yes, well, the generosity of the Terran government is extraordinary," General Ounimbango said as Overseer Pahhal approached his desk.

The general had retreated to his office to field a personal call when Pahhal arrived at the bridge, and the Overseer felt obligated to follow him. Anything was better than resuming his position on the bridge, waiting nervously for news of Jennings and the lost soul. Ounimbango looked angry, or rather like he was trying to keep his anger in check. He was sweating and gritting his teeth as he exchanged what were supposed to be pleasantries with someone on the other end of a communication signal. Apparently, the other person signed off, and the general slammed the vid screen down with unnecessary force as Pahhal sat himself in a chair opposite the general.

"I have news," he said gravely to Pahhal.

"About Captain Jennings?"

He grunted an affirmative. "My contacts tell me they know where Captain Jennings is headed, and it is not the Barnard's system."

"Where then?" Pahhal demanded.

"She wouldn't say."

"She? Petrova?" Pahhal almost snarled. With a deep breath, he regained his facial composure quickly, but still his tone remained quite dark. "If your *relationship* with that woman has in any way jeopardized my mission, I intend to see you spaced. Is that understood?"

Ounimbango gulped and instinctively began to breathe more heavily. Pahhal smiled savagely. All sentient spacefaring races had the same reaction to vacuum written in their DNA. Something about the absence of air or the sucking of space hit them so viscerally.

"Now, where are they, general?"

"Petrova said she would call us back to hear our answer in five minutes," he stammered.

"Our answer on what?" Pahhal spat.

"Petrova wants two hundred thousand for the location, and another three hundred if we are able to catch Jennings at that location. She has also offered to ensure we catch him at that location for five hundred thousand additional," he said. "I told her it was ridiculous to expect so much for one girl."

"Pay it," Pahhal interrupted.

"W-what?" Ounimbango stuttered.

"Pay them whatever they want," he said. "I want that girl now."

~

General Ounimbango's face vanished from the viewscreen, and Vosler allowed himself a slight smile. "They actually paid it. We should have asked for more."

"Oh, there are other *vays*," Anastasia Petrova said from her seat in the center of the *Grey Vistula's* bridge. "The Gael only *vants* the girl."

"I don't think there's a bounty on Captain Jennings," Vosler pointed out. "Or any of his crew."

"I'm sure there's someone who might be interested in him- someone whom Jennings recently angered," she led.

"Santelli?" Vosler asked after a moment. "Jennings gets in the way from time to time, but do you really want to give him over to that psychopath?"

"*Vhy* not?" Petrova said, her eyes scheming. "I've no loyalty to him. He's a competitor, and it was he who attacked Santelli's ship. Anything brought down on him *vill* be of his own doing." She paused. "Besides, the money *ve* extort from Santelli for Jennings *vill* be fair revenge for the trick he tried to pull on us."

Vosler muttered something about professional courtesy which Petrova ignored. "Get me Santelli," she purred, clearly savoring the conversation to come.

~

Vesper Santelli clicked off the communications screen, attempting to contain the fury carefully hidden behind his eyes. He had remained calm as Petrova practically mocked him and then pretended to offer him a bit of charity- Matthew Jennings in exchange for over a million dollars. The presumption of the little bounty hunter infuriated him.

He looked up from his overly ornate desk at his home office and asked of one of his many lieutenants who had been observing, "Did we get a trace?"

A man whose name he did not know, pushed up his glasses and said in a nasally singsong, "She thought she stayed on too short a time, and that she scrambled her position too well for us to be able to do anything with it."

"You better be about to tell me she was mistaken," Santelli growled.

The tech nodded. "We got her. Couldn't pinpoint her exactly, but she's in Beta Durani."

Santelli turned to his most trusted man in the room, Salvador Rocca. "I want a dozen ships in Beta Durani now."

Rocca merely nodded, snapped his fingers at the other lackeys and escorted everyone out of the office. He paused for a moment and turned back to Santelli. "Captain Jennings? Do you want him brought back?"

"Yes, I want him alive," Santelli said. "Some things you have to do yourself."

"Of course, sir," Rocca said, bowing his head as he did so. "I'll see it is done."

# Chapter 20

"Marquis, if you keep cooking like this, I might just marry you one of these days," Matthew Jennings said with a smile as he delved into a steak, an honest to goodness steak, with parmesan crusting, a horseradish sauce, mashed potatoes, and fresh asparagus.

Lafayette simply rolled his eyes, but Michelle saw he allowed a small smile to cross his face. She could not say she disagreed with Jennings as she too ate with gusto.

They sat in the ship's mess hall only about an hour outside of the asteroid they were headed for. Michelle was trying not to focus on the fact that it meant there was only an hour and a half of air left in the auxiliaries and then two hours of emergency back-up. She had fallen asleep in Jennings's arms after she finished crying, and he had not moved for four hours until she woke up. When she asked him why, he blushed and said something about having to check something on the bridge. Given the situation, it was about the sweetest thing anyone could have done for her.

"Well, *dis* little feast represents the last of our fresh stock," Lafayette said. "It's going to be bottles and cans and prepackaged goods from here on out." He sounded wistful. "But I couldn't let these beautiful cuts go to waste."

"Is nae half-bad," Fix said.

"Not half-bad?" Lafayette echoed. "I suppose it would be worthless to point out to you *dat* you are eating a piece of culinary artistry."

"Doesn't taste like art, tastes like steak," Squawk said excitedly. "Steak!" he shrieked again before tearing into the last of his portion.

"He really likes steak," Jennings pointed out to Michelle, who was somewhat shocked at the little Pasquatil's outburst.

"I noticed," she said.

"They don't have anything like it on their homeworld," he said. "The first meeting between humans and Pasquatil was done over a steak dinner. Supposedly, the steak was good enough to seal a treaty."

"Steak." The word was said as a reverent prayer by Squawk slowly, as he savored his last bite. He swallowed, appeared perplexed for a moment, and then unleashed a bulkhead shaking belch. "Excuse me," he added sheepishly as everyone burst out laughing.

"That one came from down in the soul," Fix said, laughing heartily. The others seemed to regard his laughter as a strange sound- perhaps no one heard it very often.

"Quite a crew you've got here, Captain," Michelle said.

"Yeah, well, they're cheap, sort of clean, good in a fight, mostly trustworthy, and cheap."

"You said cheap twice," she pointed out.

"They're really cheap," Jennings said.

Lafayette chortled through a sip of red wine, choking as he did so. This drew more laughter from everyone.

"God, you're almost a family," she said.

Everyone slowly stopped laughing and eating, except for Fix, and turned to her. "I suppose we are at that," Jennings said as he looked around the table slowly. "I've known Marquis here for twelve years. I've got more memories of him than I do my own mom."

"But I changed more diapers," Lafayette added.

"Picked up Squawk toward the tail end of the war," he said. "Most Pasquatil didn't want to serve in the Force, and those few who did were mostly disdained by the humans and Uula we fought with, but I saw something else in the little guy."

The Pasquatil's face beamed with pride.

"He was an assistant repair tech in one of the fighter bays our unit used," Jennings said. "I noticed that whenever his team was assigned to my ship it would outperform the specs by fifteen or even twenty percent. I thought the lead tech was some sort of genius and asked him about it. He said he didn't know what I was talking about. That night, I came back to the bay after hours and found this Pasquatil working on all the ships, customizing them, improving them. I made it a point to get to know him."

"I take it you did," she said.

"He told me his life story in about three seconds, then got back to work," Jennings said. "I didn't think I'd made much of an impression on him, but I sought him out after the war to see if he wanted to sign on with us. Didn't think I would have much of a chance, figured there would be other offers for him, but he jumped at the chance."

"Jumped," Squawk said. "Ships like this ship always need tweaking, always can be made better."

"And what's your story?" Michelle asked Fix.

"I answered a want ad."

"Really?" she asked.

"Really," all three men said.

"You must like the job then," she said.

"Had worse."

This drew a laugh from the others interrupted only by a beeping noise coming from the bridge. "All right, let's wrap it up," Jennings announced. "We're laughing our way right to the grave." Michelle shot him a questioning glance, and he said, "We're coming up on our destination."

~

Asteroid fields were not how people who had never seen them pictured them. Typically, they imagined hundreds of rocks filling space the way stars filled the sky, and that only the greatest of pilots could successfully navigate the chaos. In truth, a blind chimpanzee could probably do it. The average distance between most asteroids in a field was about a hundred miles. Occasionally, a few would clump together drawn in by the weak gravity of a slowly spinning rock, but they would form orbits like any other natural satellite. As such, as the crew of the *Melody Tryst* watched their approach to the asteroid, their path was easy and unimpeded.

"I want a kill order in place on the batteries," Jennings said. "As soon as we set down and are suited up, I want to save whatever life support we have."

Squawk shook his head rapidly. "Only a few minutes saved. Barely any air."

"Yeah, but I want to live for the few minutes," Jennings said.

They were getting close, and the mining base became visible as a gray shadow forcing its way across the brownish-red rock. Details became more evident as they approached: the mine itself attached to a rectangular processing station, which was connected to a hangar cut out of a mountainous rock formation towering over the complex. Connected to those buildings by a steel tube was a tall reinforced-plastic dome, which would have housed the living facilities for the mine's workers and their families.

"Two minutes," Lafayette announced. "Hangar doors are closed, and I doubt they have power. I'll have to set down in that landing area there, and we'll need to take a stroll."

"All right," Jennings said. "Marquis, you have the bridge. Everyone else down to the cargo bay and suit up. Join us once we're set down, Remy."

Lafayette turned and eyed Jennings curiously at the use of his actual first name, but only said, "Aye, captain."

The other four headed down to the cargo bay and started putting their EVA suits on. Michelle was shaking badly as she tried to suit up, so as soon as Jennings finished putting on his head gear, her walked over to her. Taking her hands in his, he helped her put her gloves and helmet on.

"You all right?" he asked.

"Aren't you scared?"

"We're not dead until we're dead," he said, allowing himself a small smile. "I'll worry then."

Jennings felt the slight change in the sensation of movement as the *Melody Tryst* slowed and then a jolt of impact as Lafayette set her down. A moment later, he joined the group and suited up quickly. "Sorry about that," he added as he put his helmet on.

"Next time, I drive," Jennings said. "Alright, everyone, O two on." A series of beeps sounded as everyone engaged their suits internal oxygen feed. "Squawk, shut it down."

Even though he should not have been able to feel it, Jennings would have sworn he could tell the oxygen had stopped being churned through the *Melody Tryst*. Maybe he just knew his ship was dead. Of course, the lights going off a second later made it all the more obvious. He turned on a hand lamp and led them over to the umbilical exit. They would not be able to go out through the cargo bay doors as they did not want what little oxygen they had saved to go rushing out into the vacuum. Jennings went first, followed by Squawk, whom he had to catch and lower to the ground and then Michelle, whom he helped because it was the gentlemanly thing to do. Fix and Lafayette were out last.

Jennings took a look around, and what he saw did not inspire confidence. Fine layers of dust covered all of the complex. Pieces of the dome in the residential structure had been cracked and other areas had been caved in. Scrapped bits of random short-range ships lay strewn across the landing pad. They looked like they had been sitting there for the better part of a century.

"Well, the habitat area is out," he said through his intercom unit. "There's no way we'll get that repaired in time." He pointed to the gaping holes in the dome. "Let's check out the ore processing center. Hopefully, they designed it without windows in mind."

Gravity was lighter on the surface of the asteroid, and they hopped as quickly as they dared through the field of debris and made their way to what appeared to be an emergency hatch in the side of the building. There was no front door, but Jennings supposed that was because anyone leaving would have been headed to the adjoining mine or the hangar, or would walk through the tube to the habitat dome. The tube was cracked in multiple places as well.

"No power to the hatch," Fix said. "My sensor's nae reading any atmosphere on the other side either."

"We expected as much," Jennings said. "We'll just have to hope we can bring it online. Squawk, can you get power to the door?"

The engineer crawled up Fix's back and out onto his arm so he could reach the control panel for the door. If this bothered Fix, he did not show it. Squawk carried a small suitcase device, which he connected to the control panel via a set of wires he stretched out of the case on a retractable spool. As soon as they were connected, he pushed a red button on the side of the case and then punched the control panel. The door slid open. As Squawk disconnected the portable battery system from the door, Fix confirmed aloud that there was indeed no atmosphere or power in the building.

"We've got to find a central control room." Jennings stepped into the inky maw which his hand lamp only barely cut through. "If we can bring their computer online, we might be able to see what would be needed to restore power and life support."

"How the hell are we supposed to find it in this?" Fix asked.

"Split up," Jennings ordered. "Michelle, come with me. Squawk, stay with Lafayette- take the floor above. Fix, you're on your own and you get two above. We'll join you after we've searched down here."

"Too bad Minerva went down before we thought to ask for a layout of this place," Lafayette muttered as he, Fix and Squawk headed up a stairwell.

Jennings and Michelle made their way through a doorway leading from the hangar into a sprawling, open room. Their lamps did not illuminate any walls for as far as the beams would go, showing only heavy equipment, conveyor belts and a lot of dust. Between random hanging chains, bulky machinery, and the darkness, it was pretty damn creepy.

"What is this place?" Michelle wondered aloud, a little bit of terror in her voice.

"An ore processing center," Jennings said. "There's probably a diagonal shaft somewhere which feeds into this room with a large conveyor, bringing up ore ingots from the mines below. They get fed to the smaller conveyors where these machines do various things to rocks you would probably need to have worked in a mine to understand."

"You assume I won't understand?"

"Actually, I meant I don't know what any of this stuff is for," he clarified, drawing a chuckle from Michelle. "Then it all goes to the hangar, loaded on ships, and away it goes."

"Oh... Hey! What's that?" she interjected, pointing into the distance.

Jennings followed the trail of her light and saw it reflecting off several windows set high up in the air. "I don't know."

"Could it be a control station?" she asked. "Wouldn't they want it set high over the work floor like that? Be able to see everything?"

Dumfounded for a moment, Jennings quickly just said, "Um, yeah. Sure. Let's check it out. Good thinking."

The room was built against the far wall of the production floor and was raised a good thirty feet off the floor, taking it all the way up to the ceiling of the massive first floor room. They took an open-air metal staircase up to the room and swung the door open. Jennings allowed himself a small smile- it was the control room.

He flipped on his comm set. "Marquis, do you copy?"

"*Capitaine*," the reply came. Lafayette's voice was tense.

"Marquis, what's wrong?"

"The second floor is some kind of crew quarters," he said. "Locker rooms, bunk beds…"

"Get to the point," Jennings demanded.

"We're not alone," he replied ominously.

Instinctively, Jennings took out his plasma pistol and charged it. "Do you know what it is?"

"Her name is Suzie," he said ominously.

"Huh?"

The tension vanished from Lafayette's voice. "It's a blow-up doll."

The sentence hung between them for a moment. "Are you fucking kidding me?" Jennings finally demanded. Even Michelle was laughing at him.

"Technically, yes," Lafayette said, his laughter barely being suppressed.

Jennings glared daggers out into space. "Do you want a fist in the mouth?"

"*Non, merci.*"

"Then haul your asses back down to the first floor all the way across from the entrance. We found the control room," he said.

"En route."

"Fix, did you copy?" Jennings asked.

"You could nae hear me laughing up here?" .

"Anything on the third floor?" he asked.

"Supply closets, maybe even some O two tanks. Hard to tell without lights though," he said.

"Alright, make your way back here," Jennings said.

Michelle glanced at him through her faceplate. "Are we going to make it?"

"Too early to tell."

Thirty minutes later, Squawk was feverishly punching commands into a portable CPU he had hardwired into the ore processing center's own processor. The system had no power, but the computer did not appear to be in a state of disrepair. The engineer clicked his tongue against his teeth in what could only be a dialect of the Pasquatil language, most likely some elegant form of cursing, Jennings supposed.

"Done," Squawk said in a high-pitched squeal of excitement.

"What's done?" Jennings asked, but the question died in his throat as slowly some lights started fluttering on in the control room. There was also a dim glow beginning out on the work floor as the larger ceiling-set halogens took longer to warm up. "Squawk, you brilliant bastard. What do we have?"

"Main power!" he said. "The entire complex powered! Cut off and redirected any power from inessential areas just in case."

"Less chance of a burnout. Good thinking," he commended, patting the Pasquatil on the shoulder. "What about life support?"

"Charging. Charging. Four hours until air levels are breathable." The zeal left his voice.

"Why so long?" Jennings asked as a heavy weight seemed to plant itself on his chest.

"Mine and ore processing interconnected. Not designed to be set up separately," he said.

"Dammit," Jennings spat. "The situation set itself up perfectly. For some reason, the company left the power and life support hardware in place, there's no breeches in this building open to space, and we're still fucked."

"Hold on a second," Michelle said, laying a hand on Jennings's EVA sleeve, but looking at Fix. "Didn't you say you found some oxygen canisters on the third floor?"

"Might have, but I could nae tell," he said. "Could've been acetylene."

"Let's check it out," Jennings said.

~

They made their way up to the third floor together, Michelle following Jennings closely. The processing center seeming less haunted and frightening with the lights kicking on. Many were out, so large patches of darkness enshrouded places, but it was still much more amenable than the pure dark which had embraced them only a few minutes before. Fix led them back to a small room with only one door and no windows. The door was a massive steel monstrosity set on hinges like an old-fashioned bank vault door. The others seemed very excited when they saw this, but Michelle had no idea why.

"Let's hope some of these tanks are still full and the machinery still works," Jennings said excitedly.

The three men and one Pasquatil started inspecting the gas tubes propped against one of the walls. They started talking excitedly, and Michelle did not feel like trying to keep up with their conversation. They kept finishing each other's sentences and snapping their fingers, making excited exclamations and jabbering in some kind of techno-babble she had no hope of understanding. Engineering was nowhere near her major in college.

The room was relatively small, about ten feet by fifteen with a row of benches on one side and the equipment everyone was so interested in on the other. The far wall had a refrigeration unit and a series of shelves that once probably housed food stores. *What was this room? Some type of emergency shelter?* Michelle thought to herself. She turned around and looked at the wall dominated by the vault door. In addition to the door's control panel, two electronic panels flashed messages. Stenciled above the left hand one was: Processing Center Atmosphere. The message flashing in red below it said: NONE. The other panel read Safe Room Atmosphere. It flashed the same message.

"This is a Safe Room?" she whispered.

"Yeah, in the event of a breech in the building, you've only got a minute or so to make for this room and get the door shut," Jennings said, looking up at her.

"Air supply connected," Squawk said.

"Fix, the door, if you please," Jennings said.

As Fix swung the massive vault door shut, Michelle stared at the board. The one on the left still showed no atmosphere, but the one on the right flashed another message in yellow: SELF-CONTAINED.

Squawk turned a handle on the oxygen tank and punched a few commands into the control pad on the wall as Jennings continued, "This room is completely self-contained and is designed to be an emergency station for personnel to get to before the entire complex becomes a vacuum. There's probably one on each floor and some in the mines."

"It's small for an entire complex," she said.

"Probably not a lot of people on this level, *n'est-ce pas*?" Lafayette said. "Maybe they have bigger ones we missed on the other floors?"

"Maybe they don't care about anyone on the lower floors," Fix muttered.

A new message started flashing on the right-hand screen: OXYGENATING. It only took a moment for the red letters to vanish entirely, replaced by green letters which read ATMOSPHERE ACTIVE.

"Is it safe?" Michelle asked.

"This would be a bad time for there to be a malfunction in the sign," Lafayette said.

"Everyone, keep your helmets on," Jennings said. "I'll test it first."

Tentatively, he shut off the oxygen feed for his own suit and removed his helmet. Jennings held his breath, apparently instinctively, for a moment. At last, he let it out and breathed in again. He coughed suddenly and then sneezed.

"God, it's dusty in here." He inhaled deeply again and gave a satisfied sigh. "All right, everyone, helmets off. Save your suit's air. Amazingly enough, we are still alive."

# Chapter 21

The next three and a half hours passed very slowly for Captain Jennings and his crew. There was nothing to do in the small emergency room, but sit and chat, but none of them felt much like it. It was a strange sensation- knowing you were going to die. Jennings had been through it twice before in combat, times when he could not see a way to survive. He obviously had in both instances, but afterward the same lethargy overcame him. For some reason, being about to die really took it out of you.

Michelle fell asleep with her head on his shoulder, both of them leaning against the wall, Jennings staring off into space. From one of his pockets, Lafayette produced a deck of cards and after getting no takers for poker, began playing solitaire. The boring, repetitive nature of it must have been appealing. Fix's eyes were closed, but he was not asleep. Perhaps he was praying, Jennings thought. Fix had a weird sense of piety when he thought no one else was looking. Even the Pasquatil was out of it. The normally hyperactive Squawk had fallen into a heap on the floor and now was snoring loudly. They were all so out of it, they almost paid no mind when the screen displaying the Processing Center Atmosphere started reading SELF-CONTAINED: OXYGENATED.

Jennings's eye caught it first. "Alright, everybody up," he said with as much energy as he could muster, standing slowly and stretching as he did so. "Come on, up! Squawk, wake up! Squawk!" The Pasquatil remained snoring. Jennings turned to Lafayette. "Marquis, get his helmet on him. Helmets on everyone. I'll open the door and test the air. Assuming I don't get spaced, we can assume we're okay."

Once everyone was ready, Jennings swung the pressure door open and stepped through into the hallway. A couple of deep breaths of cool, musty air swam into his lungs. He coughed a little but did not decompress, explode or instantly freeze, which he took as a good sign.

"God smiles at us for a change, *non*?" Marquis said as he pulled off his helmet.

"Try not to jinx it," Michelle said.

This drew a grimace of annoyance from Jennings's first mate.

"I guess Squawk isn't going to wake up any time soon," the captain said. "Let's leave him be. Fix, Marquis, make for the hangar bay, make sure it is pressurized, and then start working on a way to get the *Tryst* in."

"Aye, Cap'n," Fix said.

"Michelle and I will head back to the control room and see what we can find on this place. Maybe there are some parts we can salvage," Jennings said. "We'll set Squawk on the repairs once he's conscious."

"What then, *mon capitaine*?" Lafayette asked as Jennings turned to leave.

Jennings glanced back over his shoulder and said, "We get out of here," before resuming heading into the hallway.

Lafayette lingered. "And the girl?"

The captain came to a stop and turned to Michelle, who was staring at him quite intently, certainly wondering what was to become of her now that their lives had been spared. "She goes free. I gave her my word."

"*Oui, mon capitaine.*"

Michelle and Jennings headed back to the stairs, the latter taking them two at a time down to the first floor. "Do you trust the Frenchman?"

"He's Cajun actually," Jennings said as his long strides carried him toward the first-floor ore processing room. "And I trust him with my life. I take it you don't."

"He doesn't seem pleased that I'm not going to the Gael," she said as she caught up to him.

Together they emerged into the processing center and walked past the long conveyor belts, headed toward the control room. "He's just trying to watch out for me." With as much false bravado as he could muster, Jennings added, "He knows I can be too honorable for my own good sometimes."

"You don't think he would hand me over to the Gael against your orders?" Michelle pressed.

"Once I ordered that man to hold a position against fifty Gael. With only five men. Had he not held, our flank would have been rolled and the entire regiment destroyed. He held. I don't if he's capable of disobeying an order. So, to answer your question, you need not fear. There's no chance he would sell you out to the Gael." As they took the stairs up to the control room, he added, "Fix on the other hand…" They stepped into the control room, and Jennings pulled a faux leather chair up to the computer console and started bringing up a diagnostic menu.

"Fix doesn't seem as perturbed as Lafayette," she pointed out as she pulled up a chair next to him.

"That's what would worry me," Jennings said. "I haven't known him as long, and I barely know him personally at all. I know he was in prison, and I get the feeling he wouldn't want to go back. If things go south after we let you go, that's exactly where the four of us are going to end up. That's assuming they don't space us."

The data Jennings was looking for at last popped up on the screen, and he pulled out his comm unit. "Marquis, do you copy?"

"Go ahead, *mon capitaine*."

"Internal sensors confirm you have power and atmosphere in the hangar," he said. "External door should open and force fields should be in place."

"Lot of shoulds in there," Fix grumbled.

"We're at the hangar entrance now, proceeding in," Lafayette reported as a door audibly swung open accompanied by a harsh, "*Merde*."

"Problem?" Jennings asked.

"Place is a mess," he said. "We'll need to clear some space before we can bring the *Tryst* in."

"*Le temps, c'est l'argent, mon ami*," Jennings said in grade school passable French.

"*Oui, mon capitaine*."

"They'll be a while sounds like," Michelle said.

"So will we," Jennings said.

Michelle raised an eyebrow. "Doing what?"

"We've got to go through the schematics for the power systems here and the inventory screens for anything left behind which might fix the power plant and turn the *Tryst's* engine back on," he said. "If we can't do that, we're going to be here for a mighty long time."

~

Getting the hangar bay clear involved a lot of annoying, onerous work. Bits of scrap metal, used fuel containers, lots of items Lafayette could not identify and categorized only as junk, and one amazingly still-running power loader crowded the hangar. Once they discovered the last, the job became a lot easier. The bull-dozer like power loader pushed all the miscellaneous garbage to the far side of the hangar, giving them just enough room to fit the *Melody Tryst* inside. Now, they just needed to deal with the problem of getting her in.

The grav-locks were shot on the towing emitter beams, so an electronic lock was impossible. The *Melody Tryst* had so little power left that trying to get her into the bay on her own power would likely result in a crash of some kind, or she would not even get off the ground. Finally, Lafayette found some industrial strength tritanium cable which they could run from the power loader to the *Melody Tryst*. Normally, a power loader would not be strong enough to tow a ship of the *Melody Tryst's* size, but there was no atmosphere on the outside and therefore little resistance. Lafayette realized if they depressurized the hangar bay, they should not have any trouble bringing her in.

A quick search of some of the maintenance lockers in the hangar revealed some full O two tubes for their spacesuits. After getting the suits restocked, and resealing themselves within, it was an easy enough matter to depressurize the bay and tow the *Melody Tryst* inside. The relatively small ship, within the grand scheme of things, seemed massive in the hangar bay, its nose nearly scraping the back wall and the aft engines barely contained within the now closed hangar door.

The hangar was now re-pressurized, and Lafayette eyed his ship with an expression of amazement and gratitude.

"What's that about?" Fix asked.

"What?"

"Why are you staring at her like you've nae ever seen her before?" Fix clarified.

"I didn't think I would ever see her again," he said nostalgically walking underneath one of the wings. With a sense of reverence, he reached up and touched the metal gingerly. "*Merci.*"

"She just about died on us," Fix pointed out.

"*Non,*" Lafayette countered, shaking his head. "She stayed alive long enough to get us where we need to be."

Fix snorted. "I'll nae ever understand the weird relationship you have with this bird."

"You don't have to," Lafayette said with a smile. "Come on. Let's get this lady a drink."

Together, they lugged several power connection cables hardwired into the base's electrical supply over to the *Melody Tryst's* belly section and attached them. There were a few moments' pause before the control panel next to power conduit came to life in a series of dull colors, quickly growing brighter. The ship would not be able to maintain power on its own without a new plant, but the whole ship could be run at least while plugged in. After a moment, Lafayette punched in a command, and the hydraulic presses began lowering the loading deck for entry into the cargo bay. A hiss filled the air as some of the hangar's more oxygen rich atmosphere rushed into fill the ship.

"We'll have to give it a little while to equalize," Lafayette said. "But we should tell the captain."

"Go ahead then," Fix replied.

"Lafayette to Jennings," he called.

"Go ahead, Marquis."

"Good news, *mon capitaine*," he said. "She's breathing again."

Lafayette could almost hear the captain's smile on the other end. "Good work, Remy. We may have some more good news if Squawk ever decides to wake the hell up. The processing center's auxiliary power system might actually serve nicely as a primary for us. At least until we can get into a real port and buy some real parts, that is."

Not wanting to think about when they might actually be able to afford real parts, Lafayette said, "The ship should have full life support soon. Fix and I will go aboard and start running diagnostics."

"Understood. Keep an eye on the space above us too," he said. "I want some warning if anyone else shows up."

"*Oui, mon capitaine.*"

~

Four hours later, things were looking amazingly up from what Michelle could tell. The Pasquatil engineer had awoken from his near comatose state and agreed with Jennings's assessment that the back-up power generator for the ore processing center could be removed and jury-rigged into the *Melody Tryst*. The computer system Jennings called Minerva agreed with that assessment and was discussing the matter over the radio with Squawk as the Pasquatil and the other two humans attempted to disconnect the auxiliary power plant from the station.

Michelle stood on the bridge with Jennings, where he was working on prioritizing a list of other repairs which needed to be done. Minerva had interfaced with the processing station's computer and performed a much faster analysis of items that might work as components on the damaged *Melody Tryst*. Some of the items would need to be passed on, but Jennings repeatedly said he would not leave without the power plant, shields and at least some functioning weapons.

For her part, Michelle just tried to keep out of the way. The captain suggested she go rest in one of the cabins, but she told him she was not tired. The truth was she was rather afraid to be alone; afraid she would fall asleep and they would all be gone when she woke up; afraid this would all be a dream and she would wake up with her tormentors on the *Brigandine*, the high rollers on Strikeplain, or with the Gael themselves. Captain Jennings brought a very calming presence which made her feel safe for the moment. Despite everything they had been through, he never panicked, never lost his cool. She hoped his word was as good as he claimed, but she almost instinctively knew it was.

A loud banging over the radio interrupted her thought process.

"Everything all right?" Jennings asked.

Fix was evidently trying hard not to laugh. "Lafayette just dropped the power unit on his foot."

Jennings smiled. "Is he hurt?"

The answer was drowned in a caterwauling siren coming from one of the consoles.

"Minerva, kill that damn noise and report!" Jennings thundered.

The cool voice of the computer responded, "Ship on approach. Vector indicates no other destination but here."

"Can you identify?" he asked.

"The ship is the *Grey Vistula*. Registration belonging to one Anastasia Petrova," Minerva confirmed.

"Son of a bitch, I hate being right," Jennings muttered. "How long until they reach here?"

"At present speed, twenty-three minutes."

"How long would it take to get the power plant installed?" he asked.

There was a slight pause while Minerva calculated. "The fastest possible completion time considering all factors would be two hours four minutes."

Jennings eyed Michelle, a concerned expression on his face. "We got problems."

In the next few minutes, Jennings began issuing orders like mad. "I want the three of you back in the ship now. Lafayette, start pulling weapons when you get here. Fix, I want back-up oxygen for our suits and any other supplies we might need: rope, lights, water, consumables. Squawk, I need you to prep the *Tryst* for lockdown. I want to be able to access Minerva still, but I want the ship sealed up tight."

"What about the power plant?" Lafayette asked.

"Leave it," he said quickly. "Company's coming, and we're not going to have enough time to get it installed."

"Understood, *mon capitaine*."

"Minerva, I'm going to have to ask a lot of you," Jennings said.

"That which I love to hear," Minerva replied.

Michelle would have sworn some amusement laced her tone.

"I need maps," he said.

"Downloading to handhelds," Minerva said. "Although, these are official blueprints. Historically, many mining operations have side tunnels, emergency shafts, exploration corridors, and testing sites not indicated on maps as they are not part of the original plan."

"We'll worry about that when the time comes," he muttered. "Also, I need you to encrypt the processing center's system. We can't have them turning off the lights or God forbid the air on us. They'll have a hacker with them- be better."

"Of course, captain."

"Stay on station," he added as he stood up. "You're going to be our eyes and ears topside." As Minerva gave an affirmative, Jennings pulled Michelle to her feet. "C'mon, we need to go."

"What are we going to do?" Michelle asked as he pulled her down the gangplank and into the cargo bay.

"We've got no surface-to-space weapons on the *Tryst* functioning, so we can't fight," he said as headed over to one of the weapons lockers. "We also can't run because the *Tryst* still can't power herself. So, we're left with one other option, we fight."

"Then why the maps and the talk about topside and Minerva being the eyes and ears?" she asked.

"Counting you, we've got a crew of five. Two of which are, no offense, inexperienced when it comes to firefights," he explained as he grabbed a medium-size plasma rifle with eight rotating barrels, checked the charges and armed the weapon. "This area is way too big to defend. They'll overwhelm us with a frontal assault or use the weapons on their ship to reduce the ore processing center to slag. Either way, we wouldn't hold for very long."

"So, where are we going?"

"Into the mine," he said as he handed a small pistol to her. "It has a laser sight on it, but don't switch it on until the shooting starts. They can track it right back to you if you're not careful." A resigned expression of grim doom crossed her face as she accepted the weapon and tucked it into her belt. Jennings stood up and grabbed her shoulders gently. "In the mine, they won't be able to send their full force at us at once and the weapons on their ship can't hurt us. We can turn the terrain into our favor. We can harry them, harass them, pick them off one at a time. We can bleed them until they realize the folly of their ways and leave this place."

"And if they don't leave?" she asked.

"Then we make them wish they had," he said with a smile.

The rest of the crew arrived and started grabbing supplies and weapons. Squawk moved over to one of the computer consoles and began furiously typing commands into the system. Fix started handing backpacks to each of them containing water, food, ammo, medical supplies and any other gear that might become relevant. Lafayette passed out the weapons. He armed them to the teeth, and when given a questioning look by Jennings, he shrugged. "Better to have it and not need it, then need it and not have it."

Jennings shrugged. "Heard that before. Minerva, time to contact."

"*Grey Vistula* entering final planetary approach," the computer said. "Eight minutes until landing."

"Squawk?" Jennings then demanded.

"All preparations prepared," he reported before accepting a small rifle from Lafayette.

"Alright then," the captain said gravely. "Let's move like we want to live."

Michelle followed Jennings as they headed down the cargo bay and back out into the hangar, laden down rather heavily with supplies. The ship's entrance closed behind them, the doors locked, and the access code scrambled when Squawk pressed a button on the exterior control panel.

Michelle's backpack weighed a ton, and she wondered why they were burdening themselves with so many items. As they re-entered the ore processing center, she asked him as much.

Jennings explained, "Not certain how long we will be down in the mine. According to the maps, the place is vast, and we might be able to hide for a while. Who knows how long it will take for us to either shake Petrova's goons or take out enough of them that the Russian bitch gives us up as more trouble than we're worth."

Something about his tone made her think the latter was unlikely. She had only briefly run into Petrova on Strikeplain, but she did not strike Michelle as the giving up type. If they wanted to get out of there alive, it meant killing every last one of her people. To do that though would take time, and she supposed time required ample supplies.

The corridor leading to the mine entrance ran off the second floor of the processing center. According to the schematic Minerva had provided each of their handhelds, there was a long tunnel underneath of it that held a series of conveyors which sent ore from the mine depths to the processing center. The tunnel ran at a smooth diagonal down to the entrance base for the mines. The corridor they walked down led to a lift that would take them to the same place. The area was strewn with random garbage and a fair bit of dust, but Michelle was happy to see that the lift was still in serviceable order. The idea of trying to climb down a conveyor belt did not appeal to her in the slightest.

With a grunt of effort, Jennings opened the sliding grate as Michelle hit the call button for the lift. The doors opened immediately, and Jennings motioned everyone inside. Once he had grate closed again, Michelle hit the button labeled MINE ENTRANCE, and the doors automatically closed. A few moments and a few unhappy groaning noises from the lift later, they were headed down into the mine.

# Chapter 22

The *Grey Vistula* settled down gently over top of the tracks the *Melody Tryst* had made in the rock dust when it set down at the Comet Corporation mining colony. "Did we miss them?" Vosler wondered aloud, studying the tracks in the viewscreen.

"No," Petrova said quickly. "Tracks lead into the hangar over there, but there are none leading back out. Sensors show the ore processing station has power."

"Captain Jennings has been busy," Vosler said. "That man escapes death like no other I've ever seen. His ship is fried, limping, all but dead, and he not only finds a safe port in the middle of nowhere, but gets it powered. He's probably in a whirlpool, smoking a cigar, surround by naked women."

This earned a guffaw from the *Grey Vistula's* bridge crew. Petrova did not smile. "Let's hope so, Vosler. He might be easier to catch."

Nodding grimly, Vosler asked, "How did you want to do this?"

Petrova studied a readout for a moment. "*Ve'll* leave the bridge crew here. Everyone else *vill* come with us. The habitat area has no power or atmosphere according to the sensors, so they'll be in ore processing. *Ve'll* do a systematic search and take the girl into custody."

"Sounds easy, but there's one problem," Vosler said, peering over her head at the computer terminal.

"*Vhat's* that?" she asked. "This should be a clean sweep."

He pointed to a small corridor leading from the second floor of the processing center to an elevator. "What if they went into the mine?"

~

The lift led out into an entryway cut out of the rock with tables and lockers sat in the corners, probably a staging area for the miners, Michelle thought. Passing beyond a stone archway, they stepping into an expansive cavern which served as a switching station. At least a dozen tunnels sprang off in all directions, many having inlaid metal tracks. The tracks led to a central circular switch in the middle of the room with several lines then headed to a second cavernous room with a conveyor belt leading to the surface. Imprints in the rock indicated there may have been some kind of heavy machinery stored in that room to move the rocks from the mine carts to the conveyor belt, perhaps valuable enough for the Comet Corporation to actually take it with them.

The air reeked of must and fine rock dust which threatened to make Michelle cough with each breath. Captain Jennings noticed her difficulty and pulled a bandana from one of his pockets. Gingerly, he wrapped it around her face while the others pulled their shirts over their noses or produced similar bandanas. Only Squawk seemed unaffected.

"Aren't you going to need it?" Michelle asked.

"I'll be fine." The captain turned around and did a quick reconnoiter of the cavernous room before speaking again. "Alright, this is the best place for our first ambush."

"Where do you want us?" Michelle asked excitedly.

Jennings smiled. "As far away from here as possible. Marquis, you're going to take tunnel Alpha 7. That one over there." He glanced up from the schematic on his handheld and pointed. "That'll take you pretty far to the north here. At the end of that tunnel, there's a spiral shaft heading down to the lower level. Take that and meet me at this junction."

"*Dat's* quite a hike," Lafayette muttered as he studied the route.

"This place is huge. Everywhere's quite a hike," Jennings pointed out. "My plan is to hide in tunnel Alpha 2, wait for them to show themselves and see how many I can take out before I have to fall back."

"You'll be outnumbered," Fix said.

"By a considerable margin," Jennings agreed. "I'm hoping they won't expect it. I should be able to distract them nicely and slip away in the confusion. Even if they are following me, it's only a short run to Junction 35. From there, I've got eight directions to go. Unless they are right on my heels, they won't find me. I'll be free to meet back up with you."

"What if they find us before you do?" Lafayette asked.

"Keep the girl safe. Split up if necessary."

"*Bien sur, mon capitaine,*" he said.

"How long are we supposed to keep this up?" Fix asked.

Jennings eyed him curiously. "What?"

"Our grand plan is to hopefully pick them off one at a time?" the Scotsman demanded incredulously. "Until they pack it up and go home?"

"You got a better one?" Jennings's voice remained calm, but the anger coming off him was palatable.

"Aye, I've got a better one," he said as his eyes moved over to Michelle.

Jennings stared at him coolly for a moment. "That's not an option."

"Just nae one you're willing to consider," he corrected.

"As you say, and I'm in charge," Jennings fired back.

"My bony black arse," Fix swore. "On the ship, you're in charge. Out here, it's everyone man for him-"

Jennings drew on him before he could even finish the sentence. Fix's body flinched like he was going to go for his weapon as well, but the captain was so fast, he would have been dead instantly.

"Every man for himself, is it?" Jennings asked. "That being the case, why don't you head back up the lift and see if Petrova is hiring? Because if you're not with us, then you can fuck off."

Fix held up his hands placatingly. "Just a suggestion."

"Noted," Jennings said as he re-holstered his weapon. "Now all of you get moving. It's not going to be long before the Russian bitch and her lickspittles are upon us."

Lafayette gestured to Michelle, Squawk and Fix to follow him. "Oh, Fix," Jennings called after them.

"Aye?"

"Let me have those grenades, will ya?"

~

Anastasia Petrova let loose a string of what Vosler assumed were curses in Russian. He did not blame her- he was starting to like their chances of finding the girl less and less. They only had so many hours before General Ounimbango arrived, and if they did not have the girl, they were out quite a bit of money. The thirty men with them had torn apart the ore processing center, the hangar, and the other two levels and found exactly nothing.

Sure, the *Melody Tryst* sat like a wounded duck in the hangar, but they could not access the ship without blowing her up. As doing so would probably rupture the air seal on the hangar and depressurize the entire area, he managed to talk Petrova out of it. Likewise, they had no luck trying to access the now online and functional computer system of the station either. Apparently, Captain Jennings had some aptitude with ciphers. Bulgara, the rake thin, punk-haired, breast-less hacker Petrova employed had been unable to do anything with it. All they had were the sensors on the *Grey Vistula* and hand units to try to find their quarry. All the same, Vosler was relatively certain Jennings and the girl were not in the station. They had enough people to comb every square inch of space, and there was not so much as a heat signature anywhere.

"They're in the mines," he said at last.

"I know that," she growled.

They stood on the third floor near the emergency decompression chamber. From the empty food containers and the imprints in the dust on the benches, Jennings clearly had been forced to come here first. That probably explained why they were not able to make the needed repairs to their ship in time. They were much more interested in breathing.

"If they're in the mines, they're gone," Vosler said. "We can't hack into the computer, so we don't have any maps of the area. And if the mining company abandoned this facility because it was tapped out, then it means there could be miles of tunnels in there."

"*Ve* could shut down the air," she spat.

"Without the computers?"

"*Ve* could blast the power plant to dust," she growled.

"Then the girl is dead, Ounimbango is a little furious, and we don't get paid. Or worse." With an ominous sigh, he added, "The best thing we can do is take up position outside the mine. We keep them contained and let the TGF go in and roust them out."

"*Ve* lose out on our fee," she said. "More than that, *ve* would have failed."

Vosler recognized the steely tone of resolution his boss got from time to time. It almost always meant something he would not like. "What do you want to do?"

"Get everyone together," she ordered. *"Ve're* going in."

~

*Waiting was the worst part of any ambush,* Captain Jennings thought.

He had never been a patient man. Even his mother teased him about it growing up, when he would pace around their home whenever he needed to wait for someone else. It was all the worse when you injected a life and death situation into the equation. Senses ran at high gear, and time seemed to slow down while waiting for the battle which would eventually come.

It had been two hours since they split up, Lafayette leading everyone else deeper into the mine. Jennings had no idea how long Petrova would be searching for them, but there was one thing he was confident on. She would come into the mine after them.

Jennings did not truly know Petrova, but he understood the compulsions that drove her. Understanding your enemy was an integral part of any battle, and understanding battle was one of the few things Jennings felt he did naturally well. Even now as he waited, the coming firefight unfurled before him in his mind.

They would be coming down in a minimum of three groups as the lift only carried about eight. That ship of hers could only comfortably carry about forty men. Leaving some behind to garrison the ship and to hold the hallway above the elevator meant she could only bring about thirty against him. The real question was when to strike. Did he attack the first wave down? Petrova was not likely to be in that group- she was far too smart for that. Once he attacked, the element of surprise was gone. The next groups down would be ready for an attack and would probably come out shooting. His entire plan was based on hitting them hard and fast once, and then fleeing into the mines.

*No*, he said to himself. He would have to wait until they were all down in the mine and then attack. "Waiting on top of waiting," he grumbled to himself.

For what must have been the thousandth time, he checked his weapon's charge, made sure the safety was off, went through his back-up weapons, and checked the primers on the grenades he had taken off Fix. Once again, he checked the overturned steel mine cart he was hiding behind. It was fairly solid and should absorb several hits before turning to slag.

The high-pitched whirring of machinery coming to life distracted him for a moment, but then caused a smile to cross his face. The elevator was returning to the surface, and Jennings was about to have some visitors.

~

Vosler and Petrova were among the last to head into the mine. They left four men behind them to hold the corridor and sent twenty-five before them to take control of the mine below. Vosler knew Petrova would not be one to poke around the guts of an asteroid looking for her prey, but she would prefer to bark orders and organize the details of the search. That suited him just fine, even though he thought this plan was pure folly. Some might think Petrova allowed her lust for money to get the better of her, but Vosler knew the truth. She just did not like to lose, and letting someone else take money that was in her mind already hers- that was a loss Petrova would not bear.

That was why she had taken such a hard line on Matthew Jennings. He had proven himself to be a fly in the ointment on several occasions, but Petrova pursued him with a vendetta suited only for a cold, cruel Russian, even if she was several generations removed from the Siberian wastes. Jennings in his own way had dared to defy her: taking commissions that should have been hers, working jobs successfully where she had failed, forcing her to take marks from him in order to collect the bounty she believed she was entitled to. Not dealing with Jennings herself and waiting for Ounimbango and the TGF was a slight on her honor. And not even her unshakable lust for money rivaled her need for honor.

The lift rumbled to a stop, and they exited along with another four of her men, heading through the staging room and into the main cavern. Vosler observed those they had brought and found himself grimacing. These were no soldiers with them. They were all hired guns and bounty hunters. Maybe a few had put some time in with the military during the war, but they were not the professional caliber they needed for this type of mission. Rather than securing the perimeter and the multiple entrances and exits to the switching station, they huddled together in groups of four and five near the entrance to the staging room, chatting or swiveling their heads around, barely even looking for a threat. *These men were too used to the quarry only running*, Vosler realized. They were not ready for one which would fight back.

The thoughts were barely in his head for a moment when he glanced up and saw a spiral of black and green flying through the air. Something was strangely familiar about it. Just as it landed, recognition took hold of him, and he dived into Petrova knocking them both back into the entranceway.

"Grenade!" he roared just as the explosion rocked the subterranean cavern.

A storm of shrapnel hissed through the air, ricocheting off the rocky walls of the mine. A cloud of dust and smoke filled the cavern and puffed into the staging room, but even through it and the chaos of the explosion still ringing in his ears, Vosler could see the unmistakable flashes and hear the roar of plasma cannons ripping through those men still standing. He would have returned fire, but there would have been no point. In the smoke and dust, he had no way to find his target and even more, the firing had stopped. Their ambusher was already gone.

Vosler pulled himself to his feet slowly, knocking the detritus and rubble from his clothing, and then extended a hand down to Petrova. She had a small gash in her forehead, but she did not appear any else the worse for wear.

"Are you all right?"

"Furious," she said. "But my *vounds vill* heal." She grimaced as she tried to take a step forward and then allowed herself to fall back to the ground. "I'm a little dizzy. Find out how bad it is. How many *ve* lost. Then secure a perimeter with anyone *ve* have left. I don't *vant* any more surprises."

"Of course," he said before he left to go see how many survived and help tend to the wounded.

Immediately, he ordered anyone still standing and unhurt to take up sentry positions in the corridors. As the smoke was cleared by the station's air processing system, he was able to take stock of how bad it was. Captain Jennings had killed eight in his attack, most of them with the grenades, although two bodies had been ripped apart by precision plasma fire. There was also a half-dozen injuries, not counting the numerous scrapes, cuts and other random bleeds that most of those still standing had. Their corpsman had been one of those killed, so Vosler attended to the wounded.

Two of his men were definitely going to die, but the others seemed likely to recover if they got back to the ship. One even stated he was good enough to carry on, picked up his weapon and joined the other sentries. Petrova had found her balance and emerged from the entranceway, walking slowly over toward him. The same steely determination was on her face, and Vosler shook his head slightly. As determined as she was, she kept underestimating Captain Jennings. That unfortunate habit would get them all killed.

"Vosler," she said quietly.

"Yes, Ms. Petrova."

"Call the *Vistula*," she ordered. "Tell them to send someone over with the skimmers."

Quickly, Vosler checked out the height of the tunnels and their width, and felt a smile come over his face. "The skimmers, ma'am, aye." He pulled a comm unit off his belt and prepared to make the call.

~

It felt like they had been running for days when Lafayette at last called a break, and Michelle fell to one knee trying to catch her breath. She had lettered in three varsity sports and she jogged every day- or did until she got caught up in this mess- and she had never felt so out of shape before. Fix had barely broken a sweat, and Lafayette was not gasping for air the way she was. And he was fairly old and had a bit of a gut to him. Only Squawk seemed to be having the same trouble as little wheezes kept coming from the Pasquatil.

Fix tapped her boot with his. "A break means we walk."

Annoyed, Michelle pulled herself to her feet and started after them. How they could tell where they were going, she had no idea. Maps had never been one of her strong suits, and the environment in the mines never changed. The roof was too low, the walls were timbered, and the ground was smoothed over rock with a pair of rail tracks running through it. Occasionally, they turned left or right into another tunnel, somehow knowing this was the correct one and not the other dozen they had passed.

"We're almost to the rendezvous," Lafayette said.

"Hooray," Michelle muttered sarcastically.

All the same, she felt a little better when the tunnel emerged into a second transfer station. There was a roundabout for the mine carts, and a half dozen new tunnels led in different directions. Unbelievably enough, cut into the rock face was a small bar with Rockhead's Roadhouse stenciled in crude white letters on the rock above. A half dozen stools were bolted into the ground, and it looked like there had once been tables on a raised bit of stone near the bar. Gratefully, Michelle sat on one of the stools, feeling the aches in her legs lessen slightly.

Lafayette walked over to the bar and stuck his head over. "I never would have thought there'd be a cantina inside the mine."

"Looks like you picked the wrong line of work," Michelle said.

Ignoring her comment, he let out a sigh and plopped down next to her. "*Merde.* They left the stools, took the bottles." After a moment, he added, "And no, I don't think this would've been for me even if you're allowed to mine shitfaced. Really, *dat* has to be in violation of some kind of labor law."

"You gonna have a beverage or do you wanna help secure the perimeter?" Fix demanded. The Scotsman had been in an unpleasant mood since his confrontation with Jennings.

"*Excusez-moi,*" Lafayette said politely as he stood to go help Fix.

"Rocks and stones," muttered a tired voice to Michelle's left.

Turning around, she found Squawk trying to pull himself up onto a stool without any success. "Do you want some help?"

"That would be helpful."

Grabbing him under the arms, she hefted the surprisingly heavy engineer onto a stool. "Thankful thanks," he said and let out a long whistle that could only be the Pasquatil equivalent of a sigh.

"Buy you a drink?" she asked, passing him her canteen. "It's only water, but I think you'll like it all the same."

Squawk nodded his thanks and took a small sip. "A strange place."

"How so?" she asked.

"Big hole in the world. Seems pointless."

"They were digging for something useful, I would imagine," Michelle said. "Ores, minerals, metals."

The Pasquatil was clearly not impressed. "If we need it, why is it so far away? If it's buried, we're not supposed to have it."

"That's an interesting way of looking at it, I suppose," she said.

"There's more than one way?" he asked, confused.

A light laugh escaped her lips, and she covered her mouth for a moment. "Don't worry about it."

She had never had a conversation with a Pasquatil before, but had heard that many humans found them aggravating- their insistence on taking everything literally, their inability to grasp when to use synonyms, and their complete indifference toward understanding why things work had driven many an ambassador crazy when humanity first met the Pasquatil. All the same, she found the wide-eyed amazement he tended to find in the simplest of things amusing. After a few moments' rest, he was already hopping over to the roundabout, chattering to himself and occasionally muttering in English on how to improve it.

Here they were, probably about to die and Squawk was still busy trying to improve everything. *There was probably a life lesson in that somewhere*, Michelle thought.

Her thoughts were interrupted by Lafayette walking back over to her. "We should be safe here for a little while. Did you feel that tremor a moment ago?"

"No," she said, honestly not having any idea what he was talking about.

"It was light, barely a tickle. But definitely *le capitaine*."

"What do you mean?" she asked.

"Grenades," he said as if it were obvious. "The Russian's in the tunnel, and he just struck the first blow."

"Let's hope he walks away from it," she whispered.

"He will," Lafayette said. "*Dat* boy just doesn't know how to die."

"Let's hope that's a lesson none of us learn here today," she said.

Nodding solemnly, Lafayette headed back to the roundabout where Fix was trying to set up some kind of barricade. Michelle knew Jennings had picked this as a good location for them to rendezvous because there were so many different paths they might take from here, but it did not make her feel any better. That just meant there were so many different paths Fix and Lafayette needed to cover.

~

Captain Matthew Jennings was beginning to worry. His plan of attack had been based on being able to flee into a corridor with so many branching tunnels and passageways that he could very easily get lost. This was a brilliant plan except for the station's map neglecting to mention that many of the tunnels had collapsed, been caved in, or were otherwise impassable. Since he started running, he had been traveling in what was essentially a straight line, and it would not be difficult for Petrova's men to know exactly where he was going. Finally, he came to a fork in the pathway and took the rightmost immediately. He was already so off course that his new plan was to be as erratic as possible. Checking the map and figuring out where he was could come after he was certain he was not going to get shot in the back.

The tunnels started to show him more of what he wanted- more branches that were still open. These forks in the road never offered more than one alternate option though, and he kept picking up some kind of weird buzzing sound bouncing off the tunnel walls. It sounded distorted, but mechanical and vaguely familiar though. He turned left at another fork in the tunnel only to arrive at a dead end. Cursing loudly, he pulled up his handheld and checked his location on the map. Sure enough, he was nowhere near where he was supposed to be and would have to go back several tunnels to find a shaft that would lead him eventually to his compatriots.

Tucking the handheld back into its pouch on his belt, he drew his pistol once again. That noise was back, and this time it sounded louder. He heard the telltale roar of a hovercraft engine, and his eyes darted fervently, looking for cover. There was none to be found. His only advantage was that it was dark and his tunnel had dead-ended about fifty feet after a sharp turn. They would not see him until almost on top of him.

Moving quickly, he ran to the wall at the curve, pulled out the eight barrel rotating plasma cannon and primed it. Listening carefully, he pegged the skimmer car about two hundred feet away. One hundred feet. At fifty feet, he tensed his body and prepared to make his move. At twenty-five, he threw his body around the corner of the curve and opened up full with the weapon, its barrel rotating rapidly and spitting green fire in the general direction of the rapidly approaching skimmer. Jennings noted only a few splashes against the light shielding the skimmer carried, but he was not trying to kill anyone onboard.

Cries of surprise echoed from the two men onboard the skimmer, and the pilot wrenched the stick hard over to avoid the attack, causing the skimmer to bounce off the left-hand wall where the wall curved back to the right. The pilot tried to correct again, over-corrected as he attempted to take the curve well, bounced off the right-hand wall, then failed to fire the retrorockets as the nose of the skimmer slammed into the cave-in which had walled off the mine tunnel.

As soon as the last sickening crunch of steel and shield hitting rock sounded, Jennings was on his feet, his rifle tracking through the darkness. A slight shudder appeared in the space around the skimmer, one of the men aboard had deactivated the shields. The same man dizzily hopped out of the cockpit and then fell to the ground. The pilot's head was bleeding badly, and as Jennings moved closer, weapon still at the ready, he found the skimmer's gunner lying back in his seat, his head flopped over on his neck in a grotesque manner, suggesting his neck was broken.

"Oh God," the wounded man said as he sat up and reached for a radio comm on his chest.

"Nope." Jennings fired once hitting the henchman in the hand reaching up to the button. "I wouldn't do that."

The man cried in pain and grabbed hold of the wound with his other hand. Jennings let go of his rifle, the strap keeping it around his neck, and drew his pistol as he moved towards Petrova's wounded henchman.

"Ditch the weapon," Jennings said, indicating the pistol at the men's belt. "Slowly."

The man complied and tossed the weapon.

"What's your name?" Jennings asked.

"Li Bao."

"How many skimmers are there?" he asked.

"Blow me."

Without a moment's hesitation, Jennings redirected his pistol aim from Li's head to his knee and fired. The plasma flashed through his knee ligaments, and Li cried out in pain, his still functioning arm grabbing toward the wounded knee.

"Fuck you!" Li spat with as much venom as he could muster, drool and blood dribbling down his chin.

Jennings clubbed him across the face with the pistol, knocking him flat on his back. Li hit his head on the stone floor of the mine hard, and his eyes rolled back into his head. Kneeling down next to Li, Jennings stuck his fingers into the hole in Li's knee. Li immediately sprang back to consciousness, his core muscles tightening, causing him to burst into a sitting position. Immediately Jennings placed his pistol directly against Li's forehead while keeping his fingers in the man's knee.

"Last chance," Jennings warned.

The muscles in Li's face quaked with tremors as he gritted his teeth and tried to deal with the pain Jennings knew must be nearly unbearable. "Five more."

"Was that so hard?" Jennings asked as he removed his fingers from Li's open wound. "Now, I want to talk to your boss."

Gingerly, the man reached for his bandolier with his one still functioning arm and grabbed the comm unit, which Jennings took without taking his eyes off Li. "Ms. Petrova?" Jennings said into it.

"This is Petrova," the harsh, accented voice replied. "Tell me you have something."

"Oh, I have something all right," Jennings said. "One of your men with a gun to his head."

There was a moment's pause. "And you think that buys you something?"

"I was going to propose a trade," Jennings said.

"Nothing you have is *vorth vhat* the girl is *vorth* to me," Petrova said. "No deal."

"Just curious to see what value you placed on the lives of your own crew," Jennings said. "I wanted all of your people to know how expendable Mister… What was your name again?"

With the radio extended out to Li's mouth, the wounded man barked, "We're in the…"

Jennings fired and Li's head snapped back, his face melted by the heat of the plasma shot. "Oops," Jennings said into the radio. "Well, that's it for Mr. Li and his friend here, Ms. Petrova."

"You'll regret this, Captain Jennings," Petrova's angry voice responded after a moment's silence.

"Think so?" Jennings said as he dropped the radio onto Li's corpse and headed over to the skimmer.

The skimmer was an open-air vehicle about eight feet long with three seats, one in the front where the controls for steering and auxiliary firing control were located and two in the back with consoles for controlling the main weapons systems and the shield system. It looked vaguely like an old-fashioned motorcycle except it had two wings extending out from in between the front and rear seats and was kept in the air by repulsor lifts. Each wing carried twin plasma cannons which could be rotated by the gunners. The pilot was protected by a cone of metal and transparent hard plastic shielding that also served as the vehicle's Heads-up Display. The nose of the small craft contained a small rocket launcher.

Jennings grabbed the collar of the dead gunner and threw him out of the seat. Swinging himself up into the pilot's position, he then did a quick check on the skimmer's systems. The shields had taken a bit of a pounding from the skimmer bouncing off the walls, but they had been recharging for the last few minutes and there was no structural damage to the craft.

He connected the portable CPU into a flashport on the skimmer. "Minerva, are you connected?"

"Of course," came the NAI's reply.

"This is a minimum two-person craft, so I am going to need your help," he said.

"Do you wish me to use the weapons while you steer?" Minerva said through his earpiece.

"No, you're the one with the maps memorized, which I trust you have been updating as I have been sprinting through this maze," Jennings pointed out. "Besides, I'd rather do the shooting."

"As you wish, captain."

"Alright then. Let's cut a path to the crew," he said enthusiastically.

~

Anastasia Petrova swore so violently that Vosler took a step back from her. They still stood in the entrance to the mine, the lift directly behind them, three men in front of them crouching behind makeshift barricades between the switching station and the entranceway. The rest of her men were currently scouring the mining tunnels with skimmers, looking for the girl.

"Damn that man!" she swore. "I may kill him myself rather than give him to Santelli. The satisfaction of strangling him *vould* be *vorth* foregoing the profit."

"At your discretion," Vosler said. "But I'm going to have to insist you head back to the ore processing center."

"*Vhat?*"

"Jennings is coming for us," he said. "I can capture or kill him, but I can't do so and protect you at the same time."

"*Vhat* makes you think I need protection?" she asked.

Vosler braced himself for the tongue lashing he was about to receive. "Anastasia, you are fiercely brave and no one doubts your… tenacity." He cleared his throat slightly. "But you're not a soldier. This is not a criminal who might fire a few potshots in your direction.

Jennings was a military officer and one of the finest ones I have ever seen in action."

"You fought *vith* him?" Petrova asked, her brow furrowing.

"In the war," Vosler said with a slight nod. "Now, I have to kill him. And you need to head up the lift."

Petrova crossed her arms and turned back to one of the men manning the barricade. "*Vhat's* the status of our skimmers?"

One man turned to her. "They are making fast work of exploring the tunnels even with one down- should find the girl soon."

"Very *vell*," she said as she walked past Vosler and into the lift. She turned on her heel as the steel gates clanged shut in front of her and locked eyes on her subordinate. "Keep me apprised."

~

Michelle swiveled on her stool nervously and watched her two defenders continuing to work to make their position more defensible. They managed to pull the wooden bar to block one tunnel and dragged over several mine carts to serve as cover if Petrova's men came out of the tunnels to their right. The tunnel behind them went deep into the mine, and there was no way for Petrova's men to get there without going through the cavern in which they now stood. It also served as their only escape egress if their position got overrun.

A strange thrum like an engine revving caught her attention, and she looked over to the others to see if they heard it. Fix glanced up from where he was checking the charge on an automatic plasma rifle with a long clip and a secondary handle for his off-hand.

"Which one?" he asked of no one in particular as he readied the weapon and started pointing it toward the different tunnels.

"Hard to tell," Lafayette muttered as he set down the sandwich he had somehow made out of the rations they brought with them. Grabbing his own rifle, he primed the charge on it and started tracking from tunnel opening to tunnel opening.

"What is it?" Michelle asked.

"Get behind the barricade!" Lafayette ordered as he took up position behind the bar.

Michelle grabbed the small pistol Jennings had given her and yanked it out of her belt as she did as she was told.

"You've got to prime it," Fix said next to her as he set down the rifle and picked up a pump-action plasma cannon that fired explosive rounds. "Button on the back. Might want to take the safety off too."

She flicked the button that turned the safety off and pressed her thumb on the primer. The gun felt alive in her hands as it powered up, emitting a soft whirring noise as it did so.

"Skimmers, you think?" Lafayette asked Fix.

"Aye."

"Venture 2600 DXCs," Squawk said as he too took cover behind the bar, his own rifle looking strange and out of place in his hands.

"They have shields?" Lafayette asked before interjecting, "Wait, you can tell what kind they are just from the sound?"

"Yes. Yes."

"Nae good," Fix muttered.

Michelle threw a look to the large, black maw behind them. "Do we head down the escape tunnel?"

"If they have skimmers, we'll never outrun them," Lafayette said as he tightened the grip on his gun. "Get ready. Here they come."

~

Jennings depressed the trigger and sent a plume of blue energy racing down the tunnel ahead of him. "Minerva! Go evasive!" he shouted as he saw a missile streaking in his direction.

Minerva, who Jennings had given full control of the steering to, sent the skimmer banking around the circular tunnel's walls as they continued speeding recklessly toward one of Petrova's skimmers. The missile rushed past as Minerva sent the skimmer barrel rolling around around the ceiling and back to the floor, Jennings firing the entire time.

The skimmers continued racing at each other, both firing, both sets of shields holding, and Jennings found his lips forming a grim smile. "Hold course, Minerva."

"This is unwise," came the reply in his ear.

"Hold course!"

"I calculate only a forty-seven percent chance of this succeeding," she said calmly. "Five seconds to impact."

Petrova's men swerved to avoid the impact, trying to pass him by climbing the wall. Jennings quickly redirected his shields so all power was directed precisely at the enemy skimmer. The shields of the two vessels smashed off each other, and the enemy skimmer bounced awkwardly into the wall, smashed into the roof of the cavern, and then rolled over several times, its repulsors failing, before it crashed into the ground and exploded.

"Nicely done," Minerva's voice said in his ear.

"Nice driving," he said. "How did you know we could turn this thing upside down like that?"

"I calculated a sixty-seven percent chance based on the craft's specifications, the local gravity, and the velocity at which we were traveling," Minerva said calmly.

Those odds did not thrill Jennings. "That's reassuring. We need to get to the…"

Jennings was interrupted by a salvo of fire coming from the right-hand most of several tunnels in another interchange. Two more skimmers raced out from that tunnel, and Minerva accelerated their skimmer down a new corridor as his sensors confirmed the skimmers were following him. More fire splashed off his shields, and he checked their power: forty-two percent and falling. He would not last much longer.

The tunnel Minerva guided them down had a lot of curves and a lot of intersections, so they were able to keep far enough ahead of the enemy skimmers to prevent them from getting a missile lock. Jennings could not lead them on a merry chase forever, however. Sooner or later, he would run into a dead-end or get splashed. And besides, he was supposed to be making his way back to the others to help them out.

"Minerva, do you have any idea where you are taking us?" he asked as the shields took another hit and she turned the skimmer hard to the right followed by an immediate left.

"I am attempting to navigate a circuitous route so we might lose our trails, but this has only a twenty-two percent chance of succeeding," she said.

"Great," Jennings muttered.

"There is more bad news," she said as the skimmer dove into a downward sloping tunnel and then swung to the left.

"This gets worse?" he asked, his tone laced with sarcasm.

Another blast from behind stole his attention for a moment, so he did not hear Minerva's response. He activated the rear camera on his HUD and swiveled the cannons so they were facing aft. He fired some scattering shots, hoping to slow down his pursuers, but he did not hit much. It was hard to target when he was not in control of the direction the skimmer was going.

"Say again, Minerva," he said as they swerved once more and he lost sight of his targets.

"I calculated the longest possible variable route, but we are about to encounter several problems," she said.

"What problems?"

"In sixty-two seconds, we will enter a long straightaway," she said. "Our pursuers will have almost a full minute with which to attack us."

"We won't survive that," he pointed out.

"There are no alternatives," she said. "Also, the straightaway leads directly to where Angus Ferguson, Remy Lafayette, Michelle Williams, and Squawk are hiding."

Jennings swore. "So, I'm about to die and I'm leading the enemy to my crew? Wonderful."

"Entering straightaway in fifteen seconds," Minerva said, her voice sounding too sweet for Jennings's liking.

The skimmer shot into the straightaway, a long tunnel whose end Jennings could not see. He knew he would only have a few moments before Petrova's men had a clear shot at him. His shields were no longer strong enough to survive even a few more solid blasts of plasma cannon fire, let alone a direct shot from a rocket. No sooner had that thought passed through his mind than Jennings thought to his own rockets in the nose of the skimmer. Without enough time to wheel about and fire, he decided he might have enough to throw up a road block. Switching the targeting on the rockets to manual, he aimed the launcher at the ceiling just as Petrova's skimmers roared into the tunnel behind him. Jennings fired, and the rockets detonated just in front of him in the ceiling. As the skimmer shot past the falling debris, he fired again and again until the rocket launcher was empty.

The rear-view display on his HUD showed the tunnel ceiling collapsing in a pile of rocks, timber and dust. Two fireballs joined the collapse a moment later as Petrova's two skimmers crashed into the rubble.

"That worked out rather nicely," Jennings said.

"Against all probabilities," Minerva said.

"All right, let's get the rest of the crew and get the hell out of here," he said. "Petrova's got to be running short of bad guys by now."

~

The first skimmer sent a missile into their cavern before it was even in sight, sailing well above Michelle's head and detonating against the far wall, but still managing to shower all of them with bits of rock, forcing them to duck their heads behind the bar. Before they were able to bring their weapons back up in a defensive position, two skimmers were in the room, hovering side-by-side in a tunnel egress, and a second rocket blew apart the roof of the tunnel that was supposed to be their escape route, causing a cave-in.

Fix was the first to open fire, sending explosive rounds into the shields of the nearest skimmer. The blasts knocked the shields out, and Lafayette opened fire with his rifle, taking down two of the three men in the skimmer. The third man jumped out of the way and threw his body behind the skimmer, using it for cover, as the driver of the second skimmer moved his vehicle in between them, allowing its shields to cover him.

The gunner on the second skimmer opened fire at the barricade, targeting Fix. The skimmer had enough firepower to rip through the entire barricade easily, but Michelle supposed they were holding back as they were specifically trying to take her alive. Fix rolled down to a new location behind the bar, leapt up and fired. His move had been anticipated by the skimmer gunner, and a blast of energy tore the barricade up in front of Fix, who was thrown backward, his weapon clattering on the ground.

"Fix!" Lafayette roared.

Leaping to his feet, he poured fire into the second skimmer's shields, screaming curses in French. He did not notice in time the lone survivor from the first skimmer jump to his feet and lob a cylindrical metallic object over the barricade. Michelle called out a warning as she tried to move toward where Fix lay, but her cries were subsumed in the firefight. As the object tumbled in the air toward them, Lafayette drew a bead on the man who threw it and blasted him backwards.

The cylinder clanged off the floor followed by a light so bright that Michelle could no longer see anything, even after the light faded. She smelled something noxious and began coughing violently. Lafayette and the Pasquatil began doing the same.

Michelle heard the sound of boots falling on rocks near her, and she clumsily held the pistol, desperate for her vision to return and give her a target to shoot at. The sound of a single shot rang out, and Lafayette cried out in pain and fell to the ground. It was followed up by the sound of a boot meeting a small body and the slamming of someone into the barrier they had erected. Squawk let out a whimper, and Michelle let loose a roar of fury. It almost instantly died in her throat as she felt something hard and heavy come down on her head, and everything went black.

~

Matthew Jennings emerged from the straightaway tunnel into the crossroads where he had ordered his crew to meet him, and his heart immediately seized in his throat. One of the tunnels was collapsed, the bar that had been used as a barricade had been shot to pieces, smoke still hung in the air, and two bodies lay behind the barricades. He leapt off the skimmer and raced over to Fix, who was the nearest.

"Fix?" he asked as he fell to his knees.

"They got her, Cap'n," he said weakly, blinking some blood out of his eyes. "Go get her."

"What about you?" Jennings asked.

"Mild concussion and a few cuts," he said. "Be fine once the room stops spinning."

"Marquis?" Jennings demanded, throwing a look through the smoke to his first mate.

"Shot and bleeding," came a weak, squeaky voice he recognized as Squawk's.

Jennings left Fix and raced over to where Squawk hovered over Lafayette. "*Merde*, it hurts, *mon capitaine*," Lafayette said. "But it's just my shoulder. Fix is right. Go get the girl, *mon ami*. We'll be right behind you."

Nodding, Jennings spun about and raced back to the skimmer, leapt into the pilot's seat, and ordered Minerva to take him to the mine entrance as quickly as possible. Jennings rocketed past an abandoned skimmer he assumed belonged to the three dead men who lay around it.

"Minerva, I need a time to target," Jennings said as the skimmer accelerated down the tunnel and he started tapping furiously on the weapons console.

"Two minutes nineteen seconds," she said. "There is a high statistical probability that a rear guard would have been left in the mine entranceway."

"Well aware of that, Minerva."

The NAI's voice remained calm, but added a tone of curiosity. "May I ask your intent?"

"I'm turning this into a bomb," he said as he continued the process of setting the skimmer's plasma cannons to overload.

"One minute thirty seconds," Minerva advised as they rounded a corner and the tunnel turned into a straightaway and headed in an upward trajectory. Jennings continued to work. "Forty-five seconds."

"Got it," he said just before they emerged from the tunnel into the mine entrance.

Three men waited behind cover, and they immediately opened fire on him. His shields were still strong enough, although barely, to fend off the attack. There was no sign of Michelle or anyone else in the entrance as Jennings raced toward Petrova's men. At the last moment, he flicked a button that dropped his shields and threw himself off the back of the skimmer. His body bounced and rolled across the cavern floor just as the skimmer crashed into the bounty hunters' cover and the weapons system overloaded. The explosion threw all three men back into the cavern wall in a varying number of pieces. The force of the blast pushed Jennings across the floor until he slammed into the far wall, his breath knocked out of him.

Moving slowly, he pulled himself to his feet and forced himself over to the lift. The large elevator was still moving upwards, lumbering slowly. Michelle might still be on it, he thought to himself. It had taken a few minutes for their descent into the mine- he might still have time.

*To do what?* he wondered to himself. Glancing around desperately, he spied the second cavern, where the conveyor belt which ran from the mine to the ore processing center was. Moving as fast as possible with the numerous bruises, aches, and pains plaguing his body, Jennings made it to the room and hit a green button in a console next to an upward sloping tunnel with a conveyor belt. The conveyor roared to life, and Jennings let loose a cry of triumph as he jumped onto it.

~

Vosler was extremely thankful this job was over. They had lost dozens of men, thousands of dollars' worth of equipment, and he was pretty certain Petrova was about to lose it. The semi-conscious Michelle Williams hung slumped in between two tall bounty hunters carrying her. *She had better be worth it,* he thought to himself.

"Vosler to Petrova," he said into his comm.

"Go ahead."

"We have the girl," he said. "We're in the lift, about to exit now."

"I had to head back..." she began, but was interrupted by the chime of the elevator arriving at the ore processing station and the door sliding open.

"Surprise, motherfucker!" Jennings shouted as he opened fire with the eight-barrel plasma cannon he carried.

~

No one else had a chance to react as Jennings poured fire into the elevator, keeping the stream of plasma bolts at a height that would not hit Michelle. In just a few moments, all of Petrova's men were dead except her lieutenant, who had been hit in his chest armor and in his exposed arm and shoulder. The impact of the blast sent him flying into the back of the lift, and he slammed his head against the metal wall. Thinking he recognized the lieutenant from somewhere, Jennings walked into the elevator and picked up the now stirring Michelle Williams.

"What happened?" Michelle asked.

"You're all right. I got you," Jennings said as he put his head under her shoulder and helped lift her to her feet. "Let's get you back on the *Tryst,* and then I got to go back for..."

A blast from the other end of the hallway struck Jennings in the gut, punching through his body armor. He fell to his knees, Michelle slipping from his grasp and hitting the floor as well. Anastasia Petrova strode forward, a small plasma pistol in her hand, her eyes cold and murderous.

"Was that really necessary?" General Dominic Ounimbango growled as he strode around the corner of the hallway at the end of the corridor. A dozen TGF soldiers accompanied him. "He did not offer any threat."

Petrova laughed darkly. "I'm done underestimating when Mr. Jennings does or does not offer a threat."

Ounimbango shrugged as she stepped forward and removed all of Jennings's weapons, tossing them back in the direction of the general. Ounimbango gestured to two of the soldiers with him to pick them up. Petrova strode away from the groaning and writhing Jennings and walked into the lift. She studied the bodies on the floor for a moment before offering her hand to her lieutenant, who took it and was pulled to his feet.

"My man Vosler needs medical attention," Petrova said to Ounimbango.

"And we shall provide it." Overseer Pahhal swept in from behind the TGF forces, his robes flowing. His dark eyes bore into Petrova. "We would do the same for all our prisoners."

"What?" Petrova and Ounimbango demanded simultaneously.

"Take Madame Petrova and her associate into custody," Pahhal ordered one of the TGF soldiers. "And Ms. Williams as well, of course."

"On *vhat* charge are you arresting me?" Petrova demanded hotly.

"I must protest," Ounimbango said.

"If you must, then you may join her in a cell," Pahhal said darkly as he glared at the general.

Ounimbango immediately began sweating, and he turned back to his men. "Take those three into custody."

Reluctantly, Petrova dropped her weapon and placed her hands behind her back as did Vosler. Binders were placed on both their hands, and they were marched away by a trio of soldiers. Michelle still appeared to be woozy, so although her hands were bound, she was half-carried by her captors out of the hallway. Jennings was now powerless to help her.

"Make sure you arrest the remainder of Petrova's crew," Pahhal ordered Ounimbango, who was already turning to leave. "We'll take her ship as well. I don't want any evidence of this operation left behind."

"It won't fit in the bays of our runabout," Ounimbango said uncertainly.

*Perhaps the newfound rancor from the Gael and the talk of eliminating evidence had the general nervous,* Jennings thought. Ounimbango was not exactly known for his steel spine.

"Then tow it," Pahhal snapped.

Ounimbango nodded, turned on his heel, and then left. A small smile crossed the Gael's face, and he took long, deliberate strides toward where Jennings still lay on the floor, his blood pooling under him. Both Jennings's hands clutched his stomach, and his face had turned white. His eyes stared straight at Pahhal, and they conveyed a pure loathing for the Gael.

"I wish I could say I was sorry it ended this way," Pahhal said. "But that is the price of betraying me."

Jennings spat at him.

Pahhal laughed. "Such an indomitable spirit. It's what I have always admired about some of your species. That ability to fight against impossible odds, to stare death in the face and laugh. Under different circumstances, I would have liked the Gael to be allies to the humans."

"Then, why…" Jennings rasped.

"That's a long story," Pahhal said. "And unfortunately, you don't have the time. But I am willing to forgive your little betrayal, because I can't help but like you, Mr. Jennings."

"Captain Jennings," he retorted weakly.

Pahhal laughed. "Yes, this is exactly what I mean." He clapped his long-fingered hands together. "As I like you so much, I will not shoot you in the head right now. I have ordered General Ounimbango's men to destroy the life support system of this little mine here. I would say you have a few hours of breathable air left. Why not try to live that long at least? Can you do that? Can you stop yourself from bleeding to death so you can suffocate? Can you laugh in the face of death now?"

Jennings smiled weakly. "Be seein' you."

~

Overseer Pahhal gave a final derisive chuckle to Jennings and turned away with a sweep of his robes. He walked down the corridor, following the path Ounimbango and his prisoners had taken, headed out to the Terran Gael Force runabout. More importantly, it was the same way the one hundred and eleventh soul had been taken. *The one hundred eleventh soul*, he repeated in his own mind. *At last, he finally had her*, he thought to himself. They were all going home.

## Chapter 23

Fix did not often consider himself lucky, but he supposed it was maybe time to start changing his opinion. Petrova's skimmer had sent at least a dozen shots into his position hiding behind the bar they had repurposed as a barricade. The shots splintered and ripped through where he had been positioned and somehow the only things that happened to him were a ton of cuts from flying debris and a bulbous knot forming on the back of his head where he smacked the ground as he landed. How he did not actually get shot he had no idea, but he was willing to chalk it up as some sort of divine intervention.

Just as Jennings went speeding off down the tunnel in pursuit of the girl, Fix managed to pull himself to his feet and staggered over to his pack of supplies buried under a fine layer of dust and rock. Opening the pack, he pulled out his black medical kit and pulled the zipper. He snapped open a small pill bottle labeled omniox, removed a small purple pill, and swallowed it. Omniox was a drug developed for professional sports teams and the military to deal with head injuries. Almost immediately, he felt his head clearing, and he carried the pack over to where Squawk and Lafayette lay.

"Any damage?" he asked the Pasquatil.

"Hurts," Squawk said. "But systems are operating."

"Right." After rummaging in his medical kit, Fix handed him an orange pill. "Safe for Pasquatil."

As Squawk devoured the pill, Fix evaluated the wound to Lafayette's shoulder. The plasma had burned through the flesh of Lafayette's left upper arm and exited, leaving two holes in the Cajun's arm. Removing an aerosol can from his kit, he sprayed a pink foam onto both wounds.

"How bad is it?" Lafayette asked.

"Platelet foam will help close the wound. Once we're back on the *Tryst*, I might need to get you a transfusion." The medic handed him a pill of his own. "Perimescaline. For the pain."

Lafayette swallowed the pill and allowed Fix to help to his feet. "Get our supplies, Fix. I'll check out the other skimmer. C'mon Squawk."

~

With some movement abilities coming back to his arm, Lafayette pulled himself into the pilot seat of the skimmer Petrova's men had left behind as Squawk hopped into the back and started typing furiously into his display. The skimmer's shields were completely gone, but the engines and the repulsors functioned perfectly.

"Squawk, can you do anything about the shields?" Lafayette asked as Fix arrived and jumped into the seat next to Squawk, carrying two packs which contained their supplies.

"No tools. No time. No time. No tools," the Pasquatil said quickly. Apparently whatever Fix had given him had him feeling good enough to start talking a mile a minute again.

"All right, we'll just have to hope *le capitaine* cleared the road for us," Lafayette said.

A press of a few buttons later, Lafayette had the skimmer's repulsors engaged and its engines rumbling. He throttled up, and the skimmer took off down the corridor, not at the breakneck speed Minerva had been able to do for Jennings, but still as fast as he dared. They had taken out a few of Petrova's men, and he would have bet Jennings killed a good many more, but the captain had still gone after the girl by himself. He would need their help; Lafayette was certain of it.

About ten minutes later, they arrived in the entrance to the mine, and Lafayette took a moment to observe the destruction. A fire still burned in the center of the room, and the burned-out hulk of a skimmer lay on its side amidst a pile of debris that had been a bunch of mine carts.

The Cajun gave a whistle. "Looks like *le capitaine's* work."

"Aye," Fix agreed as he swung out of his seat and grabbed the supplies. "But where the bloody hell is he?"

"Must be top-side," Lafayette said as he jumped out of the skimmer's pilot seat and headed through the entranceway and over toward the lift.

Squawk bounded past him, hopped over some debris, and then jumped up and pressed the button to call for the lift. They waited for several minutes, seemingly an interminable length of time, but Lafayette and Fix both busied themselves with readying weapons, just in case Petrova had left them any surprises in the lift. The elevator at last arrived, its chime warbled as if damaged in some way. The doors swung open and the lift was empty of living beings. Several dead bodies lay inside, riddled about the head and face with plasma burns. *More of Jennings's handiwork*, Lafayette thought to himself as they piled inside and Squawk hit the button to send them to the ore processing center.

"Minerva, are you there?" Lafayette asked after activating the link to ship's NAI on his handheld.

"Of course," came the voice, and Lafayette would have sworn Minerva sounded worried.

"Is there something... wrong?" he asked her.

"Captain Jennings... I think he might be dying."

Fear gripped Lafayette, and he tightened his grip around his weapon. "Where is he, Minerva?"

"In the corridor outside of the elevator."

Lafayette and Fix both brought their weapons to bear. "Is he alone?" Lafayette asked.

"Affirmative. The others have left the ore processing center. Both ships have left the moon."

"Both?" Lafayette echoed.

"A TGF runabout-class vessel landed approximately twenty-two minutes ago," she said. "It took off one minute ago with the *Grey Vistula* in tow."

Lafayette kicked at the doors of the elevator. "*Plus vite!*" he raged at the machine.

At long last, the lift reached the ore processing station and the doors opened. Captain Jennings lay in an otherwise empty hallway, a pool of blood underneath him. All three of his crew raced forward and fell to their knees around him, Fix immediately taking out his medical kit.

"Fucking Russian bitch shot me," Jennings said, his voice hoarse. "Again."

"Hang on, Cap'n," Fix said as he and Lafayette studied the wound for a moment.

The shot must have been some sort of armor-piercing round as it had burned a hole though the armor and punched a hole in Jennings's left side, Lafayette thought. There was no exit wound, but shots to the torso were not shots to the arm or leg. Where the shot went in, Jennings would almost certainly have massive trauma to his left kidney. That was not the sort of thing that could be repaired without surgery.

"First things first," Fix said. "We need to keep the captain from bleeding to death."

The medic pulled out the same aerosol can he had used to treat Lafayette's wound. Fix sprayed the wound full of a bio-engineered substance designed to facilitate the rebuilding of human tissue while binding it together, specifically the body's capillaries, veins and arteries. Lafayette had seen enough wounded soldiers in the war to know it was effective at covering up holes in organs, but not at repairing them.

"They took Michelle," Jennings managed as Fix pulled out a large syringe and a vial and started filling it. "Ounimbango was here and so was the Gael."

"Minerva told us," Lafayette said. "I'm sorry we couldn't stop them."

Jennings waived away his apology. "Gotta hurry. The Gael ordered the TGF to destroy the life support system."

"Minerva?" Lafayette asked.

"Confirmed," the ship's computer said. "My link to the mining station's computer advised that the life support system was destroyed eleven minutes ago. Three hours and forty-eight minutes until oxygen levels drop below requirement for minimum human living."

"Got to get the captain back to the ship," Fix said as he injected the needle into Jennings's arm. "Pure adrenaline. Should help you walk."

"*Mon Dieu*, he can't walk," Lafayette protested. "We'll carry him."

"No," Jennings said sternly. "Fix is right. You and Squawk need to complete the repairs on the *Tryst*. If she's not ready to go in the next three and a half hours, all of us will be dead."

Gingerly, Jennings allowed Fix and Lafayette to pull him to his feet. The effects of the adrenaline were almost immediate and Lafayette would have sworn the captain looked better. Jennings allowed Fix to put his head under his arm, and the two started walking slowly down the hallway.

"C'mon, Squawk," Lafayette said. "We need to get *dat* power plant installed."

~

The Cajun and the diminutive Pasquatil raced back through the ore processing center as fast as possible, given the extent of their injuries. Lafayette was glad to find the auxiliary power plant in one piece, afraid the Gael might have thought to destroy it as well. Perhaps they assumed the *Melody Tryst* was damaged beyond repair, or they did not have an engineer with an instinctive ability to turn duct tape and matchsticks into a working power system.

It was a lot harder to get the bulky piece of machinery onto the anti-grav sled with Squawk's limited help as opposed to Fix, but after about five minutes of wrestling it, Lafayette got it into place. Activating the controls on the sled, he sent the power plant on a slow wend through the ore processing center in the direction of the hangar.

"You're certain you can install this thing in time?" Lafayette asked.

Squawk chattered animatedly to himself in his own language for a moment before he said, "As long as no complications complicate things, yes. Yes."

Five minutes later they had the sled making its way up the ramp and they stepped back into the ship. "Fix, we're back onboard," Lafayette called up the gangplank.

"Aye," was the only response he received from the upper level.

"*Vite, vite,* let's get this to the engineering section," he said to Squawk, who immediately bounded in the direction of engineering.

In the short time it took Lafayette to power the anti-grav sled from the cargo hold to engineering, Squawk had put on his engineering coveralls again, wrapped a tool belt on his waste, and thrown two bandoliers containing pockets with various parts, pieces, and components over his shoulders.

The engineering section was small and cramped with the rear of the compartment completely dominated by the solid steel bulkhead with a door set in it which separated the room from the actual engine. The engines had been off for hours, so it would have been safe to go into their control room on the other side, but that would be fatal to anyone if the engines had been operating recently.

"Are you sure the engines are all right?" he asked.

Squawk stared at him. "The overload caused an electronic pulse to be sent to the power plant, which caused a critical and inevitable destruction in the plant. The engines themselves were not harmed. Probably."

"A lot riding on probably," he pointed out.

"No power. No engines. That is certain," Squawk retorted in a staccato fashion.

"*Mon Dieu, nous aidez-vous s'il vous plait,*" Lafayette prayed. "Where do you want the power plant?"

"Here," Squawk pointed at a spot on the floor. "No time to install it as the primary. Will need to run it through the old system. Yes. Yes. Yes."

Lafayette wrestled the power plant into the position Squawk requested, and the tiny engineer immediately used a bolt gun to lock it into position. He then turned to dismantling both the *Melody Tryst's* failed power plant and the new one and began ripping the guts out in a haphazard way. Were it anyone else, Lafayette would have assumed the Pasquatil did not know what he was doing, but he knew better.

"What do you need me to do?" he asked as the Pasquatil began cutting the protective sheath off various wires and tying their ends into each other.

"Wiring," Squawk said. "The wings. System shot for controlling weapons. Communication system won't communicate."

"You said we don't have the components," he pointed out.

"Look. Look. Look."

"Fine," Lafayette said. "I'll check on *le capitaine* and then see what I can find."

Leaving engineering to the happy sounds of the Pasquatil whistling contentedly as he banged a sledge hammer on something, Lafayette hustled up the gangplank and made his way to the medbay. The captain lay on the one surgical table, a unit of saline and one of blood being run into him via intravenous lines. Fix was studying a three-dimensional picture on the holo-imager and shaking his head.

"What is it?" Lafayette asked the medic.

"Cap'n's a lucky son of a bitch."

"I don't know if I'd call losing a kidney in the war necessarily lucky," a stronger sounding Jennings said.

"You'd probably be dead if you had one now," Fix said. "Russian bitch shot you right where your kidney should have been."

Lafayette's concern was not assuaged. "So, what does that mean?"

"Apart from the blood loss, Cap'n's in good shape," Fix said. "Gave him some antibiotics to prevent infection, but otherwise..." He shrugged. "Once the blood transfusion is done, he should be fine. The cell sealant I injected in him has repaired the damage to the capillaries, and he is no longer bleeding internally. A few more hours, and he'll be fine."

"How's the ship?" Jennings asked.

Lafayette made a non-committal noise. "Squawk's installing the power plant, but we still have no weapons and no comms. I'm going to search around the hangar and see if I can find some wiring we might use to replace ours that shorted out, but I don't know if I'll find anything."

"Weapons first, Marquis," Jennings said. "And start thinking of a way to disguise our ship to sensors."

Lafayette blinked in confusion. "Why?"

Fix eyed the captain wearily. "The girl."

"You want us to go after her?" Lafayette's tone was incredulous. "All due respect, *mon capitaine*, but *dat* is insane. The *Tryst* is on her last legs, and we'll be lucky to be able to get her to a safe port for some real repairs; no one among the crew isn't wounded; and by the time we get off this rock, assuming we can, the Gael will have a four-hour head start or so. And you're talking about going after her?"

"Do you remember the first thing I said to you when I took command of our platoon, Remy?" Jennings asked.

Grimacing but nodding, Lafayette said, "*Oui*. You told us you wouldn't fail us."

"I failed her," he said.

Lafayette crossed his arms. "You did everything *dat* you could. Dying for her won't do anything to help her."

"I have to try," Jennings said. "I can't leave her at the hands of the Gael. You know I would do it for any of you."

Fix and Lafayette exchanged a glance. His back to Jennings, Fix held up a needle which Lafayette assumed was full of a sedative. The first mate gave a quick shake of his head, and Fix shrugged, putting the drug back into his medical cabinet. Lafayette looked back to the captain, who was still pale, but whose eyes were filled with stoic resolve. Lafayette's options were not many: he could betray the order of his captain and lose a friend (and maybe his life depending on how angry that made Jennings), or he could listen to the man who had guided him through more than one narrow scrape over the course of all the years he had known him. The thought of saving the girl never entered into his mind. His decision all came down to whether or not he trusted the captain and whether or not he would do for his friend what Jennings would have been willing to do for him. There was no decision to make in the end.

"*Merde.*" Shaking his head, Lafayette said, "I can't believe I'm about to say *dis*, but I hope you have an *incroyable* plan, *mon capitaine*."

"You might start with those canisters of core samples I saw on the way back to the ship," Jennings said. "Might be full of moon dust."

Pondering that for a moment, Lafayette was not certain what Jennings meant. The core samples were probably just shattered rock, silt and dust, no different from any other lifeless lump of rock that passed for a moon, an asteroid, a meteor, or a comet. The realization struck him suddenly, and he could not help but allow himself a smile.

"You are a crafty *lapin, mon capitaine*," he said with genuine awe. "*Dat* might actually work."

"If it doesn't, we probably won't live long enough to rue it," he replied with a wry grin.

~

Two hours later, Jennings was gingerly back on his feet, thanking Fix and singing the praises of modern medicine. Lafayette had finished installing cans of rock dust onto the ship and rigged them to release on a signal from the bridge, so the captain sent him to take his turn on the table to get a fresh transfer of blood. The Cajun insisted he was fine, but while Fix was short on words and never really seemed to care too much about what was going on, he was strangely and persistently stubborn when it came to insisting on his recommended medical treatments.

While the captain recuperated, Squawk had finished jury rigging the mining station's power plant into the *Melody Tryst*, and Jennings saw an insane number of wires, cables, and conduits running from the stolen power plant into the ship's now defunct one when he inspected the situation. His engineer was busy chattering animatedly and punching commands into a diagnostic computer, testing that the modifications he had made to the crippled unit would allow it to function as an intermediary between the working plant and the ship's systems.

"Almost ready?" he asked Squawk from where he stood in the doorway to engineering.

"Tests have finished testing," he said with a tired salute. "Power will drop in the transfer, but the engines will work."

"What about weapons? Communications? Shields?" he asked.

"Time, more time," Squawk answered tiredly as he pushed a series of buttons on his engineering console and the *Melody Tryst's* engines sputtered and then roared to life.

"You're bloody brilliant, Squawk, you know that?" A sense of joy and relief surged through Jennings with the ship's engines running again. "Not to throw more work at you, but Marquis found some electrical cabling. It has seen better days, but it might give us some weapons or comms."

Squawk whistled sadly, the Pasquatil equivalent of a sigh. "Do what I can, do what I can."

"You're going to have to do it in space though," he said. "We don't have time to stick around and make more repairs."

"Life support will support life," Squawk said, clearly confused. "Don't need station's life support. We can stay and repair."

"We're over two hours behind Michelle and the TGF forces that took her," he said.

"The girl," Squawk said. "Aye, aye, captain."

Turning to leave and head up to the bridge, Jennings called, "I'll send Lafayette to help you as soon as I can."

Leaving engineering, Jennings walked briskly across the cargo bay, an odd sensation in his side coming from the bio-engineered adhesive holding his insides together while expediting the healing process. Stepping past the cables Lafayette had managed to salvage from a derelict and damaged cargo shuttle, he headed up the gangplank in the direction of the bridge.

"Minerva, are you online?" he asked as he walked into the bridge.

"Standing by, captain. It is nice to see you walking around again."

"Don't get used to it," he said as he sat in the captain's chair. "I'm about to do something stupid again that will likely get us all killed."

"Charming," Minerva said.

"Do you have a reading on the TGF runabout that took Michelle?" he asked.

"Not any longer," she said. "The TGF runabout left sensor range approximately one hour forty-seven minutes ago."

"But you can hack into the military channels and find out where they are taking her or at least find out where Ounimbango's ship is," he pointed out.

"With no communication systems available, I cannot access the Nucleus and therefore cannot make any effort toward that endeavor," she reported.

"Good point," Jennings admitted, somewhat dejected. They could not go after Michelle if they did not know where she was or where she was going.

"I can, of course, give you probabilities based on their attitude and trajectory at the time they left sensor range," she said. "Based on all available information, there is a sixty-three percent chance the *TGFS Intrepid*, flagship for General Ounimbango, is still located at Barnard's VI."

A smile crossed Jennings's face. "Minerva, I could kiss you."

"You could."

*Why would they wait at Barnard's VI though, and why did the TGF just bring a runabout to come after the girl? A TGF cruiser had a more powerful FTL engine and would have been able to get here faster than the runabout,* Jennings mused. The captain peeked over his shoulder to make sure Lafayette was not around and then moved over to the navigator's seat.

"Should you not leave the calculations to Monsieur Lafayette?" Minerva asked.

"I'm not calculating our course," he said. "I'm curious about theirs…"

His voice trailed off as Magellan spit out the telemetry for traveling between the asteroid they were on and Barnard's VI. Now, he understood why they took the runabout. The positions of the asteroid and the current location of the carrier would have entailed jumping around a lot of planetary bodies. Although the TGF carrier would be faster if it could travel in a straight line, it was less maneuverable and was far more likely to have to make multiple FTL jumps in order to navigate to the asteroid. Bigger ships needed a longer recharge time on their engines with each FTL jump. The runabout would be able to take a shorter, less circuitous route, and it would have shorter recharge times on its jumps.

"Minerva, talk to Magellan and show me what the likeliest course the TGF runabout is taking," he said. "Assume Barnard's VI as a final destination."

"Of course." After a moment, data appeared on the screen and she said, "Magellan is now displaying the most likely course, a seventy-two percent chance."

"Time to Barnard's VI, based on that course?"

"Six hours thirty-nine minutes," she said.

"*Sacre bleu!*" Lafayette exclaimed. "*Qu'est-ce que faisez-vous?*"

Jennings jumped out of the navigator's seat and into his own. He flashed an apologetic smile at Lafayette and held up his hands. "I swear I wasn't programming any jump coordinates."

Lafayette sank into his seat. "What were you doing?"

"Trying to figure out what way Ounimbango went," he said. "So you can get us ahead of them."

"We're not that much smaller than that runabout," Lafayette mused as he punched commands into Magellan. "I don't see how we're going to find that much quicker of a route." After another few minutes of tapping, he shook his head. "Sorry, *mon capitaine. Pas possible.*"

"Minerva," Jennings said. "Lay in the other possible routes for the runabout to have taken."

"I cannot comply," the NAI said. "Magellan safety protocols eliminate the third highest probability."

Jennings glanced at Lafayette. "Override the safety protocol, I want to see this."

"Not a good idea, *mon capitaine.*" Despite the protest, Lafayette did as he was ordered.

A much straighter course appeared on Magellan's screen. "Time of that route, Minerva?" Jennings asked.

"Three hours thirty-seven minutes."

"All right then," Jennings said as he strapped into his chair.

"*Mon capitaine, pas possible!*" Lafayette protested.

"Squawk!" Jennings barked into the intercom. "Engines warmed up?"

"Engines are hot," came the excited reply.

"Fix! Get up to the bridge or buckle in!" Jennings warned as he started pressing buttons on his console.

"En route," Fix said.

"Minerva, depressurize the hangar," Jennings said as Fix came in and grabbed a seat next to Jennings. "Engaging repulsors. Repulsors functioning. Everyone strapped in?" He received affirmations from all the crew on the bridge and Squawk, who was probably strapped into his small chair bolted to the wall of the engineering section. "C'mon, darling..." Jennings laid a hand on the console in front of him, speaking directly to the *Melody Tryst*. "Show me what you've got."

He engaged the aft thrusters, and the *Melody Tryst* started forward slowly until she cleared the hangar. Jennings then pulled back on the stick while engaging the sublight engines. The ship shot forward with ease without any atmosphere to overcome, and a brief sense of acceleration quickened his blood before the inertial dampeners kicked in. Jennings studied his readouts for the engine functionality for a moment: they were green. Immediately, he started charging the FTL engine.

"Lafayette, are you ready?" he asked.

"*Mon capitaine,* you are going to get us killed," Lafayette protested.

"Not if we get the shields repaired in time," he said.

"Chance of succeeding is thirty-three percent with the assumption of shields being fully restored," Minerva chimed in.

"See," Jennings said, clapping Lafayette on the shoulder. "Minerva says we'll be fine."

"*Dat's* not what she said," Lafayette protested.

The two continued their arguing as a warning klaxon sounded and the viewscreen suddenly filled with a dozen ships.

"We might have a larger problem," Fix pointed out.

# Chapter 24

Salvador Rocca stood with his arms locked behind his back as he stared at the viewscreen, watching the starlines as the *Claymore* flew through space at the speed of light. Vesper Santelli's lieutenant was in his late fifties and had let himself go slightly from the fit, muscular man who had been a simple crewman on Santelli's first ship. That was back when Santelli was a simple smuggler and not the kingpin of both the largest legitimate and criminal shipping enterprises in the nine systems. In those days, Rocca had been good in a fight, a hell of a deadly shot, and someone who saved Santelli from arrest or death on multiple occasions. Those actions earned the amity and respect of one of the hardest men Rocca had ever met. He was godfather to Santelli's children and served as his most trusted councilor, not because he offered sage-like advice, but because Santelli trusted him to be honest and because Rocca trusted Santelli not to kill him for being so. (Criminal masterminds, like any corporate executive, did not like being told the truth if it reflected negatively on them. CEOs just fired you; men like Santelli killed you.)

Now, Rocca carried the belly of a man who enjoyed a good meal a little too frequently, the white hair of a man approaching retirement, and the wrinkled skin of someone who enjoyed sun bathing in the tropics a little too much. However, the man projected an aura, a sensation of power. Santelli was one to shout, scream or gesticulate wildly when he became angry. Rocca spoke quietly and calmly at all times, and only by listening to how deliberately he spoke, could his subordinates tell how furious he was.

The *Claymore* was one of the newest transport ships in Santelli's fleet, and like all of his ships, they were designed more for illicit cargo transportation than for military uses. That meant they were fast, carried a lot of shielding, and bore enough firepower to be intimidating. *Certainly enough to deal with Petrova and Jennings*, Rocca thought to himself.

"One minute to the asteroid we tracked Petrova too," the helmsman said from his position in front of Rocca, sitting just before the viewscreen.

A half dozen other men, all sitting at stations making a rough rectangle around the captain's chair which Rocca stood in front of, all turned to him simultaneously, and he spoke in a calm voice. "Full power to the weapons and raise the shields. Prepare to drop out of light speed and pass the word along to the other ships."

A flurry of activity from the crew preceded the *Claymore's* FTL engines cutting out and the sublights activating. "Mr. Rocca, I have a contact leaving the asteroid's surface," one of the crewmen said.

"Is it the *Grey Vistula*?" Rocca had studied Santelli's file on Petrova during the journey from Earth.

"Negative," the crewman said. "It identifies as a ship called the *Starlight Minstrel*."

Rocca nodded knowingly. "It's a fake." The *Starlight Minstrel* was one of the fake ship IDs Matthew Jennings had used in the past.

"Confirmed," the crewman agreed. "We have a match for the *Melody Tryst*."

Nodding with the slightest hint of approval, Rocca turned to the ship's gunners on his right. "I want her crippled, but not destroyed. Mr. Santelli wants the pleasure of killing Captain Jennings himself. I would hate to have to tell him it was any of you who prevented this."

Most of the crew knew the wrath of Vesper Santelli far too well.

"Remind the other ships of the same," Rocca said. "And by all means, commence the assault."

~

"Now, who the hell are these guys?" Jennings muttered.

"Based on the hull registries, they are vessels belonging to Vesper Santelli," Minerva said.

"*Merde*," Lafayette swore.

Jennings took evasive action as the lead ship opened fire with a plasma cannon burst, which the *Melody Tryst* narrowly avoided. Fix hit a control to raise the shields and expressed a slight concerned that they only came up at nineteen percent. Jennings rolled over hard to the left as more ships joined the attack.

"Our defenses are minimal," Fix pointed out.

"That's why I'm not letting them hit us," Jennings fired back while shooting a glance at Lafayette. "Is Magellan ready?"

"Need a minute."

"Don't have a minute," Jennings retorted.

Santelli's ships cut off every avenue of escape Jennings tried and then formed in a near perfect half-circle around him. Normally, Jennings would make a charge at one of the ships, pound them with fire, and then use the *Melody Tryst's* superior speed to flee. Without any functioning weapons, that would not be possible.

"They're cutting us off," Jennings said.

"Magellan can't calculate a course with you jumping all over the place," Lafayette countered.

"You and that fucking computer are really starting to get on my nerves," Jennings spat as he wrenched the controls hard over again and narrowly avoided being splashed. "Dammit!" Gritting his teeth, he took in a deep breath and prepared for the worst. A sudden idea popped into his head, however, and he turned to his first mate. "How much of that rock dust did you load onto the ship's hull?"

"Four canisters. Connected to two triggers."

Jennings turned to Fix. "Trigger the first one."

"Triggering," Fix said, his tone not sounding exactly impressed that they were launching dust at the enemy.

Suddenly, the firing stopped, and Jennings was able to straighten out his course and take a straight path away from Santelli's ships, which continued to hover in space as if they could no longer see the *Melody Tryst*. Lafayette let out a cry of triumph as Magellan finished calculating their course, and Jennings engaged the FTL engine.

"Ha-ha!" Jennings cried in excitement. "I knew that would work."

"What the hell just happened?" Fix asked. "Why did they stop firing?"

Jennings leaned back in his chair with a satisfied grin on his face. "Do you have any idea how much interstellar dust is out in the galaxy?"

"Nae off the top of my head," Fix said.

"In the galaxy, there is approximately..."

"Minerva," Jennings groaned.

"A lot, *n'est-ce pas*?" Lafayette said. "Enough to make most ship sensors go haywire if they didn't have a way to filter it out."

Fix raised an eyebrow. "They couldn't see us because there was enough dust around us to make their sensors filter us out?"

"Yep," Jennings said.

"Bloody nice," Fix said with the slightest of nods of respect in Jennings's direction.

"Fix, you have the conn," Jennings said. "Lafayette, Squawk, and I need to get the shields up and running before my navigational skills get us all killed."

~

"What do you mean you lost them?" Rocca demanded. "Did they use their FTL to escape?"

"We would have seen that," the sensor tech said just as an alarm sounded on his console. His voice seemed to vanish in his throat. "Mr. Rocca, the sensors just read an FTL engine engaging... Behind us."

"How did they slip behind us?" Rocca asked quietly and deliberately. "A sensor malfunction?"

The communications tech shook his head. "All other ships also reported losing contact with the target vessel."

Rocca shook his head and a small, tight-lipped smile crossed his face. Captain Jennings wanted to make this fun. He turned to the helmsman. "Can you plot his course and estimate his destination?"

The helmsman started punching commands into his Magellan computer. "Yes, sir," he said, his voice full of amazement. "They appear to be heading to Barnard's VI, but I don't think they are going to make it."

Rocca's eyes narrowed, and he stalked over to the Magellan interface to check out the course the computer had plotted. "Captain Jennings is a crazy son of a bitch." His tone was near reverent, before his steely demeanor returned. "Plot us a course to Barnard's VI."

"The same course?" the helmsman asked nervously.

After a moment's contemplation, he said, "No. We can't be foolhardy about this. Jump around the intervening system. If we miss him at Barnard's VI, we can at least pick up his trail there."

Rocca left the bridge as the fleet began to get into position for the FTL jumps. He was not looking forward to the conversation he would need to have with his boss as he stepped into a lift and headed down to the crew quarters level.

# Chapter 25

So far, Michelle Williams had not been hurt, and she found that to be strange and a little bit of a relief. A small part of her thought the Gael would execute her immediately on sight for her supposed crime of terrorism. However, they had merely placed her in binders, forced her into a spacesuit, and marched her out of the ore processing center and into a ship about five times larger than Captain Jennings's *Melody Tryst*.

After being marched up the ship's gangplank along with Anastasia Petrova, a man named Vosler, and about ten or so more of Petrova's men (all those left to guard the *Grey Vistula*), she was led through a cargo bay, a shuttle bay, and then to a very small corridor with four rooms leading off of it and two armed security guards sitting behind a desk at the end of it. Both the general whose nameplate on his uniform read Ounimbango and the Gael accompanied them to what Michelle realized was a brig, albeit a small one. The general directed Petrova and Vosler into the first cell on the left and seemed to even mutter an apology under his breath to her when the Gael was not looking. Petrova's remaining ten men were crammed into the two cells on the right, which was then sealed shut by the slamming of a black metal door with an electro-magnetic lock. Petrova's cell too was sealed and the guards then led Michelle to the last door on the left, one of them beckoning for her to step through. As she did so, she felt the Gael's eyes bearing on her hard and she was certain an emotion settled on his face, something like elation.

The door slammed shut behind her, and she sat on the bunk in the small cell, which also contained a sink, a toilet, and a station set into the wall that appeared to control the lights, dispensed water and rations, as well as controlling the sliding shelf that held a change of clothes (orange jumpsuits) and bedding for the bunk. Not feeling hungry in the slightest, but overcome with a wave of self-pity, Michelle made the bed, placed a pillow at is head, and then lay down.

She thought she might fall asleep right away, but the image of Captain Jennings being on the other side of the lift doors, firing at the men who had taken her, rescuing her yet again kept flashing before her eyes. That was a horrible moment, she realized. It was a moment that had given her hope. In that moment, she was saved, and Jennings was going to fulfill his promise and set her free. In that moment, the charges of terrorism did not matter, the fact that her life had been turned upside down did not matter, because at least she would go free.

Captain Jennings being shot changed all that of course, and that image would not leave her mind either. Granted, he had initially been willing to sell her to the Gael, but she had trusted him when he promised to let her go and when he said he believed she was no traitor. Once she had been captured, there was no reason for him to come back for her, to try to rescue her once again. And yet he had. *Unless he was trying to capture you again so he could hand you over to the Gael himself,* a cynical voice in her head spoke.

"No," she whispered, tears running down her cheeks and staining the pillow. "He wouldn't do that."

*Why else would he have tried to save her?* the cynical voice demanded. *She was nothing to him. People were not noble, riding to the rescue of damsels in distress, simply because it was the right thing to do, were they?*

But Jennings had. She was certain of it. Michelle was fairly certain she would never know what prompted Jennings to attempt to save her from Petrova's clutches, but she was positive his intention had been noble. That only made it worse in her mind though, because that meant it was her fault he got shot and probably killed. A furious stab of anger shot through her when she thought of the smug, self-satisfied look on Petrova's face as she pointed her gun at Jennings, his body already slumping and going down to the floor, his hands clutching the smoking wound. The idea that the woman who shot Jennings was only one room away from her, and that there was nothing she could do about it, made her even more furious and drew a frustrated sob from her. She took small comfort in the fact that if she was to be executed, there was at least a small chance Petrova would be as well.

Her thoughts turned to Lafayette, Fix and Squawk, the three beings who defended her only because Jennings ordered them to.

*Would they find Jennings in time to save him? Were they already dead? Would any of it matter as the Gael had destroyed the mine's life support?* The last question sprang to her mind unbidden because it was one she knew the answer to, and yet somehow she still clung miserably to the small hope it provided. *Would they come for her again?*

*Jennings might have if he had not been killed*, she thought to herself. If she was right about him, that suicidally brave sense of honor of his might have led him to come after her, but the others were a different story. Fix would not care enough to risk it, and Lafayette, while he was more amiable, was certainly not about to take on the Gael in an effort to save her, someone whom he was not entirely convinced was not a terrorist. *No, there would be no rescue coming this time.*

Eventually, Michelle completely gave in to her sorrow, and the tears would not stop coming. She cried for what felt like hours, until at last exhaustion seized her, and she fell into a fitful sleep. Nightmares of Matthew Jennings being repeatedly shot in front of her tormented her, and then she was shot by the Gael as he stared down at her with cold black eyes.

~

"Minerva, time!" Jennings called.

"Four minutes, eighteen seconds."

Jennings pulled himself out of the port wing crawlspace, where the ship's port shield generator was located and fell to the floor on the top level. Scrambling to his feet, he kicked aside some of the spent power cabling he had just spent the better part of several hours replacing and hotfooted it back up to the bridge. He jumped past Fix into the pilot's chair.

Punching the intercom, he shouted, "Marquis! Report!"

After a moment, the Cajun's voice came on the line, "Bow and starboard generators online, *mon capitaine*, but aft…"

His voice trailing off told Jennings all he needed to know. The aft generators would not be ready in time.

"Compensating for the lack of one generator puts shields up at seventy-two percent," Fix said.

"Minerva?" Jennings demanded.

"Based on Magellan data, seventy-eight percent shielding would be required to successfully navigate this hyperspace vector, captain."

"Cap'n, you need to pull us out of FTL," Fix said. "In two minutes, the ship will be fried."

"If we don't take this route or if we stop to make repairs, the girl is gone," Jennings argued.

"You can nae do her any good if you're bloody dead," Fix pointed out, his Scottish accent becoming more pronounced as he became agitated.

"One minute thirty seconds," Minerva said. "Binary stars of Castor and Pollux now within sensor range."

The two suns were magnified in the viewscreen as the *Melody Tryst* raced down a narrow vector, trying to slingshot in between the two gravity wells of intense heat that no sane man would ever try to navigate through, let alone while going faster than the speed of light. Jumping from his chair, Jennings moved to Lafayette's and started punching keys on Magellan.

"Cap'n, that is nae a good idea," Fix said.

"You don't even know what I'm doing," he pointed out.

"I know it's nae a good idea," he countered.

"Minerva, Magellan says our course takes us in between the binary stars at a slightly oblique angle, confirm," Jennings said just as klaxons began to blare and warning lights indicating gravity wells imminent began to flash.

"Confirmed."

Keeping an eye on the navigational details on Magellan, Jennings said, "Can you rotate the shields so we are reading seventy-eight percent full across the port and then cut that seventy-eight percent over to starboard when I tell you?"

"Aye, but Cap'n, we need to stop," Fix protested.

"Readjust the shields to port now!" Jennings roared over the klaxons and alarms.

"Portside shields now at seventy-eight percent," Fix said. "Starboard down to sixty-four. Command is set to reverse when ordered."

"Actually, Minerva, I need you to do this one," Jennings said. "It will happen too fast for a human to do." Jennings punched a series of coordinates into Minerva's interface. "At those co-ordinates, I need you to flip the shield strength from port to starboard."

"Yes, captain," she said. "Forty-five seconds until stellar gravity. Stand-by for temporal anomalies."

"Everyone!" Jennings announced over the intercom. "Brace yourselves! We're going in!"

Ships with FTL drives did not want to go anywhere near stellar masses for many reasons: the colossal amount of gravity tended to cause ships to crash into suns, heavy temperatures incinerated hulls, and solar flares tended to be strong enough to blast their way through radiation shielding while poisoning all the people onboard a ship. That was why most ships had automatic safeguards to prevent a ship from coming too near a large gravity well while traveling at FTL speeds. The *Melody Tryst's* safety device was currently overridden.

A more puzzling and disconcerting sensation, although certainly less fatal, was a secondary side effect of traveling at the speed of light near a massive gravity well: time for all appearances slowed down. It was not the actual amount of time that changed: thirty seconds was still thirty seconds, but everything seemed to move in super slow motion, but the human brain did not. Jennings had read about it before, but was about to see it first hand, assuming of course his plan with the shields worked and they were not killed.

"Entering solar gravity now," Minerva said, her voice warbling on the last word so it was drawn out in slow motion.

The twin stars Castor and Pollux, massive yellow balls of helium and hydrogen, not dissimilar from Earth's own sun, which had only been visible by sensor magnification, suddenly filled the *Melody Tryst's* entire viewscreen. Castor was closer, on their immediate left with its equator slightly beneath the *Melody Tryst*. Pollux was on the right and slightly above the ship. Their planned path threaded a needle between the two stars and would allow them to catch up with the TGF runabout, which had most likely chosen to jump around the system, rather than go straight through it on its way to Barnard's VI.

The *Melody Tryst* hit the full force of Castor's gravity well, and a dozen warning lights started blinking in slow motion, new klaxons blared so slowly that they sounded only like background noise. The ship shook as if in a bad storm with wicked turbulence. If it felt like that in slow motion, Jennings was fairly certain he did not want to know what it was like at full speed.

Fix roared something that sounded like, "Dampeners overloading! Thermal overload imminent!" But his voice was stretched out and strained.

All of a sudden, there was a half-moment when everything stopped, the ship was no longer shaking, time seemed to re-accelerate, and Minerva started to say, "Re-setting shields," before her voice was lost, time slowed down again, and Jennings was rocked against his safety harness as the *Melody Tryst* hit the gravity of Pollux. All around him screens shorted out, bright sparks flashing slowly like fireflies dancing in front of him. A vent above his head burst, and steam poured slowly into the room moving like the tentacle of a very lethargic squid.

"Almost there," Jennings kept repeating in his mind as he saw Pollux vanish from the viewscreen and pass behind them.

Time re-accelerated, and the ship seemingly jumped forward, resuming its course at FTL speed once more. A cacophony of warning noises greeted Jennings, and he immediately began running systems checks.

"Fire! Fire! Fire! In Engineering!" came Lafayette's voice over the intercom.

Jennings made to jump up to go help, but Fix was to his feet first. "I'll go. Keep us flying."

"Minerva, talk to me," Jennings said as he frantically began scrolling through damage reports at the engineer's station.

"Hull breach in the right wing," she said. "Emergency bulkhead in place and appears to be holding."

As he checked on the FTL engines, he asked, "Shield status?"

"Shields buckled as we left Pollux," she said. "But generators are still online. Shields are recharging."

"Engines look good," he said to himself. "Jury rigged power plant is functioning as good as it was." He punched the intercom. "Fix! Marquis! Report!"

"*Pas de probleme,*" came Lafayette's voice in reply. "We had a minor coolant leak which shorted out one of the sublight engines. The internal housing caught fire, but we have it taken care of."

"Anyone hurt?" he asked.

"Negative."

"Tell Squawk I want a full damage report," he said.

"*Oui, mon capitaine.*" With that, he signed off.

"Minerva, how are we looking for our intercept?" he asked.

"Based on current projections, we will overtake the TGF runabout twenty-five minutes prior to their rendezvousing with the TGF capital ship." After a moment, the NAI added, "Congratulations. Unless I'm mistaken, which I'm not, this is the first time a human has made a successful FTL flight in between a set of binary stars."

"I'm probably the first human stupid enough to try," Jennings pointed out.

"Incorrect," she said. "Fourteen known attempts have been made. All resulted in the loss of the ship and all hands."

"Glad I didn't know that at the time," Jennings muttered. "Do you think you can keep an eye on things until I can get Fix up here?"

"Of course."

"Oh," he added almost matter-of-factly. "Between the *Tryst* and the runabout, do you know which has the better sensor system?"

Intuitively, Minerva read into the question and gave a slightly different answer than Jennings expected, but it was technically the one he wanted. "At one thousand one hundred kilometers, the ship will still be in our sensor range, but we will be invisible to it."

Jennings smiled and looked around the cockpit of the *Melody Tryst*. "That's my girl."

~

A few minutes later, Jennings gathered everyone into the Caf, giving him a moment to get a good look at his crew. All of them had been wounded in some way or another in the past few days, the most minor of which was the bad bruising Squawk took from getting kicked in the ribs by one of Petrova's goons. Jennings probably came across as the worst of all of them. When adrenaline was not surging through him, he walked with a slight limp from the shot he had taken in the leg; his side still ached horribly from the shot there; and bruising mottled his chest from where his armor had stopped the blast the first time Petrova's goons shot him.

They were tired. Each man carried dark bags under their eyes and could probably sleep for a week. Only Squawk had gotten any decent sleep since Strikeplain, and he looked like he might pass out at any moment. Fix got up and headed to the medbay for a moment and came back with a bottle of pills.

Distributing one to each of them, he merely said, "Pep."

Squawk eyed him forlornly.

He smiled. "Safe for Pasquatil."

Squawk took his and belched.

"Everyone has earned a rest, a meal, and a vacation," Jennings began. "That's what I'd like to be saying to you now, but that's just not possible." He hated that he was asking them to do this. "I'm sorry I've dragged you all into this." Jennings shook his head and struggled to find the words. "I've almost gotten us killed multiple times because I couldn't let an innocent girl die at the hands of that Gael. I know that doesn't mean as much to all of you as it does to me, or you might not even believe she's innocent…"

"Fuck'em," Fix interrupted.

Jennings did not expect that response. "What?"

"Fuckin' Gael left us to die on that mine," Fix said. "Left us to die slow, gaspin'. That's worse than throwin' a man in a steel cage. That's bloody buryin' a man alive. No one fuckin' does that to me. Nae anymore." Everyone stared at him, surprised. Not only was this one of the longest strings of conversation Fix had ever uttered outside of the medbay, it was also the first time anyone recalled seeing him even a little emotional over anything. Fix was not deterred by their surprise. "Petrova shot the Cap'n twice, and her crew shot the Cajun, brained me, and beat up Squawk. I say we go and kill as many of those fuckers as we can. We rain the bloody apocalypse down on their houses. If you want to pick up the girl while we're fuckin' doing that, Cap'n, I've nae got a problem with it."

Jennings smiled at Fix and then turned to Lafayette.

"*Mon capitaine, mon capitaine.* When have I not followed you willingly? No need to apologize. We're with you."

"That's what I just said," Fix said to the Cajun.

"Marquis did it more succinctly," Jennings countered amiably.

A smile crossed the Cajun's face. "I trust there's a plan."

"Of course." Jennings started pacing, the pep pill taking hold of him. "Well, the beginning of a plan anyway. I'm pretty sure I can get us onto the TGF carrier, but after that, we're going to have to make it up as we go."

He explained his plan to them as quickly as possible, while still giving necessary details. Once he was finished, he said, "Thoughts?"

Lafayette coughed. "It will have the virtue of never having been tried, *mon capitaine*."

"Mental," Fix said.

"That's what I said," Lafayette said.

"Just crazy or just crazy enough to work?" Jennings asked.

Lafayette and Fix glanced at each other. "Hopefully the latter, since we won't be able to dissuade you of *dis* anyway," Lafayette pointed out.

Jennings gave a sardonic smile. "You know me so well. All right, Fix, you're on weapons detail. We lost a lot of gear on the asteroid and in Strikeplain, so let me know where we stand ASAP. Lafayette, you and Squawk get me the *Tryst's* weapons and communications in that order and anything else after that. Squawk, once phase one of the mission is complete, you're staying with the ship. Repair anything else you can and try to get that hull breach sealed."

"Aye, aye," he said as he jumped up with a series of overly emphasized salutes and then bounded away to head back down to engineering.

"Are you sure that pep pill was safe for Pasquatil?" Jennings asked.

Fix shrugged.

"It's a great idea in theory to get the ship as fixed as possible," Lafayette said. "But we don't have much left in the way of components for repairs. Anything that's blown out can't be replaced."

"Use spit and duct tape," he said. "I can't have a ship with no weapons and no communications."

Lafayette grumbled a few choice words under his breath. *"Oui, mon capitaine."*

"Now, I'll come by to assist you each in turn, so you can rotate through the mess, get some food, clean yourselves up, change wound dressings, whatever you need," he said. "Let's move like we've got a purpose."

~

Several hours later, things aboard the *Melody Tryst* were not going as well as Captain Jennings would have liked. Their weapon inventory had become a joke. There were no grenades, and most of the weapons they did have had no ammunition. They had one repeating plasma rifle with a half-full charge, two pistols with a couple of charges apiece, a sniper rifle with a few rounds, and Fix's crossbow.

Repairs were not particularly fruitful either. Squawk managed to get the one sublight engine and its coolant tank patched and operational, and Lafayette and Jennings had gone through every bit of shot wiring they had to find enough to be patched together to give them a few shots of plasma cannons and the ability to launch a couple of missiles from one of the left-wing launchers before it probably shorted out too. Jennings had something else entirely in mind for the second left wing launcher, and it would require no power running to the launcher to achieve, just the missile bay door, which was still functioning. Long-range communications were completely fried, but they had re-established short-range comms. There was also no use trying to get anything to the right-wing weapons with a hull breach there. Jennings could only hope Squawk would be able to finish more repairs while he and the others searched for Michelle.

Everyone had been given the opportunity to grab some chow, Lafayette going first and making enough for everyone as he was the only one who could make anything edible. Jennings went through his rotation last, grabbing a very fast shower, just enough to wash the dried blood off his body and perk himself up a bit. He got dressed in a fresh pair of boxer shorts, khaki cargo pants and an olive-green T-shirt, pausing for a moment to apply fresh bandages to his knee and his left side. Once dressed, he swallowed a few more of the painkillers Fix had given him and paused for a moment, resting on his bed, waiting for them to take effect.

"Captain," Minerva's voice interrupted him.

"Go ahead."

"We are approaching the TGF runabout," she said.

"Bloody brilliant," he whispered under his breath. "Good work, Minerva. Match velocity with the runabout at eleven hundred kilometers. All crew to the bridge."

"Aye, captain," the NAI said before relaying his order throughout the intercom system.

Lafayette was already on the bridge when Jennings arrived and slipped into the pilot's chair. Squawk came bounding in a moment later, followed by Fix, who said something about preparing a medical kit they would almost certainly need during the operation.

"We have matched velocity," Minerva reported.

"Good," Jennings said. "As long as we are in a sensor blind spot, they won't be able to see us until we're ready to make our move."

"When will that be?" Lafayette asked.

"Following standard Terran Gael Force practice for arrival at Barnard's VI, they will need to drop to sublight here," Jennings said, pointing to a set of co-ordinates he had sent over to Magellan.

"We drop out of light speed at exactly the same time and engage our dust shroud," he said. "We should be invisible. And the *Tryst* is faster than that TGF piece of shit. We should be able to overtake them."

"Should?" Fix echoed.

"Depending on where the carrier is relative to where they were required to drop out of light speed," Jennings clarified. "And a few other factors."

"Would you like to know the percentage chance of success?" Minerva asked.

"No," three voices said at once.

"Just kidding," she said.

"We really need to talk about your timing," Jennings muttered.

A light on the Magellan interface began blinking and a countdown began. "Five seconds until the runabout is at the specified co-ordinates," Lafayette said. "Cutting out FTL engines... now."

Starlines shrank to stars, and the massive gas giant Barnard's V dominated their view to the left. Barnard's VI was a smaller planet visible on the right. Immediately, Jennings triggered the last of the rock dust Lafayette had attached to the hull, and the particles, attracted to the small amount of gravity their ship created, surrounded them and followed them even as Jennings activated the sublight engines.

"Do you have a reading on where that carrier is?" Jennings asked.

"Yes," Fix said. "Twelve minutes away. Moving to intercept runabout."

"Damn, everyone's so impatient these days," the captain said. "Time to our intercepting the runabout, Marquis?"

"Five minutes."

"I better go suit up then," he said as he stood to leave. "Marquis, you have the conn."

"*Bon chance, mon ami,*" Lafayette called to him as he headed up the gangplank to the Caf, where his space suit now hung.

Quickly, he got dressed, attached the plasma pistol to his belt, and Fix's specially modified crossbow to his back, before climbing into the access hatch for the left wing. Moving as quickly as the bulky suit would allow him, he made it into the wing and said into his comm, "I'm inside the wing, open the missile door."

The emergency bulkhead separating the wing from the rest of the ship came down, as it always did when a missile tube was going to be opened. Once it finished locking into place, the missile door opened, and space appeared in front of Jennings. He moved his body into position on top of the missile auto reloader system (all of the remaining missiles in the left wing had been repurposed into the one working launcher), and he prepared himself, grabbing hold of the missile door opening with both hands.

"Two minutes," came Lafayette's voice through the comm.

Jennings gritted his teeth as he stared ahead, forgetting one small part of his plan. With all the glittering rock dust they were using as a shroud, he could not actually see the location of the *Grey Vistula* where it was being towed behind the TGF runabout. He was about to jump out into space, from a moving location, trying to hit a moving target, and he would not be able to see where he was going until clear of the field.

"Forty seconds, *mon capitaine*," Lafayette said. "Five seconds to optimal launch. Four. Three. Two. One. *Allez!*"

Not taking a moment to think about it, knowing he would not be able to do it if he did, Jennings pushed off with his legs and threw himself forward with his arms. He shot out of the missile door and soared through the rock dust as he left the *Melody Tryst* behind. As soon as he was clear, he knew he would miss the *Grey Vistula*. He was going to pass by overtop of it.

"You're off course, captain," Minerva's voice came in over the comm.

"I know, dammit."

The *Grey Vistula* was passing by underneath him now, and Jennings was about to become lost in space. Grabbing the crossbow off of his back, he took aim and fired at the *Grey Vistula's* hull, where the arrow stuck and a line of high tensile fiber stretched from the hull to the crossbow's handle. Fix had fitted the arrow with a magnetic cap, allowing it to lock onto the hull. Pulling hand over hand on the cable, Jennings began dragging himself closer to the ship almost effortlessly in the limited gravity. Once in range, he activated his magnetic boots and locked onto the hull.

Thanks to some good aim on Jennings's part he only needed to take a few steps across the hull to arrive at an emergency hatch. Dropping to one knee, he inserted his portable CPU into the flashport, allowing Minerva to override the system and gain him entry. The hatch swung open easily, and Jennings maneuvered himself inside, swinging the hatch shut behind him. Once closed, artificial gravity kicked in, and his boots hit the floor. A computerized voice, much more robotic than Minerva's, announced the room was re-pressurizing and atmosphere was being restored.

"I'm in, better start getting the ship into position," Jennings said.

"*Oui, mon capitaine,*" Lafayette said.

The computer announced that the airlock had been matched to internal conditions, and the inner airlock door swung open. Jennings stepped through and found himself in a clean, contemporary corridor painted in cream and taupe colors which ended in a T-Junction not far ahead. It was somewhat eerie being inside a completely empty spaceship, especially one much larger than the *Melody Tryst*, but Jennings put that thought to the back of his mind as he raced to the end of the corridor, his magnetic boots thumping loudly on the floor.

Turning left, Jennings made his way down another corridor which terminated in a lift. Pushing the call button, he was met with an elevator a moment later. The elevator was comfortably padded, and Jennings wondered what possible purpose that served. Rather than having floor numbers, a touchscreen computer monitor gave different options including C&C/Officer Quarters, Crew Quarters, Medbay/Cells/Storage, and Bays, the last of which Jennings selected. The lift let him out in a room eighty feet tall which ran the length of the ship. This ship model was designed to allow for multiple shuttles to dock while still carrying a good amount of cargo. It was ample space for the *Melody Tryst* to hole up in.

"Marquis, are you in position?" Jennings asked as he ran over to an enclosed area which housed all the docking bay controls.

"*Bien sur.*"

"Stand-by one," Jennings said.

The *Melody Tryst* pulled up within a few feet of the *Grey Vistula*, expanding its shroud cover to the very end of Petrova's ship. If someone on the runabout specifically looked at the very tail of the *Grey Vistula*, they might wonder why they could not see it on their sensors, but that was unlikely. Besides, without the shroud cover, the runabout was much more likely to notice the *Grey Vistula's* cargo bay doors opening.

Jennings punched in a series of commands, and the bay doors opened to space. A low powered shield kept the atmosphere in, but was not strong enough to keep the *Melody Tryst* out as Lafayette navigated her into the cargo bay. The shield captured all the rock dust, but that trick would have been done for once they hit the cargo bay's artificial gravity anyway. Plus, it continued to keep the *Grey Vistula's* aft shielded until Jennings shut the cargo bay door.

With a few key presses, the door closed, and Jennings glanced up at the *Melody Tryst*, sitting in the belly of one of his fiercest rival's ships. He could not help but allow himself a small smile. The first phase of the mission was going perfectly to plan. That was until he felt the muzzle of a plasma pistol being shoved into his back through his space suit.

"Don't move," a female voice said to him.

# Chapter 26

Selena Beauregard was not altogether unaccustomed to being in tight spaces, literal and figurative. It was a necessary evil in her line of work as security tended to be the most lax around areas where nobody thought another human being could fit. That led to a fair share of ventilation ducts, drainage pipes, and exhaust systems in her years as an elimination specialist. Dozens of times she had almost been caught by security and the police or had been thwarted by her own target, but she had always come through.

This was the first time she had failed so monumentally in her career. First, those lackwit bounty hunters blew her cover at the fraternity party and got the information she needed from Jacq Clemmons, and then they managed to give her the slip after she attacked them in space near Strikeplain. The worst indignity of it all though had been when Anastasia Petrova, who tried to hide her scumbaggery behind an expensive pantsuit, actually managed to capture her and now held her in a force field sealed cell.

Once in custody, she tried a few of the old gambits: trying to seduce a guard and pretending to be ill, but Petrova's warders were either too well trained or had seen enough movies to know better. Beauregard then tried to find some sort of fault in the security system on the cell, but put little energy into it as the guards would simply gun her down if she did get out. She even had a few surprises in compartments hidden in her boots that usually helped her escape prisoner situations, but they had been confiscated. *There would be another opportunity*, she told herself. She simply needed to be ready for it. With that thought comforting her, she fell asleep on the blanket-less bunk in her tiny cell.

When she awoke, it was because some strange commotion was going on in the hall outside her cell. She heard a lot of shouting and the unmistakable sound of a fist striking flesh. A brief moment of weapon's fire echoed in the narrow space, stun guns from the sound of it, and then came the thud of a body hitting the deck and the clattering of a weapon rattling away from someone's grasp.

Uncertain what to think about this development, she quickly glanced around the cell for a place to hide. Something about what was happening did not feel right, and she did not want to be caught in a small cell with some lout about to put a plasma bolt between her eyes. Under the bunk was too obvious and she was still likely to be seen, especially if they actually came into the cell to search. Her eyes next travelled up to the seamless ceiling of the narrow cell and then the open-air doorway. At the ceiling above the doorway, there was a foot long slab of steel hanging down which housed the force field emitter.

Smiling slightly to herself, Beauregard jumped off the floor, turned her body horizontally in mid-air and pushed out as far as she could with her feet and hands. Her hands and feet found opposite walls of the cell, and she tensed her entire body, locking herself into place like she was merely a plank or a shelf extending from one wall to the other. Looking to her right at the cell door, she realized she had not gotten high enough up and began the labor-intensive process of shimming herself higher up, trying to go as fast as possible without losing contact with either wall.

At last, the ceiling touched the small of her back, and she started to move to the right, shimmying until the steel force field emitter pressed against her ribs. She held her position, her muscles aching, knowing she was now invisible to a cursory glance from anyone outside the cell and that she would be able to get the literal drop on anyone who came in.

The stomping of boots reached her ears, and she braced herself for an attack.

"Clear!" she heard a voice shout and then another and a third.

"Hold!" a fourth voice snapped. "Force field is on in number six."

"No prisoner listed in the log," a voice answered from down the hall. Beauregard counted her lucky stars that Petrova's people were not particularly diligent in the area of paperwork.

"Looks empty," she heard one voice say.

"Open up six," the same voice who reported the force field as being up called down the hallway to the man at the control station.

The force field came down for a moment, and a man dressed in Terran Gael Force black combat fatigues, holding an automatic plasma rifle stepped into the room. His black battle helmet was only about a foot underneath of where Beauregard was pinned up against the ceiling. She was just about to spring into action when the TGF soldier knelt down, checked under the bunk, and then turned as he rose and strode out of the cell.

"Empty," he said to one of his fellows.

Beauregard allowed herself to start breathing again, although she did it in controlled quiet breaths. *What in the world was going on? Why were TGF forces onboard the ship of Anastasia Petrova, and why did they seem to be attacking the crew?* She pushed those questions out of her mind as she allowed herself to drop nimbly back to the floor of her cell. A quick look outside the corridor of the cell block revealed it was empty. Fortune smiled on her again. The TGF had not only done her the courtesy of opening her cell door and missing that she was in it, but they had apparently also completely removed her captors and themselves.

Before she left her cell though, the *Grey Vistula* gave a sudden shake and then lurched, sending Beauregard falling onto the bunk. She felt the ship's course stabilize as the inertial dampeners kicked in. There was no hum of engines however. Every ship had a background hum of the engines which drove it, but the *Grey Vistula* was completely silent. It was being towed, she realized. She needed to find out what was going on.

Moving quickly down the cell block, she found a weapon that had previously belonged to one of her jailers and picked it up, putting it into the pocket of her black pilot's jumpsuit. At the end of the corridor, a security substation sat with the only egress from the cells behind it. The door was currently open. Settling into the chair at the substation, she punched a few commands into the computer and the door behind her slammed shut and locked.

Feeling a lot less exposed, she started typing new commands into the computer. Annoyingly, the computer did not have access to the main bridge, engineering, or log functions, but it was wired into the ship's onboard Nucleus. With that, she spent about ten minutes hacking her way into the *Grey Vistula's* other functions. It would have been faster, but apparently someone tried to put a lockout on the main computer. While hastily done, the lockout still took Beauregard a few minutes to circumvent.

What she learned answered a few questions, but raised many more. The *Grey Vistula* was currently empty of lifeforms, save for herself, and it was being towed by a TGF vessel in the direction of Barnard's VI. She also discovered the cell bays were shielded from sensors, which explained why she was not found in the sensor sweep the TGF vessel almost certainly did before boarding the *Grey Vistula*. Apparently, Petrova valued keeping her prisoners private. That made sense, Beauregard supposed. One never knew when some crazy maniac, like Matthew Jennings for instance, might try to break into a ship to rescue someone.

Things became murkier from there. The *Grey Vistula* had set down on an asteroid where Michelle Williams was supposedly taken by Captain Jennings, and Petrova had ordered her men into the mines where Jennings and the girl were hiding. Sensor logs showed the arrival of a TGF runabout, which did not surprise her. Petrova might have sold the location of the girl to the Gael and then tried to capture Williams herself in order to squeeze a few more dollars out of them. What surprised her was the next turn of events though. The TGF forces stormed the *Grey Vistula* and arrested everyone onboard. Then they decided to tow the ship away and left the system. They would only leave the asteroid if Williams was in custody, but the arresting of all of Petrova's men made little sense to Beauregard.

With no one around to ask questions of though, she put those thoughts out of her mind for the time being and started focusing on the *Grey Vistula's* communication system. Sending a direct missive would have been tantamount to attempting to simply commandeer the vessel and escape, being foolhardy and certain to end up in her death. (Not that she had not originally considered it, but based on the *Grey Vistula's* speed, shielding and weapons compared to the runabout towing her, she would not have stood a chance.) Instead, she kept a close eye on the transmissions going from the runabout to the TGF carrier. Every fifteen minutes, the runabout spent approximately three minutes on the horn with the carrier, updating position and logs for safekeeping. She loved TGF precision. All she would need to do was wait for the next transmission, piggy back off its signal, and she could get a message through. She typed in a series of commands and waited for the next transmission to begin before she executed them.

After spending about one minute on security challenges, the face of Major Geoff Paulsen appeared on the screen, and he flinched in surprise. "Selena? I wasn't expecting to hear from you ever again."

There was a note of threat in the last part of his sentence, but she ignored it. "I've got less than two minutes, so listen fast. The TGF has Michelle Williams."

Paulsen gritted his ugly teeth. "Damn."

"But I can tell you where they're going," she said.

"Probably some impregnable military installation," he muttered.

"A single TGF carrier," she said. "You would have to move quickly, but if you truly want her dead, it may still be an accomplishable task."

Paulsen seemed to consider this for a moment. "Where is this ship?"

"You've yet to ask my price," she pointed out.

"I would think that this piece of information would go a long way to earning the forgiveness of the Resistance," he pointed out. "We're not generally understanding when our contract employees bungle an operation so badly. Some may have even been known to disappear."

"Save the threat," she spat. "I'll be dead pretty soon in all likelihood anyway without some help, so here's the price. I tell you which ship she'll be on, and you send a rescue party for me." She glanced at the clock counting down on the computer. "I'll contact you again in twelve minutes for your answer." She then signed off without giving him a chance to respond.

Thirteen minutes later, she was reconnected with Paulsen who appeared as excited as the normally calm Englishman could be. "You have a deal. Your location and the location of the girl?"

"She's in a TGF runabout being taken to the *TGFS Intrepid*, currently in orbit around Barnard's VI," she said. "I'm in a commercial vessel being towed behind it at the moment."

"How long until you reach Barnard's VI?" he asked.

"A few more hours."

"I'll do what I can to get you out of there," he said. "But if they get you aboard the carrier before my strike force can get there…"

"Once your attack begins, I will steal this ship, a shuttle, a life pod, something, anything," she said. "You'll just need to cover my escape if I'm in a ship or pick me up if I'm in a pod."

"Very well," Paulsen said. "I'm sending you a coded communication channel to use to communicate with the Resistance strike fleet should you need it. I will pass along orders that you are to be aided in every way possible."

"Very good." With that, she signed off and then leaned back in the chair. "Very good."

~

A few hours later, Beauregard was starting to feel anticipation creep up in her. The ship dropped out of light speed and began approaching Barnard's VI. Sometime soon, she hoped, the Resistance would be launching an assault on the *TGFS Intrepid,* and she was running through possible scenarios in her mind. The easiest solution was to wait aboard the *Grey Vistula* until the shooting started and then make her way out to the *Intrepid's* hangar. If for some reason, they decided to search the vessel, she planned several avenues of escape. From there, once the shooting started, she could easily steal a fighter, a shuttle, or an escape pod.

Her planning was interrupted by a flashing light displaying an airlock opening. "What the hell?" she muttered to herself as she called up the internal sensors. Sure enough, there was one life sign in the corridor on the command deck. It could not be a rescue attempt from the Resistance. They would not take a chance revealing themselves before starting the battle. She took a look at her external sensors and was still reading no vessels, but even as she stared at it, she noticed a small sliver of the *Grey Vistula* itself had disappeared from its sensors.

*Some kind of cloaking device?* she wondered. That was the only explanation. She turned back to the internal sensors and saw that the one other person onboard the ship was using the lift now, headed for the bays. That person's presence aboard the *Grey Vistula* was already risking being noticed by the TGF if they decided to scan for life signs, so she did not think anything of pulling the pistol out of her pocket and leaving the shielded cell block.

Rather than taking the lift, she found a ladder well and slid down the rungs until she arrived at the bottom of the ship where the cargo and hangar bays were. Emerging from the ladder well, she saw the hangar bay doors open and another ship coming through. *Some of Petrova's people, trying to mount a strange rescue operation?* she wondered to herself.

Not wanting to take any chances, she used the noise of the arriving ship to cover her movements and sneak up behind the man standing at the bay's control system. As soon as the ship landed and the bay doors were closed, Beauregard placed her plasma pistol into his back and told him not to move.

# Chapter 27

"What do you suppose all that was about not wanting any evidence?" Vosler asked in a forced calm tone.

Anastasia Petrova had been pacing about their tiny cell for several hours, ranting about the unfairness of it, cursing in Russian, ranting some more, plotting her revenge, and more than once treading on Vosler's feet. On the latter front, she either did not realize she had done so or did not care to apologize. After being wounded by Captain Jennings, Vosler decided it was best to sit and rest in their cell as there was nothing they could do about their present situation anyway. He found that less taxing than attempting to engage his boss on any of her diatribes, but as this had been going on for hours, he finally felt obligated to say something that might lead to conversation more productive than curses and threats.

"*Vhat* did you say?" Like always, Petrova's accent was thicker when she was upset.

"When they dragged us away and took the *Grey Vistula*," Vosler began. "The Gael said something about wanting to get rid of all the evidence."

"The evidence of *vhat*?" Petrova asked.

"That is my question," Vosler said, mulling over the idea. "It seems a little extreme to arrest and… dispose of everyone involved in a simple terrorism case. None of us had anything to do with her crimes, and none of us care about what the Resistance is doing. Plus, we've captured dozens of Resistance fugitives for the Gael. Now, all of a sudden, we're no longer useful… We know too much?"

"I don't see how they can think that," Petrova said with a sigh as she collapsed into a seated position on the bunk next to Vosler. "*Ve* don't know much of anything apparently."

"Bastard Gael," Vosler spat angrily. "Can't even have a civil business relationship with them based on mutual interest and loathing?"

Petrova laughed quietly. She allowed silence to develop between the two of them for a few minutes before she asked a question she probably already knew the answer to. "They are going to kill us, aren't they?"

"Most likely," Vosler said. "We're of no use to them and clearly whatever they want that girl for is a lot more important than any of our lives."

"*Vhat* could she be that you *vould* kill everyone who knows of her just to keep the secret?" she wondered.

Vosler considered the question, came up with nothing, and shrugged. "Whatever they want her for, she's going to be at the forefront of the Gael's mind, no matter what. Whatever they want her for, it must be huge."

"So?"

"So..." Vosler led. "There may come an opportunity for us to slip out of this little trap we find ourselves in at the moment. If that opportunity presents itself, not only should we take it, but I think we should get the girl out as well."

"*Vhy vould ve*...?" Petrova began.

Vosler cut her off with a wave of his hand. "If the Gael are so focused on the girl..."

"They'll be so busy chasing her that they won't even bother looking for us," Petrova finished excitedly, before her expression soured again. "A fine theory, but *ve* have to be given an opportunity to escape."

"We will be," Vosler said confidently. "There's always a moment for every prisoner. It might be nothing short of running when they go to shoot you and hoping they miss, but there's a moment."

"Not much of a moment," Petrova comment.

"Worked for me once before," Vosler said quietly, remembering a time he had escaped from the Gael during the war. They executed three of his squad members in front of him, and he had just taken off at a run. The Gael fired at him and missed. They chased him, but he eluded. He finished his moment of reflection. "Besides, I have a hunch that Captain Jennings might just give us the opportunity we need."

"Don't speak to me of that annoying man," Petrova snapped. "Besides, he's almost certainly dead."

"Didn't we have a talk about not underestimating him?" Vosler reminded her. "If he's alive, he's coming after the girl."

"*Vhat* makes you say that?"

Vosler thought to the effort Jennings had expended in keeping Michelle Williams and then the suicidally reckless manner in which he almost succeeded in re-capturing her from them. One did not do so in pursuit of a mark. It made no business sense for one. But more importantly, Matthew Jennings was a man of honor. Men of honor allowed criminals to be taken to the authorities even if it meant them losing out on the bounty. No, Jennings must believe Michelle Williams to be innocent, and it would be a stain on his honor if he allowed her to be captured when he knew it was unjust.

Vosler did not express any of this to Petrova. As much as he liked his boss, it was something she would just not understand. Instead, he said, "Call it a hunch."

~

Salvador Rocca had spent the better part of an hour being yelled at by Vesper Santelli. He knew it would not be a pleasant conversation going into the communication, and he correctly guessed it would be worse when Santelli answered the comm in his bedroom with a half-naked twenty-something standing in the background. If she had been fully naked, Santelli might have been in a better mood and less annoyed at being interrupted with bad news.

"What do I pay you again for, Rocca?" Santelli demanded, the veins in his neck and forehead throbbing.

Rocca was too savvy to answer the question directly, but also smart enough to know he could not keep his mouth shut. "My job is to bring you Jennings. That job has not changed nor has it been abandoned. The process is just taking a little longer than expected."

"Don't attempt to smear bullshit over your mistakes, Rocca!" Santelli roared.

"Of course not, sir," he responded calmly. "This is merely a delay, not a failure. We will continue to hunt Jennings down, capture him and bring him to you to be killed if that is what you still want."

Santelli's brow furrowed, and he crossed his arms. "Why the fuck wouldn't I want that?"

"No reason," Rocca said. "But I find myself liking Captain Jennings the more I learn about him."

Santelli almost bared his teeth at Rocca. "Are you forgetting that Jennings crossed me and destroyed my property?"

"Not at all. But how many smugglers do we employ who could have gotten away from twelve larger, more heavily armed and armored ships?" Rocca asked. "How many shipments are lost each year to our captains and contractors being forced to drop their goods and run before they get boarded? Perhaps someone with the natural inventiveness of Jennings might help reduce those numbers."

Santelli dismissed this observation with a wave of a hand. "Even if I were inclined to let his transgression pass, when the word gets out that not only have I let Matthew Jennings live but that I also have him in my employ, my enemies will declare it open season on us."

"Very well," Rocca said quietly.

Santelli stared at Rocca, his eyes narrowed like they were trying to drill down into Rocca's words. "Salvador, why are you so keen on Captain Jennings all of a sudden?"

Rocca allowed himself a slight smile. "I like his style. And there is that other outstanding matter. The one yet to be resolved."

His employer mused on that for a moment and shrugged his eyebrows as if to concede the point. After a moment, he said, "Just bring me Jennings, Salvador. No more mistakes!" With that outburst, he stood up and walked away from the communications console.

He did not disconnect the line, and Rocca was unfortunately able to see a few minutes of Santelli taking out some of his anger in a rather aggressive posture of love-making to the woman in the room before he could cut out the comm line. Rocca left his quarters and made his way back to the lift that would take him to the bridge. He had no idea how the next few hours would play out, but he was fairly certain they would be interesting.

~

Commodore Noichi Akira's dispassionate and severe face studied the information sent to him from Major Geoff Paulsen in the Midway Resistance cell with utterly pure concentration, desperate to not miss any details. His dark eyes scanned every line of the file, his hands subconsciously going to his slicked back black hair to make sure none were out of place.

He was seated on the bridge of the Resistance ship *Tora*, impeccably dressed in his old navy blue Terran Federation uniform. Noichi was the first officer of the *Tora* back when it was one of the few T-Fed cruisers that made it out of the war intact while also not being turned over to the Gael, known then as the *TFS Tora*. The *Tora* had been one of many ships the Terran Federation had thrown out in a last desperate attempt to defend their planet, even after Major Dominic Ounimbango sold out his own people and planet by giving the Gael the codes necessary to shut down Earth's defenses.

The ship had been captained by a fellow Japanese officer, Captain Oh Nobou, an aging veteran of the T-Fed navy, who could trace his ancestry back to Japanese aristocracy and who took his adherence to the code of bushido and the ancient Japanese ways of the Samurai very seriously. When the Gael fleet brushed aside the majority of the T-Fed force relatively easily and launched its devastating aerial bombardment of Midway, Captain Oh had turned to his first officer and handed him the katana that had been in his family for generations. Despite it being technically against T-Fed uniform regulations, Oh was never without the blade. Noichi accepted it with a bow and then watched as his mentor drew a dagger from his belt and rammed it into his own guts.

This had drawn gasps from the crew who stopped paying attention to the battle outside as their captain committed seppuku. Although Noichi had not been one for bushido, and he was a descendent of simple fishermen, he locked eyes with Oh as the captain went down to one knee, his teeth gritted and his breath coming in rapid, quiet gasps. An unstated demand appeared in Oh's eyes, and Noichi understood it almost immediately. Noichi had witnessed it in films about the history of his land and people, and had never understood it before. In that moment though, he thought he understood. Drawing Oh's katana from its scabbard, Noichi let out a cry and sliced off his captain's head.

An uproar came from the bridge officers, but Noichi silenced them with a cold stare. "To end his pain. To save his honor."

Noichi had sheathed the sword, sat down in the captain's chair and taken control of the *Tora*. He fought tenaciously, taking down two Gael cruisers in the process before the surrender order at last came through. When his superiors ordered him to stop firing at the intruding Gael, Noichi wondered if he should not join his captain in death. Death would certainly have been preferable to the dishonor of surrendering to the enemy.

While that was clearly Captain Oh's opinion, Noichi chose a different course. Refusing to comply, he ordered his ship to evacuate Terran space, crippling a Gael destroyer in the process. Noichi believed that a time would come when the Terrans would throw off the yoke of their Gael oppressors, and he wanted to face the Gael on that battlefield.

When the Resistance was formed, he offered up his ship to it and had been given overall command of one of the Resistance's four space-bound battle groups. With the job came the title of commodore, a meaningless designation to signify he had slight command over the other captains in the battle group. He was the most experienced space officer in the Resistance, and he wanted the title of Admiral and the ability to make decisions that came with it. That would have meant leaving his ship behind though as Resistance Admirals sat on the Resistance Council and did not actively participate in missions or the fighting.

Noichi craved the ability to direct some of the Resistance's action, because he was beginning to despise the direction it had taken. Most of the Resistance's hostility was directed against human collaborators, even civilians, and not the Gael themselves. The Gael did not often present targets, of course, but that mattered not in the slightest to Noichi. As far as he was concerned, killing other humans only turned people against them and made the Gael more sympathetic. They needed to be recruiting followers to their cause, swelling it with numbers so great that a second Gael War could be declared and won.

That was one of the reasons he hated the orders he had just received from Major Paulsen. The limey had ordered his battle group to Barnard's VI to attack a Terran Gael Force carrier in order to ensure the death of a woman the Gael had captured. Noichi had read the Resistance's file on her. The Gael wanted her alive for some reason. Their manufactured reason was terrorism and Resistance affiliation, but the Resistance claimed no knowledge of her. Besides, if she were really a captured Resistance agent, she would have taken her suicide pill and been done with it.

Noichi shook his head as he finished re-reading the file. The Gael wanted her alive, so the Resistance wanted her dead, and to do so, they had ordered him to kill an entire carrier's worth of humans. The end of his official orders bore the words: no survivors. Although he found it abhorrent, he ordered the *Tora* and the battle group based at a Resistance-constructed base, located in the middle of nowhere between systems, well away from the shipping lanes, to deploy. Ten ships and their fighter complements were now streaking toward Barnard's VI at light speed, their commodore wishing he did not have to fulfill his orders and that he had a real enemy to fight.

# Chapter 28

The cargo bay to the *Melody Tryst* opened, and Lafayette, Fix, and Squawk strode down it, looking around until they spotted Captain Jennings at the *Grey Vistula's* hangar bay control station. The captain hoped they would find it odd he was still in his spacesuit and prepare accordingly. They did not.

"*Mon capitaine.*" Lafayette waved as he started striding over to him. "I must say of all your plans, this has to be the craziest we've ever tried. Can't believe it's working so far."

"It's not exactly working," Jennings said as he jerked his head backward toward the woman behind him.

As they got closer, the others finally could see the woman dressed in a black flight suit holding a plasma pistol to Jennings's back. Lafayette and Fix immediately went for weapons holstered on their hips.

"I wouldn't," Selena Beauregard cautioned. "He'll be dead long before you get a draw on me."

Jennings's crew hesitated for a moment and exchanged glances while Beauregard stared at them. "Wait a minute." Indicating Fix, Selena said, "I know you. From the fraternity party. You dosed Jacq Clemmons and got him out of there." She dug the gun into Jennings's back a little more. "I'm guessing that makes you his partner."

"Technically, he's my partner," Jennings said.

Beauregard laughed mellifluously.

Fix nodded slowly, staring at Beauregard. A slim grin crossed his face. "Did nae recognize you without a barely post-pubescent teen's crotch attached to your arse. Or chunder all over you."

Beauregard shot him a dirty look. "I thought you were some more of Petrova's people or TGF."

"Sneaking back onto a ship the TGF has captured?" Lafayette pointed out.

"You can't possibly still be seeking the bounty," she chided, giving them a little tut-tut with her tongue. "Persistence in this instance will get you killed."

"We're not here for the bounty," Jennings said.

The assassin clucked her teeth as she apparently considered that for a moment. "What are you doing here then?"

"Rescue op," Jennings said.

Beauregard laughed even deeper. "Oh God, that's good. Let me guess, she fluttered those pretty eyes or maybe shook those big tits in your face and got you to sway."

"It's not like that," Jennings said darkly.

"Oh, so you're just the big hero, is that it?" Beauregard continued to laugh as she tapped the gun against the back of Jennings's head. "Not very smart, hero."

Moving faster than Beauregard probably expected, Jennings dropped to the floor, taking his head out of the line of fire. Beauregard instinctively fired and missed, sending a plasma bolt into the ceiling high above them. Jennings kicked out at her shin, and Beauregard cried out in pain, but still bore her weapon down on Jennings. A shot sounded across the expanse, and Beauregard screamed, her left hand instinctively going to the smoking skin on her right arm. The plasma pistol flew from her hand, straight up into the air. Jumping to his feet, Jennings caught in, primed it, and placed it in Beauregard's face.

"Nice shot, Fix," Jennings said.

Fix placed his pistol back in its holster. "Aimin' for her head, Cap'n."

"Guess I'm lucky he's a bad shot," Beauregard said to Jennings as she sank down to the floor, still clutching her wounded arm.

An annoyed sigh escaped the captain's throat. "You're lucky he's a doctor."

An inscrutable expression crossed Fix's face. "You want me to fix her up? I just finished shooting her."

"What's your name again?" Jennings asked of him, throwing a stern glance Fix's way.

"Aye." Reluctantly, he pulled out his medical kit and knelt down to start tending to the wound on Beauregard's arm.

"What a gentleman," Beauregard said sarcastically as she continued to stare up at Jennings, who shrugged in response. "Oh God, you really buy into it, don't you? You think you're a hero."

"Could you please shut the fuck up? You've got to be the most jaded person I've ever met," Jennings growled. "Not that we've actually met, of course. But I'm guessing you were in the stealth ship that attacked us when we were leaving Strikeplain."

"Very good, Captain Jennings," she said. "Selena Beauregard."

Jennings laughed explosively. "Selena Beauregard? Really?"

"Yes, you've heard of me?" she said with an appreciative smile.

"No, that's just the most ridiculous name I've ever heard," Jennings said. "And you clearly made it up. Didn't have a cool enough name for the Resistance, so you fashioned a new one?" Selena flinched like she was insulted and opened her mouth to speak but Jennings held up a hand. "No, no, wait a sec. If you were in the Resistance, you would have spat out some ridiculous rank before your name. Those idiots have a bunch of corporals calling themselves colonels and some civvies parading as admirals. No, I'm guessing you're working for them, but you're a freelancer. Am I right? You don't have any ideals, and you laugh at those who do. You don't believe in honor, and you therefore call yourself a capitalist. Any guilt you ever felt for your crimes has been bought away or rationalized that you were not making the decision, and that if you didn't do it, someone else would."

Beauregard stared daggers at him as Fix finished putting a bandage on her arm. He stood back up and stepped away from her. "She'll be fine."

"Personally, I don't care why you do what you do," Jennings said. "I won't even hold it against you for trying to kill us back on Strikeplain. But we are here to take back Michelle Williams away from the Gael, and if you get in the way of that, then you and I are enemies."

"His enemies tend to spring leaks," Fix muttered darkly.

Beauregard pulled herself to her feet. "I don't have any interest in the girl any longer. My contract with the Resistance expired right around the time Petrova captured me."

"How come the TGF didn't capture you when they took Petrova's ship?" Lafayette asked.

A derisive sneer crossed her face. "They didn't search the cells too thoroughly. And the Resistance doesn't hire me to be simple eye candy."

"If you're not working for them to kill the girl, you could always help us," Lafayette pointed out.

Beauregard laughed, and Jennings shook his head at Lafayette. "I don't think we could afford Ms. Beauregard's services."

"Too true," she said.

"But you're stuck on this boat with us," Lafayette said as he walked around to the control terminal and called up a general ship status report. "And pretty soon, we're going to be docked inside a TGF carrier. Not the best place for you to be."

"I'm pretty resourceful," she said. "And I've already made a deal to get myself out of here."

Jennings glanced to Lafayette, his eyes set with meaning which Lafayette did not appear to understand. The captain turned back to Beauregard. "How long until they get here?"

"Until who gets here?" Lafayette asked.

"Beauregard squared herself away with the Resistance by giving them Michelle's position," he said. "They've probably got one of their ragtag little fleets on the way here now. Am I wrong?"

She shook her head. "Even managed to arrange a little transportation out of the deal."

Fix drew his weapon again. "Can we kill her now?"

Jennings held up a hand. "No, but we can lock her back in the cells again. She'll find it harder to catch a lift from there."

The confident smirk vanished from Beauregard's face. "Look, I'm sorry, but the girl is gone. You'll never get her away from the Gael and certainly not before the Resistance turns that carrier to slag. Once the runabout is docked, we can take this ship and get out of this system before they are able to launch anything against us. Hell, we could even use the ship as a decoy and make a break for it on your ship there. Everybody wins."

"Except Michelle Williams," Jennings said.

Beauregard let loose a cry of exasperation. "Fine. What level of help do I have to give you to stay out of the cells?" Defiantly, she crossed her arms and stared angrily at Jennings.

"How much is your life worth to you?" Jennings asked.

Grumpily, she said, "I think you know the answer to that."

"Good," Jennings said. "Because you're about to participate in a four-man assault against a ship crewed by over one thousand."

"Fine," Beauregard muttered. "But could you tell me what the hell is going on here?"

Jennings raised an eyebrow. "I wouldn't think you would care."

"Well, as long as I am going to do something stupid, I would like to catalogue the full extent of my stupidity," she said.

~

Twenty minutes later, Jennings had told Beauregard everything he knew about the situation- it was not much. All he knew was that Michelle Williams was not a terrorist, the Gael really wanted her and he had no idea why, and the Gael suddenly decided everyone associated with this bounty needed to be either killed or arrested. It sounded from what Jennings overheard from Pahhal that they would destroy any and all evidence regarding the retrieval of Michelle Williams.

"Makes sense," Beauregard said.

"I'm glad it does to someone," Jennings said.

They were sitting on the *Grey Vistula's* bridge, going through Petrova's files, looking for anything useful in the ship's inventory: weapons, components for the ship, and supplies. Jennings had already sent Squawk to a mechanic's locker on the bay level, and the amount of material and tools available sent Squawk into a near fit of joy. Fix and Lafayette had been sent to the weapons locker. In the viewscreen in front of them, the *TGFS Intrepid* loomed and a fighter wing streaked in front of their view.

"I take it Operation Aurora is something with which you are unfamiliar, captain," she said.

"Doesn't ring a bell."

"My Resistance contact told me about it. How they got it, I don't know," Beauregard said. "They have hackers working non-stop trying to break into TGF files, and they have moles within the TGF who are sympathetic to the cause."

"What is it?" Jennings said.

"A list of one hundred and eleven names," she said. "All of them have been accused of treason, terrorism, or mass atrocity. All of them are supposedly associated with the Resistance."

"Let me guess," Jennings said as he glanced up from his computer console. "Your Resistance contact confirmed none of them are actually in the Resistance, right?"

She nodded.

"Based on what I learned about Michelle, I managed to guess as much about her," he said. "But if none of them are Resistance members, why the hell do the Gael want them?"

A shrug was the only answer she gave at first. "Don't know. Don't really care either." After a moment, she added, "Oh, but there's something else you might be interested in. They already have one hundred and ten of the people on the list. Michelle Williams is number one hundred eleven. We are at their endgame, which is probably why they are cleaning up after themselves so diligently. Whatever the Gael are seeking, they have it now."

"Not for long," Jennings said.

Beauregard laughed. "You're insane, Captain Jennings. And against my best instincts, I find myself liking you." She stood up from the navigator's seat she occupied and walked closer to him, her beauty and shapely figure nicely silhouetted against the stars of the viewscreen. "Maybe if we survive this…" She bent over to lock her eyes onto his eyes, giving him a peek down the top of her flight suit, which she had left partially unzipped.

"Don't take this the wrong way," Jennings began. "But if I went to bed with you, I have the sneaking suspicion I would end up dead."

Beauregard took the offered rejection in stride. "That's right. Besides your heart clearly belongs to another."

Jennings was about to protest again, but the runabout suddenly surged forward toward the *Intrepid*. "The runabout is docking. We're probably next."

"Wonderful," she said. "Let's get this suicide mission of yours over with."

# Chapter 29

In the brig of the *TGFS Intrepid's* runabout, Michelle Williams noticed a number of subtle differences in their journey. There had been a brief sensation of deceleration, where she assumed they had dropped out of light speed. It was the second time they had done so, but the first had been followed by a near immediate acceleration as they jumped back into light speed along a new course. This time was different. She had the impression they were now cruising along at sublight speed, which probably met one thing: they had arrived at wherever they were taking her.

With no clocks in the brig and her not having a watch, she guessed it took twenty or thirty minutes before a loud rumbling echoed across the runabout's hull. Michelle's parents had been wealthy enough to afford interstellar vacations, and they frequently took her to Mars, Europa, and even some of the outer world colonies. Whenever their star liner arrived at a fueling station or an orbital spaceport, she would hear that same sound when their ship was captured by a magnetic beam.

The sound lasted for a few minutes as she sensed they were being drawn into something cavernous. A strange buzz of static electricity passed over them. Michelle recognized it as passing through a weak electro-magnetic shield. The runabout settled on its landing legs, sending a slight jerk throughout the entire ship, and the sensation ceased.

Michelle had no idea how long it would take for them to come for her, but as it turned out, it was not long. Ten minutes after they touched down wherever they were, Michelle's cell door slid open. A half-dozen TGF guards stood at the ready outside, as did the African general from the asteroid mining colony. Next to him stood the Gael, who stared at her as if appraising something he might devour.

"Come on out of there, girl." General Ounimbango beckoned her forward with his hand.

Shooting all of them a look of what she hoped was purest loathing, she nonetheless complied and emerged into the corridor. To her left, another dozen TGF soldiers were fitting a huddled bunch of bounty hunters with wrist manacles connected by high tensile wire to the next pair of manacles. It forced the prisoners to march in a single file line as they were led out of the brig. The last one in the line was Anastasia Petrova, the woman who shot Matthew Jennings. Petrova flashed a savage grin in her direction, and Michelle forgot entirely where she was.

Charging across the open space in between them, she reached Petrova before the guards even reacted. Grabbing the bounty hunter by the hair, Michelle simply dropped down to the ground, dragging Petrova with her, the bounty hunter crying out in pain. The manacles connecting all the prisoners caused a domino effect where the first four men chained in front of Petrova fell to the ground before one of the prisoners at last braced himself and kept himself upright.

Letting go of Petrova's hair and noting with some satisfaction that some hair came off into her hands, Michelle turned Petrova around and punched her square in the face. She was not certain if Petrova's nose broke, but immediately a stream of blood ran down the Russian's face. Michelle shook her hand vigorously. That was the first time she had ever punched someone. No one told her it hurt as much as it did.

"Get off me, you stupid girl!" Petrova screamed.

Michelle responded by slapping her across the face with her other hand. "That was for Matthew." She reared back to smack her again.

A strong hand grabbed her by the wrist and pulled Michelle to her feet before she could strike. She almost wheeled about on the person who held her, but saw a man with an armored helmet, holding a plasma pistol in his other hand, and thought better of it.

"That's quite enough of that, my dear," the Gael Overseer Pahhal said.

"You'll pay for this," Petrova spat, unable to wipe the blood away from her face because of the hand manacles.

"Take them to the *Intrepid's* brig," General Ounimbango ordered.

One of the TGF soldiers grabbed the front man in the line of chained bounty hunters and started pulling on him. Slowly, all of

Petrova's men fell into line, one behind the other, trailed lastly by their furious and bleeding leader, who continued cursing in Russian at Michelle. They marched slowly out of the runabout's brig, paced on each side by a half dozen TGF soldiers.

"Now, Ms. Williams, I would appreciate it if you would let my men put manacles on you without any further... violence," Ounimbango said.

Michelle nodded, and one of the soldiers stepped forward with a pair of binders in his hand.

Pahhal raised a hand. "That will not be necessary."

"There are protocols," Ounimbango said nervously. "All prisoners going to the brig must be bound."

"True," he said. "But she's not going to the brig."

Ounimbango blinked in surprise. "What?"

"I will take custody of her." Pahhal stepped forward and removed a device from his robe which like a metal collar. Stepping forward, he said, "This should keep Ms. Williams from running off while my guest."

"What is that?" she asked, her tone nervous.

"A little invention of ours for helping to encourage compliance," Pahhal said. "You can allow me to put in on you, or I can have General Ounimbango order his men to force it on you. Which would you prefer?"

Reluctantly, Michelle nodded. Pahhal stepped forward and wrapped the collar around her neck, snapping it closed.

From the exit to the brig, a demeaning voice called, "The slave collar is a good look for you." Anastasia Petrova was still marching slowly out of the room. "Shockingly good."

Michelle made as if to take another run at Petrova, but Pahhal caught her by the arm. "I wouldn't recommend that." Michelle struggled for another moment to break free of the long-fingered grasp of the Gael, but he calmly said, "With that collar in place, if you get more than twenty-five feet from me, you will know pain the likes of which you have never experienced."

Michelle stopped struggling and turned back to the Gael.

"Apologies, but I feel a demonstration is in order," he said as he pressed a button on a device in his hand.

Michelle screamed as electricity poured into her, and she dropped to the floor, her entire body contorting in spasms of pain. It lasted no more than a few seconds, but left Michelle with tears streaming down her face, her breath coming to her in ragged gasps, and every muscle in her body aching. Pahhal reached a long arm down to help her to her feet, but she ignored it and pulled herself up on her own.

Pahhal smiled wickedly. "If you stray fifty feet from me, it will be your death."

"I understand," she spat, still breathing heavily.

"Excellent," Pahhal said before turning to Ounimbango. "General, thank you for your assistance, but I shall not be needing you or your men any longer to help me escort Ms. Williams."

The Gael made an "after you" gesture with his hands in the direction of Ounimbango and the TGF forces. Ounimbango gave a dubious frown regarding the proposition, but he was apparently used to taking Pahhal's suggestions as orders. With as much dignity as the beefy man could muster, Ounimbango marched himself past Michelle, his TGF security forces falling into line behind him.

"I will be honest with you, Ms. Williams," Pahhal said as soon as Ounimbango was out of earshot. "I will be quite happy to be done dealing with that obnoxious human being now that Operation Aurora is at last complete."

"Operation Aurora?"

"All in good time." With that, Pahhal took her by the arm and led her out of the runabout's brig.

The Gael led Michelle Williams to a lift which descended to the lowest level of the runabout, then to a gangplank about twenty people wide. The sheer size of the space Michelle walked into was like nothing she had ever seen in a spaceship before. Two areas were open to space, covered by full energy shields when no ships were entering or leaving the hangar and shields only strong enough to contain atmosphere when a ship docked or launched. The runabout had entered through the cavernous opening to space on the starboard and had pulled into a parking space specifically set aside for it to the right of that opening, toward the fore end of the ship. Next to it was the ship Michelle recognized from leaving the mining colony. It must be Petrova's ship which, for some reason, the Gael had hauled back with them.

To the left of the opening sat a group of smaller shuttles and a series of maintenance bays. Spare parts and tools lined the walls, and a few fighters appeared to be in varying stages of being taken apart and put back together. The wall opposite of the starboard opening to space was riddled with small hangars, stacked two high, each of which housed a fighter or bomber.

Directly in front of the wall of fighters was a long lane created by two sets of blinking lights that each ran the entire length of the hangar, terminating at the bow egress into space. *It must have been the launch ramp for the fighters*, Michelle thought to herself as Pahhal continued to lead her across the vast space.

She spied the long line of prisoners moving toward a different section of the ship, but she chose to ignore them and instead focused on her surroundings. Every hundred feet or so, she passed a column which ran floor to ceiling with a series of ten-foot-tall lockers built around it. The labeling on the lockers read: Emergency Decompression.

Pahhal led her to the far side of the hangar, far away from either of the openings to space, and into a lift. He pushed a button for a level marked Officer Quarters, Intrepid Club, O Fitness. *Life must not be too bad as a TGF officer*, Michelle thought to herself. *All you needed to do was not mind working for the Gael, the race which subjugated humanity.* She chanced a look at her captor, but Pahhal paid her little mind. He had a strangely serene expression on his face as they arrived at their level with a cheerful ding from the elevator.

The doors opened, and they proceeded down the hallway, passing a few men in TGF uniforms, who nodded or bowed slightly to the Overseer as they passed. They continued by a restaurant or bar and then a fitness club before they entered a corridor with doors every twenty feet or so. It reminded Michelle of her parents' condo in Seaboard or of a luxury hotel.

At last, they arrived at a door at the end of the corridor. Pahhal punched a series of commands into the control pad, and the door slid open, revealing an empty room. It was carpeted richly despite being without adornment, and illumination came from soft yellow lighting recessed into the walls and ceiling. There was no furniture even though clearly designed as quarters for a high-ranking member of the crew. The kitchen, which was open to the room they stood in (what Michelle assumed was the living room), looked like it had never been used, although she could say that about all the rooms.

"I apologize for the Spartan nature of the environs," Pahhal said as the door closed automatically behind him. He turned and punched a series of new commands into the control pad on this side of the door, locking it. "My kind do not see the same need for relaxation and comfort as yours does." His eyes glanced to a bedroom door. "Or perhaps we just experience it differently, I should say. Our free time is not spent in the same way."

"Where do you sleep or eat?" Michelle asked, unable to keep from being a little curious.

"My kind do neither," he said as he walked toward the door set in the wall on his right, the one he had eyed previously. "Kindly sit down here." He pointed to the floor against the wall next to the door.

Michelle walked over to the place he indicated, pointed at the floor, and asked in an annoyed voice, "Right here?"

"Humans cannot pass through this door." With a wave, he indicated the one right in front of them. "They will be killed instantly by the defensive measures in place." Satisfaction passed onto the Gael's face. "I'm going into this room for a while by myself. If you'll remember what happens if you stray too far away from me, you'll appreciate my recommendation of where you sit."

Nodding, Michelle sat where Pahhal indicated, and the Gael Overseer opened the door to what would have been a bedroom if this were a human's quarters. Michelle tried to get a glance into the room, but the door shut behind Pahhal almost immediately and she saw nothing.

~

Immediately, Pahhal headed into the center of the room as the silver discs imbedded in the wall began sending out their purplish-black energy. Pahhal felt himself encased in the ball of energy, his mind completely engaged by the Construct. His mind whirred as fast as he had ever found it doing, spurred by the excitement he felt churning through his thoughts as his mind sought connection to the Gael military collective. Pahhal fired off the passwords required with incredible speed and was soon connected to Fleet Admiral Varenhas.

"Pahhal?" Varenhas's voice echoed throughout Pahhal's mind.

"I have her!" Pahhal said excitedly.

"You do?!? We have all one hundred and eleven of them?" Varenhas's mind spoke excitedly.

"Yes, my friend," he said. "We are finally there."

"We are going home," Varenhas said. "After all this time, we are going home at last."

"Indeed. We need to get the one hundred and eleven humans to Gael space as quickly as possible," Pahhal said. "The supercruiser you promised me?"

"In your area and will arrive soon," Varenhas said.

"Very well, I will transfer the humans to it and come aboard, then the supercruiser will destroy this vessel," Pahhal said. "I will suffer no chances of failure in this endeavor."

"Of course," Varenhas said. "I look forward to seeing you at the Great Gate, my friend."

"To you as well." Pahhal disconnected his mind from the Construct, and the dark energy which filled the room vanished. "The Great Gate shall open at last... After millennia of failure."

~

Michelle spent her time when Pahhal was in the bedroom by himself wondering what the hell was going on. Since meeting Matthew Jennings on Strikeplain, she had been moving so quickly that she had barely considered again why this was happening to her. The charges of terrorism had clearly been orchestrated by this Gael, as it was he who wanted her. But none of it made any sense. He said she was the last of the humans he was looking for. *Why would he be interested in her? What could he possibly want her for?*

The questions kept swimming around her head, and she focused on them in order to avoid dwelling on her grief. She had not particularly known Matthew Jennings well, but he saved her from sexual servitude on Strikeplain. And while his motives had not been purely for her benefit at the time, he believed her and tried to protect her. Before being shot, Jennings had come so close to getting her back from Petrova. Seeing him on the other side of the elevator doors when they opened had felt like the greatest moment of her life. and it had been very fleeting.

The other thing she avoided dwelling on was the sense that she would be killed. The Gael had charged her with a crime which bore the death penalty, but they clearly had no intention of going through with a trial. Therefore, whatever the Gael wanted her for was almost certainly going to result in her death. She just hoped it was painless.

The door slid open, and Pahhal emerged, full of energy and smiling down at Michelle. "You have been comfortable, I trust?"

"I want to know something," she said, ignoring his question.

"Yes, this will end in your death," Pahhal said quietly. "But it will not be uncomfortable."

"I already assumed as much," she said as she stood up to face the Gael. Receiving the confirmation of what she already suspected should have made her scared or depressed, but instead gave her some steely resolve. "I want to know why."

Pahhal stared at her for a moment, before he said, "Yes, I suppose that is only fair. But not here. There's something I must show you first."

# Chapter 30

Fix and Lafayette had raided the weapons locker onboard the *Grey Vistula* and apparently came away from the experience quite satisfied. They stood rather proudly in the *Grey Vistula* hangar bay right next to the *Melody Tryst*, a plethora of weapons and gear spread out across a black cloth tarp.

"Let's be glad Petrova believes in keeping a well-stocked cupboard, *non*?" Lafayette said as Jennings and Beauregard approached him.

The latter sized up the weapons cache with an appreciative expression. "You guys don't believe in subtlety, do you?"

"Subtlety has its points," Jennings said as he knelt down, grabbed a gun belt and stood back up. "What it has to do with this line of work is beyond me though."

Petrova apparently believed in buying her firearms in bulk, so there was a decent deal of symmetry to the weapons they had procured. Each of Jennings's crew now wore weapons belts which carried two plasma pistols with ammunition for each and crisscrossing bandoliers attached. One bandolier had a back holster for a double-barreled grenade launcher and additional grenades which could be used in the launcher or armed and tossed by hand. The second bandolier had ammunition for the automatic plasma rifles each now carried.

"How do you expect to sneak around the ship armed like that?" Beauregard asked.

Jennings pressed a button on his handheld instead of answering her. "Minerva, how's your hack coming?"

The computer NAI responded, "Frankly, I'm disappointed by how easy it is to hack into a Terran Gael Force military computer."

"Your computer has quite the attitude," Beauregard said.

"The same could be said of you," Minerva responded coolly.

"Oh no, I offended the machine," Beauregard retorted.

"Not nearly as offensive as your taste in fashion," Minerva fired back. "That dress you wore back at our encounter at the Colonial Triangle, what dead whore did you pilfer it from?"

Beauregard steamed with fury and opened her mouth as if to say something, but Jennings held up a hand. "You're arguing with my tablet, Ms. Beauregard. Besides, you don't want to be on Minerva's bad side. She knows a lot about everyone, and she can be brutal... I mean... honest."

Catching movement out of the corner of her eye, she turned to Fix and Lafayette who were nodding in agreement with Jennings. Crossing her arms angrily, Beauregard nevertheless bit her tongue and said nothing more. Jennings gave her a look which he hoped expressed something akin to gratitude.

"What did you find, Minerva?" Jennings asked.

"I have a full layout of the ship and access to the internal sensors," she said. "It is after midnight standard ship time, so the hangar is mostly empty. Sensors show a large number of people leaving the hangar approximately two minutes ago."

"That would be the prisoners," Jennings reasoned.

"Currently, no mechanics are on duty per the logs, and only a half-dozen life signs are present," Minerva said. "All of those are located in a small room located off the maintenance bays. There is a high level of carbon monoxide and nicotine in the atmosphere."

"Techs playing cards and having a smoke?" Lafayette suggested.

Jennings nodded. "What about security, Minerva?"

"Minimum security in place currently. Standard roving patrols and fixed guards in high security areas. A patrol should arrive in the hangar level in approximately ten minutes. Security cameras monitor the entire area however."

"That will make things a little more difficult," Lafayette said. "The minute we're spotted this entire operation is blown."

"Minerva, can you short out the cameras?" Jennings asked.

"I could, but doing so would trigger an ultraviolet alert," she said. "Armed security would be placed in all areas until video is restored."

Fix grunted. "Any ideas, Cap'n?"

Beauregard gave a loud and annoyed sigh. "Minerva, can you tell me if a pilot's ready room is nearby?"

There was no answer for a moment.

"Please," she added.

"Yes," Minerva said. "Approximately two hundred feet from your current location."

"Are the security cameras fixed or do they sweep?" she followed.

"Sweeping."

"Could you be a nice, smart computer and plot a course with a series of blind spots and hiding places so I can get to that ready room?" she asked.

Minerva remained silent while calculating. "Eighty-two percent chance of avoiding being seen, considering all variables."

"You can only give me eighty-two percent?" Beauregard chided.

"All of the variables are a result of your abilities, not mine," Minerva said coldly.

Beauregard shrugged her eyebrows. "Touché."

"You'll need to start at the belly hatch in the center of the hangar," Minerva said. "And captain, you'll need to give her a comm unit."

"What's your plan?" Jennings asked the assassin as he handed over an earpiece.

A wry grin crossed her face. "Why spoil the surprise?" she said as she accepted it, placed it in her ear, and then jogged off toward the center of the hangar.

~

Opening up a hatch in the floor of the *Grey Vistula*, Beauregard saw the plain gray tarmac streaked with yellow dashes of paint of the *Intrepid's* hangar floor. It was about an eight foot drop down to the ground, and Beauregard crouched next to the opening.

"The underbelly of the *Grey Vistula* is completely invisible to the cameras," came Minerva's voice in her ear.

Immediately, Beauregard dropped down to the floor below, landing gracefully in a crouch. Glancing around, she took stock of her situation. She knelt in the middle of a triangle formed by the *Grey Vistula's* three landing legs. To her left was the *Intrepid's* runabout, and across from her was the massive hangar wall which storied the *Intrepid's* fighters. The fighters were stacked two high except in one location. One of the fighter bays was covered in glass and had a door set into it next to the window. The pilot's ready room, she realized. There was not a lot of cover between where she now crouched and her destination, just a few drum barrels which probably carried avionics fuel and a couple of columns with Emergency Decompression lockers surrounding them.

"First goal is the column twenty degrees to your left," Minerva said.

"Which side?" she whispered.

"You will need to get into the locker," Minerva said. "Next window in five seconds. Four. Three."

Beauregard tensed her entire body, and when Minerva said, "Go," she sprang forward, racing across the space between the *Grey Vistula* and the locker. As she approached the locker, she barely slowed, allowing her body to crash into the locker door. Hurriedly, she threw it open and forced her way inside, shoving aside atmosphere suits and oxygen tanks. Minerva had been giving her updates as she ran, but she heard none of them. Beauregard reached back and closed the locker door, sealing herself in darkness.

"Well done," Minerva's voice appeared in her ear. "You made it with one point four seconds to spare. Do you need a moment to rest?"

"No."

"Very well. Destination two is a set of aviation fuel barrels. There will be a very brief pause, and then you will need to make for the second locker. Make sure you close the locker you leave," Minerva said. "You don't want to leave anything out of place."

"Right," Beauregard muttered.

"Now."

Beauregard kicked open the locker door and slammed it shut behind her. Taking off at a sprint, she made for the set of black and green barrels and slid across the slick flooring as she approached them, popping up into a crouch as soon as she was in position. She had barely taken a breath before Minerva told her to go again, and she raced across the hangar to the second set of lockers, throwing herself inside quickly and slamming the door shut.

"You'll need to cross one hundred yards in fourteen seconds and key in the passcode at the pilot's ready room door," Minerva advised.

"And I trust you've hacked that passcode?" she said in between deep gulps of air.

"Four-four-four-three," she said. "Not particularly creative. Window is in fifteen seconds. Are you ready?"

"Yes." Beauregard tensed her body again and placed her hand on the locker door handle.

On Minerva's word, she threw herself out of the locker and sprinted across the fighter launching lane, racing toward the ready room door. Crashing into the door hard, her hands fumbled for the control pad and she hit four-four-four-four, as her twitching muscles caused her to hit the four one time too many.

"They can see you," Minerva said calmly as Beauregard rapidly punched in the combination and pushed open the ready room door. She slammed it shut behind her and leaned back against it, her chest heaving as she tried to catch her breath. Her panting almost drowned out the NAI saying, "The good news is that no alarms have been sounded. Whoever is keeping an eye on the video must not be as vigilant as they should be."

"Any cameras in here?" she asked.

"Negative," she said. "Pilots change in here- they probably want to give them their privacy."

"Right."

The room stretched into the distance with rows of lockers and benches headed away from where Beauregard stood. Looking down one of the rows, she could see racks of bunks in the area beyond the lockers and showers even further back. The room was completely empty though. Beauregard started forward, opening lockers as she went, until she found what she was looking for. After seven lockers, she found it.

Quickly, she kicked off her boots, unzipped her flight suit and shrugged her lithe, muscle-toned body out of it. Standing in her form fitting navy blue underwear, she grabbed one of the green Terran Gael

Force pilot jumpsuits off a hanger and got dressed. She put her boots back on, tied her blonde hair back in a ponytail so it was up to TGF military standards. From the same locker, she grabbed several more jumpsuits, discarded them as being either too large or too small, and grabbed several more. At last, she had what she needed, and she stuffed the uniforms into a black duffel bag she had found.

Looking like a TGF pilot now, Beauregard was unconcerned with the *Intrepid's* surveillance as she strode back out of the pilot's ready room and made her way across the hangar back to the *Grey Vistula*. Heading back to the belly hatch, she tossed the bag up through the opening. Two hands appeared out of nowhere to catch it, and then Matthew Jennings's face appeared in the hatchway.

"Minerva said you were on the way back," he said as he extended a hand down through the opening.

Beauregard leapt upwards and caught Jennings's hand, somewhat surprised at how easily Jennings pulled her up through the hatch. He led her back to where the others stood around a computer monitor that appeared to be sitting on a short easel. As she approached, she realized the Pasquatil was supporting it as the Cajun spoke animatedly with a disembodied female voice. The Pasquatil pulled the monitor back down to his eye level and started punching some commands into it.

Squawk saluted Jennings enthusiastically. "Overrode passwords. Installed better passwords."

"What was wrong with the *Tryst's* passwords?" he asked.

"Not the *Tryst*, this ship," Squawk retorted, using his thin arms to indicate the space all around them.

"Just in case, *mon capitaine*," Lafayette said. "We wouldn't want one of Petrova's people stealing our ride."

Jennings gave an acidic chuckle. "I don't have any intention of letting her out of the lock-up."

"What we intend and what happens is nae usually the same," Fix pointed out.

"Good point." Jennings opened up the duffel bag Beauregard had brought along and passed out the flight suits. "Put these on over top of your weapons. We won't stand up to more than cursory scrutiny, but we should be able to get to the brig at least."

Jennings, Lafayette, and Fix put the flight suits on over top of their clothing and weapons belts. Jennings advised them each to put one of their plasma pistols inside the jumpsuits' pockets. He collected the automatic plasma rifles and threw them into the duffel, before slinging the bag over his shoulder. He noticed Fix doing the same thing.

"What's in there?" he asked.

"Symtex," he said. "Just in case."

"*Dis* is a good fit," Lafayette observed, pulling on the jumpsuit's sleeves until they settled around his wrist where he wanted.

Beauregard winked at him. "I know how to size up a man." She threw her dark eyes toward Jennings, who suddenly shifted uncomfortably and checked the charge on his weapon. In response, she laughed again.

"Minerva has been providing us with the best possible path to the brig," Jennings said. "We're only two floors down from it."

"We have a few problems though," Lafayette said.

"With this plan?" Beauregard responded sarcastically as she placed a hand on a hip. "You jest."

"The brig is located in the heart of security," he said. "So, we'll need to deal with that. Plus, you have two very heavily guarded areas on either side of security. Engineering to the aft and storage to the fore."

"Storage is heavily guarded?" Beauregard asked, her tone disbelieving.

"For some reason." Jennings picked up the computer tablet from Squawk and showed it to Beauregard. "This area especially for some reason. There isn't even access from the security side. It's a completely isolated room."

"Fascinating, but not exactly pertinent," she pointed out.

"We can't go through it to get to security, and we'll have trouble getting through engineering without raising suspicion," Jennings clarified.

"Then we walk in the front door," Beauregard said.

They all turned to her for a moment. Lafayette stared at her, mouth agape like she was nuts, and Fix wore a muted stare, but

Jennings had a smile crossing his face. "My kind of girl." Turning to Squawk, he said, "I want my ship in good working order by the time I get back."

"That would be a miraculous miracle," Squawk said, but not without enthusiasm.

"And if I give you the order to do so, you take the ship and run for it," Jennings added, a slight tone of affection in his voice.

The Pasquatil wrinkled his nose in confusion. "You're friends," he said in a way which suggested he would hear nothing more on the matter.

"I want you to save yourself if there's no chance for us," he insisted.

"Can't leave friends," Squawk said, shaking his head energetically. "No, no, no. You go get friend Michelle. All together, we leave."

A surge of affection filled Jennings's face, directed at his diminutive engineer. Beauregard found that odd. As the others finished prepping for their suicide mission, she pulled Jennings aside and said, "I've never seen a human with a Pasquatil friend before. Most people tend to find them annoying."

"Well... it's kind of funny, I suppose," Jennings said. "After all we've been through, Lafayette's friendship comes easy; and Fix has his own strange sense of loyalty; but I never truly considered Squawk. He's always willing to go with me, always willing to do what I say no matter how insane. I always assumed he stayed with this crew because he enjoyed tinkering on the ship. Honestly, until Squawk said that a moment ago, I never considered whether the Pasquatil was a friend, but I also never considered what the Pasquatil race's definition of friendship was. I'm glad that he's with me more out of friendship than anything else."

Beauregard eyed him, not certain what to think as the rest of the crew finished getting ready. "I don't know if I've met someone as odd as you, captain," she said.

With a shrug, Jennings sized up his crew for a moment. "Alright, you heard the man... er... Pasquatil. Let's go get her."

# Chapter 31

Pahhal led Michelle out of his quarters and back to the lift. He selected the level designated Storage (Authorized Personnel Only), Security (Authorized Personnel Only), Engineering (Authorized Personnel Only). Pahhal needed to punch several codes into the lift's control pad in order to get to the level he was leading her to. When the lift doors opened, she saw this was just the beginning of the security. They stepped out into a small room which reminded Michelle of an airlock. There was a door in front of them, but the control pad next to it did not have any power until the lift door behind them closed. Once the elevator door sealed, the control pad lit up, displaying even more security challenges.

Pahhal walked over to it, punched in a series of codes, had his retinas and fingerprints scanned, and then breathed into a small tube to provide a DNA sample. The door at last opened, and he led her through. They strode down a sprawling corridor lit faintly by halogen lights. To her left and right were doors with various signs indicating they housed clothing, food, water, or parts. Each was locked and required multiple security accesses in order to access.

"They really don't want people stealing food," Michelle muttered to herself. "Is it that big a problem?"

"Not when everything is going normally, no," he said. "But imagine yourself on a ship with a thousand other men with no chance of resupply. Control of items, such as food and water, keeps control of the ship."

Pahhal led on as they passed different storage rooms until the corridor terminated in another airlock. The Gael needed to go through the same series of challenges to enter the airlock, and then once the door sealed behind them, he entered a second series of passwords to get back out of the security station. The door opened up into a short corridor, and Pahhal grabbed her arm to keep her from entering.

"Remain here while I deactivate the security system for this corridor," he said.

"What security system?" she asked.

"This part of the ship was specifically designed and installed by the Gael," he said. "If a human being sets foot in the hallway while security is active, poison is immediately released, and you will be dead."

"Would it kill you too?" Michelle asked as she took a step toward the corridor.

The Gael laughed coldly. "The poison is not harmful to Gael," he pointed out, and Michelle stopped moving forward. "Once a Gael enters the corridor, he has thirty seconds to traverse the length of the hallway and deactivate the security, otherwise plasma cannons will obliterate any lifeform in the corridor."

"Right. I'll just wait here then," Michelle said. "But isn't that more than fifty feet away?"

Pahhal smiled and held up the control device for the slave collar. After pressing a button which she hoped deactivated the collar, he headed down the hallway quickly to where he once again passed a bevy of security measures. Turning back around to her, he called, "The system has been deactivated. Step forward and see what all of this is about. The answers to your questions are inside this room."

Michelle tried to step casually down the hallway. She did not want the Gael to see the fear she felt. As she caught up to him, he reactivated the slave collar, and they stepped into the room beyond. The room reminded Michelle of a warehouse, its ceiling approximately twenty feet high. Rows ran off to both the left and right, serving as walkways between twenty-foot-wide sections of walls glowing a cold, eerie blue. The room was freezing, and Michelle clutched her arms tightly around herself.

Pahhal passed her a jacket. "Every so often, I have to let human technicians in here for maintenance. They too cannot tolerate the cold."

"You treat this place so secretively," she said. "I'm surprised you would let even technicians in here."

"They're not given the opportunity to speak of what they have seen," Pahhal said, his tone ominous.

Michelle shivered, and she did not think it was because of the cold. She turned to the right and headed down one of the rows, studying the walls carefully. The walls were not walls at all, but were machines of some kind, stacked three high. Each displayed a control panel with a temperature readout, brain wave measurements, blood pressure monitors, pulse readings, and what Michelle thought might be electrocardiograph displays. Those panels were to the right of a small door which reminded Michelle creepily of the time she went to the medical examiner's office with her mother to identify her grandfather's body. He had been kept in a similar refrigeration unit until the coroner opened it and rolled the body out. The machine Michelle now regarded was a lot more complicated, and there was also a small window set inside the door.

Michelle was fairly certain what she would see when she peered through it, but she still found herself compelled to. Inside the machine, a small child, maybe six or seven years old, lay unconscious, a breathing mask placed over his face, his skin tinged slightly blue, a dozen or more sensors placed on his body, connected to wires which ran into the interior tube's walls.

She wheeled on Pahhal. "A child?"

"It was not we who chose these people," Pahhal said. "We are only doing as we must."

"Why?" Michelle nearly screamed.

Pahhal gave a contemplative frown and appeared disconsolate for a moment. "To understand that, you must understand something about the Gael which no human knows."

"And I'm guessing you don't mind telling me because I'm about to go into one of these… what? Freezer units?" she demanded.

"Cryonic devices," he said. "And no, you won't be going into one. You're the last, and soon we shall all be going to Gael space together. You're correct in that I don't mind telling you because we are so close to the end." He took a deep breath. "First, you must understand, Michelle, that the Gael are not from this realm of existence."

"What does that mean?"

"We are from another dimension," he said. "And we were banished here long, long ago."

"Why were you banished?" she asked.

"It has been so long that no one even remembers," he said. "Very few records exist from our initial time in this galaxy, but those things that are remembered are quite important. The dimension from which we were expelled was our... heaven, to use a Terran word. Nirvana, paradise, Eden... None of these words quite describe what our home is. The Gael are intrinsically tied to this place. Why this is, I cannot say, but I know we are instinctively linked to our home, and we feel its absence every moment of every day. I believe it was a twentieth century religious figure who espoused his concept of damnation as the complete absence of your God. Our damnation is the complete absence of our home, and we as a people, therefore, are confined to this place... this hell."

For a moment, Michelle began to pity the Gael who stood before her. Then she remembered what this alien planned to do to her and decided that hell might be the best place for him.

"The second thing you must understand is a passage exists between this universe and our domain," he said. "It is an island on our current homeworld which we call the Great Gate. It has been locked to us for millennia, and it cannot be opened without a key."

"I still don't see what this has to do with one hundred and eleven humans," she said.

"We are getting there, I promise," he said. "You are asking me to condense thousands of years of strife and struggle into a few minutes' conversation. Be patient."

She made a non-committal noise.

"We know those who banished us to this realm did not construct the Great Gate and that they had no control over the key," he continued. "As such, the key cannot be kept on the other side of the Great Gate, it must be kept in this dimension."

"How long have you been looking for it?" she asked.

"Ten thousand years. This mission has led to all of our technological developments, the unification of our race behind a united goal- we have become what we are because we seek this one goal together. And now, we have found it."

"Where?" she asked.

He gestured around the room and gave a dark smile. "Right here. Right in this room. We scoured the planet we now call home for the key, and then we went to space to search for it. Imagine our surprise when we found it in this backwater berth of a stellar system."

"If you found it, why do you need us?" she asked. "Why do you need one hundred and eleven humans?"

"Our wardens were cunning," he said. "They split the key into pieces. One hundred and eleven of them to be precise."

Michelle's eyes widened. "W-w-what?"

"The key to the Great Gate is the soul of a living being," he said. "Those who put us here hid the key in your race when it was brand new, barely sentient. Those one hundred and eleven pieces of the key have been born and re-born over the generations of your people and now they reside in the one hundred and eleven souls in this room."

"That's not possible," she protested.

"I won't even begin to describe the lengths we have gone to find your race, Ms. Williams," he said. "The other civilizations we have carved from the skies in search of a way home. We went to war with your people and brought them to our heel, all in our effort to find you and your compatriots here."

"How did you find us? The souls you needed?"

"The soul is not so separate from the body it inhabits as your people tend to think," he said. "Your soul is you. It shows in your DNA... in your genetics. It was very kind of your people to voluntary create a catalogue of all human beings' DNA- it made our job much easier. Our leaders decided we should move slowly. No mistakes could be made. No deaths. Who knew how long it would take for a soul to cycle back around to be born again should one be killed? I must confess this transmigration of souls remains something we don't truly understand."

Michelle could think of nothing to say. It seemed too far-fetched to be true. *Would a race really go to war, commit atrocities all for a chance to go to a home they had not seen in ten thousand years?* But then she realized something else. If the Gael finally had what they wanted, had finally found a way home, they would leave this dimension, and humanity would be free of them.

Pahhal smiled. "I see you have worked it out. That is why it will not be necessary to freeze you, Ms. Williams. We studied all of the one hundred and eleven souls with considerable detail. You are a patriot- a true believer in the cause of humanity's liberation. You now have the chance to rid them of the hated Gael once and for all time. I think you'll take advantage of that opportunity. You're going to come with me willingly, won't you?"

Michelle took a deep breath and nodded.

"Thank you." Pahhal strode over to her and placed both his hands on her shoulders. "It would be difficult for me to explain, our emotions are quite dissimilar from yours, I think, but there is a reverence I feel for you, for all of you, my dear Ms. Williams. I am not foolhardy enough to believe the people in these cryonics units would willingly make the same sacrifice for their people, but what you are doing for your people does you a great service. And even though I know the salvation of the Gael means little to you, your sacrifice will still mean everything to my people. When we have transcended once more to the other side of the Great Gate, we will honor and sing the praises of the one hundred and eleven souls who made it possible for us to return to our home."

Michelle did not think she could take any more of his platitudes and was about to tell him so, when a caterwauling alarm began to echo through the room. Pahhal glanced around wildly and raced over to a computer monitor set into the wall by the door.

"What?" Michelle asked. "Is it a problem with one of the cryonic tubes?"

"No, it's a general alert," Pahhal said. "There are intruders aboard the ship."

# Chapter 32

Matthew Jennings led his small force of four infiltrating one of the largest ships in the Terran Gael Force through the belly airlock of the *Grey Vistula* and down to the tarmac of the flight deck. Carrying the bag full of automatic plasma rifles, he motioned for Lafayette, Beauregard, and Fix to follow him as he moved parallel to the fighter launch lane across from the wall that garaged all of the ship's fighters.

Although the hangar deck of the *Intrepid* was mostly open space, the front right corner of the hangar was dominated by the Space Traffic Control Center, which was framed by a two-story tall gray wall with inset windows. The wall ran parallel to the fighter launch lane for several hundred feet before turning at a ninety-degree angle and heading toward the starboard hull. The stern-facing windows looked down on where the *Intrepid's* runabout and the *Grey Vistula* sat parked, but Jennings led them to the side that faced to port and a door labeled Traffic Control.

The door was locked, but Minerva quickly bypassed it and Jennings swung the door open with ease. As with the hangar, the traffic control offices- the department that supervised the arrival and departure of shuttles, fighters, and runabouts- were mostly empty. With no fighters on patrol and the runabout being the only ship out, traffic control had probably been handled from the bridge when they arrived. During a cargo drop or a resupply though, this room would have been one of the busiest in the entire ship.

Interior lighting was dimmed, but a few desks still had lights on. Only one crewman actually saw them, and he nodded briefly as he peeked out of his cubicle, a sleepy expression on his face, before he went back to doing some work on his computer. They passed a set of stairs, but Jennings ignored them, knowing it led upstairs to the space traffic controller's observation area. Instead, he led them further into the maze of cubicles until they at last came to a lift and called for it.

The doors opened, and two crew members stepped out, holding hands, both women. The two groups took a moment to stare at each other awkwardly for a moment before Jennings looked intentionally to the ceiling and gestured with his head for the two ladies to move along. Looking visibly relieved, the two crewmen vanished into the cubicles, probably looking for a private place to make out or more, Jennings thought to himself. While relationships were not strictly verboten among enlisted personnel, frottage was certainly not allowed while at space. Jennings and the others piled into the elevator and hit the button for one floor above, which would take them to crew quarters.

"They thought you were going to bust them." Beauregard's voice carried a hint of laughter.

"At the next level, we need to get to the center of the ship, where a lift leads directly to security," Jennings said.

"They're probably thinking about you as they do… whatever they're planning on doing," she continued.

Jennings ignored her. "Security's built into an area completely surrounded by engineering. That should make things easier for phase three." He had told them all of this back on the ship before they left, but felt obligated to say something.

"Something making you uncomfortable, captain?" Beauregard asked.

"Can we focus please?" Jennings eyed her crossly, as Lafayette and Fix were on the verge of snickering. "You're acting as if you've never seen two pretty girls in uniform about to make out before."

Beauregard raised an eyebrow in his direction. "And you have?"

Jennings eyed her again, the barest hint of a smirk crossing his face. "I've got a few good memories of the war."

Once at their destination, they strode out into the corridor, looking for all the world as a group of fighter jocks taking a stroll through the enlisted personnel's quarters. Most of the doors off the corridor were closed as crew members caught some shut-eye, but a few crewmen milling about in the hallway chatting drew up to attention as Jennings passed. He dismissed their attention with a short salute and kept walking as if he barely noticed their existence.

They passed another group of crewmen sitting on the floor outside of their bunks and playing poker. One of the women playing was either very comfortable in her own skin or they were playing strip poker and she was terrible. When they spotted Jennings, expressions of horror froze on their faces for a moment.

"Just keep it legal," Jennings muttered as he marched on.

"You're good at this," Beauregard whispered from behind him. "Impersonating an officer, I mean. Using the uniform to play on their sense of fear, making them like you by ignoring some minor rule breaking, and at the same time making them not even question what a set of flyboys are doing in the crew quarters at this time of night."

"I am an officer," he said. "Retired."

"*Cherie*, this is not an act you're seeing," Lafayette said. "This is Lieutenant Matthew Jennings. Now, maybe you'll understand why he commands loyalty, *non*?"

Beauregard shrugged as they emerged from the corridor and arrived in an oval-shaped room which ran the width of the ship. Four corridors each led to the bow and the stern of the ship, all of which would have led to more crew quarters. There was a pair of lifts on the starboard and port sides and one in the center of the stern section of the room. It was the one that led straight to security, but it also had two guards standing in front of it.

Jennings's footsteps did not falter in the slightest, and he walked up to the two men as if he expected to run into them. Minerva had mentioned nothing about security at the lift, and they did not have a plan prepared. Beauregard's hand went into her pocket, probably wrapping around the handle of her plasma pistol. Jennings heard her thumb priming the weapon's charge as he began to speak.

Returning the salutes of the two men first, Jennings said, "I need access to the brig."

The two guards exchanged glances. "I'm sorry, sir," the first one said, who was tall, thin, and could not have been more than nineteen years old. "Standing orders. No one goes to the brig."

"On whose authority?" Jennings growled.

"General Ounimbango," the second guard stammered.

"Do you really think I wouldn't be here if General Ounimbango hadn't signed off on it?" As he acted the indignant officer, he hoped Minerva was paying attention to what was going on. "I have the orders on the computer tablet right here." He made a show of patting his pockets, looking for the display. "The two of us caught those two..." He indicated Beauregard and Lafayette. "In one of the Traffic Control offices on the hangar deck."

Beauregard looked scandalized, but Fix merely shrugged as Jennings pulled out the computer tablet. He gave it a glance before handing it over to the guard. Minerva did good work on the fly. The order appeared official, and she had even found a previous order with Ounimbango's electronic signature on it and had replicated it for the order.

"Apologies, sir," the first guard said as he passed the tablet back and stepped aside.

"No problem, son," he said as he stepped forward into the lift, Fix escorting the other two in. "Hopefully some time in the brig will teach these two to keep it in their pants until shore leave."

As soon as the door was shut, Beauregard eyed him with an annoyed expression. "Do you think it's convincing that someone who looks like me would be with someone who looks like him?"

"A black market scrap dealer finds him attractive enough," Jennings said.

"She must have terrible taste," Beauregard muttered.

"What the hell?" Lafayette groaned.

"Not a she," Jennings said, and Beauregard snorted. The lift reached the security level, and he turned more serious. "Game faces on."

The security station on the *Intrepid* did not have the soft lighting, bland carpeting and taupe walls of the crew corridors. It was brightly lit by fluorescents in the ceiling and the wall; the flooring was white and black tile; and a white desk with SECURITY stenciled across it in black letters lay before them. A single security officer sat behind the desk. The starkness of the room provided a very anti-septic, hospital feel to Jennings.

Behind the guard and the desk, there was a door which led to the brig and their ultimate destination. To their left was a corridor with several closed doors, behind which were armories, briefing rooms, evidence storage, and forensics. To their immediate right was a room with walls of shaded glass. Inside of it, three men sat with their backs to Jennings, watching four dozen computer monitors.

Two security officers stood at the desk talking to the lone guard, and their eyes followed Jennings and his crew as they strode in. The security guards' black uniforms stuck out against the stark white environs. They eyed the new arrivals suspiciously as Jennings strode up to the counter to talk to the desk sergeant. He sensed the others spread out a bit behind him, Lafayette feigning interest in what was on the security monitors, Beauregard leaning on the desk, pretending to be bored, and Fix crossing his arms impatiently behind Jennings.

"Evening," Jennings said.

"May I help you?" the desk sergeant grumbled before his brain caught onto the fact that Jennings wore a pilot's jumpsuit and that all pilots were officers. "Sir."

"I wanted to speak to one of your prisoners," he said.

The desk sergeant exchanged a glance with one of the two guards he had been conversing with before he looked back to Jennings. "No one is allowed to see the prisoners without the order of General Ounimbango."

"Of course." Jennings reached into his pocket for the computer tablet.

"In person," the desk sergeant clarified before Jennings could produce anything to show.

"That is disappointing," Jennings said as he rummaged in his pocket for another device. "Rumor has it Anastasia Petrova was one of the prisoners, and well… I know a guy."

The desk sergeant stared at Jennings in dumbfounded perplexity.

"A guy Petrova screwed over if you know what I mean," Jennings explained. "He would think kindly of my taking her on a walk around the block, if you know what I mean."

"I don't know what you mean, sir," the desk sergeant said. "And what did you say your name was again."

"Nicholas Nickleby, Lieutenant," he said, offering his hand.

Acting on unconscious instinct, the desk sergeant leaned forward and grasped it just as one of the other security officers said, "Isn't that the guy from the book?"

Jennings yanked the desk sergeant forward and jabbed his pistol into his ribs. "Not a sound."

In a flash, Beauregard hit one of the other guards with a lightning-prod, and Fix injected the other with a fast-acting sedative. Lafayette drew his plasma pistol and had the men in the observation room with their hands in the air in less than five seconds.

"What's your name, sergeant?" Jennings asked calmly to the now awake and sweating desk sergeant.

"Vlad Podolski."

"Do you mind if I call you Vlad?" he asked.

"No," Podolski answered quickly.

"Vlad, I'm going to need you to open the door to the brig, and then I'm going to need you to unlock whatever cells I ask you to," Jennings said. "Or I will be forced to start shooting your vital organs in alphabetical order."

"Nonsense," Fix said. "Appendix, gall bladder, heart, kidneys, large intestine, liver, lungs, pancreas, small intestine, stomach, testes. He'd die too quick. Testes, stomach, large intestine, small intestine, kidneys, gall bladder, pancreas, liver, lungs, heart. That's the way to go."

"We should trust him. He's a doctor." Jennings cleared his throat. "Now about the brig?"

"Right," Podolski said. "My fingerprints and retina will open it."

"Then do so," Jennings said as he released him and stalked around the desk, his pistol trained on the sergeant.

Podolski placed his hand on the fingerprint scanner to the right of the door and then his eyes to the retina scanner. The door slid open. Jennings gestured with his pistol for Podolski to enter, and Lafayette did the same with the three prisoners he had taken. The brig was a single long corridor with a half-dozen barred doors on each side. A few whispers and some cries of surprise came from the prisoners as

Jennings and Lafayette forced the guards down the hallway and to the first empty cell.

"Open it," Jennings ordered Podolski.

The guard removed a laser cut key, slid it into the lock and turned it. The barred door slid open, and Jennings shoved him and the others inside after grabbing the key out of Podolski's hand. Fix arrived, dragging the body of the guard he had drugged, and Lafayette went to grab the other one which Beauregard had shocked.

"This key works on all the locks?" he asked of Podolski.

The desk sergeant nodded. Lafayette arrived, dragging the last of the guards and dropped him in the cell. Jennings slammed the door shut and immediately began looking into the cells for Michelle. He got to the last of them and saw a far too familiar sight, a stern Russian face stretched into a smile.

"Captain Jennings," Anastasia Petrova said as she stood up from the bunk she had been sitting on. "I am surprised. And that does not happen often."

Jennings scowled. "If I were to shoot you right now, would that surprise you?"

"Not in the slightest," she said. "I *vouldn't* necessarily blame you either after *vhat* I did to you. But it *vas* only business, it *vasn't* personal."

"I take getting shot personally," Jennings growled, but he did not raise his weapon. "But I don't murder people. I would rather see you rot in this cage, but since I know there's a good chance this ship will be destroyed in a very short amount of time, I guess it's just a short stay of execution."

"*Mon capitaine, la fille n'est pas ici,*" Lafayette called to him.

Jennings snapped his attention to his first mate. "What?"

"I checked every cell," he said.

A throaty laugh escaped from Petrova as she turned to her lieutenant seated on the bunk next to her. "Vosler, I owe you some money." Meeting Jennings's inquisitive stare as she turned back to him, she said, "He bet me you *vould* show up here. He also bet that you *vould* be here looking for the girl, and I said you *vould* only come here to kill us yourself. Looks like I *vas* mistaken, *da?*"

"Keep talking and you may just win that bet," Jennings said as he leveled his pistol again. "Where is the girl?"

"*Vith* the Gael." She must have seen the contemplative look on Jennings's face, and she laughed as she shook her head. "I know *vhat* you're thinking. You're *vondering* if that computer of yours can track her down. A thousand lifeforms onboard this ship… how long *vould* it take to narrow that down?" She paused for a moment and her eyes narrowed fiercely. "If only you knew a *vay* to make finding her easier, *da*?"

"Tell me how to find her or I'll kill you," he said.

"*Nyet*," she spat. "You already told me this ship is about to go down in flames, *da*? Kill me now or I die in a few hours. I take my chances… unless you *vish* to make an accord?"

"Tell me how to find her, and I'll let you out," he said. "You have my word."

"*Nyet*," she said again. "Let me out first. Me and my men. I know you consider yourself a man of honor, but all the same, I have the cards in this hand, and I prefer speaking in free air."

"Fine. Just you and Vosler," Jennings growled. "You renege, I'll kill you twice."

Using Podolski's key, he unlocked the door, and Petrova stepped out into the hallway, Vosler lumbering not too far behind, his wounded arm hanging rather limply from his torso.

"Much better," Petrova said. Reaching out a hand, she made a motion with her fingers. "The key?"

"Not a good idea," Beauregard said.

"We've still got all the guns," Jennings said, his eyes still affixed to Petrova. "How do I find her?"

Petrova tsked, but said, "Since I did shoot you, consider this an olive branch. The Gael snapped a slave collar around her neck, Gael design, Gael power signature."

"Minerva?" Jennings said as he handed the key over to Petrova, who immediately started unlocking the cells her bounty hunters were in.

"I'm scanning, captain," Minerva's reply came in his ear bud. "Stand-by."

Jennings met the glance of Vosler who eyed him curiously. "Sorry about the arm."

Vosler glanced down at the wound and shrugged with one arm. "Just business."

"Captain, I have her," Minerva said as an alarm began caterwauling in the corridor.

# Chapter 33

Plasma fire raked down the brig corridor, hitting several of Petrova's bounty hunters as almost everyone hit the deck. Selena Beauregard was closest to the door and threw her body to the side of it. Without looking, she threw her pistol around the corner and opened fire, emptying the charge completely. She did not hit anyone, but it gave Matthew Jennings enough cover to race forward, dive through the door and fire twice at a Terran Gael Force soldier using the security desk as cover.

Jennings's second shot hit the guard in the shoulder, and he spun around and fell to the floor. The captain went to leap over the desk to disarm the guard when more rapid-fire plasma rounds ripped into the desk, and he dove down next to it. The shots had come from the right of the brig door, down the corridor where the security offices, briefing rooms, and the armory were, but Jennings was too well pinned down to do anything about it.

Lafayette spun out from the brig corridor's doorway, the automatic plasma rifle in his hand barking and sending a colorful burst of red energy into the hallway before he had to duck back behind the door frame as plasma ripped past the open doorway. Hearing a whistle, Jennings turned to look down the brig corridor and saw Fix crouching in front of the duffel bag Jennings had been carrying. The medic drew a plasma rifle from it and slid it across the floor to Jennings.

Grabbing the weapon eagerly, Jennings primed it and rolled out into the line of fire, sending a short burst of plasma to cover his movement. He rolled back behind the desk almost immediately, but he had seen what he needed to see. At least a dozen TGF security officers manned the hallway, taking turns hiding in the doorways of the rooms leading off the hall and firing indiscriminately at where Jennings hid.

"Minerva, report," he said.

He barely heard her voice over the sound of the plasma fire as Lafayette opened up again. "A ship-wide security alert has been ordered. All forces on patrol were ordered to re-take the security station. All security forces not currently on duty are mustering in armories at various locations throughout the ship and were then to report to vital areas: the bridge, engineering, the hangar bays."

"Dammit." Jennings rolled away from the desk and fired again, noting with some satisfaction that he struck a guard in the leg before he took cover again.

Lafayette lay down a burst of suppressing fire, and Beauregard sprinted from the brig corridor, dove over top of the semi-circular desk, and sprang to her feet to the left of the opening to the corridor the TGF held. Whirling around into the corridor, she fired once and immediately darted back to the side of the hall's egress. Her shot brought down the soldier who had advanced the closest to their position.

"How the hell did this happen, Minerva?" Jennings demanded.

"I'm sorry, captain," the NAI said, sounding almost sheepish. "A code needed to be typed in by the desk sergeant every ten minutes or it triggers an alert. It's not in the files or the protocols. It did not show until the alarm sounded."

"Wonderful, did you lock down the elevator?"

"Of course," she said as the desk around Jennings split in half with a new cannonade from the TGF forces. "Reinforcements will re-deploy and attempt to reinforce security from the stairs leading down from the officer quarters and the upper levels of the ship. And captain, they know I'm here. They're trying to root me out right now. If they lock me out…" Her voice trailed off.

Surely Minerva realized just as Jennings did that their entire plan was unraveling. They had counted on Michelle being in the brig. They had counted on being able to maintain stealth a lot longer. In battle, one could count on a lot of things, but van Moltke the Elder had a poetic retort on the subject: no plan of battle survives contact with the enemy. A boxer put it more succinctly in the twentieth century: everyone has a plan until they get punched in the mouth.

Jennings grimaced. "Enough of this shit."

Grabbing the double-barreled grenade launcher out of the holster on his back, Jennings stood up from behind the desk and pulled the trigger. Twin streaks of smoke leapt forward and the weapon bucked in Jennings's hand. A roar sounded in the narrow confines of the security station as a series of panicked shouts came from the TGF forces in the hallway. They dove deeper into the rooms they had been using as cover or raced back down the hallway. The grenades flew into the corridor's ceiling, exploding in a brilliant flash of red-white fire which surged back into the security station's hub, forcing Beauregard to dive out of the way, Jennings to take cover, and everyone else to dive deeper into the brig's corridor. The entire room filled with smoke and became quiet for a moment, the silence only broken by the sound of two empty grenade shells hitting the floor and Jennings ramming two live rounds into the barrels.

Holstering the launcher, Jennings drew the automatic rifle back up and moved forward into the hallway the TGF soldiers had held. Lafayette and Fix followed him, their weapons raised and ready. A massive amount of twisted steel, cabling, piping, stone, and warped plastic filled the hall, blocking the passage completely. They still had access to two of the rooms which led off the hall. The first was occupied by the man Beauregard had killed and appeared to be a briefing room of some kind. The second room was an armory with two semi-conscious TGF soldiers Jennings ordered to be thrown into the brig with the others.

Petrova and her still breathing men made their way out into the smoky air of the security station and were joined quickly by Fix and Lafayette. Jennings walked back from the armory and over to where Beauregard still lay on the ground. Appearing unhurt, she reached up with a hand, which Jennings took before pulling her to her feet.

"All right," he announced to everyone with a voice of authority. "We've got a minor problem. Security knows we're onboard obviously, and they are moving to lock down all secure areas, including the hangar bay and engineering.

Lafayette groaned. "*Mon capitaine*, a major part of our plan was blowing the *Intrepid's* FTL engine," he pointed out. To an unspoken question from Petrova, he added, "No point in escaping from here if they can follow us, *non*?"

"Got enough men now," Fix pointed out. "Could take engineering in an honest firefight."

Petrova immediately laughed. "Ah, you seem to think *ve vill* join your merry band. I think not."

"We let you out," Jennings said.

"I appreciate that you let us out of the cells, but I have already paid you for that," she said with a sly smile. "*Nyet*, I think *ve vill* take my ship and leave."

"You're going to have trouble getting away from the *Intrepid* if they still have an FTL engine," Beauregard pointed out.

"I'll take my chances." Petrova beckoned to her men to follow her to the lift.

As she passed Jennings, he called to her, "There's also the small problem with your ship."

Petrova turned on her heel angrily. "*Vhat* did you do to my ship?"

"Well, I wasn't anticipating letting you out of here," Jennings said. "So, I went ahead and changed all the access codes to the ship's systems."

The Russian blanched with rage. "You did *vhat*?"

"You know what, don't even worry about it," Jennings said, waving her away indifferently. "You've probably got a hacker in this group there. It will probably only take them seven or eight hours to break the codes. Shouldn't be a problem with TGF security running around all over the place."

Petrova let loose a series of Russian curse words, but Vosler gave a slight grin. "Very *vell*," she said after a pregnant pause. "My men fight *vith* you. *Ve* blow up the FTL engine and then you give me back my *Grey Vistula*."

"Actually, you'll be fighting with them," Jennings nodded toward Fix and Lafayette. "I'm going after the girl."

"And if you die?" Petrova demanded.

"Minerva will reset the access codes back to your originals," he said.

After considering this for a moment, she nodded curtly.

Jennings flashed a fake smile. "That's our second agreement in like ten minutes. If we keep this up, we'll be the best of friends." Petrova merely scowled in reply, but Jennings pointed down the corridor with the caved-in ceiling. "The room on the left is an armory."

Petrova and her bounty hunters went to go grab themselves arms and armor, and Jennings's crew came around him.

"The entrances to engineering will be heavily guarded," Lafayette said. "Even with Petrova's crew, we'll take heavy casualties."

Nodding, Jennings asked, "Minerva, can you find them a way around?"

"How do you feel about ventilation ducts, Monsieur Lafayette?" Minerva said.

"Ah, *merde,*" Lafayette muttered as he held the earpiece a little tighter to his ear and started listening to Minerva's instructions.

Petrova returned with four uniforms in her arms and tossed one to Jennings and each of his crew. "Security uniforms. Might give us a little bit of ease in navigating the ship."

"Thanks," Jennings said as he shrugged out of the pilot's jumpsuit and his weapons belts, and then threw on the security uniform and re-attached his weapons. The rest of his crew did the same as Petrova's men emerged from the armory dressed in the same uniforms and armed to the teeth. "Lafayette's got a back door into engineering, and Fix has got the explosives. Good luck."

"*Ka Chortu,*" Petrova said as she and her men fell into line behind Lafayette who started leading them into the monitoring room.

None of her men even flinched when Fix poured a full clip of plasma into the monitors. "Better safe than sorry," he answered Jennings's raised eyebrow.

Jennings turned away from them and walked over to the lift. "Alright, Minerva. Open her up."

The door slid open and he stepped in. Surprisingly enough, so did Selena Beauregard. He glanced at her questioningly for a moment, but did not say anything.

"Thanks," she said.

"For what?" he asked.

"For not asking me why I'm coming," she said.

"Oh, I already know." Jennings gave a wry laugh, but did not elaborate further. "Alright, Minerva, take us to Michelle."

~

General Dominic Ounimbango rubbed his temples as he stepped out of the secure lift and onto the bridge. His uniform was disheveled and his eyes bleary, like someone who had just been awakened. In point of fact, he had. The day had been far too long already with a suddenly overly-demanding and irritable Gael Overseer bothering him incessantly and undermining his authority, a sudden order from Pahhal to leave in the ship's runabout to capture a relative insignificant terrorist from what he could make of it, and a long round trip at FTL just for good measure. He was exhausted and had collapsed into bed just about the moment the runabout arrived back at the *Intrepid*. Now, he had a massive headache that was cleaving his skull in two, and his eyes kept trying to force their way shut. Making matters worse was the incessant, blaring alarm echoing through every level of the ship.

Colonel Maliq al-Ansari, his executive officer, strode toward Ounimbango as soon as the general arrived on the bridge. Al-Ansari was in his forties, but had the athletic physique of a younger man. Olive skinned with a thin moustache stretching across his upper lip, Al-Ansari's shaved head glistened as if he had the time to buff and oil it somehow before racing to the bridge.

"What the hell is going on, colonel?" Ounimbango demanded as al-Ansari saluted him and he returned the gesture.

"Not sure, sir. The call came in from security, but we have not been able to establish contact with anyone there. Sensors showed weapons fire in the security station before they went offline."

"The sensors went offline?" Ounimbango said as he led al-Ansari to the raised observation deck where his computer terminal sat. "How is that even possible?"

"There's a rogue program in the computer," he said.

"A virus?" Ounimbango asked as he settled into his seat and started pulling up information.

"This is something else," al-Ansari said. "The engineering techs are trying to isolate it or at least lock it out, but they haven't been successful yet."

Ounimbango shook his head as he studied the readout of the security logs. "Damn Petrova. Should have known she would become more trouble than she was worth."

"You think she's escaping?" al-Ansari asked.

"Of course."

Al-Ansari frowned. "General, how could she?"

Ounimbango frowned and mused on it for a moment. "She's a resourceful one... There haven't been any landings in the hangar recently, have there?"

Al-Ansari pulled out his tablet, punched in a few commands and shook his head. "No landings other than the runabout and the *Grey Vistula*. Security did not report any unauthorized landings."

"We would have seen them." Ounimbango gave a dismissive wave of his hand. "Could there have been someone we missed?" He rubbed his eyes as he pondered. "She couldn't have gotten out of the brig on her own. I want guards on her ship."

"Essential areas were staffed by security immediately," al-Ansari said. "Hangar, engineering, the bridge..."

"No!" Ounimbango snapped. "I want extra security guarding the *Grey Vistula*. If Petrova got out of the brig, she'll be heading straight there. Pull men off the engineering section if you have to."

Al-Ansari relayed his orders without question as Ounimbango continued to try to put together Petrova's plan.

"General," a stern voice announced as Overseer Pahhal's face appeared on the communications section of Ounimbango's monitor. "What is happening?"

Ounimbango explained the situation including that he had ordered more guards to the hangar bay.

Pahhal nodded. "I want plasma cannons and interceptors armed and torpedo banks flooded. If they do make it into space, I want it to be the last thing they do, general."

"Yes, Overseer, it will be done," Ounimbango said as Pahhal signed off. He hit the comm section of his computer again and relayed

Pahhal's orders to the weapons and firing teams. He then turned back to his executive officer. "Colonel, I want to know what the hell is going on in security."

"Security Chief Jacobson just reported in," he said. "Access to security has been cut off. The lift is not responding and there is no access from the stairs."

"What's wrong with the stairs?" Ounimbango demanded.

"Someone unleashed an explosive device in security, collapsed part of the ceiling," al-Ansari reported. "The corridor from the stairwell to the stationhouse is impassable."

"Tell Chief Jacobson I expect the stationhouse to be back under my control immediately, do you understand?" Ounimbango spat. "And the prisoners will be placed back into their cells. Immediately!"

~

"Problem?" Michelle Williams asked as Pahhal stepped away from a communication panel in the *Intrepid's* supplies corridor and led them back to the elevator.

"Not especially." He pushed the button for the lift. "Anastasia Petrova is proving her resiliency once more, escaping from the clutches of these pathetic idiots you humans call leaders. She will be captured and then killed or simply killed by the TGF. There is nowhere for her to go."

"We don't call them our leaders," Michelle countered as the lift arrived and she stepped in. "You do."

Pahhal chuckled slightly, but ignored her comment. "Yes, quite resilient. An attribute Captain Jennings could have used more of, don't you think?"

The elevator arrived at the officer quarters level, and Pahhal led her out into the hallway, his mocking words still ringing in her ears. "Of course, Captain Jennings displayed a great deal of... What's the human word? Tenacity?" He led her down to the entrance to his quarters and began going through the security measures needed to enter. "Yes, very tenacious up until he died." Pahhal let out a sigh that Michelle was fairly certain was fake. "To think I tried to be Captain

Jennings's friend..." The door slid open, and the Gael stepped in. "But he was more interested in fighting for the honor of a silly little girl."

A plasma pistol priming whirred to life, and a voice said, "I've got enough friends."

# Chapter 34

Alarms sounded, red lights that had descended from the ceiling flashed, and everywhere people scrambled to get somewhere as Matthew Jennings and Selena Beauregard walked briskly down a corridor through the officer's quarters. He studied a readout from Minerva on his wrist monitor, trying to bring them into a position where they could intercept Pahhal and Michelle. When they entered the lift, Michelle had been in an isolated section of the ship's supply depot, but had been on the move since then. Jennings tried to beat them to the elevator so they could stage an ambush inside, but Michelle got there first. Minerva reported the elevator was set to come to the floor they were on, the officer's quarters deck, but they could not start a fight in the middle of a hallway crowded with TGF officers and security personnel. They needed to figure out where Michelle was being taken. Jennings tasked Minerva with the job and despite protestations to the low probability of success, she found a room with security measures designed to keep any human being out. It was not an X on the map with GAEL FOUND HERE stamped on it, but it was close enough as far as Jennings was concerned.

Leading Beauregard to the Gael's quarters, Jennings found himself in a mostly unoccupied corridor with sizable spaces between each quarter's doors. "Must be the VIP section. Ounimbango, the Gael, and maybe a few rooms set aside for high-ranking officers or diplomats."

"Which one is his?" Beauregard asked.

"There." Jennings pointed at a door with additional security items built into the console to the right of the door. He led her over to it and studied it for a moment. "Minerva, any way you can get this thing open?"

"Negative, captain," she said in his earpiece. "There is no TGF subroutine in place for the opening of that door."

"The Gael likes his privacy." Jennings left the door and trotted back down the hallway to the next door down. "How about this one, Minerva?"

"Stand-by," she said. "Working."

Jennings glanced at the monitor which showed the location of Michelle- she was getting a lot closer. "Minerva," Jennings said insistently as he readied his weapon.

"Processing," Minerva said.

Beauregard took up position in the doorway across the hall, dropping to one knee. "We're going to have to hit them in this hall."

"Three dozen men will be down upon us as soon as the first shot is fired," he hissed back. "Minerva!"

"Processing." The monitor showed Michelle about to round a turn in the corridor. She would be in sight in less than ten seconds. "Complete," Minerva said as the door slid open.

Jennings darted through with Beauregard right on his heels. "Find a shared wall," he said as he leapt over a coffee table and a couch and headed into a room on the right.

The room was a bedroom left in disarray; apparently someone had left in a hurry. Clothes lay about on the floor and the bed was unmade, all illuminated by the starlight coming through a porthole set against the far wall. Another door was set in the wall ahead of him and Jennings headed forward as Beauregard entered the bedroom behind him. The room was a bathroom, large by spaceship standards, but still rather cramped. More importantly, its wall almost certainly shared a wall in the Gael's room.

Jennings grabbed the grenade launcher off his back, but hesitated for a moment as he felt Beauregard's hand clamp gently but firmly on his shoulder. "We're too close to the hull. Plus, there are better ways."

Standing on one foot for a moment, Beauregard grabbed her boot with her hands and unscrewed the heel of the sole. Inside was a tiny compartment containing a little bottle of some sort of pink gel. Jennings recognized it as Merquand blood. The blood produced by humanity's water-dwelling sentient ally, while harmless to them, could burn through almost anything.

"Why didn't you use this to break out of the *Grey Vistula's* brig?" Jennings asked as he climbed into the shower and sprayed the Merquand blood out in a ring on the wall large enough for them to fit through.

As the acid began melting through the tile immediately, Beauregard shrugged. "They took my boots. Thankfully, they were kind enough to keep them nearby."

Within fifteen seconds, the wall in between the bathroom in which they stood and Pahhal's was melted completely through and fell into the Gael's shower with a loud crash. Water gushed out onto the floor as they had apparently cut through a pipe as well. Thinking himself very lucky it was water and not sewage, Jennings knelt and stepped through the opening, Beauregard right behind him.

In the Gael's quarters, Jennings could hear the door opening and the Gael saying something about how he had wanted to be Jennings's friend. Moving through the bathroom and an empty office, Jennings stepped out into the living room and primed his weapon.

"I've got enough friends," he said as he pointed the weapon at Pahhal's chest.

"Must you take the time to be witty," Beauregard demanded as she too stepped forward and aimed at the Gael.

Immediately, Pahhal reached out for Michelle and thrust her body in between him and Jennings. He raised his right hand as if to display the controller for the slave collar for them to see and slowly tried to back toward the door. Michelle planted her feet into the ground, and both Jennings and Beauregard crept closer.

"Mr. Jennings, you're becoming quite the irritation," Pahhal said as he came to a stop. "Now, drop the weapons or I fry your little friend here." Beauregard tensed as if she were about to fire, but Pahhal tsked. "Ms. Beauregard, you might kill me, but not before I push this button and send enough charge to electrocute Ms. Williams. Your friend Mr. Jennings would not appreciate that."

Beauregard lowered her weapon but did not drop it. Jennings considered the situation for a moment, but he did not lower his pistol. Pahhal tightened his grip on Michelle, and a slight sob escaped from her lips. This brought Jennings back into the moment. Very slowly, he lowered his weapon.

"Intelligent decision…"

With lightning-fast speed, Jennings leveled the weapon and fired, interrupting Pahhal and, more importantly, blasting apart the slave collar controller in his hand. The force of the blast sent Pahhal spinning around, forcing him to let go of Michelle as he fell, still spinning, into the hallway. Jennings was already stalking forward as Pahhal spun, firing constantly. Two shots struck Pahhal in the back as the Gael continued to spin and fall back into the hall, eventually crashing back first into the door for the quarters opposite him. Pahhal's breath came in ragged gasps as Jennings came closer, moving with celerity. Stopping in front of Pahhal, he leveled his pistol at the Gael's chest and unloaded the entire charge at him. Pahhal's eyes rolled back into his head, and his body slumped over.

Jennings eyed the body for a moment before turning back around to do a cursory search of the Gael's quarters. Beauregard had just finished picking the lock on the slave collar and she let it drop to the floor. Michelle bounded toward the doorway and flung herself around Jennings. He returned the embrace, unaware he was patting her on the back with his plasma pistol.

After a moment that seemed far too short, Beauregard said to them in a cautioning voice, "Those shots are going to draw attention."

"Right," Jennings said as he let Michelle go. He changed out the charge in his pistol and holstered it, then grabbed the rifle hanging from a strap around his neck and readied it. "We've got to get to the hangars, Michelle. Fix and Lafayette are working on a distraction, and they're going to meet us there."

"Wait," Michelle insisted as they started to head out the door and into the corridor.

"No time," Jennings said as he grabbed her arm gently and tried to lead her away.

"We've got to help them," she said, breaking free of his grip.

Jennings eyed her curiously. "Who?"

"The other one hundred and ten," Michelle said.

~
Remy Lafayette was in the lead of about a dozen people, ten and a half of which he did not trust. Fix might be on his side right now, but he never really knew what went through that man's mind. They crawled their way through a ventilation duct which ran from the security monitoring room to a central ventilation hive, a vertical corridor that ran the entire height of the *Intrepid* and was equipped with a maintenance ladder for any technicians who needed to work in the vents.

A horrible acrophobia gripped Lafayette as he arrived in the hive and stared down the long shaft which would be the death of anyone who fell. At least a dozen more ventilation ducts led from this level of the hive to the rest of the ship, but their destination was one floor below.

"Get a move on!" someone snapped from behind Lafayette.

Muttering in Acadian French to himself, Lafayette grabbed hold of the ladder with both hands and tried to find a way to work his body out of the ventilation tube. There was not enough room for him to adequately turn out or even crouch so he could get both his arms and feet out of the tunnel at the same time. Gritting his teeth and tightening his grip on the ladder, he pulled himself out into empty space, relying on his arm strength to keep him from falling. His legs stretched out to find purchase and landed on one of the ladder's rungs. He sighed with relief and relaxed his arms for a moment as his foot slipped on some condensation that had formed on the ladder. A horrible weightlessness seized him for a moment as he started to fall. Lafayette cried out, his arms flailing in the air before his hands caught the ladder and his body slammed into the side of the hive. Cursing loudly, he managed to hold on and gain purchase for his feet safely on the ladder. Breathing heavily, Lafayette glanced up and saw he had fallen about ten feet.

Fix's head popped into view. "What are you yellin' about?"

"Nothing," Lafayette rasped back.

"Well, keep it down," Fix said as he too swung out onto the ladder. "Do nae want you costing us the chance of surprise."

Annoyed, but also too relieved and too fatigued to retaliate, Lafayette started making his way down the ladder. It was a short climb down to the duct Minerva told them to take, but the duct was on the other side of the hive. With no way to jump that far, his stomach got a sinking feeling. *But there must be some way to do it*, he thought. *How did the maintenance people get to the right duct?*

"Hold on up there," Lafayette called upwards as he searched around for something, anything that might help them. Then he found a small control panel just to the left of the ladder, between where he hung and the nearest duct to his left. There was only one button on the panel. "Well, here goes nothing. Hang on." With that, he pushed the button.

For a moment, nothing happened, but then Lafayette felt himself moving. The entire ladder was rotating around the shaft. It stopped at the next duct, and he hit the button on that panel, causing another small movement. He repeated the process until the ladder was where he needed it to be so he could crawl into the duct Minerva had directed them to.

Calling up to Fix, he said, "Just have whoever's next press the button on the panel in the shaft to call the ladder back once we're off."

Lafayette heard Fix pass along the message as he managed to make his way into the duct and began crawling forward. He could not wait for the others at the hive as there was little room in the duct. He would need to press on and try to keep an eye on the people filing slowly in behind him.

After what felt like an interminable crawl through the bowels of the ship, Lafayette at last saw light ahead of him and quickened his pace as best he could. After checking with Minerva to confirm the room he was about to appear in was still empty, Lafayette punched out the metal grating and squeezed out into a room full of work tables, smaller machines, tools, parts, soldering guns, and even a ceiling mounted fusion laser. The room was cluttered and messy, but completely devoid of people.

Fix arrived right after, and Lafayette offered him a hand up, which he accepted. Two of Petrova's men came out next, and they moved over to the workshop's only door, taking flanking positions on either side of it. Every few minutes, another four men would arrive and take up ready positions in the workshop, their spacing timed by the number of men who could fit on the ladder and the length of time it took to rotate it, get four more men off, rotate it again, and allow another four on. Ten minutes passed in total before Vosler and then Anastasia Petrova emerged from the ventilation system. Begrudgingly, Lafayette extended a hand to help Petrova up.

"*Vhat's* our status?" she asked of him as she straightened her clothing and tried to recapture her sense of professionalism and order.

Lafayette studied his tablet for a moment. "We're about fifty meters from the engine room, but we bypassed the entrances to engineering where security should be strongest. I would recommend we leave a couple of men to hold this room. It will be convenient for any prisoners we have to take."

"We have more convenient *vays* to deal *vith* prisoners," Petrova said darkly.

"No executions," Lafayette countered, raising his voice loud enough for all to hear. "Kill if you have to. Self-defense only."

"Your funeral," Petrova muttered before glancing over to her men. "Singh. Ingarsson. Hold this position. Everyone else is *vith* us." Holding back with Lafayette for a moment, she grabbed hold of his arm. "You do have a plan to break out of here, *da*?"

"*Bien sur*," he said, purposefully not revealing what that entailed as he followed her bounty hunters into the hallway.

The engineering section of the *TGFS Intrepid* was a massive section of the ship. It sprawled over two levels and took up about forty percent of the space in each of those levels, expanding to the point where it even surrounded the security stationhouse. Unlike the rest of the ship, there was no streamlined function or futuristic design to the engineering section. Rather than being made of molded plastic or metal, the corridor walls were a mix of different colored pipes, some with nozzles, vents or control pads, tight bundles of electrical and communications cable, and every fifty feet or so a fire hydrant which could blast fire suppressive foam onto electrical systems without shorting them out. Pale yellow lights attached to the ceiling that felt claustrophobically close to their heads cast the corridor in a sickly, shadowy sheen.

"Which way?" Vosler asked as they stepped into the hallway.

Lafayette jerked his head to the left. Going to the right would take them past the water purification tanks and the entrance to engineering where all the guards would be posted. Heading down the corridor, they passed doors for Sensor Relay & Alignment, Communications Sub-Systems, Plasma Cannon Tracking & Targeting, and Sublight Engine Control. None of the rooms were occupied, and all were protected with security fingerprint and retina challenges. The hallway was equally deserted and terminated in a hatch labeled SUBLIGHT FUEL EXCHANGERS.

Lafayette was about to ask Minerva for assistance in opening it when Fix pushed a button on the control pad to the right of the hatch and it slid open. The room they stepped into was cavernous with huge metallic cylinders connected to steel pipes running into the walls on their left and right.

"Hold your fire in here," Lafayette hissed quickly. "Those are fuel tanks. We don't want a stray shot hitting one of those or we'll all be in deep shit."

No sooner had he finished speaking than a technician appeared from around one of the fuel tanks and eyed them curiously. He wore a lab coat and thick black glasses. Lafayette sensed one of Petrova's men getting ready to attack despite his warning and knew he needed to do something.

"What do you think you're doing?" Lafayette demanded of the scientist.

The scientist cocked his head, apparently confused. "Checking the intermix ratios. It needs to be done every eight hours when we aren't at FTL."

Remembering all the times Jennings dressed him down both in the service and as the first mate on his ship, Lafayette adopted the air of an annoyed superior officer. "Did you not notice the alarms and red lights flashing, son?"

"Yeah, but I..." The technician's voice trailed off, and his face fell. "I thought it was a drill."

"It's no drill," Lafayette said. "If you don't want to end up caught in the middle of a gun battle, why don't you get the hell out of here?"

"Yes, sir," he said as he then hurried away, headed back the way they had come.

"Fast thinking," Petrova said. "Shooting him *vould* have been easier though."

"And if you missed and hit the fuel tanks?" Lafayette countered.

Petrova smiled. "I don't miss."

They headed through another hatch and into another long, cramped corridor, passing by locked doors for Temperature Control, Water Distribution, Power Consumption, and Recycling Plant. The corridor curved around a gigantic steel bulge that appeared to be a vast water reservoir, and around the corner, their hallway along with several others terminated in an open area being guarded by two TGF soldiers. The armored men stood in front of a steel door made of two massive pieces, connected along a vertical line in the center and standing at least twenty feet wide. Lafayette recognized them as blast doors, doors thick enough to keep radiation, fire, explosions, and even vacuum confined to the room which lay beyond. At last, they had arrived at the main engineering section.

The two guards straightened and tightened their grip on their weapons as Lafayette's group approached, but Lafayette tried to disarm them with a gruff, "Anything?"

The two guards exchanged glances and one replied, "All quiet." They did not lower their weapons.

"What's your business in engineering?" the second asked.

Lafayette did his best to give him an incredulous stare. "We were ordered here as back-up."

The rest of Petrova's men crept up closer to the guards, although still trying to seem as innocuous as possible. One of the guards leveled his weapon in response, not buying the pretense that they were on the same side. "We weren't notified of any reinforcements coming to the engine room. Our last was that reinforcements were going to the entrance to engineering."

The second guard also raised his weapon. "I don't think I've ever seen any of you before."

Vosler was the first to act, covering the distance between his position and the first guard with amazing speed, kicking the guard's rifle out of his hand and swinging his one good arm across the guard's chest, knocking him to the ground. Another of Petrova's men was on him in an instant and hit him with a lightning prod. Fix got to the second guard before he could react and injected him with something which knocked him out immediately.

"*Vhat* is our escape route?" Petrova asked again as the brief battle was over in a second.

"For the second time, I'm not telling you until the mission is done," Lafayette said.

Petrova scowled. "You don't have to tell me *vhat* it is or show me your little schematic your pet NAI is feeding you. I just need to know if it is in that room." She nodded in the direction of the engine room. "Or back the way we came."

"It's in there," Lafayette said after a moment's hesitation.

"Very *vell*," she said. "Rodriguez and Mason *vill* take these two back to the *vorkshop* and lock them inside. Bring Ingarsson and Singh back *vith* you." The two men left, carrying the bodies of the unconscious TGF guards. Petrova turned back to Lafayette. "Do *ve* have any idea how many guards are in there?"

He checked his monitor. "Fifteen life signs. Whether or not all are guards, I can't say."

Petrova turned back to her men and said, "Smokers."

Half of Petrova's men readied their plasma rifles and put on gas masks they had stolen from the stationhouse armory, while the others grabbed smoke grenades off their belts. "Remember, there may be civilians in here. *Ve* should do *vhat* we can to minimize collateral damage so *ve* don't upset our new friends." A smattering of laughter came from the bounty hunters as the dour Russian turned to Lafayette and nodded.

"Minerva, do your thing, *cherie*," he said as he too readied his weapon and pulled his shirt up over his mouth and nose.

With a whirring sound, the lock in the center of the two sections of the door spun around and the doors parted, retracting to the side. As soon as there was the smallest amount of open space in the door,

Petrova's men chucked their smoke grenades into the engine room and peeled back away from the door. Following a series of flashes and several loud bangs, smoke drifted through the widening doorway.

Under the cover of the dense smog now permeating the engine room, the bounty hunters moved in, their rifles tracking and looking for targets. A hail of plasma fire greeted them and two men fell. The bounty hunters returned fire as Lafayette and Fix followed them into the room.

The engine room was designed more like the bridge of a ship than what they had seen in engineering so far. Sleekly outfitted, it had a small office in the center of the room encased in retractable glass windows- the chief engineer's office- surrounded on all sides by rows of steel desks covered in tan plastic, with monitoring stations built into the desks themselves. The walls to their left and right featured screen monitors displaying diagnostics, oxygen usage, engine efficiency, fuel status, and dozens of other pieces of information on the *Intrepid*. Swivel chairs in front of them were bolted to the floor and mostly unoccupied. The chief engineer's office was empty as were most of the desks surrounding it. A dozen security guards were scattered throughout the area, firing wildly in their direction, coughing uncontrollably, or trying to take cover.

With a brief burst of fire, Lafayette brought down one of the guards, before having to duck behind one of the desks as three guards popped up from behind a station on the far side of the room and opened fire on him. The glass windows of the chief engineer's office shattered and exploded as Fix and one of Petrova's men returned fire, catching at least two of the security officers before they too took cover. Vosler led a group of bounty hunters down the right-hand side of the room, occasionally trading fire with one of the security guards, but not slowing their advance. Lafayette looked to Fix, jerked his head indicating they should go left, and slowly got up from behind his cover and started moving around the left-hand side of the room.

Quickly, they felled two more TGF personnel, and Vosler was having an equally successful time on his half of the room. The remaining TGF security squad positioned to the right of the chief engineer's office offered to surrender, and Vosler accepted. On the left-hand side, a terrified technician raced out from behind one of the desks, headed straight forward Lafayette. He was not certain if he was making a run at the exit or was trying to attack him, but Fix apparently decided it was best not to take any chances and threw a fist out into the technician's face. The man crumpled to the ground hard.

Lafayette turned to compliment Fix, but saw Petrova over Fix's shoulder aiming a pistol at him. He should have known it, he thought to himself. The Russian was always looking out for herself- there was no way he should have trusted her. She fired, and he felt the warm rush of plasma brush past his face. A sound of impact was followed by a muffled cry, and a man fell to the deck. Lafayette whirled around and saw the body of a fallen TGF soldier who had apparently been hiding behind a desk Lafayette had not yet cleared.

He turned back to Petrova and nodded. "*Merci, mademoiselle.*"

Petrova eyed him coldly for a moment before answering, "*Pojalsta.*" She turned back to where Vosler stood on the other side of the room and called, "Report."

"Five prisoners- two technicians and three soldiers," he said. "We got two men down."

"We've got this tech too," Lafayette said as four more men came into the room and caused a brief moment of raised weapons before everyone realized they were the other four members of Petrova's crew.

"Tie the prisoners up and close the blast door," Petrova said. "The shots *vill* bring the rest of security down on top of us any moment." Her men started moving to carry out her orders, and she turned back to Lafayette. "You might ask your pet computer to scramble those lock codes so they can't open the blast door."

"Not sure if she can keep them out forever, but I'm on it," Lafayette said. "Minerva?"

"One moment, *monsieur.*"

As quietly as he could, hoping Petrova would not hear it, he said, "And the lift?"

"Locked down, ready for your use," she said.

"Now, let's get on *vith* this," Petrova interrupted. "I don't *vant* to overstay our *velcome.*"

Lafayette nodded as he turned away from the closing blast door and focused on a small hallway that terminated in a steel pressure hatch opposite where he now stood. Walking in between the desks blasted apart by weapons fire and stepping on shards of broken glass from the chief engineer's office, he moved away from the scene of the battle and into the hallway, Fix following behind him. A small utility locker was set into the wall next to the pressure door which Lafayette opened, withdrawing an atmosphere suit.

Petrova studied his actions with interest for a moment from across the room. "*Vhat* are you doing?"

"Setting the bomb," Lafayette said.

The diminutive Russian let out a stunned curse in her native tongue. "Out there?"

"Obviously," Fix said.

"Unless you have a couple of tons of explosives with you, we have to mount the bomb directly to the engine," Lafayette explained as he pulled the space helmet on. "And that means taking a little walk."

Petrova shook her head. "Better you than I."

"Keep an eye on her," Lafayette said to Fix under his breath as he extended a hand to the Scotsman.

Fix rapped knuckles with him, passed him the duffel bag full of explosives, and strode back into the engine room. Lafayette turned and walked awkwardly to the hatch, his magnetic boots thumping loudly off the decking. He punched in a series of commands into a control panel, and the door slid open, revealing a small chamber and another hatch directly in front of him, emblazoned with multiple warnings. Inside the chamber, several coiled tethers were mounted on electric wall dispensers. Lafayette grabbed one and attached it to a loop on the atmosphere suit at the beltline after struggling with it for a moment. He then opened a small locker and grabbed a pair of bulky steel and plastic gloves which ran the entire length of his lower arm and had a small hole in each palm.

"Lafayette to Jennings," he said into his comm.

"Go ahead," came the captain's reply.

"About to go for a walk," Lafayette said. "How are things on your end? Did you find the girl?"

"Yes." Jennings's voice sounding a little strained. "But things have gotten more complicated."

~

"Sir!" Colonel Maliq al-Ansari called across the bridge's observation dome. "Sensors are showing weapons fire coming from the engine room."

General Dominic Ounimbango took a moment to comprehend what was said. "From the engine room," he repeated as he strode over to stand beside al-Ansari at the computer monitor the first officer stared at. "Don't you mean the entrance to engineering?"

"No sir," al-Ansari confirmed. "Sensors confirmed weapons fire in the engine room."

"How the hell did they get there?" he roared. "Get me the commanding officer of the squadron guarding the engineering entrance."

"Corporal Drake," came a voice over the comm a moment later.

"Corporal, what's your status?" al-Ansari asked.

"All quiet here."

Ounimbango quaked with rage. "Then can you explain why a firefight is occurring in the engine room right now?"

"Sir?" Drake asked, his tone surprised.

"Go down there and capture the intruders, corporal!" Ounimbango snapped. "Or you'll have latrine duty for the rest of your natural life!" He cut out the comm and turned to al-Ansari. "Order every available soldier into engineering now."

"General, we are stretched too thin as it is," he said. "Unless you want me to take men off the bridge or hangar details…"

"Dammit," Ounimbango spat.

"There are a few men with Security Chief Jacobson, still trying to clear a path into the stationhouse," he pointed out. "I could order them to engineering."

"Do it," Ounimbango agreed readily. "We've got to get this under control."

# Chapter 35

Michelle Williams raced through the hallway, headed back toward the lift, ignoring the stares of curiosity she received from the crewman still trying to make for their assigned locations in the event of a red alert. She bowled over one midshipman and barely got out an apology before she jumped up and started running again.

Matthew Jennings and Selena Beauregard raced behind her, the former bellowing, "Make a hole, people! Make a hole!"

The crewman parted to the side of the hallway, and they at last caught up to Michelle as she reached the lift and called for it. "Michelle, what the hell are you doing?" Jennings asked.

"We have to free the rest of them," she said.

"The rest of whom?" he followed.

"The other people taken as part of Operation Aurora," she forced out quickly as she tried to catch her breath from the sprint. "They were never traitors or terrorists. Just people the Gael need to go home."

"You're not making any sense," Jennings said.

"Damn it, Matthew, they have children down there!" Michelle cried out as she grabbed him by the crisscrossing weapons bandoliers and shook him, nearly sobbing while stomping her foot angrily.

Jennings stared at her, evidently still confused, but he at least recognized the sense of urgency in her voice. "Fine, lead the way. Just tell me what the hell is happening."

"Are you serious?" Beauregard said as the lift arrived and the doors opened.

Two crewman stood inside. Jennings stared at them for half a moment before barking, "Security business. Take a hike."

The two crewman hopped out of lift, and Michelle and Jennings got on. Beauregard waited for a moment, and she met Jennings's eyes. Shaking her head at herself, she glanced down to the floor, gave it a frustrated stomp, and strode onto the lift.

"I don't know why the hell I'm doing this," Beauregard muttered, but said nothing else.

"We need to go to the supply station," Michelle said and pushed the button for it, immediately receiving a prompt for a password.

She turned to Jennings who immediately said, "Minerva?"

"Multi-tasking, captain. Trying to avoid being caught, helping Monsieur Lafayette…"

"Please, Minerva," Michelle said.

A moment later, the password prompt vanished and the elevator started moving again. A combination of Minerva's hacking ability and some well-placed lightning prods got them past the electronic security and the two soldiers guarding the supply depot of the *Intrepid*.

Michelle pointed down the corridor. "This way."

"Alright, but you need to tell me what the hell is going on," Jennings insisted as they strode past the various storage rooms.

As quickly as she could, Michelle relayed the details of everything she had been told: the Gael being banished from their dimension, the locked Great Gate, those who expelled them hiding the key to the gate in the genetic material of one hundred and eleven humans, and that the Gael War had been their means to bring the human population under their control so they could capture the humans who held pieces of the key in their soul.

"Huh," Jennings said, sounding as intrigued as if Michelle had explained the virtues of a vegan diet.

"Is that all you have to say?" Beauregard demanded as she hustled behind the two of them. "If she's right, we could be rid of the Gael…"

Jennings whirled on her, and she almost crashed into him. "By sacrificing these people the Gael want?"

"There is such a thing as the greater good," Beauregard said.

"Something you know nothing about," he spat, turning back around and resuming walking.

"You've never ordered those you commanded on a suicide mission?" Beauregard pressed.

Jennings turned quickly again, this time drawing his pistol and pointing it straight at Beauregard's forehead. "I ordered grown men and women into impossible situations where their death was a foregone conclusion. But those people volunteered to defend their world in a time of war. They knew what was being asked of them and they still gave their lives willingly. We aren't at war anymore, and I'm not the Resistance. I don't sacrifice innocent people just to get rid of a government I don't like. If you disagree, then I'm afraid this is where our alliance ends."

Beauregard held up her hands. "Just saying it was worth considering."

Jennings shook his head and holstered the weapon.

"No, it wasn't," Michelle said to Beauregard as she turned and followed Jennings down the hallway.

~

Overseer Pahhal coughed and groaned as he tried to push himself off the floor and into a seated position. Every part of his torso hurt, and his hand that had previously held the shock collar controller screamed in agony. The flesh was burned black in places and covered in red blisters. Compartmentalizing the pain away, he got himself into a kneeling position and looked down at his robes which were riddled with holes and scorch marks. With his good hand, he stuck some long fingers into the holes in the robe and yanked hard, ripping the material away, revealing the severely dented armor he wore underneath.

Tossing the robe aside as he stood up, Pahhal unfastened the dented armor and allowed it to fall to the floor in the hallway. He strode over top of it and entered his quarters, his body still encased in a one-piece nylon body suit. Gingerly, he ran his good hand over his torso, noting a good number of sore spots almost certainly bruised if not sporting broken bones underneath them. Part of him wanted to thank Matthew Jennings for being kind enough not to shoot him in the face, but Pahhal compartmentalized that as well.

Jennings had the one hundred and eleventh soul, and he needed to get it back. Walking over to a computer terminal set into the wall of the living room in his quarters he punched a series of buttons, a password to unlock a compartment retrofitted from a closet in the living room. As the closet door slid open and a gray locker emerged from the compartment as if on a conveyor, Pahhal called up the internal sensors' life signs readings. He then overlaid the map with the location of every active person with a TGF transmitter and ordered the computer to filter out the results. The Gael had secretly ordered every member of TGF implanted with a microchip that transmitted their location for just these types of situations.

Of course, he had not expected there to be so many intruders onboard the ship, but the filtering process worked as well as he anticipated. A dozen or so non-TGF lifeforms were concentrated in the engineering section. Petrova and her escapees, he assumed. There were the one hundred and ten registering in the cryonics chamber, and then three more headed through the supply corridors in that direction. Jennings was not only stealing one of the souls he needed, Pahhal realized. He was trying to take them all.

With a scream of fury, Pahhal marched over to the metal locker and yanked it open. Immediately, he began removing the contents and strapping himself into it. He would not allow anyone to come between him and his people's destiny, especially not one foolish human, he thought to himself as he finished assembling the body chassis around himself and felt a surge of power as the machine interfaced with his mind.

~

Jennings followed Michelle through the supply depot's corridors, stopping only briefly for Michelle to grab three atmosphere suits from a locker labeled Emergency Decompression. "Lucky they have these all over the ship," she commented as she passed them out.

"Well, vacuum does not have a pleasant effect on the human body," Jennings pointed out. "And a hull breach is an unfortunate possibility on a warship. Why we need them now, I don't know."

"The entry to the cryonics chamber has a series of traps, one of which releases poison gas into the corridor if a human enters while security is still armed," she said as they resumed their trek.

Beauregard's shoulders slumped. "Wonderful."

Leading them deeper into the center of the ship, Michelle at last brought them to an airlock which required more Gael security clearances that Minerva hacked through. They stepped into the airlock, and the door swung shut behind them. Michelle immediately started putting her atmosphere suit on, and the other two followed suit wordlessly.

"We have thirty seconds to get down the hall and deactivate security," Michelle said.

Beauregard raised an eyebrow. "Or?"

"Pahhal said plasma cannons will obliterate anyone and everyone in the hallway," she said.

Beauregard eyed Jennings questioningly, and Jennings quietly asked, "Minerva?"

"The control for entry into that chamber is not tied into the general computer network," she said. "It's not possible for me to de-activate."

Jennings cursed before he turned to Michelle. "We have to abort. Getting killed will do nothing to help those people."

Michelle started to protest, but at a glance from Jennings, only nodded tersely.

"I can't believe I'm about to do this," Beauregard said through gritted teeth. "I'll get the bloody thing open."

An incredulous look crossed Jennings's face. "How?"

"You don't think the Resistance employees for my good looks, do you?" she said with an arrogant smirk.

"Certainly not for your personality," Jennings fired back under his breath, but he was ignored.

With some difficulty, Beauregard managed to shrug her leg out of the atmosphere suit and yank off her boot, not the one that had contained the vile of Merquand blood. With a flick of the wrist, she unscrewed the heel, and a black flash drive dropped into her hand. She tossed it to Jennings for a moment as she got her suit back on, and then took it back from him.

"You can hack a Gael system with whatever's on that?" he asked, disbelief evident in his voice.

"The person who sold it to me assured me it could," she said.

"Why would you even need something like that?" Michelle asked.

Beauregard stared at her incredulously. "In case a situation like this ever came up, obviously. Besides I don't have a pet AI that can hack into government security systems without breaking a sweat. Where did you find that anyway?"

"Came with the ship," he said with a shrug and a forced tone of indifference before turning to Michelle. "You stay here."

"Why?"

"And why do you think I need your help?" Beauregard asked.

To Michelle, Jennings said, "Because if we die in there, you can still make it out of here." He turned back to Beauregard and hefted his double-barreled grenade launcher. "I've got a back-up plan to open the door if need be. Besides, you'll be busy with the hack. You'll need someone to count the time for you."

"You can count to thirty, can you?" Beauregard teased.

"Twenty-three," Jennings said. "Using my fingers, toes, and…"

Beauregard laughed and her eyes subconsciously dropped to about Jennings's belt line. "Come on, captain. We're laughing our way to the grave."

Minerva hacked her way through the second door, and Jennings and Beauregard sprinted to the far side as a purple-pink smoke immediately began billowing from the vents on the ceiling. Beauregard reached the control panel which bore a warning flashing across its screen and slammed the flash drive into a computer port. Rapidly, she began punching commands into the monitor.

"Ten seconds," Jennings said.

Her fingertips moving at a blur, Beauregard made no acknowledgement that she heard him and continued to type away rapidly. Jennings warned her that twenty seconds had elapsed as the screen in front of them continued to flash with dire warnings and the door still remained shut.

"Twenty-five," he announced as he took a step back and leveled the grenade launcher at the door. "Twenty-six. Twenty-seven. Twenty-eight."

The door slid open as the warning on the monitor vanished. The smoke ceased billowing from the vents, and a giant sound of suction filled the corridor for a moment. The poison was being pulled out of the atmosphere as the nebulous cloud vanished from the hallway.

Michelle jogged across the short distance to meet up with the other two.

"Not bad," Jennings said to Beauregard as she pulled her jump drive out of the monitor.

She punched a few commands into the computer. "The poison is completely out of the atmosphere." Immediately, she began stripping out of her atmosphere suit, and the other two followed her example. Free of the bulky suit, Beauregard pocketed the jump drive. "Well, let's see what we just risked our lives for."

All three of them stepped into the cryonics room, and Jennings let out a short whistle. Humans had experimented with cryonics prior to the development of Faster Than Light engines, but had never been able to make it work. They could keep people asleep certainly- that technology had been around since the twentieth century- but truly freezing people in place, halting aging while the user slept was one of the Holy Grails science had yet to provide. As much as Jennings despised the Gael, he could not help but marvel at the strides they had made from a technological standpoint.

Michelle acted much less taken aback by the room as she had seen it once before. She turned to the control panel to the side of the door they had just entered and pushed a button that closed the door. Immediately, she went to the nearest cryonics chamber and studied the readouts on the monitor for a moment before she rapidly pushed a series of buttons. The cool blue light inside the tube turned red. After a minute, the door to the tube opened, and the body slid out on a plastic slab as if on a conveyor belt.

Jennings stared at the young man with dark hair wearing blue pajamas. There was something familiar about the man, and he realized who he was just as the man's eyes fluttered open and he sat bolt upright on the slab. His head jerked around wildly, trying to take in his surroundings. He looked terrified.

"Easy, we're here to help," Michelle said.

The man's eyes darted from Michelle to Jennings, to whom they locked on. "I know you. You're the one who captured me."

"And now I'm the one who's rescuing you, Ciaran," Jennings said.

"Why should I trust you?"

"No one's asking you to," Jennings said. "But I'm the only one of us with a way out of here. So if you don't want to wait and see what the Gael have in store for you, I suggest you come with us."

Ciaran O'Sullivan, the one hundred and tenth human captured as a part of Operation Aurora, paused as he considered this. After a moment, he nodded.

Michelle glanced back and forth to all of them and said energetically, "Well, don't just stand there. Start waking the rest up."

They rushed down the aisles of cryo-tubes, punching in a few commands into each monitor before moving onto the next one. Jennings found himself having to climb up ladders built into the space between every other tube to reach the third row of humans imprisoned in their cryonics chambers. He brushed aside all the questions he received from those who awoke, insisting instead they help the other humans who were waking up and making sure the ones on the top row did not fall to the ground.

O'Sullivan went through the growing number of people milling about, all with the same question, and explaining what little he knew: that they were in danger and had been captured by the Gael, but these people were here to rescue them. Michelle joined him and asked everyone to remain calm and patient, explaining they were on an enemy ship, but there was a plan to help them all escape.

~

Finishing her rows of people to awaken, Beauregard turned back toward Jennings, who had stopped and was talking to one of his crew via a comm line. She rushed over to his row and started awakening the last of the humans still in cryogenic freeze. Jennings said something about things becoming more complicated as Beauregard's last chamber opened, and an eight-year-old girl opened her eyes.

"Where's mom?" she asked with a scared expression on her face.

"We're going to take you back to her," Beauregard said with a soft smile, not certain if that was true, but not wanting the girl to cry.

The girl extended both her arms up in the air, a motion Beauregard did not understand. The child had an expectant look on her face that turned into a more desperate and insistent stare.

Realizing what the girl was looking for, Beauregard somewhat begrudgingly picked her up and carried her.

"We've got another one hundred or so prisoners we freed," Jennings said into the comm.

Beauregard was fairly certain she could hear the Cajun's French cursing through Jennings's ear bud.

"I know one hundred and twenty-five people traipsing through a TGF ship is probably going to get us caught," he retorted. "Look, I don't have time for this. We'll meet you in…"

"Captain!" an insistent Minerva interrupted his conversation with Lafayette.

"Minerva, I'm in the middle of something…"

"Something is coming down the corridor to the cryonics room," she said quickly. "Security measures are not responding."

Jennings whirled toward Beauregard. "Can you lock him out?"

Not taking the time to reply or put down the girl, Beauregard raced back over to the cryonics room's one door and jabbed her jump drive into the control panel. Immediately, she began typing away.

"Hang on to me," she said to the girl, and the child locked her arms around Beauregard's neck, freeing her second hand to type into the monitor as well.

"Michelle, get them back away from the door!" Jennings ordered as he took up a point position ten feet from the door, and Michelle started trying to herd the group of people toward the back of the room.

"Got it," Beauregard said as she ripped out the jump drive and stepped back from the door.

~

There was silence for a moment, the atmosphere thick with anticipation and fear, and then a loud bang jolted the entire room. A collective gasp escaped from the group as Jennings stared at the steel plated door which led into the room. The steel was being dented inward more and more with each blow that struck it.

"What the hell?" he whispered. "Minerva, is there a security camera in that hallway?"

"Affirmative," came the reply in his ear.

"On my monitor," he said as he let his rifle hang by its strap around his neck, and he pulled his tablet out of his pocket. The tablet gave him a view of the corridor with a focus near the security door being pounded on. Pahhal's face was visible in the faceplate of a helmet made of black and gold metal, but the rest of his body was completely covered in shining black steel armor. Servos whirred on the elbows and the knees as Pahhal stepped back and punched out again and again at the door with metal fists utilizing the superhuman strength the mechanized arms possessed.

Jennings knew all too well that on the back of the armor was a shield generator which helped to protect the Gael within, and it carried shoulder mounted plasma cannons and energy beam guns which could stun a human being into unconsciousness. He also knew Pahhal's helmet contained a heads-up display, auto targeting system, and a cerebral connection system which allowed a Gael to manipulate the cybernetic armor with his mind.

Gripped by fear for a moment, he dropped his tablet and said, "It's an HK."

Hunter-Killer was the name that human ground-pounders had given to the Gael armored infantry divisions during the war. The shield generators made them almost indestructible without artillery or weapons so massive they could only be mounted on ships or tanks. They carried enough firepower to decimate Terran legions singlehandedly. The only saving grace in the war was that the Gael did not have enough of the armor to give them to all of their soldiers. Armored Gael would have waltzed through every colony Earth had, not that it ended up making that much of a difference. Less than a hundred HK units were deployed by the Gael during the war, and they were responsible for one hundred and twenty-five thousand casualties. Only one HK had been destroyed, and that was by a squadron of bombers at the Battle of Sandrun Creek, aided by the sacrifice of forty-eight Uula who remained in position near enough to it to paint the target. They were killed in the carpet bombing of the area.

Beauregard gulped in fright and backed away from the door. "Have you ever fought one?" she asked, her voice quivering despite her evident efforts to contain her fear.

"Once," Jennings said quietly. "The Marquis and I were some of the only ones who walked away." He started looking around the room as if searching for something. "We can't go out the only door, and there's no other way out of the room." He continued mumbling to himself before his eyes at last came to rest on the wall opposite the door. "Minerva, what's on the other side of this wall?"

"The wall opposite the door abuts an open area which leads to lifts and the entrance to engineering. It's four-foot-thick steel."

"Beautiful," Jennings said as he drew his grenade launcher once more and aimed it at the wall. "Everyone take cover!"

The crowd of humans raced out of the line of fire, running down the rows of cryo-tubes and kneeling behind them. Jennings fired and twin streaks of smoke raced into the wall and detonated. After the smoke cleared, he saw he had made a dent in the wall, but had not blown his way through. Muttering to himself in an annoyed voice and trying to ignore the louder and louder pounding the door was taking, he ejected the spent grenade shells and grabbed another pair off his bandolier, penetrator rounds this time.

Sighting into the dent he had already formed, he fired again, just the one shot this time. The penetrator round raced forward and dug itself deep into the steel before it detonated, and this time when the smoke cleared, a small trickle of light came through from the other side. Jennings put five more penetrator rounds into the wall in precise points and soon there was an opening sizable enough for a body to squeeze through.

Jennings reloaded the grenade launcher with his last two rounds, normal grenades, and holstered it. Grabbing hold of his automatic plasma rifle again, he turned back to Beauregard. "I need you to get them out of here. I'll give you as long as I can."

"You need me," Beauregard said.

"They need you," Jennings corrected. "There are probably a decent number of guards between them and Lafayette." They shared a glance, and there was a message in Beauregard's eyes that Jennings chalked up to some sort of professional respect. Turning away from her, Jennings said in a loud voice to all assembled, "Listen up. Selena is going to lead you through the engineering section to where the rest of our team is waiting. Stay behind her. Do what she says, and I'll hold the Gael at bay as long as I can."

"As long as we can," Michelle corrected.

Jennings shook his head. "You're no soldier."

"And he won't kill me," she said. "He needs me."

"She's right," Beauregard said begrudgingly. "She can at least cover you while you re-load." Taking a few steps closer to the young college student, Beauregard passed over her rifle and the ammunition for it. "Safety's off. Just aim and shoot." Still carrying the child, she jogged over to the opening Jennings had made and pushed the little girl through. "Follow me, everyone!" She beckoned for the escapees to come with her then pulled herself through the opening next.

"Hurry up!" Jennings yelled as another pounding on the door bent the top half of the door down and the HK became visible for the first time.

Beams of white energy sprayed into the room, tracking the escaping humans. At least half a dozen were hit and fell to the ground stunned. Jennings pushed Michelle behind the cover of a row of cryogenics units as he opened fire with the plasma rifle. His shots were perfectly accurate, but splashed off the HK armor's shields without doing any damage or were simply absorbed. The stunning beams ceased under Jennings's assault, however, and allowed more people to escape and others to push those who had been stunned through the aperture.

"How many are through?" Jennings asked as he continued firing at Pahhal, who was now trying to kick the rest of the door out of his way so the HK unit could enter the room.

"Half," she spat back.

"The shots hitting his shield mess up his auto targeting system," Jennings said as Pahhal sent another stream of stunning shots into the room, this time only hitting one person. "When I tell you, I want you to pop out from behind there and let him have it so I can reload. When I start firing again, fall back to the next row. Now!"

Michelle popped up from behind the cryo-unit and opened fire, but her lack of experience with firearms was obvious. The weapon bucked in her hands, and most of her shots went wild, allowing only a few to splash off the HK's shields. Jennings reloaded rapidly, but not fast enough. Pahhal sent a stunning beam at Michelle, which hit her rifle and knocked it out of her hands, but left her unharmed. A stream of deadlier plasma fire tracked Jennings who was forced to race to the opposite side of the room and dive behind another cryonics unit as he finished reloading.

As soon as the new clip was in place and the charge primed, he whirled back out and opened fire. Pahhal had finished kicking down the door and now strode into the room, but the hailstorm of fire he met from Jennings slowed him down once more. His stunning beam stopped trying to hit Michelle as it could no longer track her.

"How many?" Jennings called to her.

"Just us," she shouted back as she raced by him and took cover behind the last row of cryonics units.

"Get out!" he ordered.

"Not without you," she protested.

"Dammit, girl, go!" Jennings snapped. "I'm right behind you."

Michelle took off at a run and scrambled through the hole in the wall as Jennings continued firing, stepping back slowly as he did so. In between the flashes of blue from his shots hitting Pahhal's shield, he would have sworn the Gael was smiling maliciously at him. The charge on his rifle went dry, and Jennings immediately dropped it, turned on his heel and sprinted for the opening. He expected plasma fire to mow him down instantly, but instead came the telltale sound of a rocket being launched from the forearm launcher on the HK suit. Running full tilt, Jennings dove face first into the tunnel as the missile hit the wall above the tunnel. The force of the explosion slammed into Jennings and threw him out of the hole, sending him skidding across the floor past the lifts and all the way to the door with the word ENGINEERING stenciled above it in white letters. A fireball belched forth from the wall and rushed into the lobby, sending a thousand pieces of shrapnel and debris into the air all around him, and everything went dark.

~

Pahhal should have felt annoyed by the fact Jennings had allowed the one hundred and eleven souls to escape from him, but he was not too perplexed. Mentally ordering his plasma cannon to convert into a drilling beam, he commanded it to open fire, carving a passage through the steel wall for himself to pass. There was nowhere for the humans to go, he thought to himself, and he would have them again shortly. And then he could focus truly on Captain Matthew Jennings and bring him the agonizing death he so desperately seemed to crave.

# Chapter 36

The colossal FTL engine stuck out of the rear of the vaguely triangular (in a three-dimensional kind of way) *TGFS Intrepid*, and all the jokes ever been made about the *Proto*-class carrier's asinine aesthetics came back to Remy Lafayette's mind. The least offensive of these involved the engine looking like a piece of excrement which had gotten stuck on the ship on the way out. Some people merely called it the hemorrhoid. Trying to think of all the humorous things the engine design had been called over the years calmed Lafayette as he bungeed the explosive as near to the glowing blue engine exhaust as he could. Theoretically, he could have reached over the lip of the engine casing and gotten it a little closer, but the exhaust would have probably fried him instantly.

It had taken a good while to maneuver himself into position and to mount the bomb in place as working in zero gravity with massive atmosphere suit gloves was never easy. But he was now done, and only needed to arm the device. Reaching for the yellow button that would arm the bomb and being damn sure he did not hit the red one which detonated it, Lafayette almost jumped out of his skin when his radio buzzed in his ear.

"*Merde*, Fix," he said. "You almost made me set *dis* thing off."

"We're in the middle of a firefight," Fix said matter-of-factly. "Thought you might want to know."

Quickly, Lafayette hit the arm button and turned around. Using the zero-g motion gloves, hand units which contained a small thruster that while weak, carried more than enough power to direct a human being through a vacuum, he navigated his way back toward the maintenance hatch he had left. Hitting the retract button on the tether attached to his belt remained an option, but that would have taken much longer. No longer concerned with conserving thruster fuel, he sped himself along the ship's hull, slowing down only at the last possible moment by cutting off the thrusters and then throwing his hands forward and firing them again at one-third power, using them as retro-rockets.

Lafayette forced his awkwardly bulky suit in through the hatch and then hit the retract button on the tether after he realized the hatch would not close with the tether still hanging out in space. As soon as the cord wound its way back in, Lafayette hit the button to close the hatch. It swung shut, and air was pumped back into the room as a light above the bulkhead that had previously been red, began flashing and then changed to green. Lafayette pulled off the bulky atmosphere suit, let it fall to the ground and drew the pistol still holstered on his hip.

Punching the control pad to open the inner airlock, Lafayette found himself forced to duck immediately as green plasma fire tore through the wall above him. Cursing, he crawled forward and punched up at the control panel, closing the airlock's door. That was disastrously close to a hull breach, he thought to himself as he started making his way forward.

Petrova's bounty hunters had taken up defensive positions behind the workstations in the engine room and took turns firing pot shots down several different corridors. Plasma fire was coming in from at least three of the corridors which converged in the engine room. Petrova hunkered down in what remained of the chief engineer's office, and Fix crouched next to her, occasionally firing. The two appeared to be arguing with each other as Lafayette crawled into the office next to them.

"*Ve* need to fall back," Anastasia Petrova said. "My men cannot keep them at bay forever."

"Nae possible," Fix said.

Lafayette glanced between the two of them. "What the hell are you talking about?"

"She wants to pull out and make for the hangar now," Fix grunted.

"This position is untenable," she said. "*Ve* have no ability to save anyone but ourselves, and *ve* are fast loosing that option."

"Minerva says they have ten men in each hallway," Fix said.

"We can't hit them," Vosler said as he joined them, kneeling down in the office. "They have too much cover, plus they brought up artillery. The blast that almost got you, Lafayette, came from a mounted Phalanx cannon. It's out of our range to hit, but they can pour fire down on us. I suggest we toss some grenades down the corridors and escape in the confusion."

"*Merde*," Lafayette said. "The bomb's set. We've done our job. I'll tell Jennings we're falling back and that he should meet us at the rendezvous point."

Petrova nodded.

"Lafayette to Jennings," he said. "*Mon capitaine*, come in."

"He stayed behind," a female voice said.

"*Qui est-ce?*" Lafayette demanded.

"This is Beauregard. Jennings stayed behind to buy us some time. The Gael trapped us."

A grimace crossed Lafayette's face as he thought about the possibility of leaving the captain behind. He could not worry about that now. "Where are you, Selena?"

"Headed toward you," she said. "With over a hundred civvies in tow."

Lafayette let loose a string of curse words in Frénch. "Minerva, can you tell me which way they are coming?" As he pulled out a tablet, plasma fire raked the air above them, forcing him to duck again.

"Displaying," Minerva said and a map of their level appeared.

"They're heading right down the same corridor we used," he said.

"That passage has ten TGF soldiers in it now," Fix pointed out.

"Beauregard can handle a lot," Lafayette said, hoping what he said was true more than believing it. "What can we do to clear out that passage without causing a cave-in?"

Grumbling under his breath, Fix said, "I'll handle it."

The black Scotsman stood up without a care for the fire being poured into the room and took off at run down that corridor, pouring plasma from his automatic rifle and disappearing into the passage.

"That man's a lunatic," Vosler said with a sense of admiration.

~

Selena Beauregard had been the second person out of the cryonics room and had immediately been forced to throw the small girl- who had become inseparable from her- behind her. A half dozen security personnel, armed to the teeth, had appeared out of the lift to her left and started targeting her and the child. Not giving them a chance to find out if they would have actually shot a child or not, Beauregard opened fire with her pistol, sending rapid and precise shots into the squad. She hit three of them and scattered the rest.

Stepping forward quickly, she continued to track them even as they fell or dove out of the way. As soon as each one settled in a position for more than a second, she shot them twice. The threat was neutralized before another of the humans finished escaping the tunnel leading from the cryonics room.

Beauregard turned back to the little girl. "Are you hurt?"

She shook her head, causing her red pigtails to shake comically, but she still looked scared.

"I'm Selena." Beauregard extended a hand out to her.

The little girl ignored her outstretched hand and stuck her two arms out again.

"Really?" Beauregard asked, and the girl nodded vehemently.

As Beauregard picked her up, shifting the girl's weight to one arm, so she could still wield her pistol, the little girl put her lips up to Beauregard's ear. "I'm Molly."

Two more people were out of the tunnel now, and they immediately started to help pulling out the next ones through. Every so often they would have to grab one of the prisoners who had been stunned and drag them out of the tunnel. Without it needing to be said, two of those capable of walking would take hold of the stunned human, place their heads under the arms of the unconscious person, and help carry them further away from the hole in the wall.

Beauregard kept silent count of the number who had made it out, and when they reached one hundred and ten, she shouted to everyone, "Follow me!"

She ran towards the entrance to engineering, hating that she was leaving Jennings and Williams behind, but that had been what he asked her to do. He did not say all of it in words, but the stern command implied in his expression had said it all. He did not expect to survive for too long and was willing to die for their safety. Putting Matthew Jennings's death out of her mind, she ran into the engineering section just as she answered Lafayette's radio request for Jennings.

They passed a few doors, took a curve in the corridor and then raced over a catwalk bridging two sections of corridor. Below the catwalk sat some massive tanks likely filled with water. Beauregard led them past another half-dozen rooms, before she heard the sound of gunfire and immediately stopped. The group came to a halt behind her, although without the grace she had shown. More than a few people crashed into the person in front of them.

"Wait here," Beauregard said.

"I can help you," a young man with dark hair said. He was the one who had recognized Jennings.

"Stay here," she said. "I don't need any help."

Creeping forward, she passed some fuel tanks and then started to take another curve in the passage, before she halted and pressed her body against the side of the corridor. At the apex of the passage's curve, two men crouched by and one man lay prone behind a massive Phalanx artillery cannon. Very casually, Beauregard shot all three of them in the head and dropped to the ground, slithering over to the Phalanx.

Six more appeared in front of her in various covered positions behind protruding pipes or within doorways, but they did not expect an attack from behind. One by one, she picked off the first four, before any of them realized what was happening. The fifth moved at the last instant, and she missed him. With a shout of surprise, the man whirled on Beauregard's position, expecting to yell at his comrades to watch their fire rather than actually attack. She put a dozen rounds into his chest before he got a word in edgewise.

The sixth TGF soldier had seen what happened, and he drew a bead on her and prepared to fire. She tried to swivel the massive Phalanx, but it moved too slowly and she would not make it in time. A shape in the shadows appeared behind the last TGF soldier and shot him dead. He stepped forward, and Beauregard recognized him as Fix.

"Thanks for not shooting me," he said.

"Thanks for saving my life," she said.

He shrugged and pointed at the Phalanx. "Borrow that?"

She nodded.

~

Tapping into his not inconsiderable strength, Fix hefted the huge weapon and carried it at a jog down the corridor back towards engineering. Emerging into the engine room, he swung the weapon into position and started firing, sending waves of superheated plasma down one of the corridors held by the TGF soldiers. Calling for the others to seize the opportunity to take the offensive, Lafayette grabbed his grenade launcher and sent two rounds streaking down the same corridor. The explosion had barely finished roaring before he reloaded and fired again, turning the corridor into rubble.

Fix, who had barely flinched as the explosions went off around him, placed the Phalanx into position to command the egress from the last held corridor, drew his grenade launcher, and fired a few rounds into the third enemy-held corridor. What remained of the TGF security personnel after the explosions stumbled into engineering, and the Phalanx cannon took care of them. When Fix and Lafayette were finished, all the TGF soldiers in one corridor were dead and those in the other two corridors were dead, wounded, or trapped under some rather heavy debris.

"Bring'em up!" Fix shouted down the one hallway, and Beauregard appeared at the head of a large line of people.

"What the hell happened?" Lafayette demanded as he strode up to her.

"Jennings put a dozen rounds in the Gael's chest, and he survived somehow," she said hurriedly. "Came after us in HK armor."

Lafayette flinched, and Fix raised an eyebrow. Apparently, the Cajun remembered fighting against HK armor-clad Gael far too well. "Where's Williams?"

"Michelle stayed with Jennings," she said. "They're both dead."

Lafayette held up a warning finger at Beauregard. "*Mon capitaine* does not know how to die." Activating the comm, he said, "Lafayette to Jennings, can you receive? Lafayette to Jennings. *Mon capitaine*, come in."

"What the hell are you still doing here?" Jennings's voice came over the radio.

"*Mon capitaine,*" Lafayette said with relief.

"He's coming," Jennings said. "I can't hold him off forever. Get everyone and get the hell out of here!"

"They're still alive," Ciaran O'Sullivan said eagerly. Without a moment's hesitation, he grabbed a pistol off of one of Petrova's bounty hunter's belts and took off at a run back down the passage.

"Kid! Stop!" Fix bellowed and made like he would go after him.

"*Capitaine* will get him," Lafayette said as he grabbed Fix's arm to hold him back. "We head for the rendezvous. *Maintenant.*"

~

Matthew Jennings stared with dread at the section of steel wall across the elevator lobby from where he lay that was slowly being cut away. The Gael was maybe half a minute from being able to follow the escapees. Jennings himself lay buried under a good deal of debris from the waist down, including a piece of a steel girder keeping his legs pinned.

The lobby area was littered with debris, most of the lights had burned out or been shattered in the explosion, and a half dozen dead bodies lay near the elevator. With some relief, Jennings saw they were all TGF security officers. None of the escapees were included in the casualties, but he did not see Michelle anywhere. She had not been that far ahead of him. *Had she managed to get into engineering and join the others before the explosion?*

"Matthew!" a voice exclaimed, and Michelle raced out of engineering, dropping to her knees next to him.

"Are you all right?" he asked her weakly.

"I'm fine. The blast knocked me halfway down that hall, but nothing's hurt." Michelle grabbed at the girder and tried to lift it, but it would not budge.

"Useless," Jennings said. "Go find the others before he breaks through."

As if on cue, the wall across from them fell away, and Pahhal's HK armor suit stepped through. With an even greater strain on her face and a greater sense of desperation, she pushed on the girder trying to force it to move.

"Captain Jennings," Pahhal's voice rang, amplified by the armor's in-helmet megaphone, as he lumbered forward. "I was hoping to give you a more sporting death than this. More sporting from my vantage point, I should say."

"Michelle, run," Jennings insisted. "Run now!"

Another person came sprinting out of engineering and fired a few shots at Pahhal, taking the Gael by surprise, before he dropped down next to Michelle. "Together."

Ciaran O'Sullivan and Michelle working together were strong enough to lift the girder, and Jennings was able to pull his legs free. "Get her out of here," Jennings said to O'Sullivan as he drew himself to his feet and drew his pistol.

Stepping forward, Jennings started shooting, each shot splashing off the HK's shields. O'Sullivan started trying to pull Michelle back into engineering away from the firefight, but she dug in her feet and refused to move. She called Jennings's name over and over again until she started sobbing. None of them noticed that one of the TGF soldiers Jennings presumed dead was now stirring.

The charge ran out on Jennings's pistol, and he ejected the power pack and reached for a new one. Before he could reload though, Pahhal sent the HK's right arm forward and it caught Jennings in its grip, massive metallic fingers coiling around Jennings's trigger arm and yanking him forward, causing the pistol to slip out of his grasp. He then pulled Jennings up until they were face to face.

"You fool," Pahhal spat into Jennings's face.

The TGF security guard whose nameplate read Jacobson clambered up to his feet not far from Pahhal and Jennings. He aimed a pistol at O'Sullivan and Michelle, ordering, "Don't move," as he did so.

Rage was palpable in the Gael's growl. "You could have been rid of us. You could have been free. Would you not sacrifice one hundred and eleven lives for your people?"

O'Sullivan made a sudden movement which distracted Pahhal, the bringing of his weapon up toward the TGF soldier.

The Gael must have seen the intent on the face of Security Chief Jacobson, and he screamed, "No!" as the HK's mounted plasma cannons turned to target the security chief.

The HK fired, but not before Jacobson sent a shot straight through O'Sullivan's head. Michelle screamed as O'Sullivan's blood splattered across her and then again as Jacobson was ripped apart by the HK's shot. Incredulous rage flashed on the face of Pahhal. "One of the souls has been killed," he hissed. "This is not possible. We were so careful. All this planning, all the years spent searching. We were so close." He screamed again in frustration.

"To answer your question," Jennings said.

Pahhal had apparently forgotten about the human that his robotic hand currently held in a firm grip by the arm. He looked back down and horror crossed his face as he realized Jennings had drawn a double-barreled grenade launcher with his free hand and shoved both barrels through the shield protecting the Gael.

"I'd only sacrifice one life to save my people," Jennings said as he pulled the trigger.

The force of the exploding grenades threw both Jennings and Pahhal backward, but the explosion originated within the HK armor's shield and was therefore confined completely within the shielded space, so no fireball chased Jennings across the floor. Instead, he got to watch as fire surged against the shield walls, turning them blue repeatedly as the explosion attempted to pound its way out.

The shields failed, and a flash of fire appeared and suddenly vanished, as the flames had been nearly suffocated after consuming most of the oxygen within the shield. With a loud, audible crack, Pahhal set aside the shattered faceplate to his helmet. The Gael's skin appeared to be singed in places as the broken pieces of armor and weaponry fell off his body, clattering to the ground, but he was mostly unhurt. Jennings cursed HK armor to the lowest bowels of hell.

It was strong enough to withstand two grenades even without its shields. At least, the HK suit was damaged beyond repair, he thought to himself as he tried to pull himself to his feet. The Gael had already stood and was drawing a weapon from a holster on his back. Jennings had lost his last plasma pistol, and he was fresh out of grenades.

Dropping the launcher on the ground, he raced across the debris strewn lobby, stopping only to pick up a pistol lying on the deck. Quickly, he grabbed Michelle's hand and dragged her away from Ciaran O'Sullivan's body and into the engineering section, the Gael limping behind them in dogged pursuit.

# Chapter 37

Remy Lafayette's plan for escaping the engine room was fairly simple in the long run- he would take the elevator. What Anastasia Petrova did not know, because no one thought it wise to share with her, was that one of the supposedly seamless walls in the engine room was actually the door to a massive cargo lift. Engine rooms tended to have large components, which in turn required a large elevator which ran directly from the hangar to engineering.

Everyone was onboard the elevator: Petrova's people, the crew of the *Melody Tryst,* and one hundred and nine human prisoners. It would have aroused suspicion if they all decided to take the elevator's main exit door and walked out into the hangar deck, but the lift also had a small door which opened into the Space Traffic Control offices. Lafayette hoped no one had thought to secure the area, and it was still the middle of the night, but he told Petrova to send her men in first with Fix before allowing the civilians to leave the elevator just in case.

A half dozen guards were peppered throughout the cubicles and on the second floor of the Space Traffic Control, but Fix and Petrova dispatched of them quickly and quietly, with no further alarm being raised. Lafayette ordered all of the civilians to hide in the desks while he, Petrova, and Beauregard snuck over to one of the windows looking out over the hangar deck. Security was out in force everywhere, but they were especially concentrated around the *Grey Vistula*.

"You'd think with all the havoc *dat* we have caused in security, supplies, and engineering *dat* we would have drawn some of these guys away," Lafayette said.

"They know our goal is to make it off of this ship," Beauregard said. "As long as they keep the *Grey Vistula* locked down, they still win."

"Unless we take the bridge," Petrova muttered. "Take over the entire ship."

"We have one last card to play," Lafayette said as he pulled out a small remote control. "Let's hope it's enough to draw some of them away, otherwise it's going to be a helluva fight to try and take that ship back."

Lafayette took a deep breath and hoped Fix was praying to that God of his. With a tiny press of his finger, a sudden shudder ran throughout the entire ship and then the *Intrepid* tilted crazily for a moment before artificial gravity corrected and inertial dampeners compensated. A new set of alarms blared, and most of the security officers guarding the *Grey Vistula* had been knocked off balance or even off their feet. Once standing again, several looked like they wanted to rush off and find out what was going on.

"Hold your places!" a voice roared. A short, stubby human with grey stubble and sergeant's stripes stepped in front of those trying to rush off.

"Sarge, that sounded like it came from the engine," someone protested.

"If they need you to fix an engine, boy, they'll order you to do it," the sergeant pointed out. "And if it's a major problem, believe me, there are worse places to be than the deck with all the ship's main means of escape."

The soldiers got back into their positions and Lafayette cursed.

"Plan B, *da*?" Petrova said.

"*Oui*," Lafayette said. "At least they won't be able to follow us to light speed."

"Let's take the ship back first," Beauregard pointed out.

~

Matthew Jennings and Michelle Williams made it as far as the catwalk over the vats of stored water before Pahhal caught up to them. Jennings whirled to fire but the Gael shot him in the arm, sending Jennings's gun flying behind him, clattering off the catwalk's handrail and coming to a rest on the floor in the entrance to the next passage.

"Hurts, doesn't it?" Pahhal spat with a mocking laugh. "That's the first of many pains you shall experience, Captain Jennings."

Jennings shoved Michelle backwards out of the line of fire, which distracted Pahhal for a moment, and allowed Jennings to charge forward, closing the distance between them before Pahhal could get another shot off. Jennings's arm hurt like hell, but he could still use it, and he grabbed Pahhal's gun arm by the wrist and forced him to aim the pistol into the ceiling. The gun went off several times, and Jennings decked the Gael in the face with his good hand. He followed up with a blow into Pahhal's bruised and battered torso that stole the breath from the Gael. Using both hands for added leverage, he slammed Pahhal's arm down on the catwalk's railing repeatedly until the gun fell from his grasp.

Jennings followed this by firing a rapid series of punches into the Gael's face and torso. "This is what your kind never understood about humans," he spat as he decked him again. "You have the impenetrable supercruisers and the HK armor and all the tech we don't." He threw a kick into Pahhal's shin that dropped the Gael to one knee. "But when that's all stripped away, we kick your fucking asses."

Jennings stepped forward and aimed a punch at Pahhal's throat, hoping for a deathblow, but the Gael blocked the attack with surprising speed and jumped forward, wrapping his long fingers around Jennings's neck. Returning to his feet, he lifted Jennings off the ground and stared at him with a glower of purest loathing.

"Is that a fact, you puny human?" Pahhal snarled as he tried to squeeze the life out of Jennings. "Your race is so weak we can break them with our bare hands. With our fingers."

Jennings continued to struggle, but his kicks seemed to bounce harmlessly now against the Gael, and he could not reach Pahhal with his hands. Desperately, he clawed at the hand choking him, but he could not break its grasp. Black spots appeared in his vision. It was almost over.

~

Michelle had been frozen in horror for the opening stages of the fight, and then was only able to turn away once Matthew was caught. She did not want to see what came next. But then she spotted it: the gun Jennings had lost. Jumping up off the floor, she raced over to it, bent to one knee, and grabbed it. She spun about, looking for a target, but she had no shot. Pahhal was holding Jennings's body between the two of them.

Tears began streaming down Michelle's face as a horrible laughter emanated from the Gael Overseer. The hatred she had borne the Gael had always been at best a political statement, at worst a college phase, but something much deeper and more desperate screamed through her brain now. It was something she had never before experienced. She wanted to murder Pahhal, to see him dead for the suffering he had caused. And she wanted Jennings to get out of the way so she could shoot the bastard.

A sudden lurch in the ship pitched Michelle forward as the roar of what sounded like an explosion reverberated off the ship. Pahhal lost his balance as the ship's systems attempted to correct the problem, and he dropped Jennings down to the catwalk. Michelle had been kneeling when the explosion occurred, so she was the quickest to recover, and she retrained her gun on Pahhal once more.

The Gael Overseer noticed her at last and laughed dismissively. "Put that away, child... You're hardly the..."

Michelle fired, and the plasma bolt scorched straight through Pahhal's black left eye, blasting out the back end of his head. Pure astonishment passed across the Gael's face at the moment of his death, but it vanished just as the Overseer fell over the catwalk railing, his body bouncing off the water vats several times before smacking wetly into the level below.

Dropping the gun, Michelle raced forward to where Jennings lay face down on the floor. "Matthew," she said as she collapsed on the catwalk next to him. "Please be all right."

Jennings coughed several times, rolled over, and smiled at her. "I've had enough of this fucking ship. What say we get the hell out of here?"

Michelle smiled. "Sounds good to me."

"Come in, Marquis," Jennings said into his comm as he stood up and offered a hand to Michelle, pulling her to her feet as well.

"*Mon capitaine?*" came the surprised, yet hopeful reply.

"What's your twenty?" he demanded.

"At the rendezvous point," Lafayette said.

"Stand-by, Marquis, we're on our way."

"What the hell was that?" General Dominic Ounimbango demanded to the bridge crew as he pulled himself up to his feet, one hand gingerly holding the spot on his forehead which had struck his station and was now bleeding.

The crew continued to pull themselves back into their stations, but one turned up to the General and shouted over the warning klaxons, "Explosion! In the FTL engine."

"If the FTL engine had exploded, this ship would have been vaporized," a woozy Malik al-Ansari said as he pulled himself to his feet.

"Aye, sir. An explosive detonated on the engine casing."

Ounimbango flinched. "What's the status of the engine, crewman?"

"Offline."

"I can get repair teams on it," al-Ansari said.

"With God knows how much of our ship isn't even in our control?" Ounimbango hissed.

The general had been pacing the short area of his observation station on the *TGFS Intrepid's* bridge, becoming more angry and worried with every new sensor reading and vague report he received before the explosion on the FTL engine. The men he had sent to secure engineering reported encountering resistance and then went offline. Security Chief Jacobson was no longer responding, and there were sensor reports of weapons fire throughout supply storage, a lobby on the engineering deck, and engineering itself.

"Every security team we have on this ship with the exception of the bridge and the hangar bay has gone dark," Ounimbango said. "And I'd bet your salary that Petrova set the explosion on the FTL engine."

"Trying to make sure we can't follow her when she makes her escape," al-Ansari said knowingly.

"We will not allow that to happen." Ounimbango angrily punched his own open palm. "Send a few men from the bridge detail down to the engineering deck. Try to find out what the hell is going on." He thought for a moment before he said loudly for the benefit of his crew, "Would it be too much to hope for our having communications?"

"Communications unaffected, sir," came the reply from the communications officer beneath him.

"Send a message to TGF HQ," the general said. "Explain the situation and request reinforcements. Repair ships. Marines. Everything."

"Aye, sir," the comm officer said before turning back to the two technicians in front of him.

The officer and the technicians argued in hushed voices for a moment, and the communications officer then pushed the technician aside and attempted to send the message himself.

"What's the problem?" al-Ansari demanded.

The communications officer snapped back around. "We're being jammed, sir."

"By whom?" Ounimbango asked.

"Sir!" came a cry from across the bridge at the external sensors station. "I have ten ships dropping out of light speed, approaching our position."

"TGF?" Ounimbango asked of al-Ansari who started pulling up the sensor information on his monitor.

"Definitely not," he said. "I don't have identification on most of the ships, but one is in the archive."

"The archive?" Ounimbango echoed.

"It shows as the *TFS Tora*."

"Christ," Ounimbango swore. There were no former Terran Federation ships in the TGF. The only ones which survived the war were either mothballed when their captains surrendered or fled and joined the Resistance. "They're all Resistance."

"Approaching on attack vector," the crewman called.

"Shields and weapons to maximum," Ounimbango ordered. "Magnum launch! Scramble every fighter we have now! Now, God dammit, now!"

~

Following directions from Minerva, Matthew Jennings and Michelle Williams made their way down a series of stairs, ladders, and one ventilation duct, which led them into the Space Traffic Control center. A couple of Petrova's bounty hunters almost opened fire on them as they burst out of a duct in the ceiling and crashed down to the floor.

"Wait!" Lafayette commanded as he raced over to see what the commotion was. With a grin, he reached a hand down to help his captain to his feet while Beauregard offered a hand to Michelle. *"Je ne pense jamais que je veux te voir encore, mon ami."* With that, he clapped Jennings on the shoulder.

"You can't get that lucky," Jennings replied with a tired smile. "What's our status?"

"My ship is *vell* guarded and *ve vere* planning an assault on it *vhen ve* got your call," Petrova said.

Jennings walked over to the window and peered out over the hangar bay. There was not a bloodless or easy way to do it from what he saw. Too many men guarded the ship, and he was fresh out of distractions. He resolved himself that they would have to go with a general assault when a new alarm sounded and the lights in the space traffic control center flickered on. Everyone standing at the window ducked immediately.

"They know *ve're* here," Petrova hissed.

"No, that's a scramble alarm." Jennings shook his head and threw a questioning glance at Beauregard. "Someone else is here."

"Probably," she said. "If it is the Resistance, we need to get off this boat before they blow it."

"And we need to get out of this room before traffic controllers start showing up," Lafayette pointed out.

"One second, one second..." Jennings peeked his head up to the window once more and peeked out at what was a much more chaotic scene.

Everywhere people were running. Pilots raced from the ready room and into the garages for their fighters. Technicians hustled to fuel up and loadout the fighters not currently at an alert-five level.

Launch level directors attempted to control traffic, waving lighted green wands, and sending fighters out into the launch lane. He watched two fighters speed down the lane and out into space, before a plan began to form in his mind.

Jennings turned to Lafayette. "Do you have any more grenades?"

"*Non*, but Fix does."

Without any questions, Fix passed over the grenade launcher.

Jennings accepted it and held up a hand. "Stay here until I give the signal. Then run like hell."

"What's the signal?" Michelle asked.

Jennings turned to her and grinned. "You'll know."

Terran fighters were sleek space craft with a snubbed nose and six short wings. Four plasma cannons were mounted around the cockpit, and each wing came with hardpoints for missiles, torpedoes, or bombs. They also carried impressive shield generators, but the fighters could not raise their shields until they exited their carrier. The low intensity shield which covered the open space doors would allow a ship to pass through while keeping atmosphere in the *Intrepid* sure enough, but another shielded object could not pass through.

That was why as a third fighter engaged its repulsors and prepared to accelerate down the launch lane, it did so without its shields up. Jennings calmly strode out of the space traffic control center and leveled the grenade launcher at the fighter's fuel core, or rather where it would be in three seconds. He pulled the trigger, sending twin columns of grenades streaking into the fighter as it began to accelerate down the launch ramp.

The fighter became engulfed in a fireball and crashed to the deck, skidding straight toward the *Grey Vistula* and the security detail surrounding it. The guards raced out of the way, tripping over their own feet in their rush to do so. Flaming fuel spurted everywhere from the downed craft as emergency crews rushed forward to put out the fire and to save the pilot from the cockpit.

Just as quickly, Jennings's crew and Petrova's bounty hunters ran out into the hangar, covering the short stretch of ground between themselves and the *Grey Vistula* rapidly. The TGF security personnel were scattered and still trying to figure out what happened as the ramp on the *Grey Vistula* opened and Lafayette led Fix and Petrova up into the cargo hold. Beauregard and the rest of the bounty hunters began laying down cover fire as Jennings raced across the tarmac to join them.

A voice yelled, "Okay, move, move, move!" He looked back and saw Michelle urging all the other prisoners forward, who also raced across the deck and up into the ship.

As the TGF forces continued to be distracted as well as pinned down by fire from Petrova's team, Jennings joined Michelle in extorting the escapees to hurry. At last, the one hundred and ninth one raced through the door, and both of them followed on his heels.

Once up the cargo ramp and in the bay with the *Melody Tryst* and more than one hundred escapees, Jennings called down to Beauregard, "Selena! Move it! All of you! Fall back now!"

Another two fighters launched as the rest of their motley crew made their way back into the *Grey Vistula*. As soon as the last of them- as it happened, Beauregard and Vosler- were on the ramp, Jennings ordered Minerva to close the bay and to raise the ship's shields. With no more cover fire, a few of the TGF forces tried to fire on the *Grey Vistula*, but found their shots rebounding off the shields or simply absorbed.

"Vosler, please see to these people," Jennings said. After receiving a brief nod from Petrova's lieutenant, he beckoned to Beauregard and Williams. "Selena, Michelle, we need to get to the bridge."

Thirty seconds later, Jennings sprinted onto the bridge, past the captain's chair where Petrova sat, and usurped the pilot's seat from one of her men. He punched several commands into the computer and then grabbed the ship's stick. The *Grey Vistula* moved like a dead elephant compared to the *Melody Tryst*, but that did not matter to Jennings as he steered the ship using thrusters, positioning it for a run into the launch lane.

"Three more fighters just launched," Lafayette said from where he sat at sensor control. "You've got a small window."

Jennings punched the ship's sublight engines, and the *Grey Vistula* roared forward. With a flick of a button, Jennings dropped the ship's shields as they passed through the hangar and out into space and then immediately re-raised them barely in time. The *Intrepid's* weapons began pounding away at the *Grey Vistula* almost immediately.

"Hold on..." Jennings spun the ship hard around and then dove straight down. "Spin up Magellan," he said to Petrova's man who had taken the navigation control.

"Fighters. Coming in hard," Fix said from the tactical station.

"Singh," Petrova barked. "Open fire."

The batteries on the *Grey Vistula* turned aftward and began spraying fire at the *Intrepid's* pursuing fighters. Jennings continued to loop and corkscrew his way out of the line of fire while still putting distance in between their ships. The man named Singh made a triumphant shout as one of the fighters chasing them went up in a blaze.

"We got a problem," Fix said. "Ten other ships, and we're heading right for them."

"FTL?" Petrova demanded.

"Dancing too much," her man responded.

"If they would stop shooting at us, I wouldn't have to change course so frequently," Jennings spat.

Beauregard moved forward from where she had been standing toward the back of the bridge with Michelle. "There might be something I can do. Open a channel to the lead ship." This drew a few incredulous stares from Petrova and her crew. "That is a Resistance fleet," she continued. "And I have an in with them. Let me talk to them, and I might be able to get us an escort."

"I'd suggest you let her do it," Jennings said. "The Resistance fleet isn't going to let us waltz out of here."

"Three Resistance ships altering course," Fix said. "Headed for us rather than the *Intrepid*."

"Got another one," Singh announced as another TGF fighter vanished from the scope. "The other two are bugging out."

"Hail the lead ship," Petrova said, ignoring Singh's comments.

Beauregard walked over to the communications station. "I'll type in the prefix."

A moment later, a stern Asian man was on the viewscreen staring at them. "Noichi," he said laconically.

"My name is Selena Beauregard," she said. "I believe you have orders to facilitate my rescue in exchange for me giving you this location. This ship is escorting me, and I need you to provide us a path so we can properly plot a course and make an FTL jump."

Noichi narrowed his eyes. "I do have very specific orders, Ms. Beauregard. And while your name did come up, it did so after the word kill."

Shock nearly froze Beauregard's face. "What?"

"Request from Major Paulsen," he said. "You are a liability. My orders state no ships and no people are to leave the *Intrepid* alive. Make peace with the universe." He signed off.

Jennings swore and changed course once more, but the ships were already on them. They were not yet in firing range though, and Jennings set them on an oblique course away from the *Intrepid* and the three Resistance ships pursuing them. The ships were similar in size and firepower to the *Grey Vistula*, as the TFS *Tora* was the only real warship in the Resistance's fleet, but that mattered little to Jennings. One on one, he thought he might be able to take them out, but they would pound the *Grey Vistula* to slag with their firepower combined. Since he had straightened out the ship's course though, he only needed a few seconds until the Magellan computer gave them an FTL course.

A curse from the navigation terminal took him aback, and Jennings turned to the crewman. "What is it?"

"They're using gravity generators," Petrova's navigator said. "We can't make a jump to FTL unless we can clear them."

"They're faster and gaining," Fix reported.

Jennings grit his teeth. "Open to suggestions right about now."

"I have one, Captain Jennings," Petrova said.

"Why do I have the feeling that I'm not going to like this suggestion?" he responded.

"It gives you the opportunity to do *vhat* you do best," she said. "Throw yourself into the face of danger foolishly and for others."

Jennings spun in the pilot seat to face her. "What are you talking about?"

"I'm talking about you taking your little ship and providing a diversion *vhile* my ship gets outside of the gravity *vell*," she said.

"*Sacre Bleu.*" Anger clouded Lafayette's face. "You're expecting us to die for you? After everything that's happened?"

"Not for me," she said. "For all the people you rescued."

Jennings eyed widened slightly. "You would guarantee their safety?"

She nodded.

Lafayette protested, "*Mon capitaine*, you're not seriously considering *dis*?"

"She's right," he said, turning to his first mate. "We have no chance of escaping in this ship, but one of us might buy time for the other. And since our ship can't hold all of the escapees, then it will be our ship which needs to be the distraction."

"Put Petrova in the *Tryst*," Fix said calmly.

Jennings laughed derisively. "Do you think she would sacrifice herself for us? Hell, she would probably open fire on us."

Petrova smiled thinly.

"You'll take care of the escapees?" Jennings asked. "And I don't mean finding places to sell them. I mean re-uniting them with their families, giving them new identities if necessary, helping them disappear."

"Of course," Petrova said. "I agree to your terms."

Jennings stood up from the pilot's station, and one of Petrova's men jumped back into the seat. "Take my crew wherever they want to go as well."

"*Mon capitaine!*" Lafayette protested.

"This is a suicide mission, Marquis," Jennings said. "I can't order you to come with me."

"And you can't order me not to," Lafayette argued. "I've fought beside you for every battle, and I'm not about to miss this one."

"I'm in too," Fix said. "Stinks like borscht around here."

Petrova glowered at him.

Jennings shook his head. "Alright, if I can't talk you out of it…"

He strode across the bridge, nodding at Petrova as he did so and receiving a nod in return. Lafayette and Fix both fell into step behind him as he headed into the lift. To his surprise, both Michelle and Beauregard joined him.

"No way," Jennings said to Michelle.

Michelle angrily punched the button for the hangar level before whirling about on Jennings. "There is no way after all we've been through that I'm going to leave you now."

Her tone had such finality that Jennings did not bother challenging it. Instead, he turned to Beauregard. "And what? You can't stand to be parted from my company either?"

Beauregard laughed. "You're a better pilot. And it's just a hunch, but I think I've got a better chance of getting out of here on your ship than on Petrova's." After a moment, she added, "And it does smell like borscht."

Fix laughed explosively, and they all turned to stare at him for a moment. The smile was instantly gone from his face, and he shrugged. "I like her."

They bumped into Vosler when the lift door opened in the hangar. He held a comm unit in his hand and held it up before saying, "Petrova, told me what you're going to do."

"That's the deal we made," Jennings said.

Vosler made a noncommittal head motion. "Good luck." They had already started walking past him when he added, "I'm sure you're worried Petrova won't keep her end of the deal once she has escaped." He stepped into the elevator and turned to face them. "I won't let that happen."

Jennings glanced over his shoulder. "I'm glad I didn't shoot you in the head."

"As am I, captain," Vosler responded before the lift doors closed.

The hangar was now empty as Vosler had evidently found quarters for the human escapees. The *Melody Tryst* sat alone on the deck, and Jennings led his crew over to it at a jog, heading up the cargo ramp and into the bay where Squawk waited for them.

"Please tell me my ship is repaired," he said to the diminutive engineer.

Squawk saluted tiredly. "All systems go."

"That will be a pleasant surprise," Jennings muttered as he raced up the gangplank leading from the cargo bay to the bridge.

He jumped into the pilot seat while Lafayette took control of navigation, Fix took weapons, and Squawk took damage control. Michelle glanced around as if uncertain amidst the chaos of prepping the *Melody Tryst* for launch, but Beauregard pushed a button and a small bench slid out from the wall. The assassin sat down on it and then turned to face the communications station. Michelle hit a similar button on the other side of the cockpit and grabbed the seat in front of a dedicated sensor console.

"Cargo bay sealed, repulsors engaged," Jennings said more to himself than anyone else. "Hail Petrova."

"Done," Beauregard reported as Petrova's face appeared on the viewscreen.

"We're ready for separation," Jennings said.

"Opening the hangar doors." A thin smile crossed Petrova's lips. "I don't know if I should *vish* you luck, because you never seem to need it. I don't know if I should say farewell because I don't know if I *vill* see you again or if I even *vant* to. Part of me *vants* you to die in this endeavor, part of me *vould* miss the challenge of going up against you, and part of me *vants* to hire you."

"Break your word with those people we rescued and you'll come to wish for the first," Jennings warned.

Petrova laughed. "It would be foolish of me to think you *vould* come out of this in any position to carry through on that threat. But if the past few days have taught me anything, it's that I shouldn't bet against you."

"Finally catching on," Jennings muttered.

The communication line went dead, and Petrova vanished from the screen, replaced with the view of the *Grey Vistula's* hangar and the gaping maw of space beyond the hangar doors. Jennings punched the throttle forward, and the *Melody Tryst* shot into space, racing away from the *Grey Vistula*.

"Shields up, charge all weapons to full," Jennings said. "Let's make some noise."

Jennings sent the *Melody Tryst* rocketing toward the three Resistance ships pursuing the *Grey Vistula*. The unanticipated tactic from their quarry sent the Resistance ships scrambling off of their intercept course for Petrova's ship. Bearing onto the port-most of the three ships, Jennings launched a full salvo of torpedoes at the vessel and followed it with plasma cannon fire. His aim was perfect, and the torpedoes weakened and then punched through the shields of the ship before hitting the engine. The Resistance ship went up in a brilliant explosion of red and orange.

The other two Resistance ships had apparently become angry enough at the loss of one of their own that they turned to pursue the *Melody Tryst* rather than the *Grey Vistula*. Jennings corrected his course to take them opposite of Petrova's path, hoping it would help her get clear of the gravity generators faster. Plasma fire slammed into the aft shields of the *Melody Tryst,* and Jennings threw the ship into another series of dives, climbs and rolls, trying to keep his ship as far out of the line of fire as possible.

"Aft shields at sixty percent," Fix muttered.

"Squawk, can you do anything?" Jennings demanded.

"Recharging. Diverting power from non-essential systems," Squawk answered rapidly as another salvo slammed into the *Melody Tryst*, throwing all of them against their safety harnesses.

"Might be a bad time to mention it, but two squadrons of TGF fighters are heading this way," Fix pointed out.

Finding them on his screen, Jennings yanked the controls hard over, piloting the *Melody Tryst* straight at the fighters. "Fix, switch fire control to manual. I want you to clip those birds, not incinerate them."

Fix grunted an affirmative as the *Melody Tryst* rapidly closed the distance to the TGF fighters, the Resistance ships still hot on their tail and pounding away at their aft shields with plasma cannon fire. The six fighters sent a salvo of torpedoes toward the *Melody Tryst*, forcing Jennings to roll, juke, and spin his ship out of the way a half dozen times. The fighters switched to plasma cannons as the *Melody Tryst* got closer, and a torrent of green fire raked the front shields of the ship. Jennings held his course though, plowing straight through the fighters' formation as Fix opened fire, sending a few blasts of red energy into each of the fighters, hitting engines, stabilizers, sensors or wings. The damage was not enough to destroy any of the fighters, but it sent them wobbling off course, tumbling through space. While not all of them did exactly what Jennings hoped, two of them plowed into one of the Resistance cruisers tailing them, causing it to detonate in another fiery flash.

"The *Grey Vistula's* no longer showing on the sensors," Michelle said, excitement quickening her voice. "They must have jumped to FTL."

"Alright," Jennings said as a sense of calm overtook him. "We did what we needed to, now let's beat a retreat before we get slagged."

# Chapter 38

General Dominic Ounimbango watched the battle developing with a great deal of uncertainty. While the *Intrepid* was greatly outnumbered, it outclassed all of the opposing Resistance vessels and had already destroyed two of them. His fighter wings, which had been slowed by a crash in the hangar at the outset of the battle, had recovered nicely to destroy another of the Resistance ships. The rest kept the *TFS Tora* at bay, which was the only real threat to his ship. Although they had no ability to escape, Ounimbango did not doubt they could easily overcome the Resistance fleet.

Slightly more concerning to him was the fact the *Grey Vistula* had managed to escape- but he had as much dirt on Petrova as she had on him. He could always deal with her later if he needed to. The concern was Pahhal. The Gael had ordered her taken into custody and wanted her, her crew, and her ship destroyed as a part of Operation Aurora. Ounimbango had no idea why, of course, but he also had no idea why the Gael wanted one hundred and eleven specific humans. They could always hunt Petrova down, but Pahhal should be happy he kept the girl with him, he supposed. At least she was not a part of the jailbreak.

The other concerning aspect to him was the fact that the Gael Overseer was conspicuously absent from the bridge. While he rarely made appearances, Ounimbango thought a battle might have been important enough to bring him out of his quarters. The Resistance had tried to prevent Operation Aurora from being completed several times, and this must be their last gasp effort, Ounimbango thought. If he were the Gael, he would want to oversee the battle personally, to ensure nothing got in the way of his operation.

"Sir, we're getting a report from Corporal Miller," Colonel Malik al-Ansari said.

Ounimbango was distracted by one of his bomber wings destroying another Resistance ship, and he did not hear his XO immediately. "Who?"

"Corporal Miller," al-Ansari repeated. "The leader of the security team you sent from the bridge to the engineering deck."

"I'm in the middle of a battle," Ounimbango spat. "I already know Petrova and her people have escaped. We can't do anything about that now."

"It sounds important," al-Ansari added.

An impatient growl escaped Ounimbango's throat. "Fine." As the face of a young security officer appeared on his monitor, he snapped, "What?"

"Sir," Corporal Miller said. "Engineering and the supply station are a mess."

"We can have repair crews on it once this battle is over," Ounimbango said.

"Understood, sir, but we found a body at the bottom of water reclamation," Miller said hesitantly. "The body of a Gael."

"A… Gael…?" Ounimbango repeated slowly, fear rising in him.

"And that's not all," Miller continued. "We found a room full of freezer units."

Ounimbango blinked in confusion. "We have tons of freezer units in the supply station."

"Not for humans, we don't, sir," Miller interrupted.

Fear seized hold of Ounimbango. "Where was this room?"

"In between the supply station and the entrance to engineering," Miller said.

Ounimbango was one of the few people onboard the ship aware that Pahhal had built his own private storage facility on the *Intrepid* in that room, a room only the Gael had access to. *Why had he kept some sort of cryogenic freezers in there?* he wondered to himself. *The prisoners from Operation Aurora*, he realized. That was what the Gael had picked up at Barnard's VI.

"Are the freezer units full?" he asked Miller.

"No, sir, all are empty. We think we found one of them though. There's a body over by engineering who was wearing pajamas. They aren't standard crew issue, so I thought…"

"Send me an image," Ounimbango ordered.

"Of course, sir," Miller said.

A few moments later, Ounimbango regarded the dead face of Ciaran O' Sullivan. "Any sign of a twenty-two-year-old woman there, Mr. Miller? She wouldn't have been TGF."

"No, sir. All we've found are our own personnel, the Gael, and the man whose image I sent to you."

Thinking his worst fears were about to be confirmed correct, Ounimbango pulled up the internal sensor feed from when the *Grey Vistula* departed and queried for the number of life signs aboard the ship. The sensor logs showed one hundred and thirty people onboard it. Petrova had not only broken herself out of the brig, but killed the Gael, and freed all one hundred ten members of Operation Aurora, losing one in the process. *That was not like Petrova*, he thought to himself. *She was not one to think of others.*

"What's the position of the *Grey Vistula*?" he demanded.

Al-Ansari checked his monitor. "Just jumped to FTL."

"Damn it!" Ounimbango roared.

"There's something else," al-Ansari said. "Another ship launched itself from the *Grey Vistula* before it jumped."

"Ships of that class don't carry fighters," Ounimbango countered.

"Confirmed," al-Ansari said. "The ship matches the configuration of the *Melody Tryst*."

Ounimbango's mouth fell open. "Jennings?"

*Jennings was dead- he had to be,* Ounimbango thought to himself. But now everything made a little more sense. Jennings was the type of person who would have chased down the *Intrepid* to take the girl back, sprung Petrova from the brig in exchange for her help, and helped facilitate the mass breakout of Pahhal's detainees. He had no idea how Jennings did it, but he could always ask him that in a nice interrogation chamber.

"I want that ship in our custody," Ounimbango ordered. "Now. They must be taken alive."

"The *Melody Tryst* has crippled six of our fighters," al-Ansari said.

Before Ounimbango could even curse at this latest development, a crewman barked from across the bridge, "Sir, new contact dropping from FTL…"

There was a pause.

The delay stoked Ounimbango's fury. "What is it, crewman?"

"It reads as a Gael supercruiser," he reported at last, his voice shaking.

"They're hailing us," the communications officer said. "They managed to cut through the jamming somehow."

"To my station," Ounimbango ordered, a lump beginning to form in his throat.

The face of a Gael appeared on the screen, looking relatively indistinguishable from any other Gael Ounimbango had seen. "This is Fleet Admiral Jorrarius," the Gael said. "I wish to speak with Overseer Pahhal."

Ounimbango tried to put on his most sympathetic face and most sycophantic tone as he said, "I'm very sorry to be the bearer of bad news, Fleet Admiral. It is with deepest regrets that I must advise you Overseer Pahhal has been killed." The Gael Admiral barely flinched at this statement, so Ounimbango rambled on, "I worked with Pahhal for some time and always found him to be..."

"And what of the prisoners? The one hundred and eleven prisoners?" Jorrarius interrupted. "Where are the souls?"

"The same team which infiltrated our ship and assassinated Pahhal, facilitated the escape of the prisoners of Operation Aurora," Ounimbango explained with as much an apologetic tone as he could muster.

"All of the souls have escaped!" Jorrarius hissed.

"No, no, no," Ounimbango said, terror seizing him and forcing him to search for an answer. "One of them was killed in the escape."

Jorrarrius's eyes narrowed further, and he seemed even more clouded by rage, but he did not say anything. He made a motion with his hand, and the communication cut off. Ounimbango breathed a sigh of relief. He barely heard his tactical officer shout that the supercruiser was targeting them. With a flash of light, the *TGFS Intrepid* was incinerated by the Gael supercruiser's forward weapons, the massive energy beam cutting instantaneously through the *Intrepid's* shields and armored hull, until the *Intrepid* detonated, exploding into millions of tiny pieces.

~

Captain Noichi was the lone member of the bridge crew who did not become overly excited or panicked when the Gael supercruiser dropped into the middle of the battle. The behemoth of a ship, easily twenty times the size of the *Intrepid,* which was a good deal larger than the *Tora,* was an old, familiar sight to Noichi. The elongated organic shape of the ship with its intricately curving wings that reminded him of sails on an old-fashioned Terran sailboat had been carved into his mind since the war. While he should have been terrified to go into battle against a class of ship the Terran Federation Military had never defeated, there was a certain rightness and righteousness about fighting the Gael once again. For too long, the Resistance had fought fellow humans, collaborators, or Terran Gael Force mostly. Now was the opportunity Noichi had been waiting for even as the *Intrepid* exploded- a chance to take the battle to the Gael once more.

"Gravity well generators are active and massive," his navigation officer said. "We cannot retreat."

"Nor would we want to," Noichi said before punching in a series of codes into the monitor in front of his captain's chair, opening a channel to what remained of his fleet. Six of his nine support craft had already been destroyed. "This is Noichi to all remaining ships. Focus all fire on the Gael supercruiser."

~

"Where the hell did that come from?" Lafayette demanded.

"It was the *Intrepid,*" Michelle said from the sensor station onboard the *Melody Tryst.* "The Gael ship destroyed it."

"Never thought the Gael would do us a favor," Jennings muttered as he swung the *Melody Tryst* in a new direction, away from the Gael supercruiser's location.

To his surprise, the Resistance ship that had been following them and had battered his aft shields down to twenty percent did not follow the maneuver. It continued on course, headed straight for the Gael supercruiser. Jennings checked his readings- the other remaining Resistance ships were doing the same.

"Crazy bastards," Jennings said admiringly as he set the *Melody Tryst* on a straight course away from the supercruiser. "Magellan?" He threw a glance over to Lafayette.

The Cajun shook his head. "The Gael activated their gravity well generator as soon as they dropped out of FTL. You know how strong those are. It could take us a week to get far enough outside of it at sublight."

"Not to rain on anyone's parade, but we have a dozen TGF fighters bearing down on us," Fix said.

"Throw everything you can into the aft shields," Jennings ordered Squawk.

"Nothing left."

"What about forward shields?" Jennings asked.

"Forty-five percent," Fix said.

"How long until those fighters are in range?" Jennings asked the Scotsman.

"Two minutes."

~

The Resistance fleet's few remaining ships had gotten in a few good shots on the Gael supercruiser, but the weapons on the enemy ship were monstrous. One blast and the retro-fitted freighters the Resistance used as warships were destroyed. The *Tora*, the only surviving Resistance ship, sent a full column of fire and a salvo of torpedoes at the supercruiser and barely made a dent in the cruiser's aft shielding.

The supercruiser's aft cannon opened up on the *Tora*, but Noichi's pilot was better, swerving to avoid the attack while his tactical officer sent another cannonade toward the Gael. The Gael returned fire, and this time, the *Tora* was not so lucky. It was not a direct enough hit to destroy them instantly, but it was a devastating blow. The concussion of the hit shook the *Tora* so hard that crewmen smashed their faces into their consoles or had their necks broken. The shields were knocked completely out as everywhere consoles overloaded and exploded, sending sparks and shrapnel flying everywhere.

Captain Noichi caught a piece of shrapnel in the gut, and he fell to one knee. All around him, fires broke out on the bridge. Most if not all of his bridge crew was dead, and the next hit would surely kill them. He did not intend for there to be another hit. Stumbling slightly, he made his way forward to the pilot station and pushed aside his dead crewman. Ramping up the sublight engines to maximum, Noichi sent the *Tora* on a collision course for the supercruiser, aiming for the massive blue aura that was the Gael's FTL engine. In that last moment, he finally understood his old captain's reasoning behind killing himself at the end of the battle for Earth. Some things were worth dying for.

~

The explosion of the Gael supercruiser was massive, reminding Jennings of a star going supernova. A blast of energy rushed out from the destroyed ship like a surging red-purple sphere. Lafayette let loose a cry of excitement as the Magellan computer began calculating their FTL jump.

"Course?" Lafayette asked.

"Anywhere," Jennings said, his eyes still locked on the sensor readings on his console.

The TGF fighters were thirty seconds from firing range, but the shockwave might hit them at about the same time.

"Time, Marquis?" Jennings asked.

"Twenty seconds."

Jennings distinctly heard Fix muttering something that sounded like a prayer as there was a collective intake of breath from everyone on the bridge. The FTL indicator on his monitor went from red to green right as the nearest fighter opened fire on him. Jennings punched the FTL engine activator, stars turned to starlines, and the *Melody Tryst* leapt out of the system. With a little satisfaction, Jennings saw the TGF fighters were destroyed by the blast wave from the destroyed Gael supercruiser.

Sighing contentedly, he said, "We're all clear."

# Chapter 39

A sense of celebration permeated the bridge of the *Melody Tryst* which lasted for several minutes. Jennings and Lafayette grasped hands firmly, which Squawk imitated energetically to each person in the cockpit in turn, getting even Fix to begrudgingly participate. Beauregard flashed Jennings a winning smile, and Michelle strode forward to wrap her arms around the captain then planted a kiss softly on his cheek.

"I didn't say thank you yet," she said.

"*Dis* is going to be awkward," Lafayette said, at which point Michelle turned bright red, released Jennings and sat back down.

"Well, I don't know about anyone else, but I'm starving," Jennings announced, stretching his arms over his head. "Could probably go for a nap too."

"I should probably take you to med bay first," Fix said.

"For what?" Jennings held up the arm Pahhal had shot. "For this? Please." He gave Fix a roll of the eyes.

Fix stared at him derisively. "How many times have you been shot in the past few days?"

A puzzled expression crossed his face. "Honestly, I've forgotten. Four maybe?"

Fix glared at him.

"Fine, I'll let you work your magic," he said. "As long as Marquis starts cooking something in the meantime. Some sort of victory feast."

The smile on Jennings's face vanished as the *Melody Tryst* was yanked out of FTL, and everyone seated found themselves thrown against their seat straps. Michelle was tossed forward, and Beauregard quickly caught her to keep her from flying into the viewscreen. Plasma shots erupted all around them, slamming the ship around, the *Melody Tryst's* shields barely holding. Sparks flew from the instruments, and the lights flickered ominously.

Jennings had been thrown neck first against his harness and barely managed to rasp, "Minerva, what the hell is going on?"

"We are surrounded, captain," Minerva said. "All ships showing as belonging to Vesper Santelli."

"Son of a bitch," Jennings swore. "Can't catch a fucking break."

"Shields buckling," Fix stated.

Jennings tracked the nearest target and depressed the firing trigger. Nothing happened. "Where are my weapons?" he demanded of his engineer.

"Weapons overloaded," Squawk squeaked. "Bypass failed."

Another flurry of shots hit the *Melody Tryst,* and the ship began to slow. Jennings did not need Squawk to tell him the engines had been shot up and were offline. With everything they had gone through since accepting the bounty on Michelle Williams, Jennings knew they were damn lucky to be alive. All the same, it seemed like they had managed against all odds to survive so much only to die at the hands of a smuggler's ragtag fleet. Warnings flashed all around him advising him the power plant was failing again, shields were gone, engines and weapons were offline, and then the firing stopped.

"What the hell?" Jennings whispered.

The ship lurched in a way that was not from a plasma blast- the *Melody Tryst* was caught in a magnetic beam and was being towed into the cargo hold of the largest of Santelli's ships. Jennings tried to cycle through some options, but he came up with nothing. The *Melody Tryst's* thrusters were not strong enough to break the ship free, and the ship was in such a fragile shape that he might destroy it if he tried to do so. They had no weapons and no shields; there was nothing more to be done.

"Why don't they just kill us?" Lafayette asked.

"At a guess," Jennings said. "Santelli wants to do it himself."

"Won't be quick," Fix said.

"No, but we might be able to arrange safe passage for Selena and Michelle," Jennings said. "They didn't have anything to do with the attack on the *Brigandine*. Santelli has no grudge against them."

Silence fell on the bridge as the *Melody Tryst* entered the cargo hold of a ship Minerva advised them was called the *Claymore*. Jennings went ahead and engaged the ship's landing gear- no sense in getting the ship damaged any worse by letting her belly flop on the *Claymore's* deck, he thought. The cargo bay door closed, and the magnetic beam disengaged. Jennings was ready with the ship's thrusters, and he piloted the *Melody Tryst* gently to the deck.

"Transmission coming in," Beauregard said. "Audio only."

"Crew of the *Melody Tryst*," the cold voice announced. "Consider yourself the prisoners of Vesper Santelli. Any attempts to restore power to your engines, your shields, or your weapons will result in the destruction of your ship. Explosives have been placed in the cargo bay and will detonate on my order if any of your crew set foot outside of the *Melody Tryst*. We are jumping to Earth at best possible speed. Mr. Santelli would like to have a conversation with your crew, Captain Jennings. We should be seeing him in twelve hours."

The transmission ceased.

"Well, that was depressing," Lafayette said.

No one said anything for the better part of a minute. It was Captain Jennings who was the first to speak. "Marquis, I believe we were discussing some dinner before we were so rudely interrupted."

Michelle's face screwed up in a kind of annoyed confusion. "How can you think about eating at a time like this?"

"I'm hungry," Jennings said. "That's all I can think about right now." He turned around in the pilot chair to face Michelle, who wore a disbelieving stare, suggesting she was wondering how he could have possibly given up. "Sometimes the trap is too good. I've got nothing. If anyone else has a way out...?"

No one said anything.

"Then we need to wait until one of the variables change," he said. "That probably won't happen until Earth."

~

Finally acquiescing to Fix's requests, Jennings allowed the medic to stitch up the various new wounds he had received, especially the wound to his arm Pahhal had inflicted upon him. Jennings had insisted Lafayette go first though, and so Fix improved upon the work he completed after Lafayette's being assaulted by Petrova's men back at the mining colony.

When Lafayette thanked the captain, Jennings shrugged. "The sooner you're out of the med bay, the sooner you're making dinner."

By the time Fix finished with Jennings and Fix allowed Jennings to dose him with some more anti-concussion medicine, Lafayette had come through in fine form in the kitchen. How the Cajun managed to turn canned vegetables and freeze-dried meat into haute cuisine, Jennings had no idea, but he was infinitely appreciative of the result. Most of the crew ate with a kind of resolved gusto, but Michelle was barely touching her plate.

"Not a fan?" Jennings asked her in between bites of salad.

"Not hungry," she said gloomily.

"Tradition," Fix grumbled.

"What?" Michelle said. "What tradition?"

"The condemned prisoner's final meal," Jennings pointed out.

"Goes back to Jesus," Fix added with his mouth full.

Jennings eyed him curiously, but turned back to Michelle. "What's going to happen is going to happen. No sense in worrying about it while we're waiting for it to arrive."

Squawk finished eating and let loose a huge belch. "Excuse me." He patted his belly and breathed out contently in a whistle. "Sleepy time."

The Pasquatil vanished into his quarters, moving slowly, and a few moments later, the sound of loud snoring rumbled through his closed door. Beauregard was the first to start laughing, and the others slowly joined in until no one could stop, even Fix. When the laughter died down at last, an uncomfortable silence filled the room, and there was only the clattering of forks and knives on plates as a sense of grim reality seemed to settle in over all.

~

Despite what Jennings had said, Michelle realized he and the rest of his crew were as nervous as she was. They were better at hiding it and had probably been in similar situations before, but they were just as scared. She looked over to Jennings, and their eyes met for a moment. He gave her a forced smile, and she realized that all the bravado, all the talk about waiting for their opportunity, even his sudden food obsession, were all for her benefit. Jennings was trying to keep her from being scared. She did not know if that should make her feel worse at their impending fate, or better that he would do that for her.

Michelle had almost made up her mind for the latter, when Lafayette decided to interrupt the silence, "In all the insanity, *mon capitaine*, I didn't ask you how you found out about the other prisoners onboard the ship."

"All Michelle's doing," Jennings said. "Refused to leave without them."

Michelle blushed a little bit as all eyes turned to her.

"So, she was telling the truth all along?" Lafayette asked. "And O'Sullivan too? None of them were Resistance or terrorists?"

"Oh no," Jennings said, looking over to Michelle. "It's much more insane than that."

Feeling the curious stares from those around her, Michelle opened her mouth and out came everything she had learned from Pahhal: the Gael being banished from their dimension, the existence of a locked Great Gate which would allow them to travel back to where they came from, and the key which had been built into the souls of human beings.

Fix snorted when she finished. "Bullshit."

Lafayette looked from Jennings to Michelle and then back to Jennings. "*Mon capitaine*... Do you realize you prevented the Gael from leaving Earth?"

"I do," he agreed and then he added in a stern voice. "I trust we're not going to have a problem with this."

"*Non, mon capitaine*," Lafayette responded.

"There are better ways of getting rid of the Gael than sacrificing children," Beauregard piped in, apparently having come around to Michelle's line of thinking.

"We're not the Resistance," Jennings said quickly. "We don't kill innocents for a shot at hurting the Gael."

"*Bien sur*," the Cajun agreed apologetically, shaking his head. "Getting rid of the Gael... It wouldn't be worth it."

"No, it wouldn't," Michelle agreed.

Without a word, Fix put down his silverware and stood up from the table. He started like he was headed to his quarters, but stopped and turned back to the others. "None who are innocent deserve imprisonment," he said quietly, a pensive stoicism etched on his face. "What we did here was right- justice. If it costs us our lives, I say so be it. I'll go to my Maker with my conscience clear, my soul light." Turning back around, Fix walked into his quarters and shut the hatch.

"I think Fix has the right idea," Jennings said.

"About what we did?" Beauregard asked.

"About getting some sleep," Jennings corrected with a half-hearted smile. "I'm exhausted."

~

Everyone nodded wearily, and Lafayette started clearing the table while Jennings showed both Beauregard and Michelle to their quarters. The captain returned to help the Cajun, and in a few minutes, they too were both headed to their bunks ready to get some sleep. Jennings shut the hatch to his cabin and hit the light, the room now only illuminated by the green glow of the emergency running lights. He had just lain down, exhaustion seizing his body, when a quiet knock came from his door. Jennings got back up to his feet, did not turn on the lights, and walked over to the hatch. When he opened it, he was surprised to find Selena Beauregard standing there.

"Aren't you going to invite me in?" she asked coyly with a lascivious grin playing about on her face.

"Uh, no offense, but no," Jennings said awkwardly as his face flushed with embarrassment.

A knowing expression crossed her face. "So, you and Lafayette..."

"Huh, wait, no," Jennings muttered. "No, you're nice and pretty and all that, and I'm all about the ladies..." *He never talked like this- what the hell was going on with him?* "But I..."

Beauregard smiled and raised her eyebrows at him.

"I don't... I mean, I'm not someone who..." He fumbled with his words even more, and Beauregard covered her mouth to keep from laughing.

"You're not that in to a casual dalliance, a midnight fling, a one-night stand?" she asked.

"Look, you're really pretty..."

"You said that already," she pointed out.

"And there is a part of me that wants to say yes, but I am..." His voice trailed off.

"It's all right," she said at last. "After I tried to kill you a few times... and being that you saved my life... I thought I'd offer you an amusing diversion in what might be our last hours."

"I appreciate the offer, but..."

The assassin waved away his words with a disinterested wave. "No need to finish the sentence, captain. I've seen that look on a few men's faces before in my line of work: the anguish of betrayal. You have an amazing sense of loyalty, captain." In a whisper, she added, "I hope she appreciates it."

With a sad smile, Jennings said, "No one ever does."

With that, Beauregard left and headed back to her quarters, and Jennings shut the hatch and returned to his bed. This time the door knock came before he had even lain back down. Letting loose a sigh of frustration, Jennings stood back up and opened the hatch once more.

"Michelle?" he said in surprise.

"Were you hoping it was Selena?" she asked, a hint of doubt in her voice.

"Not at all," he said. "Come on in."

Michelle stepped over the threshold and meandered through the dark until she arrived at Jennings's bed and sat on it. He closed the hatch and then sat down beside her.

"I was waiting for the hallway to be empty before I came over here," she said. "I saw Beauregard at your door."

"And you saw her leave," Jennings pointed out.

"Why didn't you let her in?" she asked, turning her head sideways to stare at him.

Jennings sighed. "She doesn't have anything I'm looking for."

Michelle turned away and stared out into the darkness of the cabin for a moment. "I didn't really thank you for coming to rescue me."

"You don't have to," he said quickly.

"Of course, I do. You risked everything for me," she said. "You didn't have to go to the lengths you did to protect me in the mines. And you could have written me off after I was captured, and you didn't have to fight a Gael Hunter-Killer. I want to know why you did that for me."

"I...I..." The words seemed to stick in Jennings's throat. "I couldn't leave you."

"Why?" she asked, her voice somewhat desperate.

"I thought of you dying... and... I couldn't imagine that," he said. "After everything you had been through... knowing you were dead would have..."

"Felt like having your heart ripped out," she finished for him. Tears glistened in her eyes in the faint green glow of the emergency lights. "That was how I felt when I thought you were dead... when I thought you'd died for me. I'd never met anyone before who would have done the same."

Her hand reached out in the darkness and found his. "Michelle..." He tried to stop himself, trying to tell himself he was taking advantage of her, but her mouth found his and kissed him hard. Their lips and tongues met and explored each other for several moments before Jennings was at last able to break away.

He was about to launch into an admonition about how they were going too fast, about how they barely knew each other, about how she was only fixating on him because he saved her life a few times, but before he could speak, she pushed him back onto the bed and had climbed on top of him.

"Have you ever... you know?" she asked.

"It's been a little while, but a few times. During the war, I lay with a few," he said. "But I've never made love to a woman before." There was added emphasis on the word love. "You?"

"Almost," she said quietly. "That was where this all started..."

She did not finish the sentence, but instead lay her body on top of Jennings and began kissing him again. He grasped her tightly with his arms, an intensity of desire seizing him as he kissed her with a renewed fury, and a moan escaped his lips. Jennings rolled over with her, so he was now on top and pulled himself up to a kneeling position so he could take off his shirt. When he had gotten free of the garment, he tossed it aside and saw Michelle had managed to get free of hers as well.

She pulled him down to her, and he gently cupped her right breast with one hand while he brought his mouth down to her nipple. His tongue flicked across rapidly, and Michelle moaned in delight. Her hands went to his belt buckle and started to unfasten his cargo pants. A shudder of pleasure ran through Jennings as she freed him from his trouser and ran her hands over his manhood.

"I want you," she said in a strong, commanding voice.

Pulling himself up to a kneeling position once more, he yanked off her pants, and she wrapped her bare legs around him, drawing him in closer to her. He kissed her deeply as he slid inside her, and she cried out in that mixture of pleasure and pain all women experience in their first time. She held him tightly as he continued to kiss her, his groans reaching a quick climax which made his entire body quiver.

Jennings let his head fall to Michelle's breast, and she wove her fingers through his hair as her legs still cradled his body against hers. The sense of exhaustion swept over Jennings like a wave, and he did not think he could keep his eyes open a moment longer.

"Sleep," Michelle whispered. "It won't get any better than this."

# Chapter 40

"Captain?" The voice seemed very far away. "Captain Jennings?"

Slowly, Jennings came into consciousness and blinked the sleep out of his eyes. "Minerva?" he whispered back, trying to allow the sleeping Michelle Williams to stay that way.

"There is another communication coming in from the *Claymore*," Minerva reported. "Should I send it to your quarters?"

"No, I'll take it at the bridge," he said.

As quickly and quietly as possible, Jennings got dressed in the dark and slipped out of his quarters. The crew area was completely empty as everyone was still asleep, and he walked briskly down the gangplank and into the bridge. He punched a few controls in the communications console and the transmission began, once again audio only.

"Am I disturbing you, Captain Jennings?" the voice asked. It was stern and masculine, but that was all Jennings could tell.

"Not at all," Jennings said. "Caught me taking a nap."

"You were asleep?"

"Sure, it's been a long day," he said.

The tone of the speaker changed somewhat, sounding more bemused. "Most people would not spend the last few hours of their lives sleeping."

"If you're assuming this is the last few hours of my life," Jennings said. "I think the jury's still out on that."

The man laughed. "I have always liked your style, Captain Jennings." After a moment's pause, he added, "Well, to business. We are almost to Terran space. I am preparing an escort, a capable and fully armed escort, to take you and your crew to Mr. Santelli once we have landed. They will meet you in the cargo bay. Until they are present, do not attempt to leave your ship as the explosives are still in play. And please do not be so preposterous as to bring any weapons with you. I would have your crew ready in fifteen minutes. Oh, and dress respectable, yes?"

The communication ended, and Jennings was left with a bit of confusion. "Why in the world would they care how we dress?"

Shaking his head, Jennings left the bridge and headed back up to the crew area. Going from door to door, he got Fix, Lafayette, and Beauregard up and told them what he had been told. It was accompanied by general frowns of incredulity and a few shrugs. Without any further explanation, he returned to his own quarters and gently shook Michelle into consciousness.

"Did I fall asleep?" she asked dreamily.

"Afraid so," he said and then he kissed her on the cheek. "Come on, we're almost to Earth. Up and at'em. For some reason, our captors have requested we dress in our Sunday best."

"I don't have any clothes," she said. "Just the T-shirts and pants you lent me."

"That's all I have too," he said as he began to change. "But I'm going to wear my nicest T-shirt."

Michelle's voice took on a melancholy note. "Are we about to die?"

"I don't think so," he said.

"You're just saying that, aren't you?" she pointed out.

He shrugged. "We're not dead yet." With that, he pulled a clean T-shirt on over his head. Seeing the concern on her face, he walked over to where she sat on the bed and kneeled down so they were looking eye to eye. "I'm not going to let anything happen to you."

"You promise?" she asked, her pretty eyes starting to water.

"I do," he said. "And I keep my promises."

"I know you do," she said.

Five minutes later, everyone was awake, dressed and in their so-called best. For the most part this involved different T-shirts, cargo pants, flights suits or camouflage, of course, but it was not like the *Claymore* had stopped by a good haberdasher on the way to wherever they were headed. By the time everyone was ready, Minerva advised them two dozen men were standing in the *Claymore's* cargo bay.

"Alright, everyone," Jennings said. "Let's do this. Try to remain calm, and no one make a move until I do."

Receiving confirmation from all of them, Jennings led them all down to the cargo hold and hit the button to open the cargo door and extend the ramp. Santelli's men were waiting at the end of the ramp with weapons ready, one of them standing in front of the rest. Something was vaguely familiar about the man's features, but the man turned on his heel before Jennings could say anything and beckoned for the crew of the *Melody Tryst* to follow. Santelli's men fell into flanking positions beside them as they were led out of the *Claymore's* hold.

It was nighttime wherever they were on Earth, and the weather was warm. The crash of waves on rocks sounded from not far away, and Jennings soon realized why. The landing pad on which they had set down was carved out of the side of a cliff which overlooked the water. The man leading them did not pause and took them on a brick trail illuminated by lights designed as old-fashioned lanterns. The path curled up and around the cliff face and gave Jennings a commanding view of the sea. Running lights illuminated a few cruise boats, rolling gently on the waves, and as they continued to circle to the top of the cliffs, music and laughter reached his ears, coming from above them.

The path let out onto a long expanse of perfectly manicured green grass enclosed by a four-foot-high white brick wall on all sides. The area was illuminated with more lanterns and rich yellow light emanating from a neo-modernist mansion that appeared to be made entirely out of windows.

Dozens of people were milling about, chatting and laughing, most of them dressed in clothing Jennings assumed would cost about as much as his ship. Their arrival as well as their escort by the two dozen men with guns did not seem to alarm anyone. They passed an ornate fountain featuring cherubim spitting water back into a pool which was changing colors via a laser show.

"Captain Jennings!" a happy voice boomed from the end of the green. Stepping down a set of brick steps leading from the home's patio was Vesper Santelli. He wore an expensive suit which complemented his tan skin tone and slicked back salt and pepper hair perfectly. "I'm so glad you could make it." As he approached Jennings, he offered his hand.

Jennings took it. "I wouldn't miss it, Mr. Santelli. Thank you for extending the invite."

Santelli flashed a smile and waved away Jennings's thanks. "It's the least I could do after you handled that mess on the *Brigandine* for me," he said in a way and a volume that the words were clearly for the assembled partygoers and not Jennings. "That is one ship captain who will not withhold money from me again. Well, please come inside, there is something you absolutely must see."

Santelli grabbed him rather forcefully by the arm and steered Jennings up the stairs, across the patio, and into a set of French doors. The rest of Jennings's crew followed him, continuing to be flanked by several dozen guards and their leader who still seemed familiar to Jennings. Santelli led them away from the windowed areas and into an expansive interior room with a parquet floor that reminded Jennings of an old-fashioned ball room. As soon as all were in the room and the door was closed, Santelli wheeled around and decked Jennings across the jaw.

Jennings fell to the floor, grasping at his face, and muttered, "Getting some mixed signals here, Mr. Santelli."

Santelli spat angrily on the floor in reply. "Keep talking, Captain Jennings, and I might change my mind about your fate."

Jennings pulled himself to his feet and wiped a little bit of blood away from the corner of his mouth. "Look, I've spent the past twelve hours thinking I was going to die. Could you be straight with me and tell me what the hell is going on?"

"Do you know how many men have stolen from me and survived? Insulted me and survived? Attacked my people and survived?" he demanded.

"Going out on a limb, I would guess none," he said. "So, why not have your boys blast my ship to pieces out in the black? Why the warm reception in front of your guests? Why make it sound like I was working for you..." Jennings's voice trailed off and he smiled. He tapped his nose twice and pointed at Santelli. "Very good, Mr. Santelli."

"What's happening?" Michelle asked in a nervous voice.

"These aren't just guests of Mr. Santelli's," Jennings explained, eyeing the bearded smuggler carefully as he spoke. "These are rivals and competitors. Oh, sure, you all have legitimate businesses as fronts now, and you may even do business with each other, but I bet you go to sleep every night plotting their downfall. You wanted them to think I was working for you when we attacked the *Brigandine*, making you no longer look weak. In fact, taking down one of your own crews might make you appear more powerful while discouraging your other employees from making a similar mistake."

"Very perceptive, captain." Santelli gave a brief nod. "Considering that pitiful little ship is inferior to almost every other ship in the nine systems and is crewed by a trio of miscreants, I didn't want my competitors thinking I was an easy target. But if I convince them all that you're working for me, all of a sudden, I have a very dangerous man on my payroll- a man who took out a crew of twenty killers almost singlehandedly."

"Still a lot of trouble to go through when I'm sure killing us was an equally viable option," Jennings pointed out.

Lafayette grabbed his shoulder and said in a hushed voice, "What are you trying to do, get him to change his mind?"

Jennings brushed off Lafayette's hand. "No need. Fifty bucks says Mr. Santelli still would have voted to kill us if it weren't for one other thing." He turned his gaze back to Santelli's eyes. "He wants us for some reason. My guess is it's a job."

"A word of warning, captain," Santelli began as he closed on Jennings and put his face directly in front of his. "I wouldn't be so flippant with my mercy. The only reason you're still breathing is that I have a contract worth millions, a contract no one wants to take. None of my employees will volunteer for the mission and unfortunately, the type of people I rely on are not known for their courage and ingenuity. The people offering the money will take failure far more seriously than I would care for, so I must be very careful to whom I entrust this contract."

Santelli stepped back and gestured to the leader of the men who had escorted them to Santelli's house. "Consider yourself lucky Mr. Rocca has been impressed with your tenacity."

Jennings turned to Rocca, and the recognition which had been nagging him suddenly clicked into place. He said nothing to Santelli's lieutenant and instead turned back to the boss. "What's the job?"

"Simple cargo transport," Santelli said, before pausing for a moment and adding two terrifying words. "To Lycos."

Jennings's eyes widened, and some groans of consternation came from Lafayette behind him. "Lycos?" Jennings echoed. "That's in the Uula system."

"I believe you're correct," Santelli agreed, smiling somewhat savagely.

"The Uulans don't care much for humans, care even less for them setting foot on their worlds," Lafayette pointed out.

Santelli turned to the Cajun, "As your captain so well reasoned, it is because of this job only that I have spared your lives. If you're not interested in the job, then we have a small problem."

The sound of two dozen weapons being primed echoed throughout the ball room, and Jennings smiled to Santelli. "We would be happy to take the job."

"Payment?" Fix grumbled.

Rocca spoke up for the first time. "I would think squaring your debt with Mr. Santelli would be payment enough."

Fix crossed his arms and said nothing.

"One hundred thousand, payable upon completion," Santelli said.

"Your ships kind of shot mine to hell," Jennings pointed out.

Santelli nodded. "It will be three days before the shipment is ready to depart. I will ensure your ship is repaired and stocked."

Jennings nodded. "I suppose we should let you return to your party."

Santelli moved to step past him waving all of his men to follow him. "Oh," he said, stopping on his heel and turning around. "Not that I don't trust you, but Mr. Rocca will be accompanying you on the mission."

Turning once more and striding out of the ballroom, Santelli returned to chatting amiably with his friends once again as all of his men save Rocca filed out of the room. Jennings appraised Rocca for a moment, before he crossed the short distance between them and offered his hand.

"Sergeant," he said.

"Lieutenant," Rocca said as they shook hands.

"I prefer captain now," Jennings pointed out snidely.

"Of course," Rocca said, a small smile playing at the corners of his mouth. "Well, captain, you've got a lot of preparation to do in the next few days. I'd offer you billets in the compound here, but somehow I think you would be more comfortable on your ship."

"It's home," Jennings agreed.

"Until tomorrow then," Rocca said as he gave Jennings the Terran Federation salute and then followed Santelli back out into the party.

Jennings glanced around at his exhausted crew. "Well, that went better than expected. Back to the ship?" he asked as he strode out of the ballroom and then back out into night air, the rest of his crew following him.

No one else said anything until they were back on the path cutting down the cliff, headed toward the landing pad where the *Claymore* was docked. Lafayette was the first one to speak. "The Uulans? He should have just shot us now."

"You can go back and ask him to if you want, Marquis," Jennings retorted. "The Uulans fought with us during the war."

"Because they hated the Gael slightly more," he pointed out.

"It's a job," Fix said in a way that suggestion the discussion was over. "A good job."

They said nothing more until they rounded a corner of the cliff and the *Claymore* came into view. The hangar door was still open and the interior lights were on, so they could see the *Melody Tryst* inside. For the first time, Jennings saw the scorch marks all over her hull and the damage done in the various fights she had been through.

"Well, Squawk, it looks like they'll be plenty for you to do," Jennings said. "You want to rest or get started?"

"Restfully rested already," Squawk said from behind Jennings. "Starting repairs."

The Pasquatil sprinted off on all fours into the *Claymore* and up the ramp into the *Melody Tryst*. Jennings could not help but smile in appreciation at his engineer as they entered the ship after him. Squawk was already doing what he loved to do, so Jennings gave everyone leave to do whatever they wanted until morning. Lafayette vanished into the kitchen, saying something about a crème Brule, and Fix vanished into his quarters without saying another word. That left Jennings alone with Michelle and Selena.

"Well, Ms. Beauregard," Jennings said. "I'm afraid this is where we say our goodbyes. It's been a pleasure fighting with you."

"You're kicking me off your ship?" Beauregard asked in a surprised tone. "After all I did? I thought I would have at least proved my ability if not that you could trust me."

"You did," Jennings said as a sense of confusion settled into his mind. "But you're not a member of my crew, you don't owe Santelli anything, and I thought you prefer to remain independent."

Beauregard chewed her lower lip for a moment, but Michelle was the first person to speak. "You want to stay."

"You could use me," she said quickly, the slightest tone of desperation in her voice. "I have quite a few talents and even a few contacts on Uula. Plus, one hundred thousand dollars five ways isn't too bad either."

She was trying to sound casual about the proposition, but Jennings was not buying it. "Why do you really want to stay? You're not one to follow orders, and if you do stay, you will be following my orders. You could earn more than twenty thousand dollars in a few hours with the skills you have, so it's not the money."

"She's afraid," Michelle said.

Beauregard eyed her angrily for a moment, but then at last nodded. "You heard what the Resistance captain said. The Resistance wants me dead. I got onto the Nucleus while we were coming here. They've posted a one hundred thousand dollar bounty on my head. Dead only."

Jennings considered this for a moment. "An enemy of the Resistance tends to be a friend of mine."

"I could pay you rent," she added quickly.

"Done," Jennings said immediately, offering her his hand, which she shook. "Welcome aboard, Selena."

Beauregard smiled. "I'll start reaching out to my contacts on Uula, see about getting us some safer passage through their system, captain." She turned to head up the gangplank to the second level but she stopped and turned around. "Ashley. My real name. It's Ashley."

"Welcome aboard, Ash," Jennings said with a smile before she turned to head up the gangplank.

Heading to the back wall of the cargo bay, Jennings put his back up against it and let himself sink to the floor. From that position, he could see the water in the distance beyond the cliffs and the stars reflecting in the seas. Michelle sat down next to him and placed her head on his shoulder. He grabbed her hand in his and rubbed her fingers affectionately.

"Do you think the Gael will keep looking for me?" she asked.

"Probably," Jennings said. "The death of Ciaran O'Sullivan means only one hundred and ten of the pieces of this key they need to open their Great Gate are currently living. That doesn't stop them from catching the rest of you and putting you on ice until that one hundred and eleventh soul shows up."

Michelle shivered, and Jennings put an arm around her, allowing her to melt into his body. Her warmth against his was a wonderful feeling of being wrapped in an old blanket, and it was awfully cold onboard the *Melody Tryst* sometimes, but he knew he had to do what was best for her.

"Look," he said. "I know you probably can't go back to your parents, but we could find you some place."

Michelle became crestfallen. "You want me to go?"

"I want you to be safe," he said.

"The *Tryst* is safe," she responded confidently. "I'm safe when I'm with you."

Jennings raised his eyebrows. "Did you miss the last few days?"

"I'm alive," she said with conviction. "Just like you promised."

"I also promised I'd let you go," he said.

"That's one promise you're going to have to break," Michelle said as she leaned in and kissed him full on the mouth.

# About the Author

Justin Bohardt became a writer because he realized early in life that creating alternative realities was infinitely preferably than living in the existing one. A former reporter, he moonlights as an auditor for a Fortune 100 insurance company while crafting new worlds in every second of free time that he can find.

His fiction has appeared in magazines such as *Hungur, Outposts of the Beyond, Potter's Field, The Drabbler,* and *Micro 100*; while his poetry has been featured in *Scifaikuest, Aoife's Kiss, The Martian Wave,* and *Champagne Shivers*. Bohardt also contributes to the occasional trade publication and teaches the occasional class. He resides in Virginia with his family.

Please visit him online at: http://gggeflat.wix.com/justinbohardt

Made in the USA
Columbia, SC
04 February 2025

3f228f9a-f97d-4a3f-a8b2-b84a7a186bffR01